Sciatu Mio

my breath

Frank J. Pennisi

ISBN: 1456305522
ISBN-13: 9781456305529
Library of Congress Control Number: 2010915995

❧ ❧ ❧

DEDICATION

This novel is dedicated to Orazio and Lina Pennisi di Floristella. When I rang their bell at the Castello Pennisi over twenty years ago, he asked me who I was looking for, I replied, "Mia Famiglia."

From that moment on, Orazio and Lina embraced my wife Carolyn and me; like true Sicilians, they opened their hearts to two strangers, and for twenty years we have been part of this noble family.

This book is also dedicated to my grandmother Santa. She gave me my passion for gardening and taught me the art of haggling. And every Sicilian cuss word I know, I learned from her.

Last but not least, I dedicate this book to my, *sciatu mio*, my wife Carolyn.

And to my five grandchildren, Joseph, Nicole, Dominique, James and Frankie: remember family is everything. *Sempre Famiglia.*

Special thanks to long time friend, Elaine Takach who has helped and encouraged with my three books.

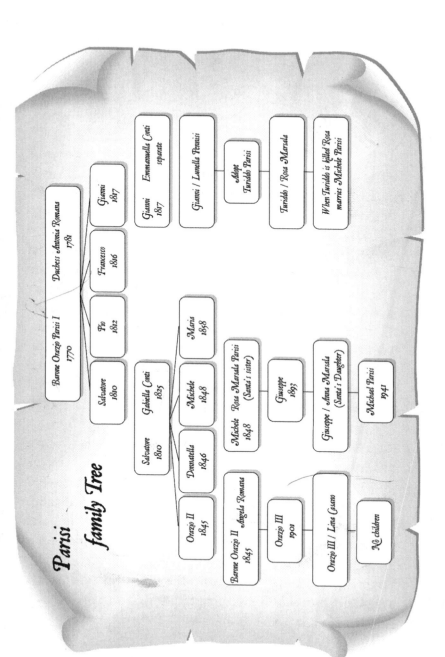

Parisi family Tree

❖ ❖ ❖

FOREWORD

It was the third day Michael Parisi was in a coma in a New York City hospital. It was January, 1986. He could hear the voices surrounding him and didn't know if they were real or if he was dreaming or dead and waiting for his placement in heaven or hell. Everything was spinning in slow motion in his head. He could hear her southern accent pleading for him to come back. He could feel his grandmother, Santa, bending over him and breathing life into his body, and then he heard his father, Giuseppe, telling him "stay away from these people," and he was right. Michael could feel a tear roll down his own cheek as he remembered when he was young hearing his father whisper to him as Michael pretended to be asleep, "*Sciatu mio*, I love you."

Forty years ago Michael was six years old and sitting on a stool in his grandmother's wine cellar, listening to Santa tell her stories. There were six apartments in the building; Santa lived on the third floor. Everyday she would walk down three flights of stairs to the basement to check on her wine. The owner of the building never gave her permission to use the basement and Santa never asked permission and no one dared to tell her she couldn't.

Santa was sitting on a stool next to Michael. "*Figlio mio*, listen to me, there is evil in this world and the devil is always behind your back waiting for you to make a mistake. And remember don't look into the mirror too long, for the devil will see you."

Michael was listening with his eyes wide open. "But *Nonna*, I got the horns, the devil can't touch me." Michael had a golden horn on a gold chain around his neck that had once belonged to his grandfather Michele.

Santa smiled, her wrinkled face showing her seventy years of hardship and sorrow. It was only her grandson Michael who could make her smile now. "*Bravo, figlio,* you are so smart, and what do you do when someone gives you the *male occhi*, the evil eye?"

"You give them the *corni*, the horns." Michael lifted his pinky and index finger and raised his arm.

"*Bravo, figlio.*" Santa got up from the stool and took her cup over to one of the wine barrels and turned the wooden sprout and filled her cup with the red wine.

"Would you like to taste the wine?" It was the first time she had asked him.

"*Si, Nonna.*"

"How do you like it?"

"I like it, *Nonna.* Pappa says you make the best wine in Brooklyn."

Santa smiled with a twinkle in her eye. "Let me tell you, in Sicily noblemen would come from miles around to buy my father's wine. In the fall when the grapes were ready to be picked the whole family would stop what they were doing and we would go out to the vineyard to pick them. I would go with my sister Rosa and our friend Maria. My father gave us each a basket to fill and we would have a race to see who could fill their basket fastest. When our basket was filled we would run to the vats to place the grapes."

"Did you win, *Nonna?*"

Santa filled her cup with more wine and gave some more to Michael. "I was the youngest, but I was the fastest. They ran like sissy girls and I ran like the wind. When the large vat was filled with grapes, all the women got in barefoot and danced on the grapes. The men played their mandolins and guitars and sang old songs, and we laughed and danced until the sun set. When we had to go to bed, the three of us would sleep together and we could hear our family and friends still singing and laughing. We would giggle and tell stories, but for some reason they would start talking about all the boys they liked. But for me there was only one, Giuliani."

Santa tried to hold back the tears but couldn't.

"*Nonna,* don't cry." Michael got up and started to wipe the tears off her face. "*Nonna,* I want to be like you and run like the wind." Michael took Santa's empty cup and filled it with wine. "Drink the wine, *Nonna,* it will make you feel better."

"*Sciatu mio,* I love you so much." Santa held onto him and kissed him.

'I love you too, *Nonna,* can I stay with you, *Nonna?*"

Santa thought long and hard. She wanted to say yes, but she knew after all Giuseppe had been through, it would kill him.

"Michele," she called him by his Italian name, "if you stay with me your father would be all alone, you have to help him and be a little man. He needs you, and for now you need him. He wants you to be smart and grow up and go to college and become a *signore,* not like these *caffones* we have living here in Red Hook. You must stay away from the *caffones.* They like to drag people down to their level. And remember, never tell anyone what you think or plan to do, you keep that inside of you. We may be poor now, but I know the day will come and you will become *signore* like your father's family in Sicily and make us all proud. I just know you will do well. I feel it in your heart." Santa tried to get up, but she couldn't. The wine was working its magic. It would make her forget for a while the sadness in her life.

"*Sciatu mio,* come here and give *Nonna* a big kiss and help me up. I need to go to sleep." Michael lifted Santa off the stool and they started to walk up the stairs from the basement to her apartment.

"My bones hurt so much sometimes I don't know if I can make it all the way up." Santa leaned on Michael. "And remember next week you take me to the farm in Bergen Beach."

"I'll take you to the farm in Bergen Beach, *Nonna*. I'll be here to help you everyday. I'm only two blocks away."

"*Grazie, figlio mio.*"

"But *Nonna*, what about my father's family? He says they lived in castles and were very rich. Is that true?"

"We will talk about that another time. Now I need to go to sleep and they can all *va fan culo.*"

✤ ✤ ✤

CHAPTER 1

It was a bitter cold February in New York and in Saint
Stevens, the Catholic church that was a miniature
replica of the beautiful cathedral in Monreale, Sicily,
was full of proud parents watching the Conformation
of their children. It was 1940, and Concetta Parisi was
getting confirmed. Her father, "Big Tony" Parisi, was
not there, but Uncle Giuseppe was, and that was more
important to Concetta. When the ceremony was over,
Sylvia, Tony's wife, went home to prepare the food for
all the guests that were expected for this wonderful
day when a child becomes closer to God.

Concetta and Giuseppe were sitting in Giuseppe's
1936 Packard, a gift from a beautiful and powerful
lady. "Okay, Concetta, we have two hours before you
have to be back for the party. I am your chauffeur,
where would you like to go?"

"Oh, Uncle Joe, I am so happy you came."

It was only three years ago when Concetta came home crying hysterically because she had been insulted by the Irish students in her school.

"*Perche? Perche?*" Sylvia wanted to know why.

"*Perche?* They call us *ignoranti, animali, stupidi.* I'm tired of being insulted every day. I cannot show my face anymore." And she broke down and cried again.

"What does your teacher say?" Sylvia asked.

"*Niente.*" Concetta continued to weep.

"I don't know why you make her waste her time in school," shouted Tony. "Send her out to work like the rest. The schools are no good; they teach them to go against us."

Sylvia ignored Tony's remark. "We are not *stupidi,*" she soothed Concetta. "Your uncle Giuseppe has more brains and education than any of the men in that school." Sylvia's eyes turned to her younger brother-in-law who was sitting reading the newspaper.

"I'll go to school with you tomorrow." Giuseppe spoke softly to Concetta as he put his arm around the child.

The next morning, Concetta and her *zio* Giuseppe went to P.S. 142 on Hick Street.

When Concetta came back home that afternoon, she was elated. Her mother had never seen her so happy.

"*Che successo?*" Sylvia asked.

"You should have been there! He spoke like a *professore,* and when he was finished, the principal treated him like a *signore.* He was wonderful."

"Cosa a detto?" Sylvia was anxious to know what Giuseppe had said.

"When we entered the classroom, they thought he had come to start trouble. The principal was called to come to the room. I don't remember everything *Zio* Giuseppe said, but he gave them a lesson in Sicilian history and culture and told them how our civilization and culture was equal to the greatest democracy of Athens."

He had spoken of the ancient temples and theaters built for the Grecian gods whose names Concetta had never heard; of how Sicily was the richest region in all of the Mediterranean world because of its inexhaustible soil and strategic location; of how it was the most precious jewel in the Mediterranean Sea, sought after by the Greeks and Romans; of how Herodotus had called it the most beautiful place in the world.

When he'd finished talking, everyone was impressed with this stranger, an immigrant who had so defiantly taken over the class. The principal asked him to come back.

"How come *Zio* Giuseppe knows so much?" Concetta asked her mother.

"Your *zio* could have been a *professore* back home, or maybe more."

"But what happened to *zio*? What makes him so sad?"

"Don't ask. My insides cry when I see him like that. Why does God hurt the good ones?"

"Concetta, I couldn't miss your confirmation. You are almost a lady now, look at you in that white dress. Why, in a few years you will be ready to get married." Giuseppe smiled. He always tried to encourage Concetta because her father didn't.

"If I get married, I want someone just as handsome and nice like you, Uncle Joe." She leaned over and kissed him and whispered in his ear, "Let's go to Coney Island. I want a hot dog from Nathan's."

Two hours later they were parked in front of Tony's home, where the party for Concetta was just beginning. "Thank you, Uncle Joe, for a wonderful day." Concetta noticed her uncle looked troubled. "Is everything okay, Uncle Joe?"

"No, but it will be in a few days. I need to talk with your father and try to settle some things." Giuseppe had asked for a meeting that afternoon with Tony and his best friend, Pasquale.

Concetta gets out of the car. "Sometimes I wonder how you and my father had the same mother. You are so kind and smart, a handsome gentleman, all my girlfriends are in love with you. I just want you to know you mean the world to me. *Ti amo.*"

❖ ❖ ❖

The basement in Tony's home was usually filled with longshoremen who came to pay their respects every Sunday to Tony. A gallon of wine would surface. This gesture meant that you would be working on the docks Monday morning. But if you were lucky and happened to bring a gallon of Santa's wine, you didn't have to go into the filthy, rat-infested bowels of the ship to unload the cargo.

As the day progressed, the wine would go down with ease and the conversations would flow. The older men only spoke Sicilian, and some of the stories were about their lives in the old country. The wife or girlfriend they left behind. Most of them talked about how one day they would leave America and go back to the simple life in Sicily. Most of them never returned.

But this Sunday afternoon there were only three men in the basement: Tony, Pasquale, and Giuseppe. Concetta's confirmation party was going on above them, and the sound of children laughing and playing games made its way to the basement.

There was only one hanging bulb for light as they sat down around the card table. Tony and Pasquale sat facing each other, leaving the head of the table for Giuseppe. "So, little brother, we are so honored to be sitting down with such a *signore*. We hear you been living in a swanky apartment in Manhattan; going to the Hamptons. Even heard you bought an ocean–front lot in Montauk and going to build a big villa fit for a prince." Tony was getting louder and louder. Just like his father, Turiddo, he couldn't control his temper. He even looked like his father: short, round, and stocky. Santa said Turiddo was evil, that the devil was inside of him.

"Listen, maybe I should leave." Pasquale was getting uncomfortable; he knew Tony was ready to explode.

"No, stay, this concerns all of us." Giuseppe spoke for the first time. He was dressed in a three-piece woolen suit tailored for him in Manhattan. One could not help but see the drastic differences between Tony and Giuseppe. One demanded respect and power; the other didn't have to demand.

"I'm leaving, I'm leaving New York. Margareta has agreed to a divorce, and I'm leaving her everything."

Tony and Pasquale couldn't believe what they were hearing. Pasquale spoke. "You know, we first lost Rosario, and last month we heard Luigi was killed in Sicily, and now, Giuseppe, without you we will lose our control of the docks."

"Listen, Pasquale." Giuseppe loved his childhood friend. They had grown up like brothers. When Pasquale's son was murdered just two months ago, Giuseppe had made the decision to get out of everything and try to move as far as he could to escape. "We don't control the docks. Harold Wilson controls the docks. All we do is give him the power."

Pasquale continued, "But we heard you were going to run for some political position in the city."

Giuseppe got up. He seemed tired and pensive. "I told Harold I wasn't going to do it. I'm going to marry Anna Marsala, and we'll be moving to Florida."

"What, Anna Marsala, that *putana!*"Tony got up in a rage, flipped the table over, and like a bull went straight for Giuseppe with one goal—to kill him. Pasquale was able to stop him, and as Giuseppe was walking out of the basement he could hear Tony shouting, "*Disgraziato, bastia!* You have disgraced this family, you should drop dead, you and that *putana!*"

Concetta heard her father and came down to the basement. "How could you say those things to your brother?"

"I have no brother." Tony took a deep breath and spat on the floor.

"You're an animal." She went up to try to say good-bye to Uncle Joe, but she was too late.

Giuseppe Parisi had gone from a peasant boy in Sicily to the leader of an insurrection that overturned the Irish hierarchy on the New York piers and placed his half-bother, Tony, and his *paisani* in control. The Parisis were one of the families in New York who made the decisions.

But all the accomplishments and all the accolades meant nothing. The one thing he wanted most he could not have—her name was Claudia and she had been promised to a prince.

For years the anguish of losing Claudia, the only woman he could love, had left a void for any other women in his life. Even the beautiful socialite

Elizabeth Wilson, whose father was the ex-governor of New York and first cousin to the twenty-eight president of the United States, Woodrow Wilson, could not mend the pain in his heart.

Around this time, Giuseppe Parisi, who was almost fifty years old, met the young Anna Marsala. Looking at him, one could not tell the sad life he had lived. He had matured very well and was considered a handsome, elegant man, especially among the socialites in Manhattan and the Hamptons. He was respected and had accumulated wealth and power along with an air of sophistication that had set him apart from the Italian immigrants in Red Hook, Brooklyn. Because of this, he was looked upon by some as a possible candidate for borough president of Brooklyn. His close friends and family affectionately called Giuseppe "the Prince."

But the Prince was not happy; he felt he was being manipulated the way the puppets in Sicily were manipulated on the strings by the master puppeteer—just like the Romans used the Sicilians as slaves thousand of years ago.

In New York, the five families held the strings, but the master puppeteer was Harold Wilson. Harold came from old money, and if there were royal families in America the Wilsons would be at the top of the list. But Giuseppe had found out Harold was all smoke and mirrors and now Giuseppe needed to cut the cords, although that would mean giving up his wealth and power.

It seemed that in New York, power and wealth for the Italians came only by brutal force, just the way Hitler and Mussolini were bullying their way toward expanding their sphere of influence and national boundaries. So when it came to making money and grabbing power, the heads of the five New York families showed the same shameless treachery. When the flamboyant Lucky Luciano, the head of the five families, was deported to Sicily, his absence left a void in the leadership in New York. Between the Gambinos and Genoveses, Lucheses, Columbos, and the Anastasias a bloody power struggle begins that lasts on and off for ten years. There was no respect for the old values anymore. They had lost their Sicilian roots and become just common thugs and criminals. Some, like Claudio un Occhio ("one eye" or "Ciclopi"), and Nicky Genovese had become animals.

With the wars starting again, the old Mafia burial grounds in Canarsi and Bergen Beach in Brooklyn were reopened.

The old art of patience in waiting for your time was gone. Everybody immediately wanted to be Mr. Big Shot. Everybody wanted to be a self-made man, and Giuseppe just wanted to get out. When he met Anna, she reminded him of Claudia, the love he could never forget. In her early twenties, Anna had a striking resemblance to the woman who had never left his heart.

Her dark eyes, light skin, and delicate beauty were a striking contrast to the peasant immigrant Sicilian family she was born into.

Married for almost twenty years and just turning fifty, Giuseppe had fallen madly in love with Anna— or was it the memory of someone else in Sicily? And why not? Anna was Claudia's younger sister. Their mother was Santa Marsala.

Many of his close friends and family thought Giuseppe had lost his mind when he took off to Florida with Anna. He gave away all his wealth and power. The Parisi family, his two half-sisters, and especially his half-brother, Big Tony, were convinced he had gone mad. "He had so much money, power, influence, and now he has nothing." He was a "*vecchio fesso,* an old fool. "He will die alone. *Comme un carne,* like a dog."

Throughout Giuseppe's rise to fortune and power he had remained humble. Some took it as a sign of weakness, but those who knew him respected him as the leader of the Parisi family even though it was the elder, Big Tony— who was anything but humble—who carried the title "Don."

When Giuseppe ran off with Anna and divorced his wife Margareta, it was a no no; divorce was not part of the Sicilian vocabulary. But there was a void in his life. He had it all, but there was no heir, there was no son, and there could never be as his wife could not conceive. They had adopted his wife's younger sisters when misfortune took the lives of their parents, but that was not enough. For all the accolades that were bestowed on him for being educated, intelligent, and humble, his Sicilian ego that demanded he have a male heir would not let him rest. The loss of his god-son Frankie, Pasquale's son, broke the camel's back.

But Giuseppe had humiliated "*la famiglia*." And Big Tony was going to punish him for it. Tony had successfully ostracized him from the rest of the family. "How could Giuseppe Parisi disgrace us by divorcing his wife and marrying that *putana*?"

CHAPTER 2

It was March 1940. The South was coming out of an unusually cold winter, there was a war raging in Europe, and Jacksonville was labeled the new "Industrial City of the South," a place where new starts and fortunes could be made. Anna and Giuseppe had leased with an option to buy a dilapidated Gulf gas station with a small grocery store that had been closed down for years. Most of the white paint had peeled off the wooden clapboard structure, and the red-shingled roof had gaping holes. The smell of mildew inside was overwhelming, and most of the hardwood floors were rotted out. The old orange and white Gulf gas pumps had not been used in years, but they were the only things that were working.

But the southern gentleman who owned the property assured them, "With a little bit of spit this place could shine." But behind their backs Ed Jerdon, the old southern owner, thought, *them Eye-talians* would be closed down in six months.

Two thousand dollars. It was all the money they had left in the world. It was the settlement he had reached with Margareta. She took the house they lived in and the real estate investments Giuseppe had made through the years with his partner, Harold Wilson. The motels and cottages in the Hamptons and the acres of ocean front in Montauk. Giuseppe wanted to make sure Margareta and the two girls would not want for anything. Margareta did not put up a fight; she knew she would lose him one day. Many nights she heard him cry out for Claudia, wake up in a sweat, and try to fall back to sleep. At first she would try to console him, but nothing she did could erase the memories of his lost love in Sicily.

With what was left from the down payment, Anna and Giuseppe needed to make repairs, stock the store, and try to survive in a southern town that did not welcome Yankees and at times did not take too kindly to foreigners. But Anna and Giuseppe were determined to make it a success. They worked from dawn to dusk. They hired some local Negroes to cart off some of the junk on the property and help with the repairs.

A local Negro, Benny "Big Ben" Williams, dressed in his Sunday best, came around with his rusted-out Ford pickup truck. Gray smoke came out of the rattling tailpipe and the engine sounded like it would conk out, but it didn't. It was a breezy, warm Palm Sunday morning, and the sky was blue and clear, a welcome relief from the three days of torrential southern downpours.

"You all the new owners?" When Big Ben smiled, his chubby face lit up and his eyes sparkled. "I work for five dollars a day and my missus here, Neddy, she works for two dollars a day, and wez good workers."

Giuseppe looked at Anna. Her cheeks, rosy from working outdoors, were covered with grease, and her long black hair had been put in a makeshift bun that kept coming apart, but she was still beautiful. His hands were blistered and splintered from ripping apart the old wooden floors and roofs. "When could you start working?"

"Theys don't calls me Big Ben for nottin', eyez been always on time." Big Ben turned off the ignition and the smoke cleared. Ben and Neddy got out, rolled up their sleeves, and started to cart off the debris.

Big Ben was always on time. Every morning he and Neddy were at the screen door by seven o'clock. Anna would have a pot of coffee brewing, and Neddy would take over in the kitchen. She'd pick six fresh brown eggs from their chicken coop, sizzle up some ham, and stir up a pot of grits. Neddy was as big as Ben, dressed in red, yellow, blue, and green floral dresses, and was always happy. Neddy had been born in the Lowcountry on Cumberland Island off the coast of Georgia. A descendant of slaves, she grew up speaking the Gullah language. Anna had a tough time understanding her dialect and Neddy had a tough time understanding the Yankees, but they bonded.

During the day Neddy helped the young Anna try to make a home out of the rubble while Ben helped Giuseppe remove the debris and repair the buildings to get the business going. In six weeks the repairs were completed, the roof didn't leak, the building was painted all white, and the wooden shutters were green. They had planted some bushes and flowers, and Neddy had helped Anna plant a victory garden behind the store. It was called a victory garden because there was a war going on and it was a way of helping the soldiers by not taking food out of their mouths and growing fruits and vegetables for their family and friends. In New York, Anna's mother, Santa, taught her how to grow and tend to a garden; something Santa and her sister Rosa had learned from their family in Sicily.

The grocery shelves were stocked and the gas tanks were full. Anna and Giuseppe were ready for business. But more important, they had found a home. Anna knew Giuseppe had wanted to leave New York and the political power struggle that was becoming deadly. But more than that, she knew he wanted a child more the anything else.

That year the summer heat and humidity came in early spring to Jacksonville. One Sunday after church, Neddy and Big Ben came around to pick up Anna and Giuseppe to take them to the colored beach on Amelia Island. Neddy had made a batch of fried chicken and okra bread and Big Ben took along his two fishing poles. The beach was only fifteen minutes away, and Giuseppe and Anna jumped in the back of the pickup. It wasn't smoking or making any loud noises anymore since Big Ben had bought a new muffler.

When they arrived at the colored beach, they could see the lone silhouette of a fisherman throwing his net into the sea.

Giuseppe didn't say much about the separation of races. He walked out to the surf by himself as Neddy and Anna prepared lunch. Big Ben threw his rig out and reeled it back in. In his silence Giuseppe reflected back to his days growing up in Sicily with his father, Michele. They had nothing, but they were happy. He thought how the life of the peasants in Sicily was similar to the plight of the Negroes living down south.

Thousands of years ago, Sicilians were the off-spring of Roman slaves. And even though back as late as the late eighteen hundreds there were no laws forbidding them to socialize with the upper class, it was understood. Sicilians were treated sometimes no better than the black slaves. There were many whose farms were taken away from them by the northern Italians, who took control of Sicily after the unification wars spearheaded by Garibaldi and King Umberto from Savoy. But once the Italians were in control, they treated the Sicilians no better than the *"ignorante animale"* of burden, the donkey. They were spat on and ridiculed. and tens of thousands were

Sciatu Mio

forced to leave their homeland with nothing except the shirts on their backs.

The locals in Jacksonville gave up trying to pronounce "Giuseppe." It would come out "Jew-sip-pi," so they started calling him Joe. They started to come in and patronize the little grocery store. Even some of the Negroes who lived nearby came in, thanks to Neddy Williams.

The store was simply called "Joe and Anna's." The first day the store was open Neddy came to the back door and asked, "Miz Anna, do I have permission to come in and shop?"

Anna looked at her almost in disbelief. "Neddy, you're my best friend. If you ever come in through that back door again, I don't know what I'm going to do with you, you hear." Anna was finding it hard to adjust. She was young and already discontented with their way of life in the South, and she needed Neddy to be her friend.

"I hear you, I just don't want to disrespect." Neddy smiled, and when she smiled she made Anna happy.

The gas station was part of the business, but it wasn't paying all the bills, so Joe was busy all day trying to supplement their income. Big Ben helped him build a chicken coop, and they doubled the size of the victory garden. Joe would stop working around noon and Anna would prepare lunch.

Neddy came into the store while Joe and Anna were eating. "I just brought over some homemade pie and collards for you two."

"Well, Neddy, why don't you eat with us?" Joe pulled up a chair and Anna put another plate on the table.

"I can't do that. It's not proper for colored folks to sit and eat with whites." Neddy knew her place in the South.

"Neddy I'm almost as dark as you." Joe got up and affectionately put his arm around Neddy and made her sit down with them. That was the first of many lunches and dinners they shared together. Neddy shared her Gullah recipes and Joe taught her how to cook Sicilian. For over a year, Joe, Anna, Neddy, and Big Ben shared their stories and became good friends. In fact, Neddy was Anna's only friend.

One warm spring day in May, a white trucker pulled up his rig at the gas pump. The truck was loaded with discarded metal to be recycled and then made into war machines to fight the evil empires, the Nazis and the Japs.

Neddy, Joe, and Anna were having lunch. Joe stopped eating and went to the gas pumps. The trucker went inside to buy some beer. When he saw Neddy eating at the table with Anna, he commented, "Niggers shouldn't be sittin' and eatin' with white folks."

Neddy started to get up, but Anna placed her hand on Neddy's shoulders to sit her down. "Mister, I don't know where you come from and I don't care. This is my place of business and my home and I don't need you or anyone else telling me who I can have sitting at my table."

"Ma'am, you ain't from these parts. You should go back north to New York where they love them niggers." He threw the money over the counter and left.

Anna was getting tired of the South, the heat, and the rednecks, and except for Neddy she didn't have any friends. The summers were too hot and she longed to be back in New York, where she felt she belonged. She knew Joe wouldn't consider it. How could he?

In New York Anna had been wined and dined by rich, older, married men who lusted for this young beauty. She was taken to Sardis' in Manhattan for filet mignon. To Vencenzo's in little Italy for the finest calamari. But her favorite was Lundy's in Sheepshead Bay in Brooklyn for lobsters. The black Cadillac limo would park in front of the old eight-family brownstone apartment house on Carroll Street. She was living in a four-room cold-water flat with her mother, Santa. But when she came out of the old dilapidated brownstone building and onto the sidewalk to get in the limo, she lit up the street. She was dressed like a movie star, the older men said, she was a knock-out like Hedy Lamar. And the New York columnist Walt Winchell had just proclaimed Miss Lamar as the most beautiful woman in Hollywood.

As Anna stepped into the limo, she always stopped to look around to take notice of who was watching. And there were many who enjoyed watching. With arms folded over their pillows hanging over the window sills, everyone watched the show in the streets, and with no televisions to entertain them in their dingy apartments the streets became their entertainment. On Carroll Street, Anna was the star. Back then it was *General Hospital* and *The Young and The Restless* put together.

The young girls in the neighborhood admired Anna and wished one day they would have the opportunity to escape their own miserable ghetto lives. They knew Anna was destined for a better life. But the older ones, who were stuck, who had no opportunity, and would not or could not leave, cursed her. And some would spit at her direction as the limo took off. They called her a "*putana.*"

When she and Joe made love she forgot everything about New York, except for the night he cried out the name "Claudia." She was his lost love, someone that Anna couldn't replace. No matter how much she looked like her sister, she couldn't erase Claudia's memory from his heart.

But Anna didn't have to make a decision; it was made for them. It was two o'clock on an early July morning and still dark when she smelled the smoke. Joe was in a deep sleep. Anna got up, and when she opened the door, a rush of flames threw the bedroom door back. The grocery store was an inferno, but

Anna managed to grab the coffee can under the bed with the three hundred dollars they had managed to save. She and Joe climbed out the window and made their way to safety. By the time they got out, the gas tanks were exploding. Joe stood there watching the inferno in disbelief.

In Sicily on April 1, 1914, the eruption of the volcano and the aftermath of destruction had almost buried his town and left thousands dead, including his mother and father. And now he was reliving the same tragedy. He had nothing, just the shirt on his back. They had lost everything. Joe was devastated.

The police determined that arson was responsible for the fire. Later that morning Anna and Joe walked among the debris. Everything was destroyed; even the chickens were charred and still smoldering. Joe and Anna had their suspicions, but nothing could be proved. With nothing left except the three hundred dollars, Joe thought he had reached bottom again.

"I don't know if I have the will to start again." He looked so despondent as he walked through the ashes, hoping to find something to salvage, but there was nothing.

Anna went over to him and hugged him. "I'm having our baby." Joe was elated. It gave him a reason to carry on.

The baby justified all he gave up. The cottages and motel in the Hamptons, the beautiful ocean-front property in Montauk he owned where one day he was going to build a home overlooking the sea—just like the view he had from his window growing up in Sicily.

But farther away from New York, Anna became more disillusioned and depressed. It seemed no matter what Joe did, it wasn't right. He couldn't find a job and his past kept closing in on him: his lost love in Sicily and his wealthy, scorned mistress, Elizabeth, in New York.

"I'm going back to New York." Anna was eight months pregnant and craving a succulent lobster from Lundy's in Brooklyn. Joe could do nothing about it. He was tired and beaten again, but this time he was like the haggard, aged gladiator who gets knocked down for the third time and thinks about not getting up.

✤ ✤ ✤

CHAPTER 3

It wasn't easy being a parent and trying to raise children in Red Hook, Brooklyn. Back in the forties and fifties it was a gangsters' breeding ground. In other parts of Brooklyn, as the children got older and started to venture out on their own, good parents would caution their child, "Don't go to Red Hook, you'll never get out alive." Others would threaten their children by telling them, "If you don't behave, I'm going to leave you in Red Hook."

Even though he lived there for eighteen years, Michael Parisi, Giuseppe and Anna's son, never felt that this was home, so it never was a question of whether he was going to leave the neighborhood; it was only a question of when. But getting out was not easy; there were obstacles and temptations to overcome. Very few got out or wanted to leave this Italian neighborhood. Some tried, but ignorance and/or fear kept many of them from even trying. Those who left and thought they had escaped found themselves locked in a time zone where life was a distortion;

they found it almost impossible to assimilate into American culture and carry the scars of Red Hook with them for the rest of their lives.

During the cold war in the fifties, no one in Red Hook was concerned about whether the Russians were coming to invade America. "No one in their right mind would invade Red Hook," they said.

In the fall of 1952, many thought the battle for the World Series between the New York Yankees and the Brooklyn Dodgers would change mankind forever; that is, if you lived in Red Hook. In every subway series, Brooklyn literally metamorphosed into a carnival. Shysters and hustlers crawled out of the woodwork knowing there would be some out-of-town sucker they could sell the Brooklyn Bridge to. The bookies made book on everything from who would hit more home runs, Mantle or Duke Snider, to who would steal more bases, Phil Rizzutto or Pee Wee Reese.

For Michael Parisi even this was a problem: he was a Yankees fan. Michael detested almost everything about Red Hook. Even the famous, lovable Brooklyn Bums.

All his life Michael Parisi wondered what it would have been like if someone had not burned down his parents' business and home. He could have been raised in the South with a refined southern accent instead of talking through his nose like a wise guy from South Brooklyn. Growing up, he wondered about that a lot. As he looked at the photo of Neddy, Big Ben, Giuseppe, and his mother, Anna, feeding chickens in Jacksonville, he thought they looked so happy. He would have liked to know Neddy and Big Ben instead of his uncle Big Tony and Crazy Joe Gallo. But the one thing he didn't regret was falling in love with Mary Madison Brittain.

But if Michael thought living in Red Hook was bad for him, he could not imagine the humiliation his father had had to endure. After walking out on his wife and giving up his prestigious position and running away with Anna, Giuseppe went back to New York with no pride left. He begged his brother to give him a job so he could support his Michael. Tony relented only because his sisters and his daughter Concetta insisted, but Giuseppe was relegated to a common longshoreman on the piers.

Four years had gone by since Tony, Pasquale, and Giuseppe had their meeting in Tony's basement. This time Tony was sitting at the head of the table. Giuseppe was dressed like a longshoreman. he didn't even own a suit anymore. His head was lowered as he fiddled with his hat, and his insides were becoming *acetto,* like good wine turning to vinegar, while Tony was berating him.

"Oh, look at him, Pasquale, the big *signore* is now a big piece of *medda.*"

Pasquale didn't say a word. He could not even look at his best friend without tears welling up in his eyes. And besides, if he showed any sympathy to Giuseppe, Tony had warned him that he would not take Giuseppe back.

"Now he comes back on his knees like a beaten dog with his tail between his legs." Tony couldn't help himself as he got louder and louder, working himself into a rage.

"You left four years ago and I stayed here. I had to fight the families, the Gambinos and the Genoveses, who wanted to take control of the docks, but I'm here, I'm still standing, and if anybody gets in my fucking way, *sono morte*, I will kill them with my fucking hands. And that includes you." And he got up and pointed to his brother.

"You will work like an animal, because you disgraced this family." Tony sent him down to the bowels of the rat-infested freighters.

But the real reason Tony was reluctant to have him back was because Tony was losing his control over the longshoremen, and he feared Giuseppe would regain the power he once had. The old-timers respected Giuseppe because he came from a noble family in Sicily. He spoke Italian and English, unlike many longshoremen who only spoke the language of the Sicilian peasants and found it difficult to assimilate into the New World with different people and languages and customs.

Giuseppe, in his forties, became their hero. He showed them that someone from their world could get out, and become a *signore*, a respected gentleman.

At this time in American society the Sicilians were considered on the same level of the totem pole as the colored. In the South the Sicilians were lynched, their homes and businesses were burned down, and they were ridiculed as being the missing link between the colored and the white races.

Harold Wilson understood the importance of having Giuseppe in his hand. With Giuseppe's popularity and the respect he commanded among the Sicilians, Harold knew Giuseppe could control the docks, and Harold needed to control the docks, for whoever controlled the docks controlled New York. But when Giuseppe left, a power struggle among the five families had started to smolder, and to say the least, Harold was not comfortable with Big Tony Parisi running the docks without Giuseppe there as his *consigliore.*

But there were other reasons why Harold was not happy: when Giuseppe left New York with Michael's mother, he left his daughter Elizabeth a scorned woman. But Giuseppe had also taken something from Harold, and Harold wanted it back, and her name was Anna.

The sun rose and set with Michael. And for the most part Giuseppe was able to turn a deaf ear when it came to the stories about Anna's infidelity, especially if it meant keeping his son. But the stories kept coming, and eventually he couldn't keep silent anymore.

When Michael was six, a terrible argument between Anna and Giuseppe changed their lives. Michael was perched on the old fireplace mantel at the flat on Sackett Street. Giuseppe was shouting at Anna. Michael felt horror for the first time in his life. There was so much anger in his father's voice he thought Giuseppe was going to kill his mother, and Michael blamed himself for what was happening.

When Giuseppe got home from work earlier that night Michael was in the apartment by himself and Anna was visiting with Mary Toscano and her three daughters who lived in the apartment above them. Giuseppe, who was becoming suspicious of Anna's whereabouts, asked Michael where he had been with his mother.

"We went for a ride in this big car and they bought me ice cream and took me to Prospect Park. I went on the merry-go-round and then I fell asleep in the back of the car. I don't remember any more, Pappa."

Anna had told Michael not to say a word, and it was the usual bribe for a six-year-old: ice cream and a ride in a nice car. But it was her intimidating look that Michael remembered so well; her eyes opened up wide and her head jerked back and sometimes she would kick Michael under the table as a subtle reminder not to say anything to his father. Because this wasn't the first time she had taken Michael for a ride with her boyfriend. Michael would be in the back seat pretending to be asleep. Sometimes he cried, but most of the time he just bit his lip while they kissed or whatever.

"I gave up everything for you, and this is what you do to me and our son? Don't you have any decency?" Giuseppe was incensed; Michael could see the anger building inside ready to explode.

"He's lying! He doesn't know what he's talking about." Anna was nervous as she turned to Michael. "Right, Michael?" She opened her eyes wide to instill that fear.

"No." Michael began to cry.

Giuseppe turned Anna around and slapped her across her face. "*Putana!*"

That night Anna moved out of the apartment. And the young boy carried this mental scar for the rest of his life.

Little Michael tried to go to sleep that night but could not. His little mind could not understand what had happened and he blamed himself. And now he heard his father crying, and Michael put his face in his pillow and wept the entire night.

The one overwhelming motivational drive that young Michael woke up with and lived with throughout those early days in Red Hook was fear. Fear controlled almost all his decisions: how he walked to school, what street he would take, whom he would meet, and whom he tried to avoid.

Red Hook was a simmering volcano, which at any moment would explode into a fight or vendetta between rival families. Sometimes they would fight over something that happened in the old country. But in reality it was ignorance and the overcrowded, depraved living conditions that fueled the flames, especially during the hot summer months. The violence was so severe that the streets would be covered with bleeding bodies and the only way to get rid of the blood would be to open the johnny pump—the hydrant—and let the red water run down the gutter to the sewer at the end of the block.

What Harlem and Hell's Kitchen were to Manhattan, Red Hook was to Brooklyn. Geographically it was South Brooklyn, and it encompassed a ten-block by forty-block rectangle filled with rows of brownstones. The farther away from the waterfront and piers, the nicer the brownstones, and Giuseppe and Michael lived near the waterfront. On the northern boundary was the polluted Gowanus Canal. Its stench stretched for forty blocks, and during the hot summer months it became unbearable—like every other thing in Red Hook. There were three small bridges over the canal, and every time you crossed a bridge you had to hold your nose. Red Hook was eighty-five percent Italians with probably fifty percent from Sicily and the rest from southern Italy. No one ever met an

Italian from Rome, Venice, or Florence living in Red Hook. Why leave Rome, Venice, or Florence?

The blacks and Puerto Ricans lived on the outskirts and were seldom to be seen walking the streets of Red Hook. They knew better. There was no sensible reason to go to Red Hook. Even people who lived in Brooklyn never went to Red Hook. It was said if you made it out of Red Hook you were either a priest, a cop or a gangster. They were right; when he was young, Michael wanted to be a priest. He prayed a lot, and he loved to go to the club.

Giuseppe hated going to the club, but now he had to pay homage to his elder brother. For some of the old-timers it was hard to see their one-time hero reduced to a common longshoreman. As Giuseppe walked in the club you could hear a pin drop as all looked up to see him coming in. His head lowered and fedora in hand, he would walk past some of the old-timers, sometimes placing his hand on their shoulders as a gesture of affection, and they in turn would show their affection for him.

But times were changing, and the newer longshoremen—some of the old-timers referred to them as wise guys or Young Turks—showed no respect. Sotto vocce they called him *vecchio fesso,* and the mean ones would call him *cornuto,* cuckold.

But for Michael it was the best entertainment in Red Hook. No matter what time of day you walked in there, it always seemed as if it was late at night. It was filled with smoke and odors from cheap cigars and cheap red burgundy, which mingled with rampart body odor and bad breath. But some of these guys were the sweetest people Michael had ever met in his life, and no one could ever imagine that some of them were hired hit men.

You had to walk down three steps from the sidewalk to enter the I.L.A. club. At the entrance were two flags, the American and Italian flag, side by side. Every time Michael walked in he saluted the flags. There were six card tables in the front room of the club, and they were always filled with players. Don Pasquale would always be sitting farthest from the front door with his back to the wall, his black cane on the table. He always had one eye on the front door and knew who was walking in before they stepped into the club. Don Pasquale wasn't a real don, but he was an elder and respected and that was important.

"*Bravo, Michele, bravo, vene qui.*" Don Pasquale always called Michael by Michael's grandfather's Italian name. "*Michele, vene qui,*come here." Growing up as children in Sicily, Don Pasquale and Giuseppe had been best of friends. Like many immigrants, Don Pasquale's life was filled with sorrow and misfortune. He lost his wife to cancer, and his only son was gunned down in the streets of Red Hook. Don Pasquale adored Giuseppe, but as fate had its way, when Giuseppe left New York, Don Pasquale was left in a bad situation. Don Pasquale hated Big Tony, but when he was asked to give his support to Giuseppe's half-brother, Don Pasquale had no choice.

When Giuseppe returned, Don Pasquale had to temper his joy at seeing his old friend, and Giuseppe took that as a sign that the friendship was over. But that was fueled by Big Tony's hatred and how Giuseppe had left the Parisi family vulnerable to the other five families. Big Tony wanted his younger brother to be ostracized from the inner circle, and Don Pasquale was in the inner circle.

Don Pasquale loved Michael like his own son and knew deep down that even though he and Giuseppe were not on speaking terms, Giuseppe expected Don Pasquale to look after him.

Every time they came to the club, Big Tony would search out little Michael and tell him, "Your uncle Tony wants you to deliver this to Crazy Joe Gallo." It was always a sealed envelope. Michael never told his father what he was doing. Michael knew Giuseppe and Big Tony weren't on good terms. But Michael always got paid, and the money was good. This was Big Tony's way of digging the dagger into Giuseppe's back. In Tony's mind, Tony had it all and Giuseppe had nothing, and he wanted to keep it that way. But Tony's hatred went deeper than that.

❖ ❖ ❖

Big Tony's father was Turiddo Parisi, who became an infamous outlaw in Sicily. It was said he had an uncontrollable temper, and when he drank he drank himself into a jealous rage. When Tony and his sisters were children, their father, Turiddo, brutally beat his wife, Rosa, and left her body out in a lemon grove in the middle of the night during a rainstorm in a pool of blood. When her friend Maria found her the next day, they thought she was dead.

Months later when Turiddo was found dead, some people said that Michele Parisi had killed him. A few months later Michele married Rosa and they had a son, Giuseppe. To Tony, it didn't matter that his father had almost killed his mother; it was that Michele had married his mother and raised Giuseppe with the advantages in life that he didn't get. In other words, as Santa would say, it was jealousy. *La gelosia a un malattia.*

Don Pasquale knew that Tony was evil and was just trying to drive a wedge between Giuseppe and his son, but Pasquale would not stand for it. However, he would deal with it in his own way. Don Pasquale was one of the few that knew the secrets of the Parisi family in Sicily.

"Evil people breed evil people, and the only way to stop evil people is to cut their hearts out." Santa would whisper to Michael.

❖ ❖ ❖

It was the winter of 1956. The Canadian cold front had settled in. President Eisenhower had his cold war and Russian Prime Minister Khrushchev to contend with, and a hot war between the families was raging in Red Hook for control of the New York piers.

"Who the fuck does he think he is?" Crazy Joe Gallo was getting a little too big for his britches, and Big Tony was about to give the orders to cut him down. Crazy Joe was expanding his numbers racket in South Brooklyn in direct conflict with the Parisi family's new business.

Michael was at the club that day when the orders were given to "cut the motherfucker's heart out." Michael was always afraid of getting too close to Big Tony even though he was his uncle. There was uncontrollable rage inside of Tony that turned him into an animal. Big Tony and his son Blackie were just like the enforcers for the Gambino and Genovese families, Nicky Genovese and Ciclopi. They were depraved, malicious, brutal thugs who had an evil streak in their genetic makeup.

Michael was told in confidence by Don Pasquale—everything Don Pasquale told Michael was in confidence—"Your father was the only one that could control Big Tony, and I wish he could come back."

One afternoon Don Pasquale pulled Michael aside. "Let me tell you something in confidence. Now don't you say nothing, *capice*? Understand?"

"*Si*." Michael promised to keep his mouth closed.

"In Sicily, a most beautiful princess was in love with your father, and he was madly in love with her, but she was promised to someone else. Your father has never forgotten her."

"Don Pasquale, how do you know so much about my father?"

Don Pasquale looked up in the air as if the answer was written on the ceiling, picked up his black cane from the table, favoring his bad leg, stood up, and started to walk away. "Because your father was my best friend in Sicily." A tear welled up in Don Pasquale's eye. "We were the four musketeers."

"Who?" Michael loved the four musketeers.

"The youngest was Rosario. He was funny, he always kept us laughing, and the women loved him. And then there was Luigi. He was the oldest and looked like a prize fighter. He was the strongest, and God forbid if anyone did something against one of us. Luigi was like our older brother. And your father was the leader. He was smart, and we all knew one day he would be somebody. He is still my best friend, but he barely talks to me."

"What happened to them?"

"Rosario died, and when he died, we thought Luigi had lost his mind. For weeks Luigi would not talk to anyone. He didn't eat or sleep, and we thought he was going crazy, and finally one day he decided to return to Sicily and join the bandits fighting the Italians to free Sicily."

"Did the Sicilians win?" Michael was enjoying the story.

"Michael, you have to understand one thing, The Sicilians never win."

"So what happened to Luigi?"

"Well, we first heard that he was killed in a town called Castenetrano."

"Did the Italians kill him?"

"In Sicily you never know. It could have been the *polizia*, the landowners, or the Mafia. Killings there are always brought about by treachery, deceit, and violence. It's the Sicilian tradition."

But the body that was found at Castenetrano was not Luigi's. Luigi had managed to escape and returned to America. When he arrived, he decided it was best to change his name because when the Italian government discovered he was alive they would pay a hefty reward for his death. So Luigi took his mother's family name, Genovese. When Luigi left Sicily and came back to New York, he expected to have his old position on the piers with Giuseppe, but Giuseppe was not running the show anymore. Big Tony was running the International Longshoremen Association.

In Tony's basement they sat, Luigi and Pasquale smoking Camels and Tony sitting at the head like some big shot, smoking a Cuban cigar. "So, Luigi, you come back from the dead and you want your old position back," Big Tony said.

"I think I deserve it. After all, let me remind you, Tony, if it weren't for me, Pasquale, Rosario, and especially Giuseppe, you would be nothing. You would be down there where you put your brother like an *animale*."

"Fuck you," Big Tony replied. "You think you can come back like him after I keep it together from the bastards like your mother's side, the Genovese. We heard you even changed your name to Genovese. So why don't you fucking get out of here and go to those cocksuckers and ask for a position?"

"You fucking asshole, you are making a big mistake." Luigi turned to Pasquale. "And what do you say?" Pasquale didn't say anything. He just shrugged his shoulders as if he was powerless.

That same day, Luigi turned to his uncle, Carlo Genovese, who controlled some gambling and the number rackets in Brooklyn, and made him an offer he couldn't refuse.

Luigi was well liked and respected among the longshoremen. Everyone knew who Luigi was. Even though he changed his name, he was still known as Giuseppe's cousin. After all, when Harold Wilson came to ask the Sicilians for help in breaking the longshoremen strike, which at the time was controlled by the Irish, it was Luigi, Rosario, Pasquale, and

Giuseppe who were the spearheads who organized the Sicilians. In a fierce battle for control of the harbor, they broke the backs of the striking Irish longshoremen, leaving the Parisi family in control.

But now Big Tony was losing control. His only approach to a problem was brute force; compromise was not in his vocabulary. If someone disagreed with you, keep beating him until he said uncle or he died.

The problem with that was the Gambino, Genovese, and Columbo families had the same mentality, and so began the bloody wars for control of the piers among the five families. Red Hook would be the battleground. The streets would be covered with blood and bodies. And Michael was about to become part of it.

✤ ✤ ✤

CHAPTER 4

The control of the New York piers had greater world political implications than most people realized. During the wars, the Wilson family and their British royal cousins overseas needed control of the shipping lanes between New York and England to defeat the Germans. And Lucky Luciano was the man they relied on to control them.

Lucky Luciano was born in 1897 in a small town in Sicily known for its sulfur mines. His family came to America in 1906. Luciano's parents settled in a Jewish neighborhood on the Lower East Side. He shook down young Jewish children on their way to school. This is where he allegedly met Meyer Lansky and Bugsy Siegel.

In 1920, Luciano met Mafia heavyweights Carlo Genovese and Vito Gambino. Together they began a bootlegging venture using trucking firms as a front. By 1925, Luciano and his partners ran the largest bootlegging operation in New York importing scotch directly from Scotland, rum from the Caribbean, and whisky from Canada. By this time, Luciano was becoming a big player in the New York mob.

Luciano and his partners became known as the "Young Turks." Like the original Young Turks of the Ottoman Empire, they formed a young, ambitious, impatient group which challenged the established order. Luciano believed that as long as money was being made, the roots of your partner did not matter. And Harold Wilson was about to become a partner.

Harold Wilson was having dinner at Del Monico's and invited Luciano to dine at the famous restaurant in the heart of the financial district of Manhattan, where the Morgans and Rockefellers made million-dollar business decisions over lavish gourmet meals, the finest tenderized steaks, and, of course, the finest French cognac in the back rooms.

"Mr. Luciano, you are developing quite a name for yourself in this city, I toast you." Harold and Luciano raised their glasses.

"Thank you, Governor, but I'm curious. Why would such a distinguished and well-known person as yourself want to do business with me?" Luciano smiled, knowing very well why he was there.

"Mr. Luciano, I need your help. The Irish long-shoremen are on strike, and we're losing millions of dollars a day because we can't get anyone to unload the ships." Harold hated to be in this position talking to some greaseball, but he had no other choice.

"Governor, I'm honored that you thought of me, but I can't help you now. You see, I got your attorney general, this Thomas Dewey, on my ass, trying to put me in jail." Luciano needed a favor too.

"I tell you what, Mr. Luciano. I put him in that office and I will take care of Mr. Dewey. You have my word on that."

"Okay, so you take care of Mr. Dewey, and so who is going to take care of me?" Luciano was always thinking ahead.

"What do you mean?" Harold was trying to show no emotions, but the greaseball was starting to get under his collar.

"I mean, Governor, what is my percentage of the business? After all, Governor, we're businessmen." Luciano knew there were tremendous profits to be made, but more important was the power that went with it.

Harold knew he was going to have to give up something. These fucking greaseballs were trying to take over everything. "Mr. Luciano, I'm prepared to offer you one percent of all the profit in and out of the port of New York. But that means we have your guarantee we have no more trouble with the long-shoremen, and you personally will oversee the entire operations." In essence the Mafia was taking over the docks, and Harold was paying for protection.

"Governor, Governor, Governor, how can you insult me like this? One percent? I should walk out of this swanky restaurant and let you sit here by yourself, but I'm interested and I have the right person to take control of the striking Micks, but I want ten percent."

"Mr. Luciano, I'm not sure if I can trust you, but if you throw the Irish out and you keep law and order on the docks, I'll give you five percent. Do we have an agreement?"

Luciano extended his hand and they cemented the deal. Luciano spoke. "There is one thing you'll have to do."

"And what is that?"

"You will have to go to Red Hook and speak with Tony Parisi and his *paisani* and tell them you need their help."

"I don't understand. Why can't you go?"

"Because Tony is not the person who will make the decision, Tony is a *caffone*. But his half-brother Giuseppe will be the one to make the decision."

"I still don't understand why you can't go."

"Let me try to explain. Giuseppe's grandfather, Barone Salvatore Parisi, paid my way out of hell. For us kids in Sicily the sulfur mines were hell. But it was Michele, Giuseppe's father, who pleaded with the barone to get me out, so I want to pay back a favor."

"I still don't understand why you can't go." Harold was getting frustrated with the Sicilian and was thinking he might have made a mistake in hiring him. This didn't make any sense.

"This family is an old, respected, noble family of principle. They go back hundreds of years. They are a proud family, and Giuseppe was raised by his father. Do you understand now?"

"Yes, if he knew you were part of this he would not take it. I'm looking forward to meeting this Giuseppe." Harold's wheels were already spinning on how he was going to manipulate this Giuseppe.

In the middle thirties, when the Irish longshoremen were on strike, Harold Wilson was about to propose a deal with Giuseppe and his Sicilian *paisani*. The deal was that if they broke the strike, he would give them control of the docks.

It was a hot and humid August night, and the country was in the midst of a great depression. To make matters worse, the Irish longshoremen were on strike against the United Fruit Company, so whatever little money the Italians made working part-time on the docks had dried up. But no matter how gloomy the situation, the men always found time to play briscola, and on this hot August night, as usual, they were playing cards at Tony's apartment.

That day, Giuseppe was sitting in a corner reading *Il Progresso*. The newspaper carried a story of another atrocity committed against Sicilians and Italians. They were lynched, shot, driven from cities in America, barred from the better paying jobs, and prevented from moving out of the slums. Giuseppe wanted to protest this humiliation of his people, but who would care? Not even his people had pride in themselves. How could they? Most were uneducated peasants unwittingly forced to live in the bowels of a foreign city that ridiculed their customs, blocked from social or economic mobility, and reduced to a status one step above the rats they co-existed with.

That night as Big Tony and their *paisani* played cards, Giuseppe watched while reading the newspaper. The room was filled with the stench of the smoke from their cheap, stubby cigars, and the odor of their perspiration mixed with that of cheap whisky and homemade red wine.

There was a strange, quiet knock at the door. The men stopped playing. Silence filled the room—even the smoke seemed to hang suspended.

Tony grunted, "*Avanti, avanti, entrate.*"

The door opened slowly, and to everyone's amazement, a well-dressed, distinguished-looking gentleman, grey stetson in hand, stood in the doorway.

"Mr. Tony Parisi?" he asked politely. The men turned their heads to Tony.

"*Si*, I'm Tony," he answered.

"May I come in?" the stranger asked.

"*Si, si.*" Tony ordered, "Luigi, give the gentleman your chair." Luigi quickly got up and attempted to clean the seat before he offered it to the gentleman.

"May I speak with you, Mr. Parisi?" he asked, indicating if it was okay to speak with everyone there.

"These are friends and family." Tony introduced everyone: his cousin Luigi and Rosario, their friend Pasquale, and the eldest, his father-in-law Giovanni.

"And this is my younger brother." He pointed to Giuseppe. Giuseppe nodded.

"Mr. Parisi, let me get down to business. I am one of the owners of the United Fruit Company. My company and many of the shipping companies in New York are losing a lot of money because of this strike."

"Why tell me? The Irish strike. What can we do?"

"Mr. Parisi, we want you and your people in the neighborhood to get together and work the docks."

"Are you crazy?" Tony said, nervous and excited. "The Irish will never let us do it."

"Mr. Parisi, the Irish do not own the docks."

"What happens when the strike is over? The Irish get the jobs back, and what happens to us?"

All the men nodded in agreement except Giuseppe.

The elder Giovanni spoke, "Then for sure we will never work the docks."

"I will guarantee that you and the rest of your people will work," the gentleman said. "If you help us break this strike, only you and the people you choose will work the docks."

The men stared grimly at one another. Then Tony spoke: "You come here dressed in a fine suit, and you say these wonderful things, but you do not have to live here. We are the ones who will face these people. There will be much blood, and we are the ones who will lose in the end."

"I gather this means you are not interested in my offer?"

"We are not interested." Tony's voice was abrupt and angry.

"I'm sorry for the inconvenience," the gentleman said and got up and started to walk out. He turned around and looked at the men. "Isn't there anyone here who can see how important this could be for you all?"

"Wait!" Giuseppe spoke for the first time. Tony and the others were surprised to see Giuseppe standing and speaking. The gentleman turned and faced him. "What is your name?" Giuseppe demanded.

"Harold Wilson," he responded.

"English," Giuseppe stated.

"Yes, that is correct." He grinned.

"We are Sicilians, not Italians, Mr. Wilson—like you come from England and not Scotland or Ireland."

Harold Wilson could see he was not dealing with an ordinary peasant. "I apologize if I offended you," he said.

"How do we know for sure that you will keep your promise?" Giuseppe asked.

"You have my word as a gentleman."

"Your word as an English gentleman means nothing to us. You people are more concerned with making profits and building empires than keeping your word."

"How can I assure you?" Harold Wilson asked.

""If you want us—as you say you do—I want a written agreement guaranteeing us the right to hire and fire the men who work the docks."

"You will have it," Wilson responded firmly.

"There will be much bloodshed before it is over." Giuseppe looked intently into Harold Wilson's eyes as he spoke. Wilson nodded as Giuseppe continued, "But if we are ever betrayed, Mr. Wilson, your blood will be there on the streets along with the Irish blood."

"I can assure you there will be no betrayal on our part."

They shook hands, and Wilson left.

Giuseppe turned to Tony, who could not believe what had transpired. *"Ma tu sei pazzo!* You are crazy!" he yelled.

"Do you want to see us all killed?" the elder Giovanni interjected. "All these years you never talk, but when you do all hell breaks loose!" Everyone started yelling and talking at once.

"Ascolti, ascolti, listen!" Giuseppe yelled over the tumult.

Now that he had their attention he was faced with the difficult task of convincing them that he had made the correct decision. "It's true I have kept quiet in the past, but I can no longer remain silent. I can no longer watch as we struggle each day to make a living in this shit while others step all over us and treat us like scum." He paused and looked everyone square in the eyes. "Our women cry when they listen to our music, remembering how beautiful it used to be back home. They work hard trying to make a home out of this garbage we live in, and they stay within these walls, not knowing what it is to breathe fresh air anymore. I see your children growing up in this filth and dirt, learning a new language and forgetting ours, because they are ashamed to say what they are or who their parents are."

Now his voice filled with anger. "But you see none of this, or pretend to see nothing. You sit here and play cards. When they tell us we can work the docks, we work two, three days. We drive trucks and make others rich or we sell fruit like gypsies and beggars. The Romans used us as slaves thousands of years ago on our own island and tried to strip us of our heritage. But the slaves fought; they rebelled. The outlaw Gaetano Giuliani," he said, pointing to Tony, "jumped off the cliffs of Taormina to his death rather than be a prisoner of the Italians and the tool of the aristocratic families. We traveled thousands of miles to escape all that, but now we are worse off; we are still being used. Look at yourselves!" he shouted. "A bunch of *immigranti, animali,* they call us! We live like animals, and we are no better off than the rats down in the cellar."

No one spoke—they didn't have to. They looked at themselves and at the crowded, unhealthy conditions that forced children and parents to share the same beds, where feuds and violence against families competing for living space in this gloomy ghetto were common.

The old man Giovanni spoke: "But Giuseppe, we do not want troubles. Maybe we are meant to be like this. At least we can eat."

"*Senti,* Giovanni." Giuseppe placed his hand affectionately around the older man's neck. "Do you think this man comes here because he likes us? No! He comes here because he is losing money. If we say no to him, he looks for somebody else to unload those ships, and then maybe we don't even work two days a week."

"Giuseppe is right," Tony said. "We have been living like beggars, and the women and children have been suffering long enough. It's time to do something."

"*Si, si.*" The rest of them shouted their approval as Giuseppe and Tony smiled and embraced one another.

"Let's make a toast—to the outlaw Gaetano Giuliani!"

"To Gaetano Giuliani!"

The night was full of excitement as the men sat down to formalize a plan. Later they tried to round up as many *paisani* as would be willing to undertake the risky project.

But Tony was uneasy with Giuseppe taking charge. His evil mind was feverishly fermenting again. But he could not help it.

"Evil comes from the devil inside of evil men. Evil men must be killed. You must take their blood from their body and run it through the town for all good people to see." (A Sicilian remedy spoken by Santa Marsala)

Giuseppe Parisi was able to organize the Sicilian longshoremen to try to break the Irish strikers' control of the piers. The four Sicilian *paisani* Giuseppe, Pasquale, Luigi, and Rosario begin making their plans to take over the piers. And Harold Wilson and his influential international associates would soon be back in business. It would be another favor Harold would owe Luciano.

But Pasquale had second thoughts. He had a wife and two children. "I'm afraid, Giuseppe," he said to his friend.

Giuseppe looked in his eyes. "Me too."

Pasquale paused, thought for a moment, and asked, "Giuseppe, what would Ulysses do?" Both men were remembering their younger years when Ulysses had been their mythical hero. In Greek mythology, the Cyclops threw three rocks toward Ulysses and his men off the coast of Acireale, their hometown.

In Sicily, Pasquale and Giuseppe had been inseparable. They spent their youth playing on these three island rocks and swimming in the warm, blue-green Ionian Sea. Their picturesque town was built along the mountainside with its small stucco homes nestled upward among each other overlooking the majestic snow-covered cap of Mount Etna ominously smoking in the background.

One day when they climbed these rocks, Giuseppe assumed the position on top of one. "*Guardame*, watch me," Giuseppe instructed Pasquale.

Pasquale couldn't help but admire his friend, standing there looking so confident, like a Greek statue on a pedestal, his bronze body reflecting the rays of the Mediterranean sun. Pasquale looked more Arab than Sicilian with a slightly hooked nose and a thin frame, and he could have passed as a rug merchant from Turkey. But Pasquale had a heart of gold.

Looking around him, Giuseppe couldn't help but wonder how many others before him had stood in the same spot admiring such beauty. As he dove off the rock he shouted, "Ulysses!"

Pasquale looked down to Giuseppe and called to him, "I'm scared."

"You can do it. Just make believe you're Ulysses, and the Cyclops is after you," Giuseppe shouted up, trying to encourage his friend. Ulysses was their hero.

Pasquale stood up on the rock and placed his foot in the same spot as Giuseppe had. He tried to swallow his saliva but couldn't. He tried to take a deep breath, but he was so nervous he started to tremble. His heart began beating rapidly and the perspiration dripped from his forehead.

"You can do it!" Giuseppe yelled.

Pasquale jumped, but his left foot slipped. His leg and hip hit the rock at the bottom before he entered the water. Giuseppe swam quickly to retrieve him, saving him from sure death.

"Don't die, Pasquale, don't die!" Giuseppe held his friend's limp body after dragging it out of the water. "Please don't die, Pasquale, please don't die." Giuseppe cradled Pasquale, rocking him back and forth. "I love you so much, please don't die."

"Did I hear you say you loved me?" Pasquale opened his eyes and smiled at Giuseppe.

Giuseppe just smiled and, with a smirk on his face, said, "Don't ever tell that to our friends."

"I will never forget this, I owe you my life." Pasquale paused for a moment and became sad. "I didn't tell we are moving to America. Since my father died in the war my mother has lost everything. My cousin in New York has a job for me and a place to live till we get on our feet."

Giuseppe was saddened. It seemed the whole island was leaving, going to America. "I can't tell you how much I will miss you." And the two young men pledged their loyalty to one another for the rest of their lives.

When Pasquale asked Giuseppe, "What would Ulysses do?" Giuseppe paused as he reflected on that day when Pasquale almost died. Then Giuseppe smiled at Pasquale. From the day he had pulled Pasquale out of the water, Giuseppe had become Pasquale's protector. "Ulysses would do it."

Giuseppe and Pasquale embraced as they prepared to carry out their plans to take over the docks. "When

I left Sicily I never thought I would see you again, and here we are together with Luigi and Rosario just like old times. I am so happy we are together again." Pasquale had tears in his eyes. He had always been the weakest of the four, but they protected each other; Luigi, being the biggest, made sure of that.

Finally everything was ready. The next night a hundred and fifty men—all Sicilians—assembled at the end of the Sackett Street pier. Giuseppe was at the head with Pasquale at his side. Rosario and Luigi were relaying Giuseppe's instructions. "Okay, I want the younger, stronger men in the first rowboats." They were crowding into large wooden rowboats supplied by Harold Wilson and the United Fruit Company.

"The bottles of gasoline will be in these boats. The next group of boats will only have oarsmen, and the life jackets and ropes will be in these boats." Giuseppe was like a commanding officer on the front lines giving inspiration to his men, patting them on the back as they got into the boats. "It's important that we are quiet. This needs to be a surprise."

"What happens when the police come?" someone asked.

"That has been taken care of. Okay, it's getting dark. Let's get started." Giuseppe and Pasquale went to the lead boat. Under cover of darkness, the men began to row upriver toward Manhattan. The harbor was filled with all types of freighters sitting low in the water waiting for their cargo to be unloaded. Many of the ships contained perishable items that had to be unloaded soon or everything would spoil.

As they reached the docks, the men quickly went to work unloading the ships and loading the trucks and railroad cars. There was much tension and excitement; a small number of striking Irish longshoremen were keeping an all-night vigil outside the locked gates.

"Okay, Rosario and Luigi, take as many men as you need and keep watch. If the Irish break through the gates, use the gasoline." Tony was going with Rosario and Luigi when Giuseppe called him, "Tony, I need you to help unload the ships. Get your gang and start on the Brazilian ship. All cargo goes on the first two railroad cars."

Tony was not to happy taking orders from his younger half-brother. "How are we going to get the trains out of here?"

"I told you, in four hours the governor will have men here to help make sure these trains get out. Now let's start unloading these ships."

Tony was skeptical and reluctantly called his gang together to start unloading the Brazilian cargo ship. Four hours went by and all the railroad cars were loaded with cargo, but there was no sight of Harold Wilson's men.

When the Irish realized what was going on, they called for reinforcements. By now they had amassed over a hundred men at the gates. As they tried to get through the fence to stop the scabs from unloading the ships, Rosario and Luigi and their men kept them at bay by tossing lighted wine bottles filled with gasoline at them. Sirens were heard in the distance, and the Irish pulled back their positions from the gates. When Giuseppe heard the sirens, he commanded the conductors to get the trains out.

Giuseppe stopped and was taken aback for a moment as he assessed the situation like a commander looking over the battlefield. Seeing the trains leaving the dock and hearing the sounds of the steam engines and sirens getting louder and louder with the gasoline bombs igniting and illuminating the sky, it looked like a battlefield during World War One. But this was New York. And it was just the first battle in the war to control the docks.

After a few days, word finally leaked out that scabs were using rowboats to get to the pier and unload the freighters. But the Sicilians were ready. Giuseppe and Luigi had prepared and organized the men well. The neighborhood became, literally, a bloody battleground with roving bands of young men from both sides marching up and down the pavements with ice picks and pipes, looking for some guinea or Mick heads to bash in. On a given night, from ten to fifty men and boys were admitted to the emergency rooms: the Italians to Long

Island College Hospital and the Irish to Holy Family Hospital.

The fighting lasted nearly two months and climaxed in a major battle that broke the Irish and established Tony and Giuseppe and the rest of the clan as the primary working force on the New York piers.

One hot August night Kathy Monroe, Rosario's lover, came to Tony's house. The men were down in the basement planning their next move. As she approached the door, a guard at the front door stopped her. "I want to see Rosario. I have to tell him something."

The guard did not understand her as he only spoke Sicilian. "*Ma che volle?*"

"I need to speak to Rosario, now!" she shouted, getting impatient with him.

Someone shouted from the rooftop above them, "*Bastiano questa e la finenzata di Rosario lascia entrata!* Kathy, he will let you in." She recognized him and waved.

Rosario was sitting at the card table down in the basement with Luigi, Pasquale, Tony, and the governor, with Giuseppe at the head with a wooden pointer in his hand. It looked like a war room with smoke emanating from the cigars and cigarettes. Papers and maps of the city were spread out on the table and the men were hunched over them.

Kathy walked in and said to Rosario, "I need to talk to you." She looked frightened and started to shake and cry. "My father and his men are planning to blow up all the rowboats tonight, with you all in them." Rosario went over and comforted her.

"How does she know, and how do we know she is telling the truth?" Tony shouted.

Rosario spoke, "First of all, her father is Charlie Monroe, the head of the Irish longshoremen. He's the one that called the strike and the one who organizes them."

They looked to the governor, and he nodded in agreement with Rosario.

"And let me say this in front of all of you and my God, when this is over, I plan to ask her to marry me if she will have me." Rosario kissed her.

"Oh Rosario, I love you so much." She continued to cry, but these were tears of joy.

"*Minca*, I guess they were hit by a lighting bolt. *Aguri*, good luck." Giuseppe went over and embraced them.

Luigi looked at Tony. "Do you think she is telling the truth now?" Tony didn't answer.

"It's true," Harold Wilson said. "One of our inside men in Moore-McCormack lines just informed me that their tugs are going to be used to break the backs of the scabs."

"*Possiamo parlare con questo qui?*" Tony asked in Italian so that Harold Wilson would not understand.

Harold Wilson quickly realized that Tony still did not trust him. Giuseppe interrupted. "Governor, please accept our apologies." He turned to the rest of the men at the table. "I think we can trust Mr. Wilson. We are in this together. If we win, we all win; if we lose, we die together. *Capice?*" He looked at all their faces.

"*Si*," they said together

"Now let's get down to business."

Pasquale spoke, "But first we need to have a toast, to the *firenzati, Cento Anni.*" Pasquale had the wine gallon opened and the glasses already poured as they all saluted the handsome Rosario and the stunning blue eyes and long red hair of the Irish beauty Kathy Monroe.

"This is good wine." Harold was surprised. Having drunk Tony's wine before, he expected it to be rough, but this was smooth and had a good aroma.

Pasquale just said, "It's Santa's wine."

There was a full moon that night in the middle of one of the hottest summers recorded. The air was heavy and deadly silent when the Sicilians boarded the rowboats as usual at the Sackett Street pier and proceeded to row up the river toward the Battery. Giuseppe, Luigi, Pasquale, and Rosario were in the last boat by themselves as large Moore-McCormack tugboats approached, filled with striking Irish longshoremen.

Charlie Monroe stood at the bow of the first boat shouting obscenities at the Sicilians: "You guinea scabs are gonna get rammed right up your greaseball asses!" He motioned the other tugboats to ram the rowboats. Tension ran high as the approaching tugboats came closer and closer to Giuseppe's rowboat.

Every boat that Harold could find in the city had been brought to the Sackett Street pier and launched into the river. It seemed that every Sicilian from fifteen to sixty had been recruited to man the boats. Luigi and Rosario had personally mobilized the neighborhood into a war machine. And now Giuseppe was prepared to attack.

Pasquale was the first to jump into the river as Luigi and Rosario helped Giuseppe light the fuses attached to dynamite and gallon wine bottles filled with gasoline they had prepared. The fuse was lit. They jumped into the river, and as the tugboat plowed into the abandoned rowboat, the makeshift bomb ignited, sending its unsuspecting Irish crew into the river.

While Charlie Monroe in another tugboat and the other Irishmen watched the inferno in awe, the Sicilians surprised them. Giuseppe's orders had been: "When the first explosion happens we need to be fast and surprise them from their rear. We'll board the tugs and burn every one of them to the bottom of the river."

The hand-to-hand fighting was fast and fierce. Bodies flew off boats in all directions until eventually the Sicilians got the upper hand of the bewildered Irishmen. At one point during the intense fighting, Giuseppe smiled when he looked over and saw Rosario climbing onto Luigi's shoulders as he used to do when they were young. Rosario jumped onto another tugboat that had come alongside to pull off a furious Irishman who was getting the better of Pasquale.

When the fighting was over, everyone jumped except the four *paisani*. As Giuseppe made preparations to blow up the tug, Luigi and Rosario jumped into the river, and Tony helped them board the waiting rowboat.

"*Subito, subito, la polizia,*" Tony warned. The Coast Guard was closing in. Their sirens could be heard across the bay as they drew near. Harold Wilson had kept his end of the bargain. Giuseppe and Pasquale were the last two to jump. They stood atop the smokestack of the burning tugboat looking out at an inferno of boats lighting up the sky with the city lit up behind it.

"Look at that, Pasquale; it's beautiful to look at."

"It reminds me when we climbed to the top of the rocks at the sea and we could see Etna when it was angry," Pasquale said.

The tug was sinking and the flames where getting higher. "Well, we better jump before this fire gets like Etna. Jump, Pasquale!" Giuseppe yelled.

"No, you first." He was getting nervous about jumping off the side of the tugboat.

"No, this time I'm jumping with you." Giuseppe grabbed his hand. Pasquale knew what Giuseppe was referring to, and as they were about to hit the water, they shouted in unison, "Ulysses!"

As promised, three weeks later Rosario married Kathy Monroe. The wedding was at Saint Stephen Catholic Church on Hick Street. The wedding party was small as no one from her side of the family showed up. Some thought her family did not go to the Italian church because they wanted the service at Saint Agnes, which the Irish attended only six blocks away.

Giuseppe was the best man and Pasquale and Luigi where the only two groomsmen. Pasquale's wife and Tony's wife, Sylvia, were bridesmaids, and little Concetta was the flower girl.

The church was full of flowers, every candle was lit, and the red carpet was rolled down the center aisle as the organ player started playing "Ave Maria".

Dressed in rented tuxedos, Giuseppe and Rosario looked like movie stars. They stood at the end of the red carpet waiting for the bride to come in. The buzz in the church was who was going to walk the bride. They were anxiously waiting to see who would usher her in because her father had cursed her and thrown her out of his home when she told him she was marrying Rosario.

Everyone was standing, and the sighs could be heard as they began their walk down the aisle. The bride looked like she just came out of a fairly tale. She was absolutely beautiful, and her smile was intoxicating—a joyous signal of a time of celebration. The governor looked charming in his pin-stripe tuxedo.

This was indeed a time of celebration; both for the wedding and the victory over the Irish. The Sicilian men stood tall with their chests out a bit, proud of what they had accomplished. As the bride made her way down the aisle, Giuseppe felt a presence of someone who was focused on him. He looked to the side and saw a beautiful, statuesque blond dressed like a Fifth Avenue fashion model in the back of the church obviously looking at him. He could not take his eyes away from her, and as she smiled at him she nodded her head and winked.

When the wedding was over and the wedding party turned to face the congregation, the celebration began. Shouts of joy and cries of happiness were showered along with the confetti and rice as the beautiful couple and the wedding party, with their arms in the air signaling a joyous victory march, tried to make it out of the church.

Giuseppe looked for the mysterious blond beauty, but she was nowhere to be found.

Charlie Monroe waited outside the apartment house his daughter and Rosario had entered, still dressed in her wedding dress and he in his tuxedo. He knew which apartment they were in but waited until he was sure no one was around. He walked up the steps and tried the door to the apartment and was surprised to find it unlocked. He silently walked through the front room and took out the loaded revolver he had concealed.

He could hear his daughter's moans. He kicked open the door and pointed the gun at Rosario's head and pulled the trigger. Then he turned the gun on his screaming daughter.

Luigi found Rosario's bloody body the next day. Kathy was not there. He dressed Rosario's naked body and refused to let anyone inside the apartment until Giuseppe and Pasquale got there. They locked the door, and the four of them stayed in the apartment for over an hour while many friends gathered outside the apartment house.

Giuseppe recalled the last few days they were together back in Sicily. They were sitting on the steps of the small church, laughing at Rosario talking about some girl he was trying to court.

They did not notice that Pasquale had stopped laughing. "I wish this would never end," he said. "I wish we could always be together." One by one they stopped laughing realizing that Pasquale's tears of joy had turned to tears of sorrow.

"*Perche?* Why must we go to America? *Perche?*" He was sobbing uncontrollably. No one said a word. Giuseppe went over to him and placed his arm around his friend.

"*Perche,*" Rosario repeated, "in two more weeks Luigi and I go to sea. Who knows where? What can we do, right? *Nienti.*"

"*Perche,* he asks," Luigi said. "What do we know? We go where the jobs are or we don't eat. This island can't support us anymore. The greedy rich bastards have taken it all."

"But America, it is so far away," Pasquale repeated.

"Luigi is right; if we stay here we have nothing. Maybe we have something in America." Rosario looked sad. "But when I think about how our families lived and died here for centuries, if we go to America we will not be buried in our homeland, which is sad."

Giuseppe got up and started to walk away without saying a word.

"Where are you going?" Luigi's voice echoed through the narrow streets, and in it the others could hear the anger and frustration they too felt. "Where is your lecture tonight, *Professore?* Tell us about this beautiful island. Tell us how we can stay and live here so we don't have to die on those goddamn foreign ships like my father. Or die working like animals in

America. Tell us. Tell us." His voice cracked, and he fell to the cobblestone pavement and started to sob.

When the door opened, Luigi was carrying Rosario's body on his back, the way they used to do when they were kids growing up.

The next day Kathy Monroe's body was pulled out of the Gowanus Canal with a bullet in her head.

Two days later Charlie Monroe's body was found, his chest cut open and his heart hacked out and the letter U for Ulysses carved on his back.

Three days later, when the Irish reported to Big Tony's house for assignment on the docks, there were no jobs available for them.

Rosario's wake was a procession of thousands of *paisani* from throughout the neighborhood. The Parisi family felt the death the hardest. Rosario had become like a brother to the Parisi family and had been godfather to their children. He had always been full of fun and enlivened the household during his frequent visits.

Big Tony used the funeral as a show of power. Rosario's body lay in Tony's front room for three days as literally hundreds of mourners and friends filled the house and showed their respect to the Parisi family.

The younger girls of the family constantly served black coffee, and the men helped themselves to drinks at the bar Tony had set up in the basement. Short women dressed in black mourned and wept all day long. Flowers flowed in until a separate room had to be set aside to hold them.

The last night, it seemed the whole world was passing through to see Rosario's body for the last time. His once beautiful face was a horrific mess. It did not even resemble the once angelic boy. Giuseppe sat in the front row of chairs between his sister Maria and his niece Concetta, as the mourners and friends moved slowly, murmuring their condolences.

A strange silence came over the crowded room as Harold Wilson entered, accompanied by a statuesque blonde with blue eyes, who looked as though she had come from a Fifth Avenue fashion show.

"I'm sorry this has happened," Harold said as he extended his hand to Giuseppe.

"This is life. We have no control." Giuseppe stood to greet Harold.

"My daughter, Elizabeth." She was the mystery lady at the church.

Giuseppe's eyes were penetrating. Elizabeth felt his warmth despite the sorrow as her dark blue eyes met his. Concetta and Maria instantly offered their chairs to Governor Wilson and his daughter.

"It's over, Joe. We've won," Harold whispered to Giuseppe. Harold was the first to call him by his American name.

"For now—until someone else tries to take over again."

"Joe, I want you to work for me. Tony can handle the piers with the Anastasia family."

"Mr. Wilson, me! A Sicilian! Work with you? My name is Giuseppe."

"Joe, I need you. I think we could work together." Giuseppe was silent, but he couldn't stifle a grin.

"Mr. Parisi." Elizabeth spoke for the first time. "My father thinks a great deal of you, and he trusts you." Giuseppe looked into her eyes, smiled, and said, "Well, we will see."

CHAPTER 5

Harold Wilson paraded him through his financial sphere of influence and introduced him to the most respected political families in Manhattan. And Harold's daughter Elizabeth paraded him through the Hamptons. She was divorced twice and had never loved anyone until she met Giuseppe Parisi. He was so different, dark and handsome but warm and sensitive, the only one who brought passion to her life.

Elizabeth's twenty-ninth birthday party was almost over. The guests were leaving the ocean-front mansion in the Hamptons, and Joe was sitting in a corner of Harold Wilson's library. He was by himself sipping a cognac and listening to the band that was playing a slow tango in the garden beside the pool. The dance floor was empty. Joe looked pensive and sad sitting there alone.

"A penny for your thoughts." Elizabeth smiled and sat down beside him.

"It would be a shame to waste a beautiful night like this with the band playing. Would you give me the honor of a dance?" Joe didn't wait for her response; he got up and put his hand out, and she followed him to the dance floor.

"I'm honored that the beautiful Elizabeth Wilson has taken the time from her birthday party to dance with me." It was a slow tango, and Joe brought her body next to his.

"You are being sarcastic, Joe."

'I'm sorry, I didn't mean to be."

"Yes, you did. You dislike me, don't you?"

"No, I don't."

"Sure you do. You think I'm a spoiled, rich bitch with no feeling or emotions. Isn't that so?" Joe didn't answer. "You sit there so calm and sure of yourself, and you silently ridicule us and what we stand for. You laugh at our weaknesses and you're glad you're not part of us. Isn't that so? Isn't it?" She was provoking him.

"You're very intelligent and beautiful, Elizabeth," he whispered softly in her ear. "I notice a lot. When you are mad, you are even more beautiful."

The band stopped playing. He kissed her, and her look of anger was replaced by a glow of passion.

Elizabeth looked into his dark eyes and took his hand and led him to her bedroom. He felt so good to her. She embraced him; his dark, firm body smothered her white, slender thighs. His powerful hands grasped her small breasts and then stroked her large, hardened nipples, and she begged him not to stop.

Every week Elizabeth would drive down to the city to meet Joe in her black Packard convertible. They went to the opera, then to a fine restaurant, later spending the night at her penthouse apartment on Park Avenue.

Elizabeth encouraged Joe to drive the Packard. They spent many beautiful, sunny days leisurely driving out to Montauk Point. The scenic, rolling hills and the charming white cottages above the glittering blue Atlantic reminded him a bit of his own home. He would stand on top of one of the high sand dunes, like a child, pointing out to her the natural beauty surrounding them. Elizabeth was amazed that anyone could get so excited just looking at the sea.

"Let's sit here for a while." Joe took the blanket and placed it on the sand and they sat down on the deserted beach, watching the waves break in front of them. The sound of the surf and the smell of the salt air were infectious.

"What are you thinking about?" she asked, holding on to his arm and brushing her face against his bare, tan shoulders.

"I'm thinking of my hometown on the other side of this sea."

"Would you like to go back there?"

"No, I don't think so, not anymore."

"Why?"

"There is nothing there for me any more but memories."

"A girl?"

"*Si.*"

"Was she beautiful?"

"Very."

"And you loved her?"

"Very much."

"And do you love me?" She looked into his deep, dark eyes. He could see her blues eyes fill with tears.

"I don't know." He caressed her long, shapely neck and brushed away her long blond hair.

"You know most men would have said yes. After all, I'm Elizabeth Wilson."

He laughed. "I'm not most men, and names and titles do not impress me. It's what's here that counts." He placed his warm hand on her heart.

"You're not like any man I've ever met." She laughed out loud, and when she stopped laughing, she said, "I love you, Joe." She kissed him, and they made love on the deserted beach.

Elizabeth could not comprehend what was happening to her. For the first time in her life she felt like a silly little girl in love. But it wasn't supposed to happen this way. Her father hadn't told her to fall in love with the guinea, just show him a good time and win him over to run for the open Brooklyn Borough president's seat.

The next day the black Packard was delivered to Joe's house on Strong Place. When he opened the card handed to him by the chauffeur, it read: "Thank you for joining the team," and was signed "Harold Wilson." But he knew it was from Elizabeth.

Giuseppe's godson was Pasquale's son, Frankie Gentile. Frankie adored and emulated his godfather Giuseppe. Giuseppe was married to Margareta, and when they found out that Margareta could not have children they adopted Margareta's two younger sisters.

So Frankie became the son Giuseppe didn't have. He showered the boy with toys and presents, took him to the movies and museums, and paraded him around Giuseppe's American friends in Manhattan at the prestigious Downtown Athletic Club and at the Sag Harbor Country Club in the Hamptons.

"When I grow up I want to be just like my godfather," Frankie would tell his parents, and Pasquale was elated that a bond had developed between his best friend Giuseppe and his son Frankie. After all, Pasquale knew Giuseppe was one of the few from their hometown who was educated.

Giuseppe looked forward to Sunday mornings; he drove his Packard over to Pasquale's apartment and beeped his horn for his godson Frankie. The two would drive to a special place Giuseppe had planned beforehand. This week they were driving to Montauk. Frankie had just turned eighteen and, thanks to his godfather, was accepted to Fordham University.

As they drove, Giuseppe talked about their little town Acireale in Sicily and the great times Pasquale and Giuseppe spent together and the hardships they had to overcome. "Our little town was beautiful. It sat along the mountainside with small stucco homes nestled among the fruit trees and flowers everywhere. It overlooked the beautiful green and blue Ionian Sea. In the distance Mount Etna would mesmerize you. Acireale was full of ancient history and Greek mythology." Giuseppe stopped and Frankie could see a tear welling up in his eye as he talked about his homeland.

"*Zio*," Frankie called Giuseppe "uncle" out of respect, "why did you all leave Sicily?"

Giuseppe paused, not really wanting to bring up the past, but he did. "We didn't want to leave, we had to leave. Children were being forced to work in the sulfur mines by greedy, powerful men, and when the Italians came, they taxed our farms and animals so we had to give up land our families had for generations. They purposely kept the Sicilians ignorant so that they would always have a work force for the noblemen's vineyards and estates."

"But *zio*, that wasn't you. My father said you came from a much respected family and you could have gone to any college, so why did you leave?"

Giuseppe wanted to end the conversation. "Remember one thing: respected families sometimes are the worst offenders of greed and treachery in their quest for power."

Giuseppe remembered how he had felt after finding out that Harold Wilson was involved with Luciano and the five families in their gambling, prostitution, book making, loan sharking, and extortion and using the longshoremen to conduct an illegal international drug smuggling trade from Latin America to Sicily and back to the United States. He wanted no part of it. Giuseppe became sick of the thought of how some manipulative, power-seeking men used people, especially the young and innocent, to feed their greed for more power. Giuseppe was sick and tired of it all.

In Sicily, it was Riccardo Conti and the infamous Don Carlo who used the peasants to increase the Contis' vast landholding and fortunes, and Don Carlo was "the Power." In New York the names were different but the game was the same.

The straw that broke the camel's back for Giuseppe came one snowy Christmas Eve in Red Hook. The Young Turks in the Genovese and Gambino families were getting restless. They were not satisfied with the status quo. So they decided to push their drug trade into Red Hook, in direct defiance to the Anastasia and Parisi families.

The black Buick pulled alongside Bryer's ice cream parlor on Smith Street. It was six o'clock and a busy time of the day. The music from the jukebox could be heard as the doors opened and closed to let the local patrons in and out. The black Buick stopped in front of the ice cream parlor. They knew Frankie was inside, and when he came out they opened fire on him. The screams could be heard for blocks. As the black Buick took off, it left a cloud of gray smoke, and when it lifted, Frankie Gentile's body lay motionless as the clean white snow around him quickly became red.

The young boy's body lay in a solid mahogany coffin in Scotto's funeral parlor on Second Place in Red Hook. It was December 28; the snow had stopped but not the wind, and it was brutally cold. Lines of mourners waited outside Scotto's funeral parlor to pay respect to the families.

Without telling his parents or godfather, Frankie had decided not to go to college. Like other young Italian boys, Frankie idolized the mobsters; it was the lure of easy money and the eventual status they could earn among their peers. "College is for the fags." That was the mentality of Red Hook.

Behind his family's backs, Frankie was making good money taking numbers and selling drugs to school kids in the neighborhood. Now Frankie had just become another of the fallen prey from Red Hook.

The mourners poured in and made their way to the coffin. After the mourners prayed they turned to the grieving family in front to express their sorrow. Giuseppe and Margareta were sitting with Pasquale and his wife and daughter when Santa Marsala paid her respects to them.

"*Mi dispiace, e piccatto,*" Santa expressed her sorrow to them. They had heard those words all day long, but when it came from Santa it came from her Sicilian soul. After all, she shared their history and faith in Acireale.

"*Questa e mia filglia,* this is my daughter, Anna," Santa said.

When Pasquale looked up, all he could say was, "*Dio mio.*" Oh my God.

Giuseppe just whispered her name so only Santa could hear, "Claudia."

Santa nodded. *La sorella,* her sister.

It was only three months later that Giuseppe left for Florida with Anna. The death of his godson had opened up his eyes to the corruption and brutal world he found himself living in, but it was Anna who opened his heart again and gave him hope, hope that one day he would have a son.

But Giuseppe had to return to New York with his tail between his legs, a beaten man; now his only reason to carry on was his son, Michael. He would have liked to move away, anywhere from Red Hook and his past, but that would have meant Michael not seeing his mother, Anna. But probably more important was that he would be denied seeing his grandmother, Santa.

Back in New York, Giuseppe reverted back into his shell. He got up early in the morning, fed his son, sent him off to school, and left for the docks. Santa would pick up little Michael from school and keep him until Giuseppe returned. Throughout the day Giuseppe rarely spoke to anyone. He worked alongside his old *paisani* and never complained about the cold, heat, or rain. He was focused on one thing: when the whistle blew he was all smiles, knowing he would be with his son.

It had been a few years since Anna moved out. Giuseppe had just finished a double shift on the docks. It was late morning and he was exhausted and wanted to go to bed, but Michael was playing stickball with the Sackett Street Dukes. He sat his tired body on the stoop in front of his brownstone, pulled out a book from his pocket, and began reading, one eye reading and the other keeping an eye on his son. Maureen Walsh, the cute, skinny little Irish girl loved Michael and always made a point to sit with Giuseppe.

Maureen never knew her father and was drawn to Giuseppe since he read to her, but today Maureen was watching Michael. It seemed as if all the people on the block were watching the stick ball game. Some were watching from their windows and some were sitting on the parked cars. It was a game against the Union Street Saxons.

A black Buick Roadmaster pulled up and double parked in front of the brownstone. The game came to a screeching halt as everyone thought it was going to be another rub-out of some Mafia thug, something that was happening more frequently in Red Hook.

The driver slowly got out and walked over to the passenger's door. At the same time two men in black got out of the back and surveyed the situation. It was Luigi Genovese, Giuseppe's cousin. Luigi had been back from Sicily a year now and had made no bones about taking what was rightfully his, and Big Tony was standing in his way.

Luigi walked over to Giuseppe, who had gotten up and ushered away Maureen. Michael had started walking toward his father, but one of the players stopped him.

There was a big sigh of relief as the two *paisani* embraced. Luigi whispered in his ear, "*Ti amo.*"

"I love you too." Both men had tears in their eyes as they embraced again.

"Are you okay?" Luigi asked.

"I'm okay."

"Do you need anything?"

"I'm fine. I got everything right here." And Giuseppe put his arm around little Michael, who had run over to his father's side.

"I'm not. This is not right what Tony did to you."

The news of that meeting spread quickly around Red Hook, and the next day not only Big Tony was hearing about it, but all the heads of the five families.

Luigi didn't change Giuseppe's mind, but that wasn't the message Big Tony got. Big Tony didn't know who or how the Genovese and Gambino families were coming after him, but he knew one thing: he feared Giuseppe the most.

But Giuseppe kept on doing what he liked best, which was sitting on his front stoop reading or translating a letter or document for a friend. There were times when Giuseppe would gather a bunch of Michael's friends on the steps and teach them games he had played as a youngster in Sicily. And of course, he told them about the mythical adventures of his hero, Ulysses. He was respected again, and by now the cruel whispers behind his back had turned to accolades of affection and admiration, and the old-timers were saying, "The Prince is back." They hoped he would take control again.

But Giuseppe had other plans. In Greco-Roman culture, the bond that developed between a father and son was considered to be the ultimate treasure of life. Giuseppe had an inner sense of pride and strength and an overwhelming love for Michael. Despite all their obvious hardships, Giuseppe was determined to get his son out of this ghetto and to make sure he wouldn't be one of Red Hook's victims or succumb to the Parisi family's temptation.

While Michael was sleeping Giuseppe would place his arm around him and whisper in his ear, "*Sciatu mio.*" These two words were the ultimate expression of love for a Sicilian. Sometimes Michael would pretend to be asleep trying to stop the tears from flowing onto his pillow when he heard his father whisper "*Sciatu mio*" and kiss him. It made him feel so special and almost made up for not having a mother.

During those early years, when Michael was younger, it seemed the winters in New York were colder, and it would snow from November to March. The two of them would watch from their window as the wind swirled around the rooftops and alleyways, creating huge white drifts. It snowed so much that parked cars would literally disappear for days.

But in their apartment, away from the gloom and depravity of the ghetto, the young Michael's days and nights were full of wonderful dreams and his imagination was unlimited. Giuseppe became his tutor, and Michael was an eager learner. The warm kerosene stove was in the center of the middle room. In the mornings Giuseppe would peel an orange and place the pieces on the stove. They played scuba and briscola, Italian card games, listened to the Italian radio station playing some the great arias sung by two of the greatest tenors, Caruso and Lanza, and the citrus aroma would linger for hours. At night Giuseppe would tell Michael stories about the Parisi family from Sicily; that they were from nobility and lived in castles and beautiful palazzos. And he would tell stories from Greek mythology and of places he had traveled throughout the world.

Michael was fascinated with Constantinople, Turkey. In Constantinople, Giuseppe was only nineteen when he got a tattoo on the inside of his left forearm. It was a beautiful naked woman with a snake wrapped around her. It was fading now, but Michael could see the initials underneath the tattoo, C.C.

"Pappa, what does the C.C. mean?"

Giuseppe got up from the table and walked to the window. "It was a girl in Sicily that I knew a long time ago."

"And where is she now?"

Giuseppe looked at his son with tears welling in his eyes. "*E morta.* She died very young." And he whispered so Michael couldn't hear him, "And so did I."

✣ ✣ ✣

CHAPTER 6

After the meeting that summer a year ago between Luigi Genovese and Giuseppe when the two cousins embraced, many thought Giuseppe would come back to lead. His influence among the elders was still there and growing. But Giuseppe's heart wasn't. Ever since his godson was gunned down in the streets of Red Hook, Giuseppe realized that Harold Wilson, Big Tony, and the Gambinos, Genoveses, and Gallos—the three G's—were evil and treacherous. They would stop at nothing to get control of the docks. Just as Don Carlo and Riccardo Conti in Sicily would stop at nothing to get control of the sulfur mines.

As Lucky Luciano said: "Whoever controls the docks, just like whoever controls the sulfur mines, controls the most power."

Giuseppe just wanted to raise his son. But someone wanted him dead. And that someone had just signed a contract with the devil.

When Minicu Persico's grandson arrived in America, he came with a horrific past. And the rotten apple doesn't fall far from the rotten tree; they called him Claudio un Occhio because he only had one eye and a black patch over the other. Pasquale called him "Ciclopi," Cyclops. Santa Marsala called him the devil.

Ciclopi was one of Crazy Joe Gallo's planted troublemakers. He was much older than the Young Turks, but he was as close as one could get to being an idiot. He was big, strong, and horrific, easily manipulated, and was used by the Gambino and Genovese families to extort monies and favors. Ciclopi was feared. Ciclopi was a leader of one of the gangs that worked the piers for the United Fruit Company, and he had been told to make sure Giuseppe had an accident.

In Sicily, Minicu Persico, was the notoriously brutal enforcer in the sulfur mines for the infamous Don Carlo, the head of the Mafia in Palermo. In the small town of Trapani, Ciclopi was wanted for the murder of a ten-year-old girl he had raped. The poor, innocent, angelic Dominique had been playing in the cemetery amongst the tombstones when she was brutally attacked. Her mother had given her a pair of scissors to cut some herbs in the *giardini* when she felt something evil behind her. When she turned around, a monster confronted her.

Don Carlo sent Ciclopi off to America before someone cut his heart out and stuffed his *cagliones* in his mouth. But a vendetta was placed on the family by the grieving mother, and all of the Persicos in Trapani that were related to this family were killed. The mother vowed to kill the evil and end the bloodline.

The daughter had taken out his eye; the mother wanted the rest. "I will not die until I get my revenge," she had vowed.

Giuseppe had worked hard as a longshoreman, and over the years his hard work paid off. The gang he had worked with for the past three years had chosen him to be their leader. It was a sign of respect and honor among the longshoremen. His gang was a mixture of older Sicilians and the newcomers to America: the Italians from Bari and Naples.

Don Pasquale still had some influence on the docks, and he made sure that Giuseppe's gang was assigned the better cargo ships; he tried to take care of his best friend in spite of Big Tony.

One day Pasquale was sitting in Marco Polo, a small Italian restaurant across from the I.L.A. Club. Pasquale was sitting by himself, but he was waiting for someone, and he was nervous about meeting this person.

The waiter came up to him and whispered, "Mr. Castellano is sitting in our private room in the back and would like for you to join him." Pasquale was relieved.

"Please sit, Pasquale, and join me." Mr. Castellano was very polite and refined, unlike some of the other dons.

"*Grazie, Signore* Castellano." Pasquale sat and moved closer to Paulie Castellano. "*Poi parlarmo?*"

"*Si*, we can talk. But let's order first. Giovanni!" He called the waiter. "I think we will start with the grilled calamari with lemon and a plate of linguine and clams in the white sauce. For the *secondo* let's try the lamb chops. Is that okay with you, Pasquale?"

"*Si.*"

"And a bottle of your finest Chianti." And the waiter left. "Pasquale, what's going on? Tony seems to be out of control and his son Blackie is not better."

"I know, Mr. Castellano, that's why I wanted to talk with you. I can no longer stay with him; he's like a volcano ready to explode, and I don't want to be there when it happens."

"Can we get Luigi to come back?"

"I've been talking to Luigi, but he'll have nothing to do with Tony."

"If only if we could get Giuseppe to come back. He's the one to end this fiasco."

The waiter came in with the calamari.

A large cargo ship from Colombia, South America, had come in on a rainy April morning. Another gang was assigned to help Giuseppe's gang unload the bananas.

When Pasquale found out that Ciclopi was a last-minute addition to this gang, he knew something was up and quickly went to the ship, but by the time he got there it was too late.

"Hey, old man, I hear your beautiful young wife is a *putana.*" Ciclopi had one purpose: to make sure that this would be Giuseppe's last day as a longshoreman. His instructions had been, "do what you have to do."

Giuseppe's *paisani* and gang were quick to come to his defense, keeping Giuseppe at arm's length. But the taunting grew louder and Giuseppe couldn't silence his aching heart. Seconds later Giuseppe and Ciclopi were facing off with picks in their hands,

The older men tried to break up the fight, fearing for Giuseppe's life, but Crazy Joe Gallo's hired thugs quickly restrained them. The fix was in, and Giuseppe was the prey.

The word spread like wildfire along the piers that a fight had broken out. It looked like a scene from the Roman Coliseum as the gladiators were pitted against one another in a struggle for life or death. Giuseppe's quickness and agility surprised Ciclopi. As Giuseppe stared at Ciclopi's monstrous face he tried to use every advantage he could to make up for the obvious mismatch.

By now Pasquale had arrived, and he immediately called out to Giuseppe, "Ulysses! Kill the Cyclops!" And his *paisani* picked up the message and started chanting, "Come on, Ulysses, *marzullo il* Ciclopi, kill the Cyclops!"

The chants became louder and louder. An angry, snearing Claudio turns to spit at them. That was the opening Giuseppe needed. Striking the first blow, Giuseppe slashed Ciclopi's nose with his pick. Ciclopi let out a scream like a wounded bear. In desperation, he threw his large body forward, leaping toward his prey. Giuseppe slipped, and Ciclopi's pick plunged into Giuseppe's chest, just missing his heart.

Two days later when Giuseppe woke up in the hospital, there was a vase of flowers on the table next to him. The card read simply, "Elizabeth Wilson Brittain." His friend Pasquale stood by his side.

"Hello, *Paisano*, it's been a long time. *Come ti senti?*" Pasquale was holding Giuseppe's hand.

"I feel like a crazy Cyclops tried to cut my heart out," Giuseppe answered slowly.

Pasquale smiled. "I missed you, Giuseppe."

"You knew where I lived," Giuseppe answered.

"*Si*, but I couldn't come." Pasquale stopped. "I really missed you. Things were not the same after you left. Your brother went crazy and no one could control him, not even Harold Wilson. When you left we almost lost everything, and now these wars for control, because Tony is *testa dura*, hard-headed. He doesn't know how to negotiate and bring people together like you did."

"Times were tough for all of us," Giuseppe barely answered his friend. "How's my son Michael?"

"Michael is fine. He's with his grandmother, Santa. I pick him up every day from school and take him to her apartment. He's okay, but he is worried about you."

"And his mother?" Giuseppe whispered.

"She visits them every day." Pasquale was short and to the point. He had never liked Anna and blamed her for all that went wrong.

"What a mess I've made." Giuseppe turned with tears welling in his eyes; he looked toward the sunlight coming through the shutters.

"How can you blame yourself? Listen, Giuseppe, let's go back, back home to Sicily, and leave this mess behind us. You deserve to claim what was yours. *Capice?*"

"They call me 'the Prince' here, and go back, go back to what? There is nothing there for us anymore, our life is here. Promise me if anything happens to me you'll take care of Michael. Promise me." Giuseppe looked into his friend's teary eyes.

"Nothing will happen to you."

"If it wasn't for his mother I would leave this place now, but at night I know he still cries for her. And after all that has happened, I can't bear to have him suffer anymore."

"It wasn't your fault; you did everything a father could do and more, and you did good; he's a good kid."

"I could do more." He became quiet for a while and looked toward the window. "I'm getting old and tired. I don't know if I have the strength anymore."

"What are you talking about? You should have seen yourself out there. You were Ulysses back in Sicilia."

"No, I was lucky. I gave everything I had inside of me. I have no more, I have no more to give."

"Stop talking that way."

"Listen, Pasquale." He reached out for his friend's hand. "I don't have much time. I don't want him to be part of this family business. I don't want him to meet the same fate as Frankie."

"*Capisco.* I understand." Both men had tears in their eyes.

Pasquale got up and pulled out a letter from his jacket. "It's a letter to you from Sicilia. It's from Claudia. *Viva,* she's alive." He placed it on Giuseppe's bed.

Giuseppe felt the pain in his chest from the pick that had penetrated his lung. But after he read the letter, he folded his arms over his chest with the letter in hand, and the tears started to flow from the pain and sorrow in his heart.

❖ ❖ ❖

CHAPTER 7

In the fall of 1959, Vice President Richard Nixon and the young senator from Massachusetts, John F. Kennedy, were bearing down for the battle of their lives.

"Now let me tell you something in confidence. *Capisce?*" Michael and Don Pasquale were driving in Don Pasquale's brand new black '59 Oldsmobile 98, just the two of them, heading for Roosevelt Raceway. The trotters were running, and Michael was running for Don Pasquale. Where Giuseppe was teaching Michael about history and literature and the appreciation of the arts, it was Don Pasquale who was teaching Michael how to survive in Red Hook.

Don Pasquale couldn't walk very well, so Michael had to place his bets at the windows. Like every gambler, Don Pasquale had a system, and it worked like this: He took the favorite horse from the first three-post positions. A look at the charts showed clearly that one of the three would win fifty percent of the time. Don Pasquale's wager depended on the odds of the selected horse. In his system, Don Pasquale put up a limit of five hundred dollars for the night. Once he reached his goal for the night they were gone.

Nice change; it sounded simple. Sometimes the bet was a hundred to win five hundred, but if he lost three of four races in a row, the bet escalated. Sometimes Michael had to place thousand-dollar bets just to win five hundred.

But Don Pasquale was up twenty-five thousand for the season. And Michael was having a ball. Three nights a week Don Pasquale picked Michael up at the club and they'd drive to the track. Sometimes Michael and Don Pasquale stayed for one race, hit the jackpot, and off they'd go to Sheepshead Bay and eat in the finest fish restaurant in New York City. Appetizers of raw clams and oysters on the half shell on a bed of ice with freshly cut slices of lemon. Afterwards they would relax in a nice leather chair and order a succulent, steaming red lobster. It took them an hour to search for all those hidden morsels.

Lundy's was a real classy restaurant, a beautiful white stucco Mediterranean building with a terra-cotta tile roof and colorful baroque stained glass windows. The ambiance of the interior was just as distinctive, with decorative Spanish tiles around faded white stucco archways that led to private dining rooms for the wealthy, influential clientele who wanted or needed privacy. No matter what time of day, the place was always crowded, and reservations were needed unless you were somebody important.

"Look at the waiters dressed in tuxedos. How nice they look; a real classy place. Your father took me here the first time." Don Pasquale and Michael were eating raw oysters at the bar. From where they were sitting they could see the fishing boats pulling into the dock.

One time they were sitting at the bar and Frank Sinatra walked in.

"Hey Don Pasquale, *come stai?*" Frankie gave Don Pasquale a big hug.

"Hey, Michael, say hello to Mr. Sinatra." Michael couldn't believe it. He was shaking hands with Frank Sinatra. And that's the way Lundy's was—you could meet anyone from wise guys to judges, and sometimes they'd end up in a private room together.

"Let me tell you something in confidence. *Capisce?*" Don Pasquale was talking sotto vocce. The wars between the New York families for control of the piers, racketeering, prostitution, and now narcotics had been going on for almost three years now. Big Tony and the Anastasias still controlled the piers, but the crazy Gallo brothers and the Gambino and Genovese families were getting stronger and wanted more control. Big Tony delegated control to his oldest son, Carmine, who they called Blackie. Blackie was the carbon copy of his father, a hundred pounds heavier and just as ruthless.

Blackie was typical of the new generation of Italians in Brooklyn. They called them the Young Turks. They thought they were made men simply by having a name or knowing someone who had a name. Blackie loved to play the staring game. Blackie stared at you till you backed down, and he always won. If you didn't back down, he beat the crap out of you. Michael hated being around Blackie. Whenever he saw him, Michael walked the other way.

Don Pasquale was sucking the meat out of the lobster claw. "I don't want you coming around the club for a while, *capsice?*" Don Pasquale knew another blood bath was about to hit the streets of Red Hook. And he had made a promise to his friend Giuseppe.

Don Pasquale cracked the claw in half with a nutcracker and then looked at Michael. "Listen, your father was my best friend. Things happened in the past that we both can't change, but I still respect your father. He has sacrificed his life for you. God knows what he's been through, and I don't want you to let him down. You will go to college and get the hell out of Red Hook. *Capsice?*"

Michael had a smile on his face. "You know you and my father sound alike." Michael couldn't finish before Don Pasquale interrupted him.

"I think you young people talk too much. Sometimes you don't have to talk. All we have to do is look into each other's eyes and we know."

The tall, middle-aged waiter, Dean "Scungadu" Demattio, came over to them. Dean used to be a golf hustler. They called him Scungadu because his legs had been broken on the orders of Carlo Genovese and he walked with a terrible limp. He no longer was a golf hustler. He waited on tables and played the accordion during weddings.

Scungadu wouldn't let Don Pasquale wait too long for a table, as it was a sign of respect. The waiter brought them an extra tray of raw clams and two more glasses of wine. Then Dean Demattio bent over and whispered, "It's complimentary, from Mr. Davis at the bar." There he was, Sammy Davis Jr., saluting Don Pasquale.

"*Grazie,* Sammy." Sammy gave him the thumbs up sign.

It wasn't the best table in Lundy's, but Don Pasquale liked it because he could see who was coming in and who was going out. And that was important, especially when your life depended on it.

It was a busy night, business as usual for Lundy's, and it was noisy as a political fundraiser was being catered in the back room for Vice President Richard M. Nixon. The place was hopping with all kinds of distinguished guest coming and going.

Don Pasquale mumbled, "I wonder who's throwing this party?" No sooner had he said that than he exclaimed, "*Dio mio!*"

A distinguished-looking older gentleman in black tails arrived escorting a young lady. They almost walked past their table when he noticed Don Pasquale and stopped. It was an awkward moment as both men tried to make small talk.

Michael knew this man was important because he saw Don Pasquale rise from his seat to greet him. He looked familiar, but Michael couldn't place him.

"How are you, Don Pasquale?"

"Fine, *grazie*, Governor." Michael realized that he was the former governor of New York, Harold Wilson. Michael couldn't believe the governor had stopped at their table to greet Don Pasquale. Michael waited for Don Pasquale to introduce him, but he never did. He seemed very uncomfortable as he kept clearing his throat.

"I want you to meet my granddaughter, Mary Madison Brittain. She's from Charleston, South Carolina, but she has decided to go to Columbia here in the big city and she'll be living with us."

Michael stopped breathing and his heart pounded so loud that Don Pasquale could hear it. Don Pasquale realized Michael had been struck by a lightning bolt. Mary Madison Brittain looked like a princess out of a fairy tale book. Dressed in a lacy powder-blue ballroom dress, her blonde hair was rolled up, and she had a diamond tiara meticulously placed like a crown on her head.

At eighteen, Michael had grown up quickly. There was no mistaking that he was Sicilian. His grandmother Santa always said he had the map of Sicily on his beautiful face. He looked like a young Giuseppe. But Don Pasquale still didn't introduce Michael. Michael tried to give him a subtle hint by stepping on his shoe, but it didn't work.

"My name is Michael, pleasure to meet you, Governor." Michael extended his hand to Harold Wilson, and as he turned to Mary Madison he bowed like a knight. "My princess, I am at you service."

Mary Madison blushed and started to laugh. She curtsied to Michael. "Oh thank you, Sir Lancelot," she said in jest. Then with the thickest of southern accents, "I do declare, I was led to believe that only fine southern gentlemen were chivalrous." She extended her hand to be kissed.

Michael knelt down on one knee in front of her and kissed the back of her hand. None of them realized that everyone in the restaurant had stopped eating to watch them. "Bravo, bravo!" they shouted in unison, making Mary Madison blush even more. By now Don Pasquale's face was probably as red as the lobster on his plate and Harold Wilson was getting a bit steamy under the collar.

Michael was still on his knee when he looked up and said, "Mary Madison, you are a beautiful princess."

She smiled and said, "And you are a handsome prince."

"Well, it seems we have a charmer here. Don Pasquale, who is this young man?" Harold Wilson seemed a bit uncomfortable with the exchange between his granddaughter and the young man. He had a big grin on his face, but it wasn't a smile.

"Oh." Again Don Pasquale was obviously having a problem introducing Michael. "This is Michael Parisi, Giuseppe's son," he finally blurted out.

The grin immediately disappeared from Harold Wilson's face as he grabbed Mary Madison. "Let's go," he said, and they were gone, leaving Michael still on his knee.

"*Che su chiso?* What happened?"

Don Pasquale looked up as if the answer was on the ceiling "*Ammunini.*" It was Sicilian slang and meant "let's go now." "Ask your father."

Don Pasquale stopped the Olds on the corner of Court and Union. They hadn't said a word to each other all the way from Lundy's. When Michael got out of the car, Don Pasquale whispered sotto voce, "Remember what I told you, *capsice?*"

Michael was disheartened; he didn't understand why his best friend Don Pasquale wouldn't explain what just took place in Lundy's. "*Si.*" Michael wasn't going to the club anyway. With Blackie there now and the family wars still going on, it wasn't the same. Besides, the old men weren't playing cards or checkers as much because they had been pushed aside by the young wise guys. Blackie's boys liked to play poker; they even brought in a pool table. Michael didn't like them—there was something sinister about them and they didn't have what the old-timers had, respect.

"Can I tell you something in confidence?" Don Pasquale called out to Michael as he walked away from the car.

"*Che?*" Michael looked at him and saw that his frown had changed to a smile.

"You know you're my best friend?" He paused. "*Ti amo.*" And he drove off.

After Pasquale dropped him off, Michael decided he needed to take a walk. He could think only of her, Mary Madison Brittain, the prettiest thing he ever saw.

It was a still, cool December night, and Michael could hear his friends Dyale Forsythe and Phil Dressler and some of the local guys harmonizing to Dion and the Belmont's hit, "Run Around Sue." They were standing around a fire in a metal can.

"Hey, Michael, come join us." It was Phil Dressler, the only Norwegian in the neighborhood, and he was Michael's best friend. Two years ago Michael and Phil were sophomores in Manual Training High School when they made varsity teams. Phil made the swim team and Michael made the baseball team.

"Where have you been?" Phil was six foot two with a swimmer's body, and he treated Michael like a protective older brother. A special bond had developed between them. They were both only children, and Phil too was being raised by a single parent, his mother.

"We were looking for you. We went to Nathan's for hot dogs and drove around Coney Island. You should have seen the girls we picked up from Bensonhurst, real *putanas*." Phil liked using Italian words.

Michael looked up and smiled. "Did you find Sophia?"

Phil always said he was looking for his dream girl, but she had to look like Sophia Loren. Phil was in love with Sophia Loren. His infatuation with her started the day that he asked Michael to go to Manhattan to the movie theater. Sophia was starring in the movie *Two Women*. That year, she won the Academy Award for best actress. She played a mother who was trying to escape the perils of war with her young teenage daughter; a company of African mercenaries viciously raped them. They watched the movie three times and Phil fell in lust with Sophia. But Phil was secretly in love with Dorothy Toscano. She lived with her mother and two older sisters in a third-floor apartment above Michael on Sackett Street.

There was one problem: Dorothy was going out with Nicky Genovese, Carlo's son.

"I don't think I'll ever find Sophia. I might have to lower my standards." They were standing by the open fire listening to the boys harmonizing to another of Dion's hits, "Where or When."

"You mean you don't think there's a nice Italian girl out there?" Michael smiled, teasing his friend.

"No, so I think I'm going to look for a nice Jewish girl to date."

"A Jewish girl? Why a Jewish girl?"

"Haven't you noticed? They got the biggest boobs and they are the sexiest girls in school. Besides, Marsha Swartz has the hots for me, and her girlfriend

Susan Meyers has the hots for you. I set up a date for the two of us. You're going to owe me big time." Phil had an infectious smile, and Michael started laughing.

"Susan will have to wait."

"Are you crazy? Susan is the hottest piece in the school. Any guy would give his right arm to get a date with Miss Boobs. She's almost as good as Dorothy Toscano."

"Walk me home." Phil started to walk with Michael. He lived in the city projects; they were three blocks from Michael's apartment. "I met this girl tonight. Her name is Mary Madison Brittain. She is so different I can't explain it. It's like we met before in a dream or somewhere."

"Ha, *amore, bella bella, tu si innamorato.*" But Michael just smiled. Phil had told him he was in love.

"She looked like a princess, she's beautiful, and when she smiles..." Michael couldn't finish.

"Listen to you, you sound like you've been hit by a lightning bolt. Who is this girl, and besides, what kind of name is Mary Madison Brittain? With three names like that I'm sure she's not from Brooklyn."

"Southern, from Charleston. Her grandfather is Harold Wilson."

"Harold Wilson the governor?" Phil was beside himself. "Are you crazy? Do you think for a moment you're going to get to first base with this Mary... whatever?"

"Phil, I'm going for the bleachers, and besides, he's the ex-governor."

"My little *paisano*, I'll have more of a chance of going out with Sophia or Dorothy Toscano, for that matter, than you with this southern belle, Mary Madison whatever her name is."

Phil and Michael were so engrossed in their conversation that they didn't realize they had walked into the Gallo brothers' turf. They were in front of Monte's restaurant on Carroll Street. Monte's looked like a hole in the wall, but it was one of the best Italian restaurants in Brooklyn.

Monte's was where the who's who from Manhattan's Upper East Side went slumming. Monte's was their number one cuisine, and even though they were in Brooklyn's Red Hook, they were safe. Lou Monte made sure of it. In Lou's later years he opened a plush international spa called Gurnee's Inn on the ocean cliffs off exquisite Montauk Point, overlooking the Atlantic Ocean. It was the land that Giuseppe had owned, where one day he had planned to build a simple ocean-front cottage on the sea.

But Phil and Michael weren't from the Upper East Side, and seven of the wise guys were hanging out in front of Monte's.

"Oh, where are you two going?" Nicky Genovese demanded. Nicky was the youngest son in the Carlo Genovese family and the one with the biggest mouth. He was dating Dorothy Toscano. She was sixteen and he was twenty-two.

"What's it to you?" Phil quickly responded. Phil hated Nicky and all the guineas but mostly because he treated Dorothy like shit. But that was the wrong answer. Michael knew they were in trouble. There was no place to go as Nicky and his boys surrounded them.

"You know who you're talking to, asshole?" The ugliest one, Ciclopi, came at Phil's face with a switchblade. He was big and monstrous and looked like a down and out old-time fighter who'd been in one too many fights. And Giuseppe had added to the monster's look when he nearly removed Ciclopi's nose a year ago. Ciclopi was now Nicky Genovese's protector and enforcer.

"Listen, we made a mistake. We're sorry, it won't happen again." Michael wanted to get out of there in the worst way.

"Listen to the pretty boy." Now Ciclopi had the switchblade pointed at Michael's face. "I know who you are. You're one of those fucking Parisis."

"Listen, I don't have anything to do with their business, I'm not with the family." Michael was trying hard not to show fear. That was the first thing he'd learned in Red Hook. But the cold December night air was getting into Michael's bones. It seemed he had lost all feeling in his feet and fingers, and now he was trying hard not to shake. Michael had witnessed enough of these wise guy encounters that he knew he and Phil were going to get a beating. Hopefully that's all it would be.

The monster started to laugh. "You're the son of the *cornuto,* that *vecchio fesso* with the young wife. Hey, guys, come meet the son of the *cornuto,* the cuckold."

Michael knew he was being baited, but he could feel the heat going to his face and his heart beating a mile a minute. As his hands started to clench, a look crossed his face that Phil had never seen before. If looks could kill, Michael had it.

"Hey, leave him alone. He's not part of the family." Phil was trying to protect Michael, but it was too late, and they were in the wrong place at the wrong time.

Michael didn't see the first punch, but it hit him squarely in the nose. It felt like the time he was playing second base and a line drive hit him between the eyes. Then the onslaught came, and a barrage of kicks and punches had them whirling around and around like an out-of-control merry-go-round. All Michael kept thinking was, *Don't let them get you to the ground.* He had seen enough beatings to know that once they got you on the ground they were like a pack of starving hyenas ripping the flesh off their wounded prey.

Michael tried to stay up, yelling to Phil, "Don't go down, don't go down!" But his warning was in vain. They were on the ground now and Ciclopi took off his garrison belt and started to beat them mercilessly. They covered up in the fetal position, and at that moment Michael thought he was going to die. As their frenzy escalated with laughter, Michael vowed that if he ever got out alive he would kill Ciclopi and Nicky Genovese.

But before any real damage was done, someone called off the hyenas. It was Sam Peppirone, called Peppe for short.

"The next one that lays a hand on one of these boys will answer to me, *capisce?*" He looked at Nicky and Ciclopi with a look that could kill. Peppe despised Nicky and Ciclopi, but that was the shit one had to put up with when one's godfather was Carlo Genovese. "Hey, the kid's telling the truth. He's not with the family. Besides, he's my second baseman and we need him for my last season."

Sam Peppe's godfather was Carlo Genovese, the head of one of the five families. Sam was also an all city first baseman for the Manual Training High School baseball team the Braves. And the New York Yankees had just given him a $25,000 signing bonus and a brand new red '59 Thunderbird.

Not only were Peppe and Michael teammates, they were good friends off the field. Peppe took Michael home in his Thunderbird after the games, but Sam had one big problem: he liked to hang out with some of the wise guys, and they liked that he was becoming a celebrity.

Michael and Phil got up very slowly. Michael felt warm liquid on his face and as he rubbed it off, he realized it was blood. His nose was bleeding badly, and Ciclopi had cut him on his cheek, a scar he would carry for the rest of his life. Peppe went over to help Michael try to stop the bleeding. "What the fuck?" Sam looked at Michael's nose, took out his handkerchief, and began cleaning his second base-man's face.

"How bad is it?" Michael always had a problem with nose bleeds; he would wake up in the middle of the night to find his sheets full of blood. In the beginning he woke up and screamed for his mother, but Anna was never there, and it was Giuseppe who comforted him.

"You'll be okay, kid. It's like the time you got hit by the line drive. Get home and keep that nose up." Peppe dusted off Michael's pants.

"Let this be a warning." Nicky Genovese was walking toward Michael like Edward G. Robinson in some gangster movie. Ciclopi stood behind him. "Tell your cousin Blackie you don't fuck around with the Genovese and Gallo boys." This was the second time their paths had crossed. If Michael had a knife he would have cut his heart out. Just like any Sicilian would have.

When Michael slowly climbed the stairs to the apartment that night he tried to be very quiet. It was the one time he was glad the bathroom was in the hallway. Michael tried to clean the blood from his face, but his nose wouldn't stop bleeding. He stuffed toilet paper under his top lip and kept his nose up like the doctor at the hospital had told him when he had to get it cauterized. The bleeding finally stopped.

Michael entered the apartment hoping Giuseppe was asleep. In the past year, their relationship had changed. Michael did not consult with Giuseppe anymore. At one point Giuseppe had been the center of Michael's world. Now he was lucky if Michael spoke to him. One time their apartment was a warm classroom—filled with laughter, playing cards, and listening to Italian music. Now it was silent and cold. They didn't agree on anything anymore. Everything Giuseppe had sacrificed and given up was precariously sitting on a pendulum with Michael's life set in the balance.

Almost a year had gone by since Ciclopi's pick had penetrated Giuseppe's chest. It was a miracle Giuseppe was alive, but it was obvious the assault and the heart attack that followed three months later had quickly aged Giuseppe. He seemed to have lost that passion for life and worried more about Michael. He was counting the days before Michael started college and left Brooklyn—and hopefully could begin to repair the damage of a broken heart that comes from being abandoned by a mother.

Lately, since Giuseppe's health had begun deteriorating, Anna had started coming to the apartment to check on them. It was a strange relationship. She was only thirty-seven with deep black eyes, long black hair, and a slim figure. She looked like Giuseppe's daughter. She would stop in in the morning to see if they needed anything and then leave for work in Manhattan. After work she would come and visit for an hour. Sometimes Giuseppe had supper ready and she would eat with them.

It was during these times that Michael realized Giuseppe would have taken her back into their world. All she had to do was say the word. But Anna was living in her own world of lies and deceit and didn't need the burden of an old husband and a young child to get in her way to riches.

"*Come stai?*" Giuseppe always asked her how she was doing. At the dinner table Michael sat between them.

"*Bene.*" She didn't talk much. She checked her watch three or four times and then said it was time to go. "Don't forget to do your homework," she reminded. Then she gave Michael a quick peck on the cheek and was out the door.

These short visits made things worse for them, especially for Giuseppe. He would withdraw, put the Italian station on the radio, and listen to some sad opera and play solitaire. He wondered where she was going or whom she was with and it tore him apart.

In the evenings, when Michael went out and left him in solitude, he would take out the letter and read it over and over. He sat there in the green recliner and couldn't stop the tears from coming. When he fell asleep he dreamed of Claudia back in Sicily. They were walking arm and arm, laughing and giggling like two lovers in a fairy tale.

But tonight Giuseppe sensed something was wrong. It was late, and Michael was still not home.

He always waited till Michael got home before he went to bed. Sometimes he fell asleep in his favorite green leather recliner and Michael would have to wake him up and help him to bed.

The only light in the room was from the TV, and Michael hoped Giuseppe couldn't see him. As he tried to wake him to take him to bed, Michael noticed a tear in his eye. *"Pappa, va dormire?"* he insisted. Michael only spoke to him in Italian. *"Deve alzare."*

"E tu, figlio?" He was waking up. "Is it you, my son?"

"Si, Pappa, farme aiutare." Michael helped him up from the recliner.

"Dove andato?" He wanted to know where Michael had been.

"Con amici," Michael answered. "With my friends."

"Che successo?" He looked at Michael's face; Michael's nose had started to bleed again. "Who did this to you?"

"I was playing with the guys and fell off the stoop." Michael bit his lips to hold back the anger and hurt, but he couldn't hold back the tears anymore. His insides were hurting so bad he thought he was going to vomit and he started coughing up blood.

"Figlio mio, figlio mio, my son, what have they done to you?" Tears rolled down Giuseppe's cheeks. "What have they done to my son?" He just kept repeating that as he tended to Michael's welted back. But all Michael was thinking about was revenge.

That night when Giuseppe thought Michael was sleeping, he came to his bed and sat next to him.

He started singing a Sicilian lullaby as he had when Michael was young, "*Figlio mio, figlio mio,* I love you so, and no matter what happens I will protect you. Fear not, my son, for I am here and always will be with you. With the last breath that I take, I will breathe for you. *Sciatu mio.*"

Michael pretended to be asleep, but he didn't know which hurt more: the pain from the vicious beating of those degenerate animals or the pain of knowing his mother was only two blocks away and wasn't there for him when he needed her.

"Revenge is what keeps me alive." Santa's words echoed in his brain.

❖ ❖ ❖

CHAPTER 8

When Michael couldn't sleep he would go up to the rooftop and think; this was one of those nights. The view from the roof was breathtaking. Across the river was the steel lady with a torch in her hand. It comforted him knowing she was always there. She reminded him of his mother with a sad look on her face. She always looked lonely, but to her left was another world, Manhattan. From this distance it looked like a mystical Shangri-La, and its glitter of lights intrigued Michael and gave him hope. It made him wonder about his life and the people who controlled the strings.

Michael thought about his day—from winning at the races with Don Pasquale and meeting Mary Madison Brittain at Lundy's, to Phil and him almost being killed by an out-of-control mobster. But the one person that mystified him the most was Harold Wilson.

The more Michael thought about Harold Wilson, the more curious he was about him. He had that

I'm-better-than-you smirk on his face when talking to Don Pasquale—something he hadn't learned at Harvard or Yale. Michael knew that Harold came from upper class East Hampton and old family money. He was well-bred, sophisticated, and from a powerful family, and yet there had been something indescribable about his reaction to Michael. It was his expression when Pasquale told him he was Giuseppe's son. There was something Harold Wilson wanted to get away from; something that maybe he didn't want his granddaughter to know, and whatever it was, Michael believed it was not good.

But the more he thought about Mary Madison Brittain, the more he wanted to know about her. When their eyes met for the first time, a strange feeling came over him; it seemed in that short period of time two strangers were able to bare their hearts and souls to one another and were no longer strangers.

But that didn't leave Michael with too many options in Red Hook, because on the other side of the spectrum he wanted to hate his family, Big Tony and Blackie and all their connections. They were *caffoni*, uneducated, uncultured, and he didn't like what they were—thugs. They had disdain for anyone who got in their way. They used fear and power to get what they wanted, and they got what they wanted while stepping on anyone who got on their wrong side. Michael suspected that Harold Wilson, with all his sophistication and class, seemed to exhibit these same traits as the wise guys. And now Michael was starting to realize that maybe he was from the same mold.

For the first time tonight Michael had known he could kill someone and walk away. He knew he had Sicilian blood and that this was what his father was afraid of. Giuseppe would warn him, "don't go to the club," knowing Tony would be up to no good.

At the club, Big Tony threw out carrots from time to time to his nephew. "Hey, Michael, come over here." Michael was playing scuba and briscola with Pasquale and some old-timers.

Michael always felt uncomfortable around Tony and Blackie. "*Si*, Uncle Tony."

"How would you like to make some extra money?" He didn't wait for Michael to respond. "Go to Fernando on Union Street; tell him you're there to pick up the envelope for your uncle. Blackie forgot to pick it up and now that *disgraziato* son of mine needed a vacation and is off to Miami with some bimbo he picked up last week in Coney Island."

"Do you want me to go now?" Michael asked.

"Yeah, go now, and when you come back I'll give you something." Tony winked.

Michael looked over to Pasquale and could see Pasquale was annoyed with him. Pasquale had his hand in his mouth and was biting down on it, basically saying, *Michael, you're doing something wrong and you're going to get in trouble.*

Michael felt that maybe Tony was doing this because he felt bad for what he did to Giuseppe?

But Big Tony, or for that matter Blackie, never had a guilty feeling between them. These people were callous, and everything to them was black or white. But Michael was still a blood relative and there was always the carrot they wiggled in his face. All Michael had to do was reach out.

Reaching out for the carrot became more and more tempting for Michael as time went by because there was plenty of money to be made. Blackie was expanding the family's numbers operation in Brooklyn and Manhattan. And the family had just purchased Plato's Retreat, the top nightclub in Manhattan where all the wannabes went to be seen with the celebrities and socialites.

With the expansion of the family business, it was only a matter of time before they stepped on someone's toes. The Genovese family was the most powerful family in Brooklyn. Carlo Genovese, the family patriarch, was a man of small stature, maybe five foot five and a hundred and fifty pounds soaking wet. He had a slender, almost gaunt-looking face with a large, hooked nose. He looked like he should be in a coffin. He was named after his malevolent uncle, Don Carlo from Palermo, and had inherited his toxic, crude, vile viciousness. One could make a case that their family's bloodline descended down to Dante's inferno.

Carlo only wore expensive clothes and shoes imported from Italy. It was a ritual every day for him to have Black Joe spit shine his shoes on the corner of Third Ave and Carroll Street, near Monte's restaurant. One day Sal "the Snake" Persico, who worked for Carlo, made the mistake of stepping on Mr. Genovese's shoes after Black Joe had just finished spit shining them.

"You stupid bastard, the fuckin' nigger just finished polishing them and look what the fuck you did." Carlo took out his gun and put it to Sal's head. "Get on your fuckin' knees and lick that shit off my shoes, you stupid guinea." Sal the Snake didn't hesitate. He got on his knees and licked Carlo's shoes. Sal Persico was also a New York City policeman.

Carlo didn't like Blackie expanding the numbers racket into his territory so Carlo decided, with the help of his sister's son, Luigi, to organize the longshoremen and force Big Tony out of the International Longshoremen Association. Carlo was about to send a final message to Big Tony and Blackie.

But instead, someone got to Ciclopi first, and instead of rubbing out Blackie he was paid to go after Giuseppe. When he couldn't finish off the old man, Ciclopi's anger fermented and boiled over like a soured wine that had turned to vinegar. And the evil was unleashed on Michael when the opportunity arose on that cold December night.

On the roof, Michael did his best thinking. At times he felt lost between two worlds: the world he was living in and the world his father lived in. Michael thought Giuseppe was becoming senile from the way he would catch his father mumbling about his life in Sicily.

Whenever things seemed to be the worst, Giuseppe would talk in general about his family riding horses and living the life of noblemen. He talked about the benevolent Maria, who fed the peasants, and Michael's great- grandfather in Sicily. According to Giuseppe, Barone Salvatore lived in a magnificent castle.

"These are the *famiglia* I want you to know. Your bloodline is that of nobility. The Parisi *famiglia* were all educated and cultured. They were famous artists and composers, not these *animale* you see here."

It was hard for Michael to imagine or believe in a Parisi family bloodline of nobility. In a way it was comical to think of Big Tony and Blackie as nobility. Here he and Giuseppe were living in a cold-water flat in Red Hook. No phones, no brothers or sisters, no family, and no mother.

To Michael there was nothing noble about their life.

✤ ✤ ✤

CHAPTER 9

B ut Michael's education in culture began before
he went to public school. When he was younger,
his grandmother, Santa Marsala, would watch over
him when his father was working. Living with Santa
in Red Hook was as far as one could get from nobility. You could not find anyone even in the backwoods
of Kentucky that was more of a peasant than Santa.

Santa did not believe in schools; according to
her, the teachers were *baccalas*. In Sicilian a *baccala*
could mean a lot of things, but in this case it meant
they were stupid. So whenever she felt like it, she took
Michael with her instead of sending him to school.

It was not a typical class trip. Santa took Michael
shopping on Union Street where all the local vendors
displayed their fruits and vegetables on wooden carts.
On cold winter days, especially near Christmas, it
was like a carnival of excitement as vendors boasted
of the freshness of their products. They sang and
chanted to lure customers while trying to stay warm
near an open fire.

Santa and Michael wiggled in and out of makeshift canvas-covered stores that easily could have been mistaken for the market in the center of Istanbul. They first walked to Angelo's and tasted a piece of apple or a thin slice of provolone and then walked off and tasted some anchovies at Johnny's fish market. Santa wasn't satisfied until they visited at least three or four vendors, and of course she would bargain.

Santa was the ultimate bargainer. She was pushing five feet, broad with shoulder-length white hair rolled up in a bun kept in place with knitting needles. First she would insult the vendor by telling him his product was inferior to Angelo's across the street. Angelo's was the best, but he had the highest prices, and Santa never bought from him.

One day Angelo had had enough of Santa's free loading. "Oh, *signora*, when are you going to buy something?"

"*Che ti credo so fesso?* Do you think I'm a fool? Your prices are too high."

"Please, *signora*, don't come here no more. I can't feed my family with people like you."

"*Va fan culo!*" and that was all she had to say. She grabbed Michael's arm and nearly tore it out of the socket as they dashed out. "*Ammunini*, let's go!" It was the last time they patronized Angelos—for that day.

But Santa always had something up her sleeves or Michael's sleeves. She would engage in heavy bargaining before she settled on a final price; meanwhile, she had instructed Michael to take an orange while she had the owner's attention. Michael's reward would be a pinelle sandwich that they would split at Fernando's trattoria and, if Michael was real good, a Manhattan special—coffee soda. When they got back to her apartment, Michael lined up the day's take: Maybe an orange or two or an apple or, depending on the season, a few chestnuts and snails. She loved the snails. They boiled them in olive oil and garlic with a little bit of parsley, *bellissimo*. The rest of the afternoon was spent picking the snails out of their shells with her sewing needles.

In 1950, Bergen Beach, Brooklyn, was a mixture of gardens, summer cottages, and burial grounds, whenever they couldn't get to Canarsi, for people who stepped on Carlo Genovese's shoes. Being a Sicilian peasant, Santa had a victory garden in Bergen Beach. No one knew how she was given the land to farm and no one dared ask. Santa lived by all the Sicilian sayings, and the one she stressed to Michael was "Don't let anyone make a fool of you." Nobody made a fool of or got over on Santa, nobody.

Michael soon began to realize why Santa took him on all her trips. She couldn't read or write; she was even illiterate in Italian. They had to take three trolley cars from Red Hook to Bergen Beach, and the trip took over an hour. Santa always bullied her way to a seat and managed to squeeze Michael in next to her. While passing through the Jewish section of Flatbush on one of these trips, the trolley quickly filled with shoppers. An older Jewish lady with two

Sciatu Mio

filled shopping bags wanted to sit. Michael tried to
get up and give her his seat, but Santa almost pulled
his arm out of his socket again as she pulled him
down into the seat.

"I think it would be nice if the young boy got up
and gave me the seat," the Jewish lady said sternly.
Santa didn't understand a word she was saying so
Michael had to translate.

Santa looked at Michael with stern eyes and said,
"Tell her *va fan culo.*"

Michael thought it best not to translate Santa's
insult, so he did not say anything, but the Jewish lady
became impatient. She insisted on sitting between
Santa and Michael and tried to make room between
the two of them. Santa shoved her back up, refusing
to move an inch.

Michael started to translate immediately as Santa
spoke. "My grandmother said it takes six people to
carry a dead person out. Can you imagine how many
it's going to take to move us from these seats?"

The Jewish lady gave up.

When the Jewish lady got off the trolley she gave
Santa a dirty look. Santa said it was the evil eye, and she
immediately checked to see if Michael had his golden
horn around his neck. It was the same golden horn
his grandfather, Michele, had worn. She was relived
to see it. Santa called out the window of the trolley car
to the Jewish woman "*putana*" and spat at her.

According to Santa, all women were *putanas,* and
Michael should take every precaution not to marry

one. She warned Michael about the opposite sex by saying, "Women, when you turn them upside down, they are all the same."

It was this reasoning that made Michael think about becoming a priest when he grew up.

When the trolley got to Bergen Beach, Santa's eyes would light up. She would grab Michael's arm, and her short legs would move so fast Michael swore his arms were getting longer. When she farmed the one hundred by one hundred-foot lot, she was in heaven as it was the closest she could be to being back in Sicilia.

Away from the noisy city and crowded tenements, they plowed the soil and planted seeds, tied up the tomatoes, pruned the fruit trees, uncovered the fig tree and grapevines. Santa would sing all day long, and her beautiful voice filled the garden with love. She sang old Sicilian peasant songs that told stories of hardships and sorrow and lost love. And Michael would work alongside her and listen.

Sometimes Michael would catch her crying and ask, *"Nonna perche gridare?"*

"Sono contento." She was happy, she said, but there was something in her past that was too sad to forget.

Before dawn approached they put all the fruits and vegetables in as many shopping bags as they could carry back. The last trolley left Bergen Beach at six and they had to be on it. One time when they were going back they met the same old Jewish lady. The trolley was pretty full, but there were two seats available on either side of Santa and little Michael. It was probably because they smelled so bad and also had a shopping bag of fresh garlic, but the Jewish lady just took one look at them, put her nose up in the air, and walked by.

Santa gave her one mean look and called her a *baccala*. A salted, stiff codfish would be the correct definition, but in Sicilian it had other connotations. Calling a person a *baccala* meant he or she could be a dummy or it could refer to a woman's privates. In this case Santa meant both.

They once missed the last trolley. It was the end of August, and they had a record number of shopping bags to take back with them. Santa started to panic. "*Che devammo fare?* What are we going to do?"

Michael remembered his mother's work number. It seemed she always worked late during the summer. They called from the little grocery store near the trolley stop. Within an hour a chauffeur-driven black Cadillac like a funeral car pulled up next to them. The limo was for them.

"*Questo machina e per e morte!*" At first Santa refused to get in. She thought it was bad luck to get into a funeral car for dead people.

"*Ma Nonna e questo o devamo caminare*," Michael told her. "If we don't take the car we have to walk home."

"*Va bene.* But before we get in we have to give it the *male occhio*, the evil eyes," so she decided to give the car the horns. So Michael and Santa had to make the horns with their fists, leaving the index finger and pinky up to ensure they were protected from evil. Then Santa had Michael kiss the golden horn. After the brief ceremony they were able to get into the Cadillac. Luckily the chauffeur was Sicilian; he understood.

Driving back, Michael wondered whom the car belonged to and how his mother knew the owner. And then he remembered he'd been in this car before. It was something Michael wanted to forget.

Santa lived two blocks away from Giuseppe and Michael, at 206 Carroll Street. The brown brick apartment building belonged to the Scotto family, who owned the funeral parlor and were connected to the Gallo family, who were connected to the Genovese family. Everybody in Red Hook was connected, or at least they thought they were, to some mob family.

Santa lived in a four room railroad apartment, and one thing Michael liked about it was that the bathroom was not in the hallway. The other thing Michael liked about it was that Santa had two dogs and, at different times, ten chicks, a parrot, and an accordion. There was no department of health in Red Hook. But even if there was, they probably couldn't condemn Santa's apartment.

Her next door neighbor, an older *signora*, once told her, "I am going to call the landlord if you don't get rid of these animals."

"*Quella putana, desgraziata, baccala, bestia, va fan culo.*" And then Santa gave her the horns. Three days later the old *signora* was dead. She died of a heart attack, but everyone in the neighborhood knew Santa put the *male occhio* on her. And nobody messed with Santa, not even Carlo Genovese or Big Tony.

❖ ❖ ❖

CHAPTER 10

Hollywood made a movie called *Black Board Jungle*. It starred a young Sidney Portier as a high school student trying to avoid the pitfalls of being black and living in a ghetto in New York City. Vic Morrow starred as the leader of an out-of-control gang in a New York City high school, and Glenn Ford was the teacher who tried to control them. The school in the movie was Manual Training High School, and in 1959, Michael Parisi and his two close friends Phil Dressler and Dyale Forsythe were seniors at this school.

The population of the school was about five thousand, almost half of them ghetto Italian kids from Red Hook. The Irish moved out to Sunset Park about ten miles away; the blacks lived in the twelve-story government projects on the outskirts of Red Hook, and the Puerto Ricans moved in wherever there was an empty apartment. Sprinkle in a few Greeks and Arabs here and there and one had a melting pot. Except for the Jewish kids; they made up about ten percent of the school. At graduation only ten percent of the graduating class went on to college, and ninety-five percent of them were the Jewish kids.

Michael, Phil Dressler, and Dyale Forsythe were among the few who were not Jewish that got accepted to a college.

It was December 1959, the last week of school before the Christmas holiday. Phil and Michael were recuperating and just getting over the beatings. They were in study hall planning their fraternity's annual party when they heard the shot go off. It happened across the hall in wood shop. Dyale yelled, "Sam got shot!"

By the time Michael and Phil got there, Sam Peppe was lying on the floor with a bullet in his side.

"Hey, you alright?" Sam looked at Michael; it took him a second to recognize him. Michael took out a handkerchief and put some pressure on the wound. The bullet had just grazed his side.

"Yeah, yeah, just a flesh wound. I'll be okay, you took a worse beating." Then he stopped and pulled Michael closer to him and whispered, "Hey, kid, I'm sorry what happened to you the other night. That fuckin' Ciclopi is crazy, and he has a hard-on for your family."

"I understand, thanks for helping me." The ambulance attendants came and took Sam out. "Hey, Michael, tell the Yankees they have nothing to worry about and come by the apartment when I'm home."

"Okay, take care."

That was Sam making a joke out of a serious situation. No one found the gun or knew who fired the shot.

Michael was walking out of school in a daze when he heard the car horn beeping at him. It was the black Oldsmobile 98. Don Pasquale rolled down the window and said, "Hey, can I tell you something in confidence?"

Michael smiled and got in the car. "Want to go to Fernando's for a pinelle and a Manhattan special?"

The first time Michael met Don Pasquale was at Fernando's. Michael was with Santa. They had just made out well at the market; Michael had taken three apples and a handful of snails.

"*Questo e mio nepputo.*" Santa was proud of her grandson, Michael.

"He looks like his father." Pasquale shook hands with Michael. "Let me pay for your lunch." Santa never refused anything for nothing.

Fernando's was a favorite place to go for lunch in the neighborhood. It was a small hole in the wall with small black and white checkered tiles on the floor. Years ago some homesick Sicilian painted a scene of his little town by the sea in Sicily on the two inner walls. The fresco was hard to see because the paintings were covered with grease from the hot black oil in Fernando's big black cast iron vat. It was said that Fernando was so cheap he never changed the oil. He said it made the pinelle taste better.

Pinelles were similar to thin, flattened potato knishes. After they soaked up all that hot oil, Fernando put them on a toasted sesame seed bun, threw a scoop of ricotta cheese on top, and finished it off with a sprinkle of provolone. It was a recipe to clog up ten arteries on any given day.

Leaving the Oldsmobile parked at the curb, Michael and Don Pasquale walked into Fernando's. Don Pasquale took a seat in his favorite position with his back to the wall watching the front door. Fernando had just brought over two pinelle sandwiches and two Manhattan specials when in walked Blackie. There was no way for Michael to avoid him. Blackie walked right over to their table.

"I'm going to cut that fucking fat bastard's balls off and stuff them in his fucking mouth and then I'm going to cut his fucking heart out." He was referring to Ciclopi. Blackie pulled Michael up from his seat, and Michael winced as his ribs were still sore.

"I won't fucking forget this, cuz, you took a beating for the family. I'm not going to forget this." It was the first time he had said anything nice to Michael. He hugged Michael and gave him the traditional two kisses on the cheek, left side first. That's how the old-timers did it.

And then he whispered sotto vocce, "I know your father is against it, but anytime you say the word, kid, we have a position for you in the family. You be set for life."

Blackie turned to leave. As he did, he reached inside his long black trench coat and took out a crumbled brown paper bag and gently placed it on the table. There was obviously something heavy in the bag. "We just sent Genovese a message. Don't fuck with the Parisi family. When you pass over the canal, pitch it."

Don Pasquale was silent, just staring at the ceiling. Michael was glad Blackie had left, but it was the first time he felt good about the family. Blackie had called Michael "cuz," and in their own way they were protecting Michael. The family would repay the Genoveses for what they had done to Michael. It was an old Sicilian thing that Santa lived by: "Don't let anyone get one over on you."

Michael began to like the feeling of power that belonging to the family gave him, and it convinced him even more that one day, when the time was right, he would kill Ciclopi.

Don Pasquale looked at Michael. Michael could see Don Pasquale was annoyed. He picked up his cane and said, "*Ammunini,* let's go."

"What's the problem, Don Pasquale?" Michael knew something was bothering him.

"We talk in the car." Michael helped him get up. It seemed his legs were getting worse in the cold weather.

The faster he drove, the faster he talked. "You don't need this, leave this all behind. When you graduate, you get out of Brooklyn and never come back. This family thing will destroy you like it did to your father. Your father was right to get out. I just wish I had been strong enough to leave before it destroyed my family and killed my Frankie."

Don Pasquale knew he was getting emotional, so he was silent for a while, thinking about what he wanted to tell Michael. Don Pasquale was like Michael's second father. "I promised your father when he was in the hospital we would not make the same mistake with you."

He came to an abrupt stop before crossing the bridge. Even though it was winter and it was bitter cold, they could smell the foul odor of the canal. "Here take this and pitch it." He gave Michael the bag. Michael knew immediately there was a gun inside of it. A moment of fear came over him as he thought *maybe this is the gun that shot Peppe.*

Michael's insides were in a knot and his stomach started churning. Only a few minutes ago he had thought of accepting a position with the family, but now the idea was repulsive. Sam had saved him from more of a beating and it wasn't his fault that he was Carlo Genovese's godson. And why did Blackie give him the gun?

A trucker blasted his horn to get Don Pasquale to move his car from blocking the bridge, startling Michael. Don Pasquale moved forward and motioned for Michael to meet him on the other side of the bridge.

As Michael was about to throw the gun into the canal, he remembered Ciclopi and Nicky Genovese. Michael remembered Ciclopi's vicious hyena laugh as Phil and he lay on the ground bleeding. He was an ugly, evil person who enjoyed inflicting pain on others, and Michael was suddenly convinced he had to kill him. Ciclopi knew Michael wasn't part of the family, but he was so irrational and sick it didn't matter. Michael remembered Peppe's words: "That Ciclopi is crazy, and he has a hard-on for your family." Michael was convinced even more now that Ciclopi would try to kill him and his father.

Michael quickly made up his mind. He took the gun out of the brown paper bag and placed it in his navy pea coat then threw the empty bag into the canal. When he got into the car he managed to hide the gun under the driver's seat without Don Pasquale being aware of it.

"Hey, can I tell you something in confidence?" A smile had replaced Don Pasquale's serious expression. "I got a tip on the sixth at Roosevelt. Number seven, Royal Hanover, driven by Stanley Dancer, a hundred to one."

"What about the system?"

Don Pasquale didn't answer, and they were off to Roosevelt Raceway. They got there in time for the first race. Too bad they lost—and they proceeded to lose the next four races. Don Pasquale was down four thousand as the marshal announced the trotters for the next race. The system called for them to play the number one horse, Moon Glow, driven by the infamous jockey Steve Bailey. The little jockey was married to the mob, and if there was a fix, you could bet he was in on it. The only problem was you never knew if someone was fixing the fix.

The horse was going off at two to one. Pasquale's system called for the bet to be two thousand. But their dilemma was Royal Hanover; the opening odds were dropping quickly, indicating a lot more people had the same tip. The horse hadn't won in twenty starts, and the best it did was third at Yonkers. But Big Tony with some of his partners had recently bought into Stanley Dancer's stables in New Jersey. And they figured the horse needed a win.

It was two minutes before the marshal called the horses to their post. Don Pasquale was having a rough time deciding how he was going to bet this race. "I don't think the horse is going to win."

"Who, Moon Glow?"

"No, Royal Hanover. I've got to go with the system." Don Pasquale had hoped he would have won a race already so it wouldn't come to this—his system versus Big Tony's horse...

"Take twenty-five hundred and put it on number one to win," he said. It was all the money he had left that night. If they lost, Don Pasquale was down big, and they wouldn't get to go to Lundy's.

Michael had twenty-five hundred in his pocket, and he was off to place the bets. There was a minute left before the windows closed. An older couple was in front of the hundred-dollar window. They were just about to leave when the old man decided to make another bet. Thirty seconds left, and Michael's stomach was starting to churn again. It wasn't his money, but he knew it meant a lot to Don Pasquale.

A strange thing happened within the last few seconds: the odds on the number one horse had risen to three to one, which meant they didn't need to put all the twenty-five hundred down. Michael took a chance and tried to quickly calculate the bets.

"Number one to win twenty times and number seven to win five times." Michael had a hunch. He knew Big Tony hated to lose.

"And they're off." Royal Hanover came out from the number seven position and stormed to the lead while Moon Glow fell back to the fourth position. By the time Michael got to the lower level where Don Pasquale was watching, the horses had rounded the half-mile track and were making their second round to the finish line.

In the last turn, Royal Hanover was ahead by five lengths, and Moon Glow was third by six and a half lengths but closing in. They were down the stretch neck and neck. Royal Hanover was losing ground, and now Moon Glow was ahead by a length. At the last minute, Steve Bailey pulled the reins back on Moon Glow, which allowed Royal Hanover to come in first place. Immediately the inquiry sign lit up.

It took ten minutes for the judges to review the films and make a decision. Michael didn't say a word.

He just kept rubbing the five tickets and praying. It was the longest ten minutes of his life. As the board lit up, the crowd yelled in excitement hoping for the underdog with high odds to come in. Moon Glow was placed fourth and out of the money, and his jockey, Steve Bailey, was suspended. Royal Hanover stood as the winner.

Don Pasquale was disappointed, but he turned to Michael, giving him a lecture on the vices of gambling. "So much for the system; you see, that's why I don't want you to bet, *ammunini.*"

Michael just smiled and pulled out five one hundred-dollar tickets on Royal Hanover to win. They were up fifty-five hundred.

"Let's go to Lundy's!" Pasquale shouted. Michael and Don Pasquale didn't know it then, but it was the last time they would go to the track.

And it was the last time jockey Steve Bailey rode in a race. Two months later, an unbearably foul stench arose from the Gowanus Canal. The stench could be smelled ten blocks away, and the New York Department of Health was sent out to investigate. They pulled Steve Bailey out early the next morning—he was attached with chains and ropes to his horse, Moon Glow.

Lundy's was crowded and noisy with latecomers from Wall Street there for the succulent raw oysters and clams. Their limos were double parked and waiting while the smells emanating from the fishing boats permeated the cool, crisp December night. The fishing boats were being washed down and rested for the night.

The maitre d', Dean "Scungadu" Demattio, was glad to see them. "Don Pasquale, I have a nice table for you by the fireplace." They sat down by the fireplace and the heat felt good.

"You know why he walks with a limp?" Don Pasquale didn't wait for Michael to answer. "Because he thought he was a hustler. He played that stupid game, what do they call it?"

"Golf," Michael interjected.

"That's it, golf, and stop interrupting me." Michael smiled, knowing he was getting another lesson in life. "He hustled everyone out of money and then they hustled him. He couldn't pay back so they broke his legs."

"Who broke his legs?" Michael smiled, knowing that Don Pasquale, in his own way, was trying to protect him.

"Does it matter who broke his legs? You young people want to know everything." Don Pasquale was getting frustrated. "I'm trying to tell you, don't gamble, don't let it get in your blood—it will destroy you."

Scungadu served a plate of raw oysters and poured Don Pasquale a glass of white wine. "*Ha fatto bene, figlio,* you did well, son." Don Pasquale was relaxed now he was sipping his wine. Michael was so excited that he hadn't realized he was sitting in Don Pasquale's position with his back to the wall watching the front door. When he realized it, he offered to change seats.

"No, no, you deserve the seat of honor, I salute you." They raised their glasses and toasted, and Don Pasquale bent over the table and whispered sotto voce, "Can I tell you something in confidence?"

He didn't wait for Michael to respond. "I wish you were my son." Don Pasquale had lost his only son, shot down in the streets of Red Hook trying to emulate one of the hoods. With tears welling up in his eyes, Don Pasquale got up from his chair and walked over to Michael and kissed him.

Michael was embarrassed. "*Ma che fai?* What are you doing?"

Don Pasquale didn't get a chance to answer. Scungadu had come to their table. "Excuse me, Don Pasquale, but the other night you and Michael were here along with a young lady by the name of Mary Madison Brittain. She left this for you." Dean handed Michael a sealed envelope addressed to "My Prince."

Don Pasquale looked to the ceiling, put his hands up to the heavens, and shouted, "*Dio mio!*"

CHAPTER 11

The next day, the weathermen were predicting a major snowfall within the next twenty-four hours. John F. Kennedy's name was on the front page of the *Daily News* and *New York Times* as he was coming to New York for a Democratic fundraiser.

That morning Michael had visited Sam Peppe at his home. He was fine; the bullet had gone in and out of his side. It was just a superficial wound. The Yankees were happy that it hadn't affected his playing baseball for them, and Michael was just happy Sam was alive. Michael didn't ask or didn't want to know if the shooting was a message to the Genovese family.

"What's up, kid, how's my second baseman doing?" Sam was lying in bed smoking a cigarette. His hair was perfectly combed, and he looked like he was relaxing at Coney Island, the beach at Bay Fourteen, that's where all the wise guys hung out. Peppe was always the center of attention and always had a fast-talking, bubble gum-popping, big-busted bimbo at his side.

"Okay, I'm glad to see you're looking good. For a minute there I thought…"

"Nah, kid, I'm okay." Sam looked pensive. He looked out his window where the elevated train passed right by. The squealing of the brakes was deafening as the train pulled into the McDonald Avenue station, just seven stops to Coney Island. Michael wondered how anyone could live right next to the elevated train station. It blocked out the light, and every half-hour another noisy train would pull in.

"I'm going to get out of this fucking place before it kills me. I just seem to be in the wrong place at the wrong time and I just can't help it. And now with this thing with the Yankees, all the wise guys want a part of me. It's like I can't get away from them. Do you know what I mean?"

The wise guys wanted a free ride, and if one of them was going to get out and become something, the way Sam was, they were going to be there for the ride. Still, there was an underlying feeling in Red Hook that if anyone expressed the desire to leave or bad mouthed the lifestyle or wanted to be somebody other than a longshoreman, a cop, or a wise guy, he was considered a traitor.

They could hear the train pulling away from the station. "I have a lot of respect for you, Michael. With all the bullshit around you, you try to keep your distance, and I know that's hard sometimes. I wish I had the balls to walk away from some of these greaseballs."

Michael looked at Sam and smiled. "You know what I wish sometimes?"

Sam looked at Michael and said, "No, tell me."

"I wish I could meet someone like Donna Reed. We'd live in a nice house, I would be a doctor, have wonderful kids, and we would belong to one of those fancy country clubs and drive around in a sports car along the coast of California."

"I like that, but she doesn't have big enough boobs. You know I like big boobs, like Susan Meyers."

Michael smiled. "I've got to go."

"Where to, California?" Sam was laughing.

"No, to meet Donna Reed."

If you took the D train to the last stop in Brooklyn, you would be at Coney Island. At one time it was the playground of the world, where rich families from Manhattan and Brooklyn Heights vacationed along the fine beach and stayed for a week in lavish hotels and frolicked on the boardwalk that stretched for miles. Private carriages paraded up and down the boardwalk from morning till midnight. Rheingold Beer sponsored elaborate fireworks displays every Thursday night from a barge across from the Steeplechase, the world-renowned amusement park. But the new wave of immigrants came and destroyed it for the rich. The remnants of a fabulous era still lingered in Coney Island, but now it was occupied by freak shows, and sometimes the best of the shows were walking the boardwalk.

But today, Michael wasn't going to Coney Island; he was going to the opposite end of the world. The D train also went into Manhattan. On certain Sundays when he finished eating, he would get on the D train and escape Red Hook to his fantasy world. The train stopped at the planetarium, where he would spend hours enjoying the heavens and wishing and praying that Donna Reed was his mother.

The train stopped at the station sign that read Metropolitan Museum of Art on Fifth Avenue, his favorite getaway. He could enter any world and any time in history and become Julius Caesar or Napoleon, visit the tombs of ancient Egypt or visit the Knights of the Round Table. But his favorite was Marco Polo. Michael dreamed of being on his caravan walking through time and meeting people of different cultures and buying and selling goods and products that no one knew existed before. It would probably be similar to going to the markets on Union Street with Santa. Michael chuckled at the thought.

Soon Michael was perched on a white horse decorated in fifteenth-century Renaissance armor in the middle of the Medici exhibition hall. Michael could hear the tour instructor in the adjacent hall explaining the historical significance of the exhibits.

Her voice was the sweetest sound he had ever heard. It had a scent of magnolia, a touch of jasmine, and the beauty of a camellia. He almost fell off the horse as he closed his eyes and took a deep breath. In the letter she had told him to meet her at the museum where she worked as a guide.

Mary Madison's voice echoed throughout the Italian Renaissance exhibit. "And here we have the famous Medici exhibition. The Medicis flourished in Florence, the beautiful city of flowers. Throughout the fifteenth century it reigned supreme among the city-states. Life in Florence was a gay tapestry-like procession woven over a red wine warp of intrigue and bloody politics, shot through with golden threads of wealth, and embroidered with rich emerald green and royal blue. She was a fortress within her walls. Florence was a mixture of medieval romance and modern realism."

As the group walked through the exhibit, no one noticed Michael sitting on the horse. "My princess, may I be of assistance?" Michael bowed.

Mary Madison Brittain had the prettiest smile. Her blues eyes opened wide when she saw him, and Michael pictured himself a wounded soldier walking down the gangplank returning home after years on the front line and she was waiting there with open arms. Michael got the strange feeling that they had been lovers in another land, in another time.

"My prince, I thought you would never come."

As they walked past the massive Corinthian columns and the regal lions down the stone steps of the museum, it started to snow. The sidewalks were already covered with a thin layer of white powder as the traffic hurried along Fifth Ave. The exodus was beginning with people looking to get out of the city as the weathermen predicted a massive snowfall.

They held hands, sharing their thoughts without saying a word as they walked through Central Park. By now all the branches were white and the meadow was a sea of snow. Leaving their footprints behind them, they stopped in front of the lake. As the snowfall intensified, the tall skyscrapers in the background looked like a fantasyland of castle towers.

She looked at him sadly. "You know my grandfather has forbidden me to see you?"

"I know, Don Pasquale told me." Don Pasquale had told Michael a lot of things, but Michael had made up his mind. He had to find out what the story was behind the ex-governor and the don.

"I told him I wouldn't, but there was something inside of me that wouldn't let me let go of you." She brushed the snow off his navy pea coat, then placed her scarf around Michael's neck and drew him closer to her, and they kissed.

"I think I have that same something inside of me. I think of you all day and dream of you at night. This had never happened to me before."

As she closed her eyes she again pulled the scarf until their lips were about to touch, then she whispered, "This is crazy, but when I first met you I felt I had been waiting for you all my life." They kissed again.

As the snow continued to fall, Mary Madison and Michael walked in Central Park, oblivious to everything around them, except the sound of the music coming from the ice-skating rink on Wolman Lake.

"Oh, Michael, I never went ice skating before. Will you teach me?" They went in.

"Let me help you." Michael got on his knees and helped her put on the ice skates.

She started to giggle. "This is the second time we've been together and both times you've been on your knees."

"They say three times is a charm." And he smiled.

"Oh, I think I'll look forward to that." She bent over and kissed him.

"I think we better start your first lesson."

It was magical; they couldn't stop falling and laughing. Every time they got up Michael and Mary Madison kissed. Michael was looking forward to falling down again.

And then a funny thing happened. The ring announcer got on the P.A. system and announced he was playing a special song for the two lovers in the center of the ring. Everyone stopped skating and looked at them. They didn't realize they had become a spectacle. He played the theme from the new movie *Summer Place*.

As Michael and Mary Madison awkwardly skated around the ring they tried hard not to fall down, and the people applauded. It was such an enchanting moment, and when the song was over, they looked at each other and she said, "This will be our song for the rest of our lives."

The snowstorm brought the city to a halt and only the subways were running. But they purposely got off at the Brooklyn Bridge exit on the Manhattan side and decided to walk over the bridge to her grandfather's brownstone in Brooklyn Heights.

Brooklyn Heights was a stone's throw away from Red Hook, but it was in another world. The people who lived there were doctors, writers, politicians, the intellectuals. Hollywood was filming *The Patty Duke Show* among the elegant brownstones, and Brooklyn Heights had the most beautiful view of the New York skyline and some of the most expensive real estate in the city.

About a year earlier, Dyale Forsythe, the son of actor Ryan Forsythe, had moved to Brooklyn Heights. His parents had split up and he was having a problem adjusting between coasts. Thrown out of three private schools in one year, he adjusted well in Manual Training, and Michael and Phil became his new best friends. Sometimes when he was in one of his sad moods he would tell Michael that he and Phil were the only friends he ever had.

The D train pulled into the Carroll Street station in Red Hook, and Michael would get on every morning at seven thirty at the Seventh Avenue station to get to Manual. Every morning Dyale would be on the same train, getting on one stop before at the

Brooklyn Heights station. Dyale always had a cup of coffee and two chocolate éclairs—one for him and one for Michael. They walked the same route along Seventh Avenue, passing the same storefronts. Every morning Mr. Lazarus's ice cream parlor was packed with sorority sisters and fraternity brothers from Manual. It was their hangout before and after and sometimes during classes.

Mr. Lazarus's place was more than an ice cream parlor. It had exquisite stained glass windows up front and a Victorian mirror behind the counter that sat ten on red velour-cushioned swivel seats. The black and white diamond tiles led to the back where screaming teenagers filled the mahogany booths singing to the music from the colorful lighted jukebox.

Michael, Dyale, and Phil were popular. Dyale being a celebrity's son didn't hurt. The girls were all over Dyale, but Susan Meyers wanted Michael.

It was the way things went in the neighborhood with so many ethic groups mixing with each other. The Jewish girls loved the Italian boys; the Irish boys loved the Italian girls; and the Italian girls wound up marrying Jewish boys. And the Italian boys thought they could love them all.

But Dyale was in love with Barbara Gittens, and Barbara was probably the best-looking girl at Manual. The problem was that Barbara was black, and being black was a problem if you lived in Red Hook and went to Manual.

Michael, Dyale, and Phil belonged to Omega Gamma Delta; it was the only fraternity that accepted anyone except blacks. Michael was the token Italian. In Manual tension existed between the Irish and the Italians as a carry-over from the waterfront fight for the control of the piers, a war their fathers hadn't forgotten.

Dyale was hard to figure out. It seemed he had everything going for him. He looked like his father, the girls were crazy about him, and he was well educated. Dyale had traveled and lived in places that most people at that time could only dream of. He was the first person Michael knew that wasn't from Red Hook.

Dyale spoke four languages, but he played it down, especially with the wise guys and girls at Manual Training. Michael found it amazing how he could turn the culture thing on and off. When they were at his mother, Donna Forsythe's, apartment, he was the perfect well-bred American boy. They spoke French to each other, and when Michael came over they would speak Italian to him.

Dyale became the fourth pitcher in the Braves rotation, and although he clearly had the talent to be number one, he didn't care. And that was a reflection of his whole attitude. He didn't care about anything. At times it seemed he was even bored with life, and sometimes Michael thought he had a death wish.

One morning the D train pulled into the Carroll Street Station. When the doors opened up Dyale was there with two cups of coffee and two éclairs. "Let's go to Coney Island." And off they went to Coney Island.

This was a Thursday. If you took a second ride on the world famous Cyclone it was half-price, twenty-five cents. And the view of the fireworks from the top of the Cyclone was spectacular. To Michael's surprise, Dyale pulled out a joint and lit it as the Cyclone slowly made its ascent.

"Come on, take a puff, there's nothing to it."

They were in the last car; Michael pushed Dyale's hand aside. Dyale took a deep drag on the joint and started to stand up as the line of cars reached the pinnacle. The fireworks at Steeplechase were lighting up the sky and Dyale started shouting, "I hate my fucking life, I hate my fucking father!"

As the last car started down, people held on for dear life, but Dyale had let go and was about to throw himself out of the car. Had it not been for Michael fighting all the way to hold him down Dyale would surely have committed suicide that night.

When the ride came to a stop, Dyale was completely distraught, holding on to his friend and crying.

About two weeks after the Cyclone incident, Barbara Gittens stopped over at Dyale's apartment just as Michael was getting ready to leave.

"Michael, stay, my mom is working late and left some food for us." Dyale took out some joints and started to smoke. "Hey, Michael, want a puff?"

"No." Michael had seen too many kids at Manuel getting high and doing stupid things, and besides, if he needed to get high he had Santa's wine.

"Here, Barbara, take a drag." Barbara took a drag. "Hey, before we eat, let's take a walk to the bridge."

The Brooklyn Bridge was a short walk from his apartment, along the promenade overlooking the million-dollar view of Manhattan. The stately brownstones were to their right and the bridge was in front of them. It looked so delicate spanning the river. They walked to the middle of the bridge and Dyale started climbing one of the cables.

"Dyale get down," Michael and Barbara pleaded with him. Michael saw the same look on Dyale's face that he had when he tried to kill himself on the Cyclone.

"You don't know what it's like. Every day for the rest of my life, I have to live in the shadow of my father. It's like a fucking ghost that haunts you in the middle of the night. I've never spoken to him without worrying that I was going to say the wrong thing or that I wasn't going to measure up to his expectations. Every place I go I fuck up, because I don't know if people like me or are just pretending."

"Dyale, get down. I love you. I don't care who your father is, just like you don't care if I'm black." Barbara was crying; she never knew her father.

Michael didn't know what to say or think. Here was his friend who he thought had it all together, someone he admired and looked up to, someone with all the advantages in life, threatening to kill himself by jumping off the Brooklyn Bridge.

Michael and Mary Madison stopped in the middle of the bridge. No one had to tell them this was a magical night. The view of the city from the Brooklyn Bridge was spectacular. The city traffic came to a standstill and it was beautifully quiet. The bright lights seemed subdued as they glistened intermittently among the falling snowflakes.

Mary Madison opened his jacket and placed her head on his chest and put her arms around him As he put his arm around her, his chain came loose and his small golden horn fell onto the snow. He was lucky it had snowed or else the horn would have fallen between the grates and down into the East River.

"What's this?" she asked as he recovered it from the snow.

"Oh, it's a Sicilian horn; it was my grandfather Michele's, and my father gave it to me when I was ten. It's supposed to bring good luck, and my grandmother says it wards off evil spirits and that if you believe in it no harm can come to you."

Mary Madison put the tiny golden horn on the chain. "Now bend down, we can't have you going around without this horn around your neck. I don't want anything to happen to you, and besides, it has brought us both good luck." She kissed him and whispered in his ear, "If I had one wish, I would wish this day would never end."

Michael looked at her. She was the second person he had ever met who didn't come from Red Hook. She was different; she didn't hide her feelings, and in Red Hook, in order to survive, you didn't let anyone know your feelings.

Santa would say, "Don't ever tell anyone you're feeling good; it will bring bad luck. And don't ever tell a woman that you love her. She will take you for a fool and take everything you have and leave you. *Sono tutti putani*—they are all whores—and watch out for the ones with blue eyes, they are the most dangerous." Santa had blue eyes.

Michael was silent; he looked out in the distance and seemed reflective.

"What are you thinking of?"

"Oh, sometimes I wonder what it would be like had I been born in Sicily."

"Why do you say that?"

"Because my father tells me our family comes from nobility and lived in castles. It's hard to imagine that, living here in Red Hook."

Mary Madison got excited. "I knew you were a prince, and now you have a castle to prove it."

"I think my father tells these stories just to keep me in line."

"I think I like your father." Mary Madison placed her head on Michael's chest. "One day we will both go to Sicily and search for that castle."

He whispered in her ear, "*Sciatu mio.*" Michael couldn't believe he said that; it came so natural to him.

She smiled and looked into his eyes. "That sounds so romantic, what does it mean?"

He smiled, almost embarrassed, and she saw a slight blush cross his face. "It's a Sicilian expression. One day I'll tell you what it means."

"I think I know already." She kissed him as she had never kissed anyone before and whispered in his ear, "*Sciatu mio.*"

That night Michael had a difficult time sleeping; his dreams seemed so real. He and Mary Madison were walking through a snowstorm when a black limo pulled up. Out came Harold Wilson with Ciclopi, and they grabbed Mary Madison and threw her into the black limo.

Now Don Pasquale was warning Michael, "You are making a big mistake." In the dream, Michael found himself walking into a castle and Mary Madison was sitting on the throne—no, no, it was the woman, Claudia. Claudia was beautiful. "Yes, come to me." She beckoned, and Michael walked to her and started to kiss her. Oh my God, Claudia was his mother, Anna. Michael woke up in a sweat.

Mary Madison's letter was by his side. He started thinking about what Don Pasquale had told him at the restaurant. "Can I tell you something in confidence?" Don Pasquale waited for Michael to reply.

"I guess you're going to tell me anyway, even if I don't want to hear it." He had received the same warning from Phil: "Stay away from her."

"A long time ago in Sicily, your father made the same mistake you're about to make now, and he's never been the same."

"I'm not my father."

"In many ways you are. *Dio mio*, Michael, I could close my eyes and when you talk like this I'm back in Sicily—Giuseppe and me. When I open my eyes and see you, I see him fifty years ago. I know he is not the same now, but part of that is due to what happened back then."

"*Che su chesso?*"

"They were in love, a beautiful princess whose name was Claudia Cavour, and your father. We told him it would never work, but your father wouldn't listen. He had ideas, he had visions, and he aspired to be something. He was so full of life and hope, but the place he loved so much cut his heart out and tore it to pieces." Don Pasquale paused and looked at Michael in a way he never had before. There was almost fear in his eyes. "The treachery of Sicily destroyed him, and it will destroy you."

"But this is not Sicily. This is America."

"*No, figlio mio*, listen to me. There's a Sicilian proverb: No matter how we think we are different, we are the same. You are your father; your blood is Sicilian."

Those words kept ringing over and over in Michael's head. "You are your father, and your blood is Sicilian."

Michael was afraid to go back to sleep. The sheets of the bed were soaked with perspiration. He decided to go to the roof. As he slipped on his pants he glanced into the mirror and even surprised himself by how much he had grown. All the years of self-doubt and teenage awkwardness had disappeared, and the reflection in the mirror showed a young man on a runaway roller coaster going full speed and he couldn't get off.

But there was a sense of shame that Michael found hard to shed and that tormented him. He loved his father, but he was old, much older than other fathers, and now his health was failing. There were times Michael felt ashamed of Giuseppe. He had heard the whispers and the name calling sotto voce, "*Vecchio fessio, cornuto,*" and it hurt. It didn't seem to bother Giuseppe as much as it did Michael.

Michael found it hard to rationalize how his father was a commoner while his brother Tony was a big shot holding the strings. How he and his father lived in a small cold-water flat and the rest of the family lived in beautiful homes in Bensonhurst. Their children rode around in fancy cars and went to Florida for weeks for a vacation while Michael went to Coney Island for the day.

Did he want that? In Michael's world the ones with the money were the wise guys in the streets. But the ones with the power who controlled the strings lived in penthouses in Manhattan or the ones watching them from their beautiful brownstones in Brooklyn Heights.

CHAPTER 12

Later that night Michael was startled when he heard the banging on the steam pipe—it was Dorothy Toscano. Michael hadn't seen her for five months. When her mother, Mary Toscano, found out she'd had an abortion she placed Dorothy in Mount Loretto, a six hundred-acre Catholic mission for problem children on Staten Island. It looked like such an idyllic place, with rolling hills and horses and cows eating in the pastures, but it was hell to Dorothy. She was beaten, but the nuns couldn't break her, and after five months they gave up.

It was two o'clock on a Sunday morning at the beginning of summer six months earlier when Michael heard the code on the steam pipe. He quickly dressed, sensing something was wrong. When he got to the roof she was crying.

"Oh, Michael, oh, Michael, I'm so ashamed." She cried on his shoulder, and he held her for what seemed an eternity. She couldn't stop crying and she couldn't stop saying she was ashamed.

Nicky Genovese had just taken her for an abortion and dumped her off in front of their brownstone like a discarded *putana*. He told her their relationship was over. That was another reason why he hated Nicky.

Dorothy was the leader of the Dukettes, a girl gang in Red Hook. At sixteen Dorothy was built like a mature Sophia Loren. She always wore her jet-black hair in a ponytail that went down to her waist. She was pretty and pursued by older boys—and unfortunately by Nicky Genovese.

When Dorothy was younger she really believed she and Michael would get married. And at one point Michael thought if he wasn't going to be a priest he would marry Dorothy. She was the brightest and best-looking one of the Toscano sisters, but she grew up too fast, like most of the girls in Red Hook.

Dorothy and Michael had a secret way of communicating: they'd bang their secret code on the steam pipe that went through his apartment up to hers. A couple of years ago yelling and screaming came from the Tuscano apartment and a frantic banging of the steam pipes. Michael, without thinking, ran upstairs. He expected the worst. When he opened the front door of the apartment, Mary's deranged ex-common-law husband, Vinny un Pazzo "Crazy Vinny," was chasing Mary around the table with a butcher knife in his hand threatening to kill her and the three girls. The three girls were huddled under the table, screaming for someone to help them.

"Leave her alone!" Michael yelled. Vinny un Pazzo looked past Michael as Giuseppe appeared right behind him.

"You heard him, Vinny, leave them alone." Giuseppe looked at the poor soul who had nothing in his life to offer anyone. The Genovese bookmakers had taken his money and alcohol did the rest. "Give me the knife before the police come and put you away." Giuseppe calmly walked over to Vinny and put his hand out for the knife.

"They took everything from me, Giuseppe, everything, and now I have nothing. I don't even have a place to sleep." Vinny started to cry. As he handed the knife to Giuseppe he put his head on Giuseppe's shoulder. "*Tu capisce?*"

"*Si,* I understand."

Five months had passed since Michael had heard the banging on the pipes and had met the crying Dorothy on the roof. He'd heard she was back from Mount Loretto, so he quickly went out into the hallway. The light in the hall was turned off, and when Michael saw Dorothy he knew why. She looked seductive, with a flimsy nightgown that was half open to her belly button slightly revealing two healthy breasts. Her body was stretched across the stairs.

"I've been thinking about you for five months. I turned seventeen today, and I want you for my birthday. Come here and give me a kiss."

Michael bent down to give her a kiss on her cheek but she grabbed his neck and opened her mouth and stuck her pulsating tongue into his mouth. This was something new; he figured she must have learned it at the mission. Michael couldn't breathe anymore and had to come up for air.

"Hold on, you're driving me crazy." It was as if she was in heat. Michael could feel her young, firm, voluptuous body pressing against his.

"Make love to me, I want you to make love to me, Michael, I want you inside of me." She unbuttoned the rest of her nightgown. Michael must have dreamt of this situation a thousand times with Hedy Lamarr, Marilyn Monroe, Brigitte Bardot, and even Dorothy Toscano.

Growing up in Red Hook, most boys became men by the time they were fifteen. Michael was a late bloomer, but over the last year he had been having a difficult time justifying wanting to become a priest. The temptress Toscano sisters were unmerciful in their attacks, escalating his feelings of lust and desire, which raged through his innocent libido. "Dorothy, I love you, but not like that. Like a sister. I can't do this."

"I don't want to be your sister. You know how I feel about you, and we were supposed to get married, remember?"

"Dorothy, things change, we were kids." Michael wanted to put his arms around her but stopped.

"Oh, things change—like my abortion?" She started to cry and he put his arms around her.

"No, that has nothing to do with it. Listen to me and stop crying." Michael gently pushed her away and wiped her tears. "I met Donna Reed."

"Donna Reed? You still in love with her?" Dorothy looked up. Her tears were subsiding. They talked half the night away. She told him about her stay in Mount Loretto. She didn't know if she hated it more than she hated Nicky, but in the final analysis it was Nicky. She wanted him dead, but she was going to have to wait in line.

Right now Michael needed Dorothy. He just needed someone to talk to, someone he could trust, and Dorothy listened.

Too many things had happened over the last few days that had changed Michael's life. Too many questions remained unanswered, such as what he was going to do for the rest of his life. He was definitely in the proverbial crossroads, and in this case the wrong decision could wind up with someone dead and that someone could be him.

He had great hatred for Nicky Genovese and especially Ciclopi for trying to kill his father, for beating Phil and him unmercifully—and had it not been for Sam Peppe, who knows how far they would have gone—and for treating Dorothy Toscano like a *putana*.

On the other side of the coin was meeting and falling in love with Mary Madison Brittain. Never had Michael felt this way about anyone. But that raised the perplexing problem of Harold Wilson and how he, Michael Parisi, fit into all this. Was Harold Wilson just being protective of his beautiful, fragile granddaughter who came from a powerful and influential family? Or was there something else, something sinister? Something Harold did not want anyone to know? Was he involved in the wars between the families? If so, what side was he on?

And how was his father, Giuseppe, involved? How could he have given up everything for Anna? And was Don Pasquale right when he said, "You are your father, your blood is Sicilian."

The uncertainties of Michael's future lay heavily on his mind. The lure of instant power and money by going to work for the family brought an unusual feeling of comfort. But the feeling of letting down the two people he loved the most bothered him even more. How could he rationalize the family to Mary Madison?

Dorothy had his head on her breast, and as he talked and told her everything, she stroked his face and tried to comfort him. "I don't like this Harold guy, I think he's a snake. I'd be careful if I were you," Dorothy said.

"I think you're being a snake now." He smiled as she put her legs around him and kissed him softly— once, twice—and started to unbutton his trousers.

He kissed her back, trying to unravel the web he was caught in. The seductress had a good hold on him, but at the same time he was completely aroused.

"I bet you Donna Reed doesn't kiss like this."

They heard the vestibule door opening on the floor below, and she quickly walked up the steps to her apartment and whispered, "Next time you're not going to escape." She threw him a kiss. "If you need me I'll be here for you. You know I love you."

Michael felt for his lucky horn; it was gone.

✤ ✤ ✤

CHAPTER 13

The holidays were a sad time for Giuseppe and Michael. This Christmas it was worse. Every holiday Anna would come over to eat with them, stay to clean the dishes, and leave. On this Christmas Day she came over with presents, they opened the presents, and then she prepared to leave.

"Why can't you stay?" It was almost as if Giuseppe was begging.

"I have to take care of my mother, she's not feeling good." She was lying as usual. Santa was fine. Michael had taken her shopping on Union Street the day before and she had gotten into three fights with the merchants.

"How much is this stale fish?" she had demanded.

"*Signora*, this is fresh fish. It just came off the boat in from Sheepshead Bay."

"Your wife's *baccala* is fresher than this fish." She pulled Michael's arm and shouted in disgust, "*Ammunini*, let's go!" And off they went to Santa's next victim.

Michael could hear the fish man yelling as they crossed the street, "And don't come back here anymore." Michael believed they had been thrown out of every place of business on Union Street. But it always amazed him how they forgot Santa's insults from one week to the next. He finally realized it was a game they played that they seemed to enjoy. The owners would usually give Michael a wink, saying they understood, but in Santa's mind nobody was going to make her a "*fesso.*"

This Christmas, Anna couldn't hit Michael's leg anymore or try to scare him with her wide-eyed warning stare. But she knew Michael knew she was lying. Santa wasn't ill; Anna was meeting her boyfriend— probably the one with the big limo. The rumors were she had a few sugar daddies that kept her in an elegant lifestyle. Her new sugar daddy had set her up in a penthouse apartment with a million-dollar view in Brooklyn Heights. The million-dollar view was the East River and the skyline of Manhattan. Anna had reached the top; she had gotten everything she always wanted—money. But in the process she had destroyed Giuseppe, the only man who loved her, and she had lost a son.

"I have to go, Santa is waiting for me." A peck on the cheek was about all the affection she could show toward Michael, never a hug. And it was just a goodbye to Giuseppe, which just about broke his heart every time she left. Sometimes Michael felt they were better off just not seeing her at all.

Michael felt guilty leaving Giuseppe alone this Christmas, but it seemed he was content being alone these days. He sat by the window with a book in his hand near the new radiator to keep warm. Two weeks had gone by since the beatings; all but a slight scar remained on his cheek where Ciclopi had slashed him. Michael had healed. But his insides had not.

Michael now understood the old-timers in the club. "You don't get mad, you get even." How many times had he heard the expression? Giuseppe had tried to reason with Michael when he uttered that sentiment and adding, "I'll get my revenge one day when they least expect it."

"You don't understand—revenge will kill you. These people have no heart, no feelings. They don't think life is important except in their own inner circle of ignorance."

But Michael had passed the point of reason and was starting to boil. Anna had just left and his anger with his mother was fueling his rage. He could feel his temper coming on like never before. Anger rushed through his veins, and all his frustration and days of contemplating his revenge just exploded.

"I don't understand you, how could you let them do this to you?" Michael demanded, frustrated and angry. These arguments had become more vehement of late, but this time he showed his rage to the one who loved him the most.

"Do what?"

"How could you have let them take everything away from you?" The frustration of living in Red Hook had just about taken its toll on Michael. "I see your brother living in a beautiful house in Bensonhurst like a *signore* while his son drives a Cadillac, and I understand you had all this and lost it."

"Michael, you are still too young. One day you will understand."

"Understand what? Why they call my father *vecchio fesso*, old fool, or better yet, *cornuto?*" As soon as he uttered those words Michael wished he could take them back. He realized he had stepped over the boundaries.

In an uncontrolled rage Giuseppe struck out. A fierce slap across his face brought Michael to his knees. It was the first time Giuseppe had struck his son. When Michael got up, his face was full of blood; his nose was bleeding again.

Giuseppe immediately tried to put his arms around his son. "Leave me alone." Michael angrily pulled away.

"*Dove vai?* Where are you going?" he asked as Michael stormed out of the room.

"I'm going to live with my grandmother." As he left, Michael realized he was wrong. He wished he could go back and put his arms around his father and say he was sorry, but he didn't. He threw a few clothes together and left.

All alone, Giuseppe looked at his reflection in the window with tears streaming down his face and said,

"Where did the years go when I just held him in my arms?" He reflected back to the time he argued with his father, Michele. He too had stepped over the line and his father had slapped him in anger, something Giuseppe had vowed he would never do to his son.

"The more things change, the more they are the same." A Sicilian proverb.

He pulled out Claudia's letter and started reading it again.

❖ ❖ ❖

CHAPTER 14

What Michael didn't get from his mother, Santa tried to make up for. Her influence on Michael was tremendous. She loved him overbearingly, to the point where she alienated the feelings of the rest of her family, but Santa didn't care. "*Va fan culo*," she told them all.

She was born Santa Columbo in 1881 in Acireale, Sicily. Her father, Carmello, was forced to work since he was seven years old in the sulfur mines at Floristella. They called them "*carusi*," young boys aged five and up. Each of them belonged to a pickaxe man and had the task of bringing up the steep slopes of the mines at least twenty-five kilos of sulfur per day. Five-, six-, and seven-year-olds sold to a pickaxe man who paid the so-called "dead aid" to the family of the *caruso*, who were so poor that they were forced to accept this sale of human flesh.

With the discovery of sulfuric acid, Sicily became the world's biggest exporter of sulfur. For the Sicilians, it was a bitter irony that they contributed to the industrial revolution with raw material but never took part in it, since the island continued to be linked to a feudal system. Sulfur created wealth for so many nations, but not for the sons of Sicily.

For ten years, Carmello was working back-breaking shifts, forced to work naked because of the tremendous heat, to inhale harmful fumes, to be constantly exposed to the risk of collapses, explosions, and leaks of deadly gases. By the time Carmello reached the ripe old age of seventeen, his body was deformed. Permanently hunched over and crippled, he was one of the lucky *carusi*. His family was able to buy his freedom.

Santa fared no better than her father. She and her older sister, Rosa, worked from the age of seven. Neither of them had any formal education—that was reserved only for the nobility, so they fared no better than Sicily's beast of burden, the mule. But the fortunes of the Columbo family were turning. Being the eldest son, upon his father death, Carmello inherited some farmland in the small resort village of Corruth. The Columbo family worked the farm for years, but it was never enough to feed Carmello's family, so with a little bit of cash paid to a local official—some call it a bribe—Santa was able to procure a maid's position at the Cavours' villa in Enna.

Carmello looked at it as an investment; it would be the only opportunity for Santa to make any contribution to her family. Carmello always reminded her of how much it had cost to get her the position and not to do anything to disgrace him.

At the ripe age of fourteen, Santa had developed a voluptuous body. In her naiveté, she was unaware of being pursued by Philip Cavour, the dysfunctional twenty-two-year-old son of Barone Franco Cavour. But Santa had already been spoken for...

Michael knocked on Santa's apartment door. The dogs started to bark and he could hear the chickens. "*Aspetta, aspetta!*" He could hear her trying to keep the dogs quiet and chasing the chickens back into their coop, just in case a nosy neighbor called the department of health.

He had a sad look on his face, and Santa knew something was wrong.

"*Che su chesso?* What happened?"

Michael started to cry, "*Nonna, ho fatto un spaglio,* I made a mistake."

"*Sciatu mio, sediti,*" and Santa consoled her grandson.

"*Come ti senti, Nonna?* How are you feeling?" Michael knew the answer before Santa answered.

"*Cosi, cosi, menza, menza.*" So-so; in Sicily, it was considered bad luck to say you were feeling fine. "You respect your father, *capisce?*" Michael was getting the same lecture from Santa. "He loves you very much."

"I know." For Michael it was almost comical. For someone who seldom spoke with anyone, Santa knew everything that went on in the neighborhood.

Don Pasquale described Santa as a black mussel: they attach someplace and want to live and die there, and for Santa, after she left Sicily, it was her apartment.

Santa did not have any friends. The only people she showed any civility to were the Favatas, a family from Bari, Italy, who lived in the apartment next door. It was whispered sotto voce that the apartment became available when the old lady died from the curse Santa put on her. And the only reason Santa showed any civility was because the eldest daughter, Linda, helped Santa thread her Singer sewing machine and the father, Mario Favata, helped Santa make her wine.

"*Vieni,* come on, you help me check the wine." Santa made the finest wine in the neighborhood. Down in the dark cellar of her apartment she had a storage bin where she kept six oak barrels of some of the finest homemade wine in the neighborhood.

It was here that Michael learned that there was a rhythm to life; the making of the wine with his grandmother also taught him to be patient. Santa stressed the importance of being slow and deliberate with the picking of the grapes at the piers. She personally picked the boxes of grapes. "*Quarda, scuitu, e sacesta,* look, smell, and taste," she would say. The dockworkers never lost patience with Santa; in fact, they seemed to enjoy her feistiness and spirit.

"*Come sono?*" She would ask how the grapes were as she fed them to Michael.

"*Sono buoni.*" Michael would laugh; Santa would give him a wink.

"*Va bene*, we take these boxes."

She always took Michael with her when she bought grapes. From Carroll Street to the dock was about twenty blocks, and they walked. Inevitably they would meet some *paisano* from the old country. "*Signora* Marsala, I haven't seen you in so long; how are you?" the older lady said.

"*Cosi, cosi.*" Santa kept walking, not wanting to converse, pulling Michael along with her, and when the women couldn't hear her she said, "*Baccala.*"

At the docks she was well known. The dock foreman, Lizio, knew her from Trapani. He always made sure she had the first pick of the grapes and saved the best for *Signora* Marsala.

"Lizio, *come e la famiglia?*" she asked.

"*Cosi, cosi.*" Lizio knew that the hardship, sorrow, and horror this little woman had endured in Trapani would have been fatal to most people. "Let me take the grapes home for you, *piacere mio.*" It would be his honor.

The first press of the grapes was the highlight for Michael as Santa always let him drink the juice from her cup.

"*Saluti.*" They toasted to the success of the making of the wine.

"Remember what I tell you, your father is your father no matter what." More Sicilian logic. She tasted the wine in a little glass she had brought down to the cellar with her. "Here, you taste." She offered a glass of wine to Michael. "So you want to come and live with me?"

They were in a small, dark cubbyhole in the cellar that was partitioned off with wood planks. Santa had positioned an old door to secure her portion of this underground.

Realizing the agony he was putting his father through, Michael was sulking inwardly. Even though he was remorse, he still intended to move in with Santa. "Drink it, you'll feel better," Santa insisted. Michael drank the red wine and she poured them another.

Santa placed her hand affectionately on Michael's face and, with tears in her eyes, said, "*Sciatu mio,* sit down and let me tell you something about our families in Sicily."

PART II

❊ ❊ ❊

CHAPTER 15

Santa painted a colorful collage from the raging red lava of a snow-capped Mount Etna, to the array of multi-hued brown and black mountainsides that descended to the warm turquoise blues and greens of the crystal clear Ionian Sea. This tropical island, where princes and barons dwelled and planted and cultivated their vineyards. The oranges were as big as grapefruits and tasted like sugar. There were a hundred churches just in Acireale filled with colorful tapestry and tiles depicting life twenty-five hundred years ago. Baroque architecture flourished four hundred years ago and surrounded itself with beautiful *giardini* and courtyards. Tall, lush tropical trees, brought in from Turkey, mysteriously concealed a three-story gray Norman-Arab stone castle that was built nearly three hundred years before.

History and legend are interwoven in the origins of Acireale. The present name of the town refers to the myth, sung by Virgil and Ovid, of the shepherd Aci and the beautiful nymph Galatea. The nymph loved and was loved by the young shepherd. But Polyphemus, one of the Cyclopes who lived on Etna, took a fancy to the girl. She rebuffed his advances. Mad with jealousy, he killed Aci by throwing enormous rocks at him, some of which reached the sea and can be seen off Acitrezza. Galatea's tears formed the river Aci, which was subsequently covered by numerous lava flows.

Settled by the Greeks then followed by the Romans and later by the Normans, Aci became important during the Arab domination, but the earthquake of 1169 forced the inhabitants of Aci to migrate inland. In 1326, the Angevin fleet of Beltrando del Balzo destroyed the town. The town had resurgence during the Spanish domination, and Aci enjoyed steady economic growth. But in 1553, the town was sold by the Spanish crown to the nobility of the region and was reduced to feudalism.

In the meantime, thanks to the ability of its ambassadors and especially great sums of moneys donated by the three barons, the Contis, the Cavours, and the Parisis of the region, Aci was able to continue growing economically. In 1651, the free market for commerce of the area was moved to the center of town, giving the town noble status.

King Fillippo IV gave the authority for the town to be called Acireale. In 1671, the Academia Degli Zelanti was opened. It was a cultural center of great importance and had one of the largest and richest libraries in Sicily. The cultivation of silkworms and the silk trade was the main economic activity until 1693, when Acireale was shaken by another devastating earthquake. The town was heavily damaged, but the nobility began rebuilding the center of town. With the efforts of the three barons, Acireale was enriched with stylish churches and palazzi. The baroque image was gaining influence, and the three barones built lavish palazzos, charming piazzas, and magnificent cathedrals—each one trying to outdo the other.

The Piazza Duomo was the heart of the town. It became the seat of political, religious, and economic power. The center of the piazza boasted stately palm trees and a seventeenth-century fountain surrounded by the busts of the three barons. The Palazzo Comunuale, the town hall, with its unique local baroque style, surrounded the piazza and made an aristocratic statement for its time. The building had an elegant portal on the first floor with ornate wrought iron railings adorning the elegant balconies.

It took twenty years to complete the cathedral; the pseudo-gothic style façade was framed between two cusp bell towers decorated with polychromatic flat tiles. The famous Blandamonte carved the marble portal, which took him four years to finish. The first mass was held in 1698, and the whole town came to the service to pray for good fortune, good weather for a good citrus crop, and for Etna to keep its lid on, but most of all they came to see the nobility. How were they dressed? Who were they sitting with? How many horses pulled their elegant carriages?

One of the most interesting palazzos in the piazza was the beautiful Palazzo Parisi. The elegant neo-classic design set the finishing touches to Piazza Duomo. The palazzo once housed King Ferdinand IV's family, descendants of the Bourbons. Probably the most remarkable private building in the town, decorated by Falcini, was said to house some of the finest frescoes in all of Italy. Salvatore Parisi and each one of his younger brothers, when they reached the age of twenty-one, were given a fifteen-room apartment in the palazzo.

In the late eighteenth century, a *castello*—a castle—was built by Barone Orazio Parisi I as a retreat from living in the palazzo in town. It took over ten years to complete the massive Arab-Norman structure. The grand *castello* was over one hundred thousand square feet. The interior was frescoed by Gianni Scuitu and designed by the renowned architect Giovanni Patricolo, who insisted that the stones to build the castle be imported from Malta because the granite there was practically impermeable. This proved to be true when, in World War II, the Germans took over the castle as their headquarters in Sicily. The *castello* withstood a British bombardment that lasted for a year.

The ceilings were over twenty-five feet high and decorated with massive hand-carved oak moldings cut down from the family's extensive landholdings near Enna. The elaborate tile work for the pool took nearly three years to complete as the artisan had to be so meticulous with the tiles. When completed, the pool depicted young men and women scantily clothed in various scenes of Greco-Roman athletic events. The family chapel and crypt were designed and painted by the famous artist/painter from Siena, Lavata, who had gained acclaim throughout Italy for his masterpieces in the cathedral in Tuscany.

During the industrial revolution, the castle was officially called Castello Parisi di Floristella (the flowering star). It perched majestically high above the blue-green Ionian Sea with the smoking Mount Etna in the background. It was the centerpiece of aristocracy in eastern Sicily.

Years after the unification of Italy was complete, a young, dark-haired, mustached, robust Salvatore Parisi was given the castle for his wedding, a present from his father, Barone Orazio Parisi I. Six months later, Barone Orazio passed away. Salvatore was the eldest of the sons. Among his brothers were Gianni, who became an artist and moved to Naxos, and Pio, who painted murals for the Vatican, and the youngest, Franco, who became a renowned composer and lived in Rome.

Salvatore inherited the title of barone. Years earlier, the planned marriage between the Parisi and Conti families united the wealthiest families and landholders in Sicily. The plain-looking, pudgy Gabriella Conti had been educated in a private school in Florence. Luckily for customs and prearranged marriages and a family who had more money and land than the Parisis, the young noble couple was married.

The Parisis wealth came from owning land and the Floristella sulfur mines. Floristella was a day's journey by horse into the center of Sicily. It was the biggest mine in Sicily and gave work to thousands of people. During the industrial revolution, it became the world's largest exporter of sulfur, and young Barone Salvatore Parisi reaped the benefits.

Salvatore's wealth and power had become notorious throughout the continent. When a rare three thousand five hundred-year-old, Greek coin was discovered in an archaeology excavation in Syracuse, no one could put a value to it. The bank of Switzerland that funded the excavation decided to place the coin on the auction block. There were three bidders: King Emanuel I of Italy, the international banker J.P. Morgan from the United States, and Barone Salvatore Parisi di Floristella. After three days of a bidding war, it came down to J.P. Morgan and Salvatore, and the barone won. When a value was established for the coin, an economist calculated the barone could have bought half the island of Sicily.

Years later, the American banker, J. P. Morgan came to spend some time with the barone. He and Salvatore would play chess all day long, smoking the best cigars and drinking the finest brandy and wines.

"Tell me, why did you want that coin so badly?" Morgan would always ask. He was still ticked off that Salvatore had outbid him for the rare Greek coin.

Salvatore never hesitated to answer. "Because I'm tired of this island being raped of its heritage for centuries by strangers who come here and take away our history, our resources, and our people. The Romans, Arabs, French, and Spaniards have come here and ruled and now it's the Italians. We have a culture and history that existed thousands of years before Rome was ever conceived. I want to preserve it, and I want the people to feel proud to say, 'I'm a Sicilian.' And that coin is a symbol of that, and I don't want to see it taken away from us."

These were the times of good and plenty for the nobility and especially for Salvatore. The three wealthiest families on the island were the Parisis, Contis, and Cavours. And one way or another, through the years, the families intermarried. These families would throw lavish parties for the nobility of Sicily and Europe. Guest lists included duchesses and dukes, princes and princesses, and kings and queens from all over the continent. The Castello Parisi became the playground for the aristocracy. The stables were filled with only the finest Arabian stallions. The meticulously cultivated *giardini* was lush with fruit trees, and the aroma of wildflowers blooming all year long permeated throughout the stuffy, ornate rooms. Three massive fountains adorned the *giardini,* and statues of family members were placed along the garden's stone paths, which led to the clay tennis courts. The tallest of palms were brought in from Saudi Arabia as a gift from the sultan. It was common at that time to see a prince from Prussia or a duke from Austria-Hungary mingling with some of the dukes and duchesses from England. But the most intriguing character who visited from time to time was the most unassuming individual. He had no title other than Don Ciccu.

Like most men of power, Salvatore had an eye for beautiful women. He had his mistress in Rome, whom he put up in a lavish villa on one of the famous hills near Saint Peter's. She was the daughter of the industrialist Wilhelm Von Frederick of Germany. She was tall, had fair skin, and was very young, slender, blue-eyed, and blond. She was every Sicilian man's dream and nightmare.

But Heidi was just a showpiece, a trophy to be shown, and Barone Salvatore understood the game. Her father, Wilhelm Von Frederick, was Salvatore's largest purchaser of sulfur. Wilhelm needed the sulfur to build an industrial empire for his Germany to prepare for war, and his daughter was the insurance that the supply would continue.

As beautiful and sought-after as Heidi was, the barone was never enthralled by her. She did not fool him. He realized everything she did was for a purpose, even faking orgasms. When they had sex she always insisted on being on top. She moaned and groaned more than any whore in a bordello. She touted how she was coming, but in reality she was as dry as the sirocco, the dry desert winds from Africa during a hot, rainless August. But the barone knew she was Wilhelm's pawn, and Salvatore played along for a while.

Barone Salvatore was recognized as an excellent statesman, a man of reason, a mediator who was able to bring Giuseppe Garibaldi, the Italian liberator and the catalyst who unified Italy in 1861, into successful negotiations with Emmanuelle II, King of Italy. It was at this time that Barone Salvatore and Giuseppe Garibaldi became friends.

As a man of principles, Barone Parisi respected Garibaldi's devotion to the cause of Italian unity, and when the time came to help his friend, the barone contributed a large sum of money to Garibaldi's army of a thousand. In May 1860, Garibaldi landed in Sicily with a volunteer force of 1,070 men. Within two weeks this force had taken over the city of Palermo and defeated an army of twenty thousand from the Kingdom of Naples. In August, Garibaldi crossed to the Italian mainland, routing the Neapolitan army in a series of victories and capturing Naples itself within a month. Garibaldi's march became one of the greatest legends of the nineteenth century, both because of the genius with which Garibaldi overcame vast military odds and, equally importantly, because of the potent political symbolism of the event in an age when ethnic and cultural groups increasingly responded to nationalism's call in a Europe still dominated by dynasties of an earlier age.

Twenty years had gone by since the unification of Italy, and Barone Salvatore Parisi had been elected senator to Rome. After his term as senator ended, he returned to Sicily to take care of family businesses. The barone already had three children. The oldest was Orazio, then Michele, his favorite, and the girl, Donnatella.

But when he returned home he was surprised to find his wife pregnant again. As a Conti, Gabriella had all the luxuries that life could offer and more; she was now a Parisi. But having it all didn't make Gabriella a happy person. It seemed all she did was complain. In the summer, it was too hot in Sicily for her. In the winter, it was too cold. She complained about the servants; they were too slow and too dumb. In Sicily when things went bad, she blamed it on the peasants. Salvatore asked his brother-in-law for help.

"I knew she wasn't a raving beauty, and I overlooked that. I knew she didn't have the most tempting body, and I overlooked that. But I didn't know she constantly complains and nothing satisfies her." Salvatore looked worn out; the three weeks since his return had taken more out of Salvatore Parisi than the unification negotiations with Garibaldi and the king of Italy.

"She's a bitch; she always was and always will be. Our mother is a bitch and our grandmother, I understand, was the biggest bitch." Alfredo was sniffing cognac and now he poured Salvatore a glass. They sat in Alfredo's library at his villa by the sea in Acireale.

Salvatore started to laugh; he laughed so hard Alfredo started to laugh along with him. "I guess these are the sacrifices we must make to keep our families and bloodline." Alfredo raised his glass and toasted his brother-in-law. "I sympathize with you."

"Alfredo, I need more than your sympathy, I need a woman." They laughed and drank. "Barone, with that German beauty you have in Rome you are the envy of all the senators." Alfredo and Salvatore were feeling no pain by now.

"She is as dry as the sirocco and colder than the top of Mount Etna in January." Salvatore stuck out his empty glass and Alfredo refilled it.

"I believe my brother-in-law needs the services of a Sicilian woman, and I just might know of such a person." Alfredo raised his glass to Salvatore. "*A saluti.*"

"*A saluti.*" They raised their glasses and toasted again.

❖ ❖ ❖

CHAPTER 16

When Gabriella had her fourth child, Maria, Florianna Rosellini came to work as a servant to Gabriella at Castello Parisi di Floristella. In Palermo, the Mafia had murdered her husband, and it was said she had to flee Palermo, but the insidious Don Carlo had sent her son, Franco "Ciccu" Rossellini, to the sulfur mines for insurance.

If an artist could capture on canvas the soul and beauty of this mysterious island, it would be in a portrait of Florianna Rosellini. She had long, black, silky hair that came down over her voluptuous body; her dark, penetrating eyes could seduce a king or drive a peasant insane. With one look, she could melt the snow off Mount Etna and turn around and put a knife through anyone who hurt someone she loved.

Florianna loved to work in the *giardini* whenever she wasn't serving *Signora* Gabriella, which seemed to be most of the day. She could often be found tending to the vegetables and pruning the fruit trees, potting the geraniums, cutting the gladiolas. The warm

Sicilian sun was kind to Florianna. During the hot days, her dress was totally drenched and her bronze skin became darker, enhancing her warm, sensual body.

The barone was having problems with peasant labor like many of the wealthy landowners, including his brother-in-law Alfredo Conti and his cousin Franco Cavour in Enna. Since the unification of Italy, there was much unrest among the peasants in Sicily. There were wildcat strikes and small revolts against the Italians and raids on villas by growing numbers of roving bandits that hid out in caves along the isolated, rocky mountainside.

Barone Salvatore Parisi's attention was focused on his problems at the sulfur mines at Floristella. There was much unrest among the *carusi*. It had been three years since Salvatore visited the mines and his family's home there, Palazzo Parisi at Floristella. He was saddened by what he saw. From a strategic position on his balcony at Palazzo Parisi, he was able to watch every phase of the mining process, the pits, the mountains of mineral diggings, the horrid dwellings of the workers and officers, and above all the *calcheroni*, the furnaces where the sulfur was burned. The liquid sulfur flowed out of these so-called mouths of death. For days the awful smell of rotten eggs was stifling.

Salvatore felt he was suffocating from the horrors these *carusi* endured. It disturbed him tremendously to see the deformed young children. The *carusi* worked ten to twelve hours a day; in some cases the money these children earned in these horrid conditions was all the poor peasant families had to live on. Some used the excuse, "It was better than death" for sending their children here. After a few days in the sulfur mines some children wished they were.

Salvatore watched the children carrying heavy sacks of sulfur from dangerous, dark, unsafe mines. Now that he was a father he could not close his eyes to this atrocity. A young boy caught Salvatore's eye because he reminded him of his son, Michele. He asked the boy his name. The boy was carrying a sack of sulfur out of the mine. His whole body was covered with dust. His pale white face had an angelic charm, but he had a morbid expression that tugged at Salvatore's heart.

It was the first time anyone of importance had ever spoken to the boy. "*Io mi chiamo Vito Marsala.*"

Salvatore arranged for Vito Marsala's freedom, and years later he arranged for Vito to marry Santa Columbo.

After a grueling three months at the sulfur mines negotiating with the foremen, firemen, carters, smiths, and wagoners, an exhausted, more slender and svelte Salvatore returned to Acireale and to the tropical tranquility of Castello Parisi. The tranquility only lasted a few moments; Gabriella had her perpetual headache and complaints.

"Sure, you go away and leave me with all the problems." It was a hot August night. They were sitting in the formal dining room being served dinner. In the dining room were two massive oil portraits, one of Cosimo di Medici and the other of the king of Italy, a wedding gift from Alfredo Conti. The heavily ornate chandelier was made at Morano, Venice, a gift from Cousin Franco Cavour.

Salvatore's eldest was Orazio II, who was twelve. The designated heir, he took after the Contis, his mother side of the family. He was very slim, pale, and meek, and it seemed he was always sick. Orazio shied away from his father and became a mamma's boy. But Orazio loved his younger brother, Michele. Michele was the sensitive one who looked like his father at ten, a little rambunctious and carefree, but he was Salvatore's favorite. There was Donnatella, very prim and proper, and now there was his little darling infant, Maria.

Gabriella kept complaining. "You know Etna exploded again and left all the lava rocks on my patio. I told the servant to get up there immediately and clean it off so that Donnatella and I could play tennis. You know these servants seem to be getting slower and slower. I swear there must be something in the cheap wine they drink that makes them dumb and lazy. I can't wait until we go to Florence so I can buy some decent clothes and drink some decent wine. Salvatore, when are we going to Florence? I just can't take the heat anymore." Gabriella pointed to her fan, and Florianna, who was stationed next to her, immediately gave it to her.

Every trait that Salvatore had been admired for—his statesmanship, his benevolence as a mediator and fine gentleman, a nobleman of compassion—was about to go out the window that hot August night. The smoking volcano had remained dormant too long, and it was about to explode.

"I've had enough. You are a bitch, your mother was a bitch, and your grandmother was a bitch." He was standing at the head of the table with fire in his eyes. Florianna had been serving dinner and now she gathered the frightened children and quickly ushered them out of the dining room. No one had seen Salvatore so enraged; it was as if everything he had gone through over the last few years with the negotiations for unification and witnessing the atrocities at the sulfur mines had taken their toll on the barone.

"You're never satisfied. There are people starving, there are children who are dying, there are families that go tonight without food, but you complain because you can't even wipe your ass by yourself." He walked closer to Gabriella and with one quick motion grabbed the table linen and pulled it, sending the silverware and glasses dancing across the long, hand-carved fifteenth-century table.

For the first time in her life Gabriella knew what the word fear meant. She started to tremble and scream uncontrollably for God to help her, shouting "*Dio mio, auiti!*" When he reached her she was kneeling and praying.

At that point, Florianna interceded. She stepped in front of him. "Barone, please, for the sake of the children, stop." The children were crying. Donnatella and Orazio were clinging to their wailing mother and Florianna held Maria while Michele silently held on to Florianna's apron.

He looked at Florianna and for the first time an impulsive passion ran through his body. The combination of rage and sexual arousal was almost uncontrollable. "Take her to her room." He pointed to Donnatella who was still weeping. "I'll be in the *giardini*."

An hour passed before Florianna came down to the *giardini* to look for the barone. By this time he had calmed down and was sitting in the gazebo by the fountain. He was ashamed of his outburst. She had poured him an amarro, a Sicilian liqueur, in a cognac glass and brought it out to him on a silver tray. She was extremely sensual. "Drink this, you will feel better."

She looked stunning. Her eyes were penetrating and they appeared to say, "Take me now." She made an impetuous, innocent mistake. She wasn't supposed to fall in love, that wasn't in the agreement, but there was nothing she could do about it.

He didn't say a word as he took the glass from Florianna's hand. His eyes never swayed from her. He took one gulp of the amarro and tossed the glass over his shoulder.

The night became enchanting for the lovers. In the distance they could hear the volcano rumbling and in an instant the starless night became inflamed in a fury of red clouds as the inferno erupted, sending balls of fire hundreds of feet into this magical night. Their eyes opened wide as they heard the pitter-patter of lava showering from the heavens upon the roof of the gazebo. The scent of wildflowers became their blanket as they lay like two intoxicated young lovers in each other's arms.

In his bedroom, Michele came to the balcony window. The red sky was awesome and enticed the young boy to go out to the balcony. He saw his father and Florianna embraced in each other's arms.

❧ ❧ ❧

CHAPTER 17

The gay, lavish lifestyle the Parisis, the Contis, and Cavours were accustomed to was being challenged. The rich were getting richer and the poor were starving. The classes were extremely divided between the haves and have-nots. Political rhetoric was always cheap, but during difficult times it became dangerous in Sicily. The European continent was drawing the battle lines and the trenches were about to be dug. The powder keg was ready to explode; all it needed was a match. And Sicily would not be spared. Sicily is never spared.

Over twenty years had passed since Salvatore had become Barone Salvatore Parisi di Floristella and the class struggles had intensified between the nobility and peasants, and as always, the Church and Mafia played their secret roles. In Sicily sometimes it was hard to tell them apart.

At this time the patriarch of the Parisi family was still Barone Salvatore Parisi di Floristella, but Salvatore was getting older, becoming less focused on family business, and losing control. He had built a small empire and now he was having problems controlling it. There was unrest in Sicily. He needed Don Ciccu.

His oldest son, the shy Orazio, was entitled to become barone. Salvatore had a difficult time entrusting him with the family's wealth and power because when the time came, it was Michele the second born who had Salvatore's heart. Michele had soul and fire and convictions, and the peasants said his tongue was sweet as *zucchero*.

But a change in Michele and Salvatore's relationship had taken place. Michele had been studying history and politics with his tutor and was discussing it at the dinning table with his father when it turned into a heated debate.

Michele was expressing the opinion of the new independent movement that was spreading all over Sicily since the unification of Italy had left control of Sicily to the northern Italians. "We have our own history and culture; therefore, we should rule ourselves."

Salvatore looked at his son and knew that the young people in Sicily hated the Italians, but Salvatore felt the Italians were the lesser of evils. "That's not so. We have no history of our own."

"True, we have been conquered. But we have never surrendered our culture and way of life. Even when the conquerors tried to impose their rules, we still kept our own. If they broke our laws, they were dealt with quickly." Michele had gotten excited as he talked.

"Sicily existed and our culture thrived a thousand years before Rome was born."

Salvatore tried to remain calm. "Our culture and way of life is that of the Italians now; those who talk of independence are foolish."

"One day Sicily will rid itself of all these foreigners, and we will govern ourselves." Michele slammed his fist on the table.

"Don't be foolish, my son. We are destined to be ruled by others. We must know who rules and play their games. Those who don't...we find them dead with their heads blown off."

Michele answered without thinking of the consequences. "It was you and your class of nobility that allowed the Italians to take over our island. How can you sit here in this castle while the peasants are starving and being raped and killed by these foreigners?"

Those indignant words, coming from his son, aroused Salvatore. He loved his son so much; he never put a hand on him, but this time he vehemently struck Michele in the face. Blood gushed out of his nostrils.

Michele looked at his father. "I will be leaving for Florence."

Michele marched to a different drummer. It was never a question of if he would leave Sicily, but when he would leave Sicily. Michele had a love/hate relationship with Sicily, but most of all he knew he didn't want to live here anymore. Sicily grabbed his inner soul and tore it apart, leaving the fragments for the vultures to pick on. But his broken heart could never be repaired because, as a young man, Michele thought he could never love anyone as much as he loved Florianna. She was everything he needed: compassionate, understanding, encouraging, comforting, but most of all she showed him how to love. And for that other reason he had to leave Sicily.

In Florence, Michele excelled in painting portraits of the Sicilian peasants in their humble surroundings. By the age of eighteen his works were being displayed in some of Florence's prestigious galleries. But Michele was very political; he absorbed life around him like a sponge. He was interested in everything but mostly in the plight of the peasants in Sicily. His sympathy for the peasants turned into a devotion to the peasants, and it was reflected in everything he painted. He became known as the peasant painter. He captured the pain in their faces and the sadness in their eyes.

His affixation of the plight of the peasant drew some heavy criticism, especially from his young cousin, Riccardo Conti. Unlike Orazio, Riccardo was being groomed to take over as head of his family's estates. The family didn't like it when one of their own sided with the other side.

When Michele received the invitation to the Conti wedding, he almost threw it away. In Florence, it was the biggest event of the year: Alfredo Conti's pompous eldest son, Riccardo Conti, marrying Antoinette Cavour, the eldest daughter of Franco and Vita Cavour. "It is a marriage deal made in heaven," according to Alfredo Conti. They were first cousins, and this marriage would further unite the three most powerful families in Sicily. But in reality more power was shifting to the Conti family, and this was the way Alfredo Conti had planned it.

Franco Cavour and Alfredo Conti were brothers-in-law, Franco having married Alfredo's sister, Vita. Unlike Alfredo, in his later years Franco decided to retire and live a quiet life at his family estate in Ragusa, Sicily. Franco was proud of his accomplishments and the prestige of his family's name. His landholdings encompassed large vineyards and estates in southern Italy, northern Africa, and the Balkans. He had hoped that one day his only son, Philip Cavour, would inherit and carry on the family name and tradition. But Philip had disappointed Franco. He resembled Orazio Parisi in statue, but that was it. Philip Cavour had a mean streak bordering on evil. He was lazy and non-productive, hated living in Sicily, and had taken up residence in Paris.

So the Conti family was given control of the Cavour family holdings. Thus the conniving, manipulating Alfredo Conti had doubled the Conti landholdings in southern Italy and Sicily. All they needed now to complete their ambitious plans to control the continent were the sulfur mines.

There were two factors that contributed to Michele's taking up the fight for the peasants. The first was the visit to the sulfur mines at Floristella. He was ten years old when his father took him and his older brother Orazio to stay at Palazzo Parisi at Floristella. It was the first time the young boy was rendered speechless. He was drawn to his father's study where he picked up a sheet of paper and charcoal and started to sketch what he saw. When his father came upon him and saw the sensitivity of the sketches and the tears dripping down his young son's face, he realized that Michele was special.

"Come here, my son, *sciatu mio,* let me put my arms around you." Michele was so overwhelmed with grief he ran into his father's comforting arms.

"Pappa, Pappa, it's so sad, it's so sad, they are children like me. I saw two boys fighting today like animals and the crowd was shouting '*marzolu, marzolu*' (kill him, kill him) Why do we do this to them?" Michele couldn't stop crying.

"It's something we inherited and must carry on. It's where our family's wealth and power come from."

"Pappa, I don't want our wealth if it comes from the backs of children."

"That's very profound for a young boy of your age to be thinking, but you see, we do not control who works the mines, we only rent out the mines."

✣ ✣ ✣

CHAPTER 18

The second factor that contributed to Michele's taking up the cause of the peasant was Florianna. Michele loved Florianna. Michele loved Florianna more than he loved his mother, Gabriella. Florianna was there every morning in the servant's kitchen ready with a biscotti and fresh squeezed orange juice from the trees in the *castello's giardini*. But more important was the hug that greeted him every morning and every night. She was always there. When he fell off the horse and tore up his leg she was there to wipe his tears and mend his wounds. Florianna showed Michele as much love as she did for her own son, Ciccu—a nickname for Francesco.

Florianna missed Francesco terribly. She blamed herself for allowing the deceitful Don Carlo to take him away to the sulfur mines. She was vulnerable, and Don Carlo was a master of controlling people and pulling the strings. But Florianna would wait for the right time to get Francesco back and get her revenge on Don Carlo.

The servant's kitchen was the center of activities at the *castello* as it was strategically placed in the middle of the first floor. It was adjacent to the dining room, which opened up to a large, formal sitting room. The rooms were ornately decorated to suit Gabriella's gaudy, expensive taste. It was Florianna's duty to make sure that every piece of crystal and silverware was polished and dusted, that every portrait hung perfectly, that every meal was prepared to Gabriella's satisfaction.

Gabriella insisted only Italian be spoken in the house. She considered Sicilian the language of the peasants and the uneducated. She once reprimanded Michele at the dinner table and insisted that all the children dress appropriately for dinner, which meant their Sunday best. Donnatella was always meticulously dressed in her finest linen. She was the apple of Gabriella's eye. She exuded nobility and had a pompous air about her, which Gabriella fostered. She never spoke casually to the servants, and when she did speak to them, her tone was always a command. Orazio was the quiet one; he observed everything and kept it to himself. Gabriella was proud to say they took after the Conti side of the family. But Maria and Michele took after the Parisi side; they related more with the Sicilians—the common folks.

"Michele, you are eating and talking like a peasant." Michele was talking to Florianna in Sicilian. Gabriella was angry, as usual. "I want you to stop that immediately. And the way you are dressed, you would think you are not part of this family."

Michele looked toward Florianna who was serving the family dinner. She did not say a word.

"I'm your mother." Gabriella raised her voice. "I want you to listen to me, do you understand that?" Gabriella was at her breaking point. It didn't take much to get her yelling and screaming and in a rage. She was an unstable person and every confrontation was a threat to her, and she saw Florianna as a threat.

"*Basta!* Enough of this." Salvatore was trying to come to his son's aid. "It's not all that bad if he speaks a little Sicilian—after all, we live here."

"What do you suggest, Barone?" Gabriella called him Barone out of frustration and hatred. After all, it had been several months since he moved out of their bedroom. "That we give up our way of life and become *animale?*" If looks could kill she gave Salvatore a death warrant.

Florianna stopped serving and cleared her throat; it was not appropriate for the servant to say anything. She was to be deaf and dumb and invisible when she served the family. "If I may, your mother is correct." Florianna was speaking perfect, grammatical Italian. "This family is looked up to by all of us here in Sicily. You are a prestigious family; you define culture and refinement for us. You are leaders, and people watch and follow what you do. So it's important that you dress well and eat properly, Michele, and listen to your mother, speak Italian."

Gabriella was so taken aback she was speechless. In fact, there was a stressfully silent moment at the table. Everyone nervously looked to Gabriella—they expected her to go off the deep end as usual. "Well, at least we have someone here with common sense. Thank you, Florianna, and you may continue to serve dinner." Gabriella had spoken, and Florianna had managed to stop Gabriella before she went on one of her out-of-control tirades.

When no one was looking, Salvatore looked over at his son Michele and gave him a wink. Michele was comforted by that and by the slight smile on Florianna's face for him.

There were times when Salvatore and Florianna's passion was uncontrollable. They were like alcoholics who became intoxicated by each other's touch, smell, or look, and they couldn't wait to be in each other's arms. It wasn't supposed to happen this way, but Florianna fell in love with the barone and he was madly in love with her. When she served the family at dinnertime they would steal a glance or a look when no one was watching. She brought tranquility to his hectic life and calmed the explosive Gabriella. The barone was spending more time at the *castello,* and when he had to leave for business, he couldn't wait to get home to see her.

Florianna kept the pregnancy a secret from everyone, even from Salvatore.

It was January; the cool winter had begun and the rainy season was about to start. Florianna was looking forward to the spring and working in the *giardini*. Michele was helping her till the soil around the lemon trees one day when suddenly Florianna collapsed to the ground.

"Florianna, Florianna, *che su cheso?*" Michele said as he came to Florianna's side.

"Call the barone, don't speak to anyone but him, *capisce?*"

"*Si.*"

By the time Salvatore arrived her water had broken. "Why didn't you tell me?"

"I didn't want you or anyone to know. I didn't want you to get hurt."

"Don't you know by now I love you?" Salvatore was holding her in his arms.

"Salvatore, it's Don Carlo's baby. *Sciatu mio*, I didn't want to tell you because I didn't want to lose you. What are we going to do?"

Michele watched from a distance, realizing how much his father loved her when he took her in his arms despite the fact that she was carrying Don Carlo's baby. In that moment Michele hated his father.

It was a premature baby boy, barely three pounds. After much thought, Florianna suggested that they give the baby to Salvatore's younger brother, Gianni Parisi, who lived in Naxos with his mistress, Lunella. At first the barone was against it. "We cannot let him go; we will find a way to raise the baby here."

"It's impossible. We will be discovered, and Gabriella will make your life even more miserable." Florianna knew Salvatore was having a difficult time trying to keep the family's vast holdings in the sulfur mines and vineyards from being taken over by others. And she also knew that there was a conspiracy by Don Carlo to destroy the Parisi family. The knowledge of this illegitimate child would surely be used against the barone.

❋ ❋ ❋

CHAPTER 19

Years ago a young Gianni Parisi, Salvatore's younger brother, had done the unthinkable in Sicily. He had left his wealthy wife, Emmanuelle Conti, the younger sister to Alfredo Conti. Like most marriages of the nobility, it was a prearranged marriage. After ten years of an unhappy marriage, Gianni gave up everything he possessed to be with the woman he loved.

Acireale was too ostentatious for the free spirit non-conformist within Gianni. He resented all the titles and pomp and circumstance the royal noble city represented. All of the nobility competed with one another as to who could build the largest villa or palazzo or who had more vineyards, but most of all Gianni resented Alfredo Conti and his son Riccardo. There were many who disliked Alfredo, but they would wisely keep it to themselves. Gianni didn't.

Gianni had it all: the lavish lifestyle, the name, his wife's wealth, a fifteen-room luxury apartment in Palazzo Parisi in Acireale, and three vineyards and a villa in Corruth. And then one day he met her. A famous puppet show from Messina was performing in their town and had set up camp near the beach. They came every year during Carnival time.

Carnival was the most important event in Sicily, taking place from the Thursday before Lent to Carnival Tuesday, with a parade of enormous, grotesquely allegorical floats made of papier-mâché and four-wheel carriages decorated with flowers built by skilled, imaginative craftsmen. Colorful masked groups represented different parts of the island culture, and there were folk bands, which added to the profusion of lights and color. Sports competitions were held, and of course fashion shows and balls for the nobility, all of which lasted till dawn.

She was picked out of a hundred contestants to be the "Queen of the Carnival." Her name was Lunella "Little Moon" Pennisi. Her family came from Messina, and her father was Don Mariano Pennisi, the puppeteer. The theater and café were the favorite pastimes for the upper classes. The lower classes had their daily entertainment with the puppet theater of Don Mariano Pennisi. The peasants would come from miles away—Catania, Messina, and Syracuse and as far off as Palermo—to be entertained by Mariano and his famous puppets.

During Carnival, Gianni sneaked out of the royal ball. This year the Contis hosted it, and it was just too stuffy for Gianni. He found himself walking along Via Parisi and wondering what life was all about.

At thirty-two years of age he started to think about what he had accomplished in life. His father, Barone Orazio I, had given each of his children enough money and property so that they never had to work. His older brother, Salvatore, was the true barone and conducted the family business as usual. Gianni was never resentful of his elder brother; in fact, it was a relief. He did not want the pressures and responsibilities that came along with the title. But Gianni found himself unhappy and unwilling to stay in the marriage. He was dying to get out of Acireale.

Gianni and Emmanuelle's marriage was a typical prearranged marriage between two noble families. The fathers in this case were Barone Orazio Parisi I and Barone Alfredo Conti. Emmanuelle Conti was sister to Salvatore's wife, Gabriella. She was an even bigger bitch than her sister, her mother, and her grandmother.

In Sicily, funerals and weddings become spectacles. The more important the participants, the more of a spectacle it becomes. In Acireale, Gianni and Emmanuelle's wedding was the spectacle of the year. It was April 14, and a beautiful day. The wedding was held at the Cathedral de Pietro e Paolo at Piazza Duomo. The Romanesque gothic façade was outstanding, but the magnificence of the cathedral was expressed by the artist who took years to complete some of the finest frescoes in any cathedral. The interior, with a Latin cross design, is composed of three aisles, divided by pillars. The vault of the nave is decorated with frescoes of the Eternal Fathers by G. Scuitu. The patron saint of the town is on the first of the ten chapels, decorated with remarkable frescoes by the outstanding artist Alberto Filocamo of Florence.

The whole town showed up to see the marriage of nobility. There was excitement in the air. As the day progressed, the frenzy escalated to a carnival-like climax. It was as if it were a marriage between the king and queen of some monarchy. The church was overfilled with curious locals, visitors from surrounding towns, and invited guests. They were standing ten rows deep. The nobility, of course, were sitting up front. The king of Italy was sitting next to Barone Orazio Parisi. The Parisi family and their royal guest were sitting to the right of the hand-carved altar. By this time Barone Orazio was almost ninety years old. He looked very pale, and many did not think he would last out the year. The Conti family and their guests were sitting to the left of the altar. The archduke of Austria-Hungary and Wilhelm Von Frederick and his beautiful daughter, Heidi, of Germany were sitting next to Alfredo Conti.

The sound and vibration of the organ filled the cathedral and silenced the masses as the chorus began to sing the beautiful "Ave Maria". Everyone stood, as the bride was about to make her pompous entrance. The groom, Gianni, stood next to his brother, Salvatore. Both men looked handsome and noble in their long tails and the family crest proudly displayed on their chests. Gianni was small in stature but had a handsome, delicate face with brown hair and light hazel eyes. He looked more northern Italian and took after his mother's side of the family. Salvatore was more robust, six inches taller than his brother, with penetrating black eyes that drove women crazy, black hair, and a nobleman's beard.

Heidi's steel blue eyes were focused on Salvatore. As everyone watched the bride, Heidi was inamorata with Salvatore. All her sexual animal senses were focused on one thing: to have him notice her. Salvatore felt this overwhelming power distracting his concentration on the wedding. He turned, and there she was smiling at him. He smiled back. Alfredo turned to Wilhelm and winked and thought, *one more step closer to the sulfur mines.*

When Gianni agreed to marry Emmanuelle, old Barone Orazio gave the young couple a vineyard and an old villa in Corruth. Corruth was a small farming town twenty miles north of Acireale on the coast. Gianni fell in love with the property, and during the first few years he devoted his life to restoring the rambling villa and changing the grape vineyard to a citrus grove. Gianni felt oranges, lemons, and limes would be more profitable at market time than grapes. He was in paradise, waking up every morning to the sweet scent of the citrus trees and flowers. From the villa's balcony he could see the beautiful Ionian Sea, and when he turned around in the other direction there she was, Mount Etna, smoking majestically in the distance.

Gianni took a deep breath and looked around him and thought, *this must be paradise.* And then he heard her voice, "*Tengo un delore di testa.*" Emmanuelle woke up with a headache every morning and went to bed at night with pains in her back and neck. Gianni thought she was just one big pain in the ass.

For ten years he lived with this pain until one day he found himself walking aimlessly through the crowded streets of Acireale during Carnival. The joyful, carefree crowd enjoying themselves during Carnival was such a breath of fresh air compared to the stuffy ball at Alfredo Conti's villa. When he arrived at the street Via Cavour, he came upon the puppet show where hundreds of people had gathered to enjoy the show. Gianni found himself mesmerized not by the puppets but by the young girl controlling one of the puppets. She had been just named the Queen of the Carnival and proudly wore the papier-mâché carnival crown. Her name was Lunella.

Two months later Gianni left his wife Emmanuelle. An infuriated Alfredo openly swore that Gianni would pay for the insult to his family.

Salvatore, who was now the barone, had been asked to come to Alfredo's villa in Acireale for a private meeting. The huge eighteenth-century villa

overlooked the Ionian Sea and resembled a miniature medieval castle with dark stones and pitched
rooflines. It was enormous, boasting over forty rooms.

"After all, Salvatore, we are the ones to preserve
the bloodline. For the past two hundred years our
fathers have amassed a vast fortune. Between our
cousins, the Cavours, and us we can control this continent. With my banking influence, your sulfur mines,
and our vineyards we have Europe in the palms of
our hands. But we must stick together; we cannot
dilute the bloodline, we must keep the wealth and
power within our families. Your son Orazio and my
son Riccardo will inherit all this and build upon our
fathers' foundation. That's how it has been for two
hundred years and that's how it will be for the next
two hundred years."

Alfredo Conti and Salvatore were sitting in
Alfredo's library. Alfredo was pouring them a cognac,
and his voice was growing more irritated until he
exploded, unleashing a verbal assault. "But what
that *disgraziato* of your brother has done is to shame
our families!" Alfredo threw the cognac glass into
the fireplace. "You don't break up the family! The
bastard left my sister for a *putana*; the whole town is
talking about it!"

"Alfredo, calm down. He has given up his rights
to all our properties and has moved to Naxos. And
your sister will get over this."

"That's not enough! I want his *cagliones* cut off."
Alfredo wasn't concerned about his sister. He knew

she was a bitch and that any self- respecting man who was married to a bitch would have a mistress or two. But you didn't leave the bitch, especially when her brother was Alfredo Conti and your name and bloodline went back two hundred years.

"Alfredo, he is still my brother." Salvatore knew Alfredo had always been obsessed with absolute power. The Contis were the last descendants of the Medici dynasty, and Alfredo was fearful that one day the bloodline would end, and the power and wealth would end with it.

"He has disgraced us. He shall pay for it, mark my words. He will live like a dog, I will see to it." Alfredo stopped his tantrum and looked at Salvatore. "Your family needs to compensate the Contis for this disgrace. I want control to the sulfur mines and I will stop at nothing until I possess them." It was obvious Alfredo couldn't care one way or another about his sister's feelings or his family's hurt pride. The outrage was to disguise the real intent: the grabbing of power. And more power.

"The more the world changes, the more it is the same." An old Sicilian saying.

CHAPTER 20

Salvatore and Florianna looked sad as they handed the tiny infant into Gianni and Lunella's open arms. With tears in her eyes Florianna asked, "What will you name him?"

Lunella kissed the infant and said, "We will name him Turiddo," which was an affectionate nickname for Salvatore. "*Si*, Turiddo Parisi."

Turiddo Parisi would grow up to be Big Tony's father.

Florianna turned to Salvatore with uncontrollable tears rolling down her face. "Salvatore, please help me get my son Ciccu back."

Florianna had never told Barone Salvatore Parisi that she had a son. Don Carlo had said that if Florianna betrayed him her son Ciccu would die, but Florianna was getting desperate and she did not trust Don Carlo. She was in love with Salvatore and knew Don Carlo would find out. It seemed Don Carlo had a way of finding out about everything.

Ciccu was a *caruso* at the sulfur mines in Floristella. Francesco "Ciccu" Rosellini was born in Palermo, the only child of Florianna Rosellini. His father, Francesco, was arrested two times for armed robbery and for stealing chickens to feed his family, and on the third attempt the Mafia shot him to death. He made the fatal mistake: you didn't steal chickens from Don Carlo.

Don Carlo used the murder of Francesco Rosellini to his advantage. Don Carlo used everything and everyone to his advantage. He made amends to the family. He gave Ciccu a position; in Sicily, one acquires a position rather than a job. It sounds nicer and is more civilized. But there was a slight problem with this position: it was at the sulfur mines at Floristella. This was as close to a death sentence as one could give a twelve-year-old. Don Carlo was uncomfortable having the boy too close to him. It was customary to kill the sons of the murdered victim and his family, but Don Carlo lusted for Ciccu's mother, Florianna. It would be a decision he would come to regret.

The night that Ciccu's father was murdered for stealing the chickens, the short, obese, greasy-looking Don Carlo came to their home. The manipulating, ill-tempered Don Carlo had always had his evil eye on Florianna. She was desired by many, but Don Carlo controlled the strings, and some whispered, sotto voce, that Don Carlo had her husband set up to be killed. Francesco never stole the chickens.

Florianna thought Ciccu was asleep. As Don Carlo came in he politely said, "*C'e permesso?*"

"Come in, Don Carlo." She ushered him in. "*Che su chesso?* What happened?"

"Your husband is dead. His body was found in a ditch with his heart cut out along with ten other bandits." In Sicily, whenever someone was murdered and their heart was cut out, it was usually a vendetta.

Florianna didn't show too much feeling since she hadn't seen her husband in over a year. He had gone to the hills to hide with the rest of the bandits. Sooner or later she knew he would be killed. Florianna had worked hard trying to raise her son without a husband. She earned some money cleaning the homes of the wealthy, and once in a while her husband secretly sent them some money through a messenger, but now that would be gone.

Florianna said, "It's a shame; he was once a respected man, with noble ideas."

"But noble ideas don't put food on the table." Don Carlo placed an envelope with money in it on the table.

Florianna looked at the money. "But Don Carlo, how can I repay you?" As she said the words she knew how she was going to pay him back, and it would be with interest. Don Carlo grabbed Florianna and kissed her. Ciccu pretended to be asleep.

Don Carlo persuaded Florianna that for his own safety Ciccu would be better off leaving Palermo and that he would secure Ciccu a safe position at the sulfur mines at Floristella. "Those who killed your husband will try to kill Ciccu." Florianna had no choice. She now knew that Don Carlo had killed her husband, and she needed to buy some time to save Ciccu.

Don Carlo was the biggest *gabelloti*, who rented a major portion of the mines and paid the owner, Barone Salvatore Parisi, a percentage of the profits. Don Carlo never liked paying the Parisi family; he felt he did all the work, and just because they owned the land they got more than he did. "I will change that," he had told his trusted aide Minicu.

Ciccu became one of the *carusi*—he would have been better off as a Roman slave. He was assigned to a gang of fifteen *carusi*. They lived under terrible, inhuman conditions. Their crude dwellings of stone were carved out of the strip mines. Sometimes there were as many as five hundred children working at a time. The living quarters consisted of one room with fifteen mattresses on a dirt floor. The children became zombies in a short time. With no parental contact, with no mother's love, with no kind words, they were one step away from being *animale*.

Every day was the identical picture of the previous day. The *carusi* were awakened at dawn by their axeman, the person in charge of the *carusi*, who had them line up as if they were in the military. They were quickly ushered to the center of the camp where the eating area was located. They were given bread and water by callous old maids who served as the camp *putanas.* No sooner had they finished the bread and water than they were thrown into the bowels of the earth via small, dark, winding caves that only the small frame of a child could enter.

Ciccu's first day was filled with horror and fear and went downhill from there—between the hot summer months and the six giant furnaces that were constantly burning, emanating tremendous heat so that they barely wore any clothing, just the essential underwear. On many days the odors of the chemicals that excreted from the chimneys were stifling; for some of the younger children it was deadly. Combining these cruel and barbaric conditions with the pungent, foul odor of week-old feces and urine in the *carusi's* one-room barrack, Ciccu thought he had died and gone to hell.

Some of the *carusi* would have probably been better off being in hell. Their poor young bodies became deformed carrying heavy loads of sulfur out of the caves from dawn to dusk. If an axeman liked one of the *carusi*, he might reduce his load and have him sit out a few shifts, but that sometimes meant the *caruso* had to sleep with the axeman.

The sulfur mines at Floristella had a clear hierarchy, starting with the *carusi* to the axemen, to the foremen, to the smiths, to the bosses, the *gabelloti.* Don Carlo was head of the *gabelloti* and controlled the Mafia in Palermo. When Ciccu was sent to Floristella he was twelve years old and bigger than most of the *carusi.* He was only at the mines three days before he was tested in the pecking order.

His name was Gaetano Giuliani; as he got older people affectionately called him Giuliani. He was thirteen years old and had been working the mines for three years. Giuliani was by far the tallest of the *carusi,* and because he was so big, after one year of going into the dreadful caves, he was delegated to assisting his axeman. Giuliani was the unofficial head of the *carusi*; the younger ones looked up to him. He was handsome in a rugged way and stood out because there was no fear in his eyes, and for that he was respected. Gaetano Giuliani had become a valuable asset amongst the hierarchy for controlling any rebellious *carusi.*

Pecking order was very important at the mines. When a new recruit came into camp, he was given a choice: go to the bottom of the pecking order or fight *numero uno.* For most of the young recruits, it was go to the bottom of the pecking order, which meant cleaning out the makeshift latrines. When Ciccu was given the option he decided to fight Giuliani.

A fight was always a welcome relief from the daily drudgery. Word spread around the camp that the new boy from Palermo had challenged Giuliani. It had been a while since Giuliani had been challenged, and the anticipation grew; even the axemen and foremen were present to witness the main event.

Giuliani and Ciccu had the same build. They were tall with dark skin, ruggedly handsome with high cheekbones and square chins; both had light brown hair, which bleached out under the Sicilian sun. Even though they were twelve and thirteen they had the bodies of young men.

It was the Roman forum mentality, and the crowd was eager to turn their thumbs down on the new boy. The *carusi* began to chant, "*Forzi*, Giuliani, *forzi*, Giuliani, *marzullo*, kill him!"

At first Giuliani was the aggressor, striking Ciccu on the side of his face and drawing first blood. That's all the *carusi* needed to stir them into a frenzy. "*Forzi*, Giuliani, *forzi*, Giuliani, *marzullo*." But Ciccu stood his ground and refused to fall. The thought of cleaning the latrines made him sick. The image of Don Carlo entering his mother's room made him angry, and revenge became his motivation after the murder of his father—and revenge is what a Sicilian does best.

After a grueling twenty minutes of non-stop combat between the two gladiators, both boys had nothing left and could barely stand. Their faces were cut and both had bloody noses; their bodies were totally drenched in perspiration. They stood silently wobbling in the bright sun waiting for their opponent to throw the next punch, but neither one could muster up enough strength to lift his arm above his waist. The crowd had grown silent, knowing they had just witnessed a heroic battle in which there was no loser. Giuliani first reached out his hand as a peace offering. When Ciccu did the same they automatically embraced, and the *carusi* started to chant, "*Forza, Giuliani, forza,* Ciccu!"

At this same time, Barone Salvatore Parisi and Michele were visiting the Palazzo Parisi at Floristella to check on the sulfur mines. A young Michele Parisi witnessed the brutal fight between Giuliani and Ciccu, and it had an everlasting impression on his life.

With tears streaming down his face, Michele went to his father and said, "Pappa, you must do something to help the *carusi.*"

Months later, on another visit to the sulfur mines at Floristella, Barone Salvatore Parisi brought Michele with him again. The trip from the *castello* at Acireale to the palazzo at Floristella took a whole day on horseback. But for Michele it was an adventure. Leaving the sea behind them, they looked to the majestic mountains and Etna in front of them. Michele let his imagination run wild likening his trip to Floristella to the exploits of Marco Polo from Venice to China.

After the long trip to Floristella, the next morning, Salvatore took Michele down to the foremen's office where two new *carusi* were being indoctrinated into the system. It was probably the same indoctrination a criminal would receive when entering a prison. They were young, maybe eight or nine, and it was sad to look in their eyes. As they stood there stark naked in the heat of the day, they trembled from fear.

The barone asked their names. "*Io me chiamo* Angelo." The little one could barely speak, so he stuttered.

The other one was just as fearful, and he also stuttered, "*Io me chiamo* Luciano."

The barone looked at his son. "I will pay for one of these *carusi* to go free, which one is it?"

"But Father, none of them should be here."

"I know that, son, but for now we do what we can, *capisce?*"

"*Si*, Pappa." Michele looked at the two boys and could not choose. His father had a rare Greek coin he carried with him. He took it out of his pocket and flipped it.

"Heads for Luciano and tails for Angelo."

'Heads," Michele called out. It was heads, and Luciano was sent home. From that day on he was called Lucky Luciano.

But Angelo was not so lucky.

Ciccu had become *numero due* under Gaetano Giuliani, but Giuliani and Ciccu had become best of friends.

Ciccu adapted as well as one could to his new environment. Ciccu was an observer; he listened very well and he rarely spoke. He observed the pecking order amongst the hierarchy from the *carusi* to axemen, to foremen, and up; he noticed that the men at the top were mostly feared but not respected. He noticed one particular foreman's strange behavior. His name was Minicu Persico; he was about forty years old but looked older and had a face that resembled a Neanderthal man. He struck terror just by his stare. He was short, stocky, and had hair all over his body. He always smelled of cheap wine and cheap cigars. Whenever a new, young, good-looking, defenseless *caruso* came into camp, Minicu would take him for a few nights. When the new *caruso* returned to the fold he no longer had a soul. Minicu Persico worked for Don Carlo and looked after Don Carlo's mining interest. Everyone feared Don Carlo and everyone feared Minicu.

Minicu had picked out a new *caruso* for his pleasure. The only problem was that this *caruso* was now assigned to Ciccu. A few weeks after his fight with Giuliani, Ciccu was given a gang of fifteen *carusi* to oversee. One day, Ciccu's *carusi* had just finished eating breakfast—the standard bread and water—and were lined up ready to begin work and enter the caves when Minicu pulled out the young *caruso*. The fragile, handsome young boy was barely eight years old. His name was Angelo and he looked like an altar boy. When Minicu picked him out of the line, the boy's face had terror written all over it. He had heard stories about this monster. Everyone knew, but no one could do anything as he worked for Don Carlo.

"I need him to work for me today," Minicu said.

"You cannot have him," Ciccu stated and pushed Angelo back into line and directed his boys to enter the caves. Minicu viciously struck out like a raging animal at Ciccu. Before he knew it, Ciccu was on the ground bleeding profusely from a gash above his eye and trying to protect himself from Minicu's vicious kicks. In the back of Minicu's distorted mind he recalled what Don Carlo had told him. "Make sure Ciccu does not come out alive."

"Remember this. The next time you cross my path, you are dead." Minicu left Ciccu on the ground with a gash across his left cheek; he would carry the scar for the rest of his life.

Some of the *carusi* went over to help Ciccu as Minicu grabbed Angelo and left. Three days later Angelo's broken body was discovered, discarded like a dead rat in a pile of rocks. Three days after that, Minicu was found dead, his heart cut out. From that day on Ciccu was called Don Ciccu. Not only was he feared, he was respected.

When Don Carlo heard that Ciccu had killed Minicu, he ordered him to be killed. He was too late. The day Ciccu's mother, Florianna, handed over the infant Turiddo to Gianni and Lunella, she had said to Barone Salvatore, "I must have my son back." Two days later Ciccu was living at Castello Parisi with his mother in the *giardini* cottage next to the stables. And Don Carlo went on a rampage vowing to kill them.

✤ ✤ ✤

CHAPTER 21

Maria Parisi was the youngest, and Salvatore's *bambina*. She had her mother's blue eyes and red hair and beautifully matured into a slender, five-foot-four young woman, an oddity for a Sicilian, who seldom reached five feet. Unlike her mother, Maria loved the Sicilians. She was gentle and kind and her beauty came from within. When it was time to pack up and return to Acireale, Maria would cry because she loved the simple way of life they led at Corruth.

Those were beautiful days for the family. They would swim to the island rock offshore, and when Salvatore had them all together, he would tell them stories from Greek mythology. He would describe how Ulysses sat on this very island before he encountered the Cyclops. And he would point toward Mount Etna, where he said the Cyclops lived. At night he put his children to bed and told each one how important he or she was going to be. Michele and Maria were last to be tucked in. He would just lean over and whisper in their ears so that no one could hear, "*Ti amo, sciatu mio.*"

As Maria matured into a beautiful, vivacious woman, she was pursued by the many young noblemen of Acireale. But Marie's heart belonged to the plight of the peasants and stopping the exploitation of Sicilian women. She was appalled when she was old enough to find out what had happened to Florianna and horrified when her two best friends, Rosa and Santa Columbo, were raped.

She was the heart of the Parisi *famiglia*. With long red hair flowing in the wind, she exuded nobility riding her white stallion along the beach, through the family vineyards, and lush citrus groves to the edge of Mount Etna. Along the way she would stop and chat with the peasants and farm workers and their families. Maria would bring the children gifts and give money to a struggling family. They loved her; deep down she was one of them.

But Maria's favorite stop was at the home of her *Zio*, Gianni. Michele would take her by horse and carriage along the seashore to *Zio* Gianni's home. It was a beautiful ride, especially on a windy day as the many forms of the black volcanic rocks stood as fortresses against the pounding blue-green iridescent waters of the Ionian Sea. They could taste the salt water as the spray cooled them down from the summer sirocco. Gianni lived in a simple stucco home twenty miles from Corruth in a little fisherman's town called Naxos. Gianni was becoming well known for his artwork and had been commissioned by the Vatican to repair some of the frescos on the ceilings of Saint Peter.

Maria and Michele spent time with their favorite uncle, who indulged them with warm hugs and kisses, and were quick to learn the ancient art of icons. He mixed his paint from the rocks and ashes that Mount Etna unleashed from its inner core. He searched for interesting pieces of wood from abandoned churches and let Maria and Michele paint one side with gesso. They were fascinated with how meticulously he peeled off the thin layer of gold and placed it on his beautiful work in progress.

Maria and Michele helped him crush the volcanic pebbles and mix them with the whites of eggs. They loved to go on these scavenger hunts to almost the top of the volcano helping their uncle search for the colored pebbles. It was as if they were finding gold and riches; it was a wonderful time for all.

Except for Turiddo:

When he was first born they thought he looked like Florianna, but as Turiddo got older he resembled his father, Don Carlo. In spite of the affection and love showered on him by Gianni and Lunella over the years, Turiddo turned out to be callous and mean; his moods would change in an instant. He lived in the shadows of Acireale, he lived in the shadows of their nobility, and he lived in the shadows of Michele Parisi, and he hated them all.

When Turiddo was sixteen years old he left Naxos and joined the bandit Gaetano Giuliani and his army of peasants. He quickly rose to power within the army of the people, which suited the misfit, illegitimate son of Don Carlo.

Maria was infatuated with the bandit Gaetano Giuliani because she believed he took up the fight for the peasants. And initially she secretly supported his cause as Giuliani took from the nobles and gave to the poor; he had become known as the Robin Hood of Sicily. There were many that supported him and his group of bandits, who did not pay homage to anyone, including Don Carlo and the Italian army. The Church and the Mafia were looking to destroy them.

Growing up in Acireale, Maria did not have many friends she liked being with. They were all too stuffy for the carefree young socialite. Her best friends were Santa and Rosa Columbo. Their father, Carmello Columbo, owned a small farm in Corruth next to the Parisis' villa. *Signore* Colombo's land was not substantial enough to feed his large family so Carmello Columbo tended to the barone's property to make extra money. Carmello and his sons tilled the rich volcanic soil from dawn to sunset. And his daughter Rosa did housekeeping chores at the Parisis' villa next door while the youngest, Santa, managed the Columbos' household.

During the summer months the three girls were inseparable, as they had grown up together in Corruth by the sea where life had a rhythm. The summer months for Maria, Rosa, and Santa were filled with wonderfully lazy long days at the beach. They would giggle like little girls and talk of their dreams and the boys they loved. But the best of times was when they stayed over a weekend during one of the many festivals with Maria at the *castello* in Acireale.

Rosa Columbo could have passed as Florianna's daughter. Her striking beauty turned many a head when the girls went to Acireale to shop and walk the piazzas. She was the bijou. Maria was the educated one, but the younger, Santa, had the street smarts, and no one was going to make a fool of her. When it came to bargaining with the storeowner, the girls backed off and let Santa do the haggling.

"*Ma tu si pazzo*," she told the owner. She was crazy if she thought they would pay that amount for a dress.

"*Quando volle pagare?* How much do you want to pay?" the older lady asked. The older lady knew she was dealing with a peasant. Her language was crude, she slurred her words. Obviously she had not been educated in Italian; she was speaking the language of the Sicilians.

"Metta—half."

The old lady smiled. "*Non se fooba*, no one will ever make a fool of you. It's yours." The three girls giggled all the way up Via Emmanuel and Piazza Cavour. They sat themselves down by *Signore* Nicolosi's outside café and ordered *gelato con ghiaccio e panni* and proceeded to watch the festival before them. The vendors came from all over Sicily to sell their crafts and articles in makeshift storefronts from horse-drawn wagons. The hot oil from the pinelle pots lingered over the bandstand as the five-piece band, dressed in typical Sicilian black and white with red bandanas, stopped to announce it was time for the young ladies to come forth to see who would be crowned Queen of the Carnival.

At that moment a young handsome man rode up on his Arabian horse, and Rosa was hit by a lightning bolt.

"*Dio mio*, who is he?"

"*Mio fratello*, my brother Michele," said Maria as he came over and kissed his sister, then turned to Rosa and just stared.

"*Dio mio*. Who are you?" he asked.

Rosa was speechless. Maria piped up, "She is my friend from Corruth, Rosa Columbo, and you, my brother, look like you have been hit by a lightning bolt too.

"You could pass as Florianna's daughter."

The bandleader called out, "This is the last call for Queen of the Carnival!" Without saying anything, Michele extended his hand to Rosa and she automatically got up as if she were in a daze and walked with him to the bandstand.

"*Signore* Nicolosi," Michele was eloquent, "I submit to you the Queen of the Carnival *Signorita* Rosa Columbo, from Corruth." Rosa was still in a daze as the crowd gave its approval and Michele placed the crown on her head and kissed her.

Sotto voce, Rosa whispered, "*Sciatu mio.*" He would be the only man she ever loved.

Maria was torn between two men in her life—the outlaw Gaetano Giuliani and Don Ciccu. In many ways they were the same. It was the mystique of Giuliani and his fight for the peasants that attracted her, but if ever she needed anything she knew Don Ciccu would be there for her like an older brother. But Don Ciccu did not want to be Maria's older brother; he was in love with Maria.

When he first came to the *castello* he was solemn and spoke only when he was spoken to. At first Florianna was worried that he would not want to stay. He was only twelve; just a baby in his mother's eyes, but what he went through at the sulfur mines would have brought most men to their knees. Instead it made him stronger, respected, and, later on, powerful.

But some nights Florianna thought she had already lost him. She heard his screams in the middle of the night, and when she got to his room he would be drenched.

"*Non me lascare*, please don't leave me anymore," he cried, holding on to her as if he lost her he would die. "Please don't leave." And he cried himself to sleep.

"*Dio mio, che ho fatto? Ha mio figlio?* What have I done? What have I done to my son?" It had been difficult for Florianna to justify sending him away, but Don Carlo had given her no alternative.

But something happened to change Ciccu. One morning Florianna was in the kitchen holding the baby Maria trying to stop her from crying and Michele was eating a biscotti when Ciccu came in quietly and sat down next to them.

The kitchen was their favorite place in the castle. It was big, with white tiles on the walls and black and white checkered tiles on the floor, but it had a good, warm feel about it. And it was the only casual place in the *castello* where they could laugh and eat and have the family come together without any pretenses. Gabriella never came into the kitchen.

Florianna said to Ciccu, "Here, you hold her while I warm up some milk for her." It was as if someone took a thorn out of an animal's injured paw. Maria stopped crying and started to giggle.

Michele looked at Ciccu. "I think she likes you."

"*Anche Io*, I think I like her." Ciccu smiled at Florianna, and Florianna could not stop her tears of joy. She knew she had her son back.

Ciccu had found his two best friends, but more important, he had found a new beginning.

❖ ❖ ❖

CHAPTER 22

It was in Corruth that Florianna and Salvatore were the happiest; they had become a family. Over the years they shared their love with Maria and Michele and Ciccu. But it was Florianna that made Corruth their home.

During harvest time, Florianna and Maria hand picked the olives from their orchard and placed them on a table where Michele and Ciccu crushed each green olive with a wooden mallet. It was fun having the whole family working together to live. The olives were placed in a jar with fresh olive oil and hot peppers and served weeks later when they were ready. The olives were placed on the table along with fresh cheeses and slices of tomato in simple vinegar and oil dressing. The ceramic hand-painted pitcher was filled with wine from the grapes that were picked by Salvatore and Florianna and the children.

Florianna had two little golden horns around her neck that she always wore. They kept the evil spirits away, and for Florianna, evil was Don Carlo. One day when Florianna was feeding Michele and Ciccu in the kitchen, to show that she loved them equally, she placed a chain with the golden horn around each of their necks and said, "I give you this as a sign of love. I love you two very much; you are my *sciatu mio,* and this will bond you as brothers."

And brothers they became. Growing up, Ciccu and Michele were inseparable. They loved playing hide-and-seek in the lush vineyard maze where they helped pick the ripe purple grapes and toss them into the large hand-woven baskets from dawn to lunchtime. And when everyone else was taking their siesta, they would rush down to their favorite place, the sea, and swim and share their dreams.

"What do you want to do, Ciccu?" Michele asked him one day. They had become brothers, and Michele loved him more than his real brother, Orazio.

"What do you mean, *Professore?*" Ciccu liked calling Michele "*professore*" because he was so educated and talented.

"I mean, don't you want to see the world and leave this place?"

"Why? I don't know what is out there. I know what is here."

"If you stay here you will probably work for my father and get into the family business."

"Is that all bad?"

"You know how terrible those mines are and how poor our people are on this island. They have no power to change things, and that's why they are losing

242

their lands and leaving, and my father and this nobility is part of the problem."

"Your father is a good man. He saved my life and has given my mother a good life. I will always be indebted to him."

"But don't you see how these people exploit the poor for their gain? Don't you think that is wrong?"

"What is wrong? Your father was given this power, why should he give it up? He is only one man. He has done good to his family and that's important."

"But life is not just the family, there is more to it."

"There is? I don't think so. There is nothing more important than the family, nothing; there is nothing more powerful than the family, nothing. One day you will leave here, Michele, because it's in your blood. You will see the world, but you will be back because you will realize this is where you belong, this is where your family is."

Michele started to laugh and shake his head back and forth. "You know, I don't think in all these years we have ever seen eye-to-eye. I don't understand how we get along so well."

"You know why?" Ciccu looked at him very seriously. "Because we are family and I love you."

As the years went on and the children got older and tried to find their way in life, Maria took on her fight for women's rights in Sicily. And Don Ciccu took

on the responsibilities of running the family's holdings. And with Michele living in Paris, Salvatore and
Florianna found comfort knowing they had found
their piece of heaven in Corruth.

The fresh fish they bought each morning was
grilled on the open pit and served by Florianna on a
beautiful hand-painted platter. It was garnished with
lemons and limes, and the aroma from the fish filled
the *giardini*. The warm crusted bread heated on the
wood-burning fireplace was placed traditionally in
the center of the table along with a large steaming
bowl of risotto and wild mushroom soup. On special
nights Etna would light up the sky with its fiery show
of red lava that illuminated the sky with brilliant reds
and lavenders, and on this night, Etna was putting
on a spectacular show.

Salvatore sat in his favorite chair in the *giardini*
for what seemed an eternity and thought to himself,
If I could control time, I would stop it right now. Knowing
that the woman he loved was by his side, he knew it
didn't get better than this.

Florianna watched him sitting in his chair, so tranquil in the *giardini* sipping a glass of wine waiting for
her to come to him so they could fall asleep in each
other's arms while watching the stars and the beautiful Mount Etna putting on a fireworks show for them.

She had been crying knowing she didn't have
long to live. She walked over to him as she usually
did and put her head on Salvatore's shoulder. "*Sciatu*

mio, I love you so much. You are the breath of my life. Thank you for everything."

"What's wrong, why are you crying?"

"I don't have much time left."

"What can I do?" Salvatore held her tightly.

"Just hold me. I want to go to sleep in your arms and never wake up."

And so she did.

❖ ❖ ❖

CHAPTER 23

Had it not been for Don Ciccu, Giuliani would have died in the sulfur mines. Ciccu convinced Barone Salvatore to pay the sum of money to free him of his bondage to Don Carlo because it would have been discovered that Giuliani helped Ciccu kill Minicu. And now that Minicu's son, a young Claudio Persico had been placed in charge, he surely would have arranged for Giuliani to have an accident.

Because of his loyalty to his friend Ciccu, Giuliani never attacked what belonged to the *famiglia* Parisi while Maria, who had grown into a sensitive and politically active young woman, felt that Giuliani and his small band of bandits were freedom fighters, that they would spearhead the fight to change this island stuck in medieval times.

When Maria asked Don Ciccu to arrange a meeting with Giuliani, he reluctantly set up the meeting with the notorious outlaw, but Ciccu knew that she had a crush on the bandit and tried to change her mind. But Maria had a mind of her own. They met in the foothills of Randazzo, a one-time Arab stronghold in Sicilia. Seven hundred years ago Randazzo saw a massive battle that thwarted the rise of the Muslims in Sicilia.

When she first saw him it was a chilly night and a large fire was burning, in the center of their camp. From the glow of the fire she saw his face and couldn't help but compare his looks to Don Ciccu. They were taller than most Sicilians, but when she turned again to look at Giuliani, his face seemed angelic in the glow of the fire.

But then she turned and saw his face: Turiddo. Her cousin had turned anything but angelic, and his stare frightened her. She thought his face had evil written all over it, and her hopes of enlisting the outlaws to help her fight for the rights of women in Sicily faded away.

Many women were infatuated with Gaetano Giuliani. The famous bandit was a notorious lover in Sicily, but the one woman who possessed him was Santa Columbo.

Santa had matured well beyond her fifteenth year; although just an uneducated peasant, she instinctively learned the ways of the world around her and adapted well. She saw everything and said nothing, absorbing all that was happening around her. She loved the farm; she could be heard from one end of the orchard to the other singing Sicilian folk songs. She had a beautiful voice, and when the time came to harvest the grapes her father would pick her to be the first one they threw into the barrel with the grapes. With her beautiful voice and glowing face she led Rosa and Maria in pounding the grapes as they danced and sang. She was the soul of the peasant women and her mother's favorite. And when her mother died and her father took another wife, it was Santa who took over the household.

Secretly, in the middle of the night, Santa would place a candle in her window and wait until her lover showed up. Giuliani was kind and passionate and told Santa all his inner fears, and the most feared outlaw in all of Italy became a child in Santa's arms. After they made love she held his body in her arms and sang to him until he fell asleep.

When her father gave her to the Cavour family as a servant she was despondent, not so much because she was leaving her family but because she thought she would lose Giuliani. But that wasn't to be.

"*Che bella,*" Philip whispered to her. Santa was cleaning the Cavours' elaborate Roman spa at the far end of the villa. Philip had checked to see if anyone was near when he followed her in. He locked the doors behind them.

"*Grazie,* Barone Cavour," she said timidly.

"Don't call me Barone. That's my father. I am nothing like him, thank God." It was only nine o'clock in the morning and Philip was drunk. He placed his drink on the large, white marble mirrored vanity and started to walk closer to her.

As he approached she started to back up, pleading with him. Unaware of how close she was to the large Roman pool behind her. Santa fell in, and not being able to swim, she started to scream for help. He watched delightedly as she floundered in the pool. Her dress became transparent, exposing her luscious young body. Thrilled by what he observed, he undressed and dived in after her. In the water, with one firm pull, her saturated dress easily ripped off.

"No, *Signore*, no, *Signore*," she started to cry like the child that she was.

He helped her out of the pool. They were both naked and dripping wet. He gently picked her up; she was so frightened she offered no resistance. He carried her to the adjacent room where he laid her trembling, naked body on the Roman couch.

She was frozen with fear, not knowing what to expect next, her heart pounding so strong she feared she'd lose her sanity. "*Dio mio, Dio mio, aiutami,* dear God, help me."

When he had fulfilled all his pleasures with Santa, he warned her, "If you say anything to anyone I'll make sure you'll never work here again. *Capisce?*"

She was so frightened she didn't hear a word. "*Capisce*?" he said louder.

"*Si, capisco.*" She understood.

"*Bene*, then I'll meet you here again tomorrow." He began kissing her again. "And tomorrow it will be better. I promise."

When Santa's father, Carmello Columbo, found out that his daughter was pregnant, he went into a rage shouting "*Bestia*, I will kill the miserable bastard!"

Santa's stepmother ran around the small cottage, pulling at her hair and crying, "Madonna, Madonna *mia*, we have been disgraced!" But no one worried about poor, frightened Santa. But Barone Cavour was a shrewd old man who knew how to handle these peasants. He sent his son off to Paris with the rest of the misfits of the world and pledged a piece of farmland to Carmello and the promise of a sum of money on each birthday for the child; the Columbo family swallowed its pride.

In Sicily, a woman who gives birth out of wedlock is a *putana* no matter what the circumstances. The baby girl whom Santa named Claudia was an extraordinarily beautiful infant, and as promised, Barone Cavour delivered a sum of money and a piece of farmland to Carmello Columbo. But life became difficult for Santa. In the small town of Acireale, known as the town of a hundred churches, Santa could not go to mass on Sunday.

"*Guarda la putana*," they whispered behind her back yet loud enough for her to hear. "*Putana, guarda.* If you didn't know what she did, you would think she was an angel."

A year later, for her own good, Santa and the baby Claudia were sent to live with the Marsala family in Trapani. Here she married Vito Marsala. It was a favor the family owed Barone Parisi for buying their son's freedom out of the sulfur mines. But it was a sad day for the sixteen-year-old as she packed up everything she owned in a small suitcase and said goodbye.

"*Ciao*, Rosa, *ciao*, Maria, I'll miss you so much." With tears rolling down their cheeks they held on to Santa, not able to let her go.

Six months after Santa was sent to Trapani, a tragedy happened to the Cavour family. The Cavours had two daughters, and when their youngest daughter, Laura, was killed being thrown off a horse there would be no continuation of the Conti or Cavour bloodline.

Antoinette Cavour, Franco Cavour's older daughter, had married Riccardo Conti, the only child of Alfredo Conti. Their first and only child was a mongoloid, and when the child was born Antoinette almost died. But worst than death for Riccardo, Antoinette no longer could conceive.

And so Santa's child was purchased in exchange for another piece of land and a small amount of money. Santa and her new husband, Vito Marsala, bought a piece of farmland, where she would sing and work and try to forget.

"*Per Piacere lascere la sua nome.*" Santa begged them to keep her baby's first name. Barone Cavour agreed, so the infant Claudia became Claudia Cavour.

✤ ✤ ✤

CHAPTER 24

In ancient times, Sicily was the center of trade in the Mediterranean world. The Greeks came to Sicily and built a civilization that was bigger and better and more powerful than the culture they left behind in Athens. Many more Greek ruins in Sicily are standing today than in all of Greece. Sicily existed one thousand years before the birth of Rome. Rome realized quickly that, strategically, whoever controlled Sicily controlled the Mediterranean world. But Rome also realized that Sicily had forests to build the Roman navy and fertile soil to feed the vast Roman Empire.

For a thousand years, Rome controlled Sicily by enslaving the peasants. From the sulfur mines, Spartacus led a revolt of slaves in Sicily. The revolt quickly spread as fumes of freedom engulfed the island and spread fear among the patricians who lived on vast estates. But the revolt was brutally crushed by the Roman army, and the Sicilians returned to their lives as slaves. Spartacus was crucified.

In the 1890s, the plight of Sicilian peasant farmers was not much better than their ancestors who were Roman slaves. The Italian government taxed their land, trees, and farm animals, and when they couldn't pay their taxes, the government took their land away.

Their choices were simple: either leave Sicily and go to the north to some foreign country for work or leave for America. Most of them went to America, but some of them became bandits in hopes of getting their property back. Gaetano Giuliani chose to stay and fight for their land.

The Italian army led by General Giuseppe Govone from Piedmonte had been sent to crush the rebellion. The Sicilians resisted, just as they had for centuries. In order to get the bandits/rebels to surrender, whole families and even villages were held in captivity and tortured by the Italian army. When the rebels refused to surrender, the Italians killed their families.

Gaetano Giuliani's mother had been raped repeatedly by the Italian soldiers while they held her captive in his home. When his father refused to surrender the whereabouts of his son, he was burned to death in the piazza, and when that didn't work, Giuliani's brothers and sisters were forced to watch as they tied their mother face down in the middle of the piazza for all to see. As the axe came down, her head rolled and stopped at his sisters feet.

When the rebels returned to find the corpses of their wives and children and parents burned beyond recognition they became incensed and savagely attacked the Italian invaders.

It had been raining for three days and was starting to get cold. It was the coldest January anyone could remember. The winds picked up as a cold front came in from the north. They were picking up off the sea, the clouds were getting thicker, and it looked as if it was going to snow, a rarity in Sicily. It was January sixth, the Epiphany, when the Italians celebrated Christmas. The train from Palermo to Messina stopped in a small town outside Mallarzzo. One hundred Italian soldiers were on the train; they planned to catch the ferry at Messina to Reggio Calabria, to spend the holiday with family in northern Italy.

They were singing, drinking, and celebrating their victory over the rebels in Cefalu. The train was slowing down, but no one noticed as the Italians continued to party. When the train came to a complete stop in the middle of the fields they realized something was wrong. But before they could react, the rebels were on top of them securing their weapons and marching them single file out into the dark, cold, windy day. And then it started to snow.

Among the rebels was Turiddo. Although some of the hardened bandits who were with him that day had seen outrageous atrocities, they had not lost their souls. Turiddo never had one. The more hideous and outrageous the killing of another human, the more Turiddo seem to take delight. He stood there with a crazed look in his eyes in the middle of the line of rebels with their rifles aimed point blank at the officer's head. "Where is your general?"

The frightened young officer declared, *"No lo so."* He didn't know.

Two shots rang out and the young officer fell. Blood gushed from his head onto the snow-covered ground.

The twenty-five bandits ordered the soldiers to undress, and one at a time Turiddo cut out their hearts while the others watched. In all there were one hundred hearts. The next day a large package was sent to General Govone's headquarters. When he opened it there were his soldier's hearts.

The more perilous their exploits, the greater their legends, and so Giuliani was loved by the masses, especially the women. Giuliani and his roving bandits' reputations as Don Juans flourished from the little *cittas*—the towns—in Sicily to the open markets in Rome. What to do about their feats was discussed in closed chambers by the ministers and politicians while their wives giggled in the *giardini* discussing rumors of the sexual exploits of the infamous bandits.

Whenever the bandits were known to be in a town, it was said a fair maiden would place a rose in her open window or light a candle hoping to entice the Romeo, Giuliani, or one of his handsome bandits. But it didn't happen that way for Rosa Columbo.

Turiddo knew Rosa was alone on the farm in Corruth. It was late October, and Rosa had been picking lemons and limes. The aroma of the fruit engulfed the groves. There was a hint of coolness in the air. Under the clear, brilliant blue sky, Rosa saw that Etna had gotten its first dusting of snow.

He rode into the vineyard on his brown stallion. The horse, gasping for air and totally wet, had obviously been ridden hard. She could smell the animal from a distance, but as they got closer she could smell Turiddo.

He looked mean and desperate and had that smirk on his face that exuded cockiness. "Ah, *la bella* Rosa."

"What do you want here?" She was frightened, but she wasn't going to show it.

"Ah, *la bella* Rosa," he repeated.

"You are on private land. Get off now," said Rosa.

But Turiddo dismounted and tied the horse to a tree. Rosa realized she was in trouble. She dropped the basket of limes and started to run, but it was in vain. In a matter of seconds he had her on the ground, and as he mounted her he started to laugh like a hyena.

"From now on you will be known as Turiddo's woman, and no other man will even dare look at you because I will kill him. You are mine."

She silently bit her lips and as the blood poured out she cried, "*Dio mio!*"

As Turiddo had his way, Rosa thought of another man, Michele, the one she loved; the one who had crowned her Queen of the Carnival.

Rosa became pregnant. Before the baby was born, Turiddo married her thanks to Don Ciccu's intervention. The boy was named Antonio Parisi and later became known as Big Tony in New York. Maria Parisi gave *Signore* Columbo a little money and the family provided a little stone cottage for Rosa and the baby near their villa in Corruth.

But the venomous Turiddo was off to his bandit's hideaway and a young, disheartened Rosa was left to fend on her own. Turiddo visited from time to time, but as quickly as he came during the secrecy of darkness he was out, and in three years she had three children and needed to work to feed them.

The young Rosa had no choice; women in Sicily usually didn't. At night she went to bed with teary eyes thinking of the man she loved and what it would be to have him by her side, but Michele was in Paris, painting and living with a rich Parisian who collected young artists. It had been many years since he left Sicily. He seldom came back to visit. She wondered what he would think of her and if she was still beautiful in his eyes.

Because Turiddo was off on his next escapade and wanted for murder and treason by the Italian army, he gave no financial support to his family. Rosa was just there to satisfy his primal urges. Rosa needed to break the cycle. So thanks to Maria, the enterprising Rosa became a servant for Riccardo Conti's ailing wife, Antoinette Cavour Conti, at their villa in Acireale.

Through all her hardships and while in the midst of raising three children on her own, Rosa had developed into a prized jewel. In her late twenties, her stunning beauty was whispered about in small, smoky cafés where men spoke of politics and beautiful women. Sotto voce it was whispered that Riccardo Conti, heir to the Conti and Cavour fortunes and last of the Medici bloodline, had made Rosa his mistress.

There was no greater disgrace for a Sicilian male than to be called a *cornuto*, a cuckold, and if that male happened to be insidious Turiddo Parisi, the infamous bandit, that insult was compounded ten times. When rumors of their liaison reached the bandits' hideaway, Turiddo went off in an explosive rage. By the time he reached the stone cottage, Rosa and the children were sleeping.

Living in caves and the life of a bandit had taken its toll on Turiddo. He looked much older than thirty-five—he was short, overweight, prematurely bald, and unkempt. He could barely breathe anymore as his lungs were weakened from years of smoking and living in damp, cool caves. At times he wondered why he became a bandit. At first it was a young, idealistic cause to take up the plight of the peasant against his ostracized father. But as he became involved with the movement, his overwhelming motivation became revenge. He was going to punish the nobility for their callous, pompous, non-productive way of life.

It was a rainy night when he stormed in, crushing in the wooden door. The children awoke and cried and screamed as they tried to stop Turiddo from dragging Rosa out into the fields.

"*Putana, putana, putana!*" he screamed in a rage with every blow to her fragile body. He beat her till her body lay limp in a puddle between the mounded rows of soil. He kicked her one more time. "This is for making me a *cornuto*." He didn't make any attempt to console the children; he just walked over her inert, bloodied body and left the traumatized children hovering over their beaten mother.

When Maria first saw Rosa lying in a pool of blood in the mud, she thought Rosa was dead. What kind of animal would do this to his wife? If she had a knife she would have plunged it into Turiddo's heartless body. "*Bestia, animale, disgraziato, figlio di putani.*" Maria used every curse word she knew, every curse word a peasant knew, not a noble lady.

Maria looked at her friend, "*Vene qui.*" She placed her arms around her and they hugged. Maria started to cry. "I'm sorry, I'm so sorry."

Rosa couldn't stop crying. "Oh Maria, I'm so afraid. If he knows I'm alive he will come back and kill me, and I'm afraid he is crazy enough to kill the children. We must get the children out of here."

It took a long time for Rosa to recuperate from the beating, and in that time a once sweet, innocent soul was replaced with bitter hatred and revenge. She wanted Turiddo dead.

Maria became Rosa's nurse at her villa in Corruth. "You will stay here with me. I have arranged for the children to be taken care of." Turiddo's exploits had become so publicized and outraged so many people that the Italian army had offered a handsome reward for the capture or death of this bandit. Not only were the children in danger from Turiddo, but also, if the Italians found out that Turiddo had children, the children would be used to capture him. So Maria made arrangements for the children to be sent to America.

In Maria's bedroom where Rosa was recuperating, a picture of Michele stood on the night table. Rosa placed the photo next to her heart and fell asleep dreaming of Michele.

✤ ✤ ✤

CHAPTER 25

Ever since the argument with his father over Sicilian politics, Michele seldom left Paris to visit Sicily. When he did, he immediately sought out his best friend, Don Ciccu, who was living alone in Acireale in a magnificent fifteen-room apartment in Palazzo Parisi in Piazza Duomo. The apartment once belonged to Gianni Parisi but was given to Don Ciccu as a reward for taking on the responsibilities of overseeing Barone Salvatore's family holdings.

Michele was a guest in Don Ciccu's elegant, palatial *apartamento*. He thought to himself that a nobleman and his family would have been very comfortable living in these quarters. But a nobleman was not living here; rather, it was Don Ciccu, and at forty-five years old, Don Ciccu was one of the most respected men in Sicily. The apartment was adorned with the finest art from Florence. The twenty-foot ceilings were garnished with celestial frescos painted by the same artist who created the Duomo. To the finest china from Venice, the dwelling oozed elegance.

The center of the apartment was the magnificent palatial terrazzo, with breathtaking views overlooking the sea from one side and Etna on the other. This was where Don Ciccu spent most of his time, and this was where Michele's paintings hung.

Michele, now in his forties, had matured into a handsome man, and even though he was not recognized as an accomplished artist in Italy, his work was well known in France. To Michele this meant he wasn't good enough for the rich Italians who looked down on the Sicilians. He never got married but was pursued by many fair ladies of the nobility. Many thought Michele would never marry; he was too involved with his work.

To the dismay of his aging father, Salvatore, Michele's visits to Sicily were becoming less and less frequent and his stays were becoming shorter and shorter. When he did come to visit the family at the castle he made sure his father was some place else.

Florianna always begged Michele to stay and make up with his father; she knew how much he missed him and how much he wanted his son back. And so did she. But even Michele's love for Florianna could not change his position; he was just as stubborn as his father.

Ever since he had witnessed the abuse of the *carusi* in Floristella, Michele had felt the need to take up the plight of the peasants. So strong was his passion to alleviate the suffering of the poor in Sicily that

Michele secretly supported the bandit Giuliani in his quest to help the poor peasants. Michele sold many of his art works to prominent families of French nobility, and in turn gave the money to Giuliani to support his small army of bandits, in hopes of defeating the Italians and establishing once and for all self-rule for Sicily.

By now the barone was approaching eighty. It was the time in his life when he was supposed to sit back and enjoy the fruits of his labor and let his son Orazio take over the reins. But the fragile Orazio was overwhelmed with all the responsibilities, and Salvatore didn't have confidence in him. Orazio reminded Salvatore of his cousin Riccardo Conti, whom he never liked.

Ever since the barone had discovered the Contis' plot to take over the sulfur mines, the relations between the families had been strained, to say the least. And because of that mistrust and apprehension, Salvatore, without justification, didn't trust his son Orazio with the controls. Salvatore thought, *Orazio looks too much like a Conti.*

In his solitude, Salvatore wished that Michele had succeeded him as barone. Michele had the passion and the people loved him. But when Michele visited his father once to pay his respect, the conversation started where it had left off years ago. "How can you and your cohorts take away people's land? How can you have children working like slaves in those mines? How can you look at yourself every morning knowing that there are people starving on this island while you go to bed with a full stomach?"

"I always knew you were different, but I never thought you would turn against your father. Leave this house; I do not want to see you again. As far as I'm concerned you are no longer my son." Salvatore wished he could take back those words.

"As far as I'm concerned, I do not want to be part of this family." Michele left the *castello*. It was the last time he would see his father alive. Michele wished he could take back those words.

"The more the world changes, the more it is the same."

It was the early 1890s. Europe was preparing for war, and the armies needed sulfur to fuel their war machines. At this time, ninety percent of the world's sulfur came from Sicily. The exportation of sulfur from Sicily was vital to sustain the industrial revolution, and now it was Riccardo Conti and the northern Italians who wanted control of the mines so that they could control the European continent with the Von Fredericks of Germany.

When Salvatore, still after twenty years, refused to give up the controlling interest in the sulfur mines to the Contis, Don Carlo and the Contis formed an alliance to destroy Barone Parisi. First there were organized strikes at the mines directed at the barone, then his vineyards were attacked by bandits, and then the Mafia tried to extort large sums of money for protection. Salvatore first turned to the Italian government for protection, but the new king of Italy took his orders from Riccardo Conti. Barone Salvatore then turned to Don Ciccu for help.

What the Italian army couldn't or wouldn't do, Don Ciccu did. Don Ciccu was able to end the strikes at the sulfur mines. He managed to negotiate with the bandits and his friend Giuliani, and the raids on the barone's properties halted. And Don Carlo and the Mafia in Palermo left the eastern side of Sicily with their tails between their legs, although the old embattled fox Don Carlo hated to lose and promised he would seek his revenge.

Don Ciccu had become a powerful made man in Sicily. He had over three hundred men in his private army that took direct orders from him. When Michele left, the barone needed help to keep his holdings intact. Most of Don Ciccu's recruits came from the sulfur mines. They were the older *carusi* whose freedom Don Ciccu, with Barone Salvatore's money, was able to buy. They respected Don Ciccu and pledged their loyalties until death to him.

"These mines will be closed until we stop using the *carusi* as slaves. From now on the younger *carusi* will no longer be used to work the mines." Don Ciccu issued the proclamation to all the *gabelloti*. Don Carlo did not like it, but he had no choice; it was either *questo o gozzi.* It literally meant either take this or what was between your legs.

In Michele's absence and with a weak son in Orazio, Don Ciccu took control of all of the barone's vineyards and business affairs. A few weeks after Don Ciccu freed the *carusi*, he was surprised to learn that Giuliani wanted a meeting with Ciccu. In Sicily, political alliances changed from one minute to the next. It depended on which way the wind was blowing.

Maria insisted on going along.

"My dear friend." Giuliani and Don Ciccu embraced. As they embraced in the middle of a ring of outlaws, Turiddo fumed.

"It's been a long time." Don Ciccu and Maria had gone where most people would have been dead by now—to the bandits' hideout in the caves on the east side of Mount Etna. In the hillsides between Catania and Enna, the valley was green and covered with wildflowers, and the sheep grazed from one open field to another. It was a serene, peaceful, pastoral setting with the sound of the sheep's "ba-ba-ing" mingling with their bells and the shepherd singing his song. But death and treachery were only a stone's throw away.

Maria thought Giuliani looked older and tired. He had aged in the past ten years and his bandits looked worn out, especially the sinister Turiddo, who was losing the support of Giuliani's inner circle and Giuliani's trust.

"I need a favor from a friend." Don Ciccu knew Giuliani was in trouble as the Mafia and the Italian army was closing in, and who best to give it than his best friend and former *caruso*?

Giuliani didn't know whom to trust anymore. The international press had interviewed him, and his photo was in every major newspaper throughout the continent. In New York among the Italians, especially in Red Hook where most of the Sicilians lived, he had become a folk hero.

But the folk hero was in trouble, pursued by the Italian army, and now the Mafia, headed by Don Carlo, had placed a reward for Giuliani's death. His enemies portrayed Giuliani as a leader of the Communist movement, but that was all propaganda put out by Don Carlo. Giuliani was a simple peasant who wanted to help the poor. Unfortunately he had become entangled in the treachery of Sicilian politics, and the traitor in his midst, Turiddo, who was stabbing him in the back. The political climate had changed when Don Carlo saw the outlaws were getting too powerful and threatened his position, and because Don Carlo was shrewd and had heard of Turiddo's temper, he used it to his advantage.

Turiddo was biting at the bit to insult Don Ciccu, so he rudely interrupted Giuliani and Don Ciccu. "Are you a friend?" Turiddo demanded sarcastically. He had never liked or trusted Don Ciccu because he was Michele's protector, and Turiddo hated his cousin Michele. Whenever Don Ciccu looked at him, Turiddo felt as if Don Ciccu could see right through him and it made him uncomfortable.

There were only three people besides Salvatore and Florianna who knew that Don Carlo was Turiddo's father: one was Don Ciccu and the others were Michele and Maria. Now Don Ciccu looked at Turiddo closely. He was bitter and unkempt, he looked greasy, he had trouble breathing, and he had a sinister look in his eyes. Ciccu found it hard to believe that they had the same mother.

"What are you looking at, Ciccu?" Turiddo refused to call him Don Ciccu. It was his way of disrespecting him, but it was just jealousy.

Don Ciccu turned and looked at Giuliani. "Do I need to answer that?"

"Don't mind Turiddo. He's been working too hard, he worries too much."

And Maria interjected, "And sometimes he drinks too much and likes to beat up defenseless women."

"I guess now the great Ciccu needs a woman to talk for him. He's been hiding behind Parisi money and become soft like a woman. I hear he's a *finoccio* (gay) in love with that Michele. Come on, *finoccio*, show me what you have." Turiddo kept taunting, pulling out a knife and tossing it from one hand to the other.

Don Ciccu looked to Giuliani. "*Ce e permesso?*"

Giuliani nodded his permission for Don Ciccu to fight Turiddo; it meant it would be a fair fight. "Are you sure you want to do this, Turiddo?" Giuliani knew Turiddo had bitten off more than he could chew. Giuliani threw his knife to Don Ciccu.

It was at this very moment that Maria realized how much Don Ciccu meant to her, how much she depended on him, how much her father needed him, and how much she loved him.

"Don Ciccu." She stood there erect with tears welling up in her eyes knowing she could not stop the inevitable. "I want you to know that whatever happens, I love you."

For a second Don Ciccu turned to her and smiled, but could not say anything as Turiddo jumped at him. It was a bad mistake. He was ready. Turiddo took a beating the likes of which he had never had in his life. Don Ciccu was unmerciful; at one point he even thought of killing him. Had Florianna not been their mother he probably would have.

"The next time you address me, you call me Don Ciccu. Do you understand?" Don Ciccu had him by the throat, and with only one twist Turiddo would have been dead.

Turiddo could barely utter the word "*Si.*"

"And if you don't, I will kill you, do you understand that?"

Blood was gushing out of his mouth and he was choking. His eyes were desperate. He thought for sure he was going to die as Don Ciccu put more pressure around his neck. "*Si,*" came the strangled word.

"And if you touch Rosa one more time you are dead. Do you understand?"

His eyes were bulging and looked ready to come out of their sockets. "*Si.*"

It took Turiddo two months to recover from the beating, and in those two months he only thought of one thing—his vendetta, how he was going to kill Don Ciccu and all of the Parisis.

In Sicily, vendettas sometimes lasted generations. Families didn't talk to one another for hundreds of years, and sometimes no one knew how the vendetta started in the first place. But more often they couldn't forget, and when that happened whole families would be wiped out, even the innocent.

As Santa said, "When someone has done something evil, he must be killed. But that's not enough. You must go to the roots and kill the family to get your revenge."

❖ ❖ ❖

CHAPTER 26

Michele arrived in Acireale too late; his father was dead. Michele looked at his father in the coffin and put his arm around him. He loved him and he hated him, and at times he didn't know why. Over the last six years his father had aged so much, had become frail, sickly, and tired. But most of all he looked sad. Ever since Florianna died Salvatore seemed to have lost his joy of living.

The day after Michele had become antagonistic and attacked his father's way of life and discredited his nobility, Michele had left medieval Sicily. He moved to Florence with his mother, Orazio, and Donnatella. He had forgotten how bad they were, and now they had become enablers for each other. But even with some success he was never comfortable in Florence. Pursued and seduced by women of nobility, he went from one woman to another.

Michele couldn't bring himself to love anyone. He tried painting in Paris and for two years lived with Brigit Varillon, a beautiful French woman who loved to collect art and young artists. When she visited the École Des Beaux-Arts in Paris, Brigit met the Italian artist Michele Parisi whose art was on display at the famous gallery.

It was Michele's first major showing and he was quite nervous. Ambroise Vollard, the famous art dealer who mostly dealt with Van Gogh, Renoir, and Monet, was accompanying Brigit around the gallery. Brigit was dressed in a tightly fitted white-lace dress that had a neck collar decorated with studded diamonds. The dress accentuated her shapely body and flared out at the middle of her thighs, barely touching the floor. The white, bird-feathered hat was almost too big for her petite face, but she managed to carry it off quite well. With a white parasol twisting around in her hand, she was the crème de la crème of style and grace in Paris.

Michele was unaware that Vollard had stopped to critique his work. "*Signore* Parisi, your style is a throwback to the post-Impressionist. You must get with the new movement if you want to make a name for yourself." Vollard had that pompous air about him. He was very effeminate and his affixation for young boys was well known.

Michele had learned the ancient art of painting from his uncle Gianni, and there were only a few artists left who went through the tedious process of making their own paint from rocks and peeling the gold onto a canvas or piece of rare wood, which Michele preferred to work with. "Excuse me, sir, but why don't you just keep on walking." Michele turned around and pointed to the exit. But as he did, his eyes focused on Brigit who was standing next to Vollard. And she smiled. "Shall I go too?"

Vollard just kept on talking. "Do you know who I am? I am Ambroise Vollard. I represent some of France's finest artists, and I shall make sure this will be your last showing in France."

"Mr. Vollard, my name is Michele Parisi. I come from Sicily, and names do not impress me, people do, and you do not impress me, and if you do not leave right now, I will take you by your trousers and throw you in the street."

"I just dare you, you cocky Sicilian bastard."

What took place next was a comedy scene: Michele dragging Vollard by his britches and tossing him into the street while Vollard screamed every obscenity in the book. Brigit just couldn't help but laugh during the entire episode. Michele came back, clasped his hands, and walked to where Brigit was standing. Michele bowed like a gentleman. "Mademoiselle, may I take you to lunch?"

Brigit looked at him and smiled. "You are a cocky Sicilian bastard."

They lived together as lovers for two years. He was the nourishment she never had, like a starving rose that never quite matured because it was shaded by a big old oak. Michele had chopped the tree down and allowed the sun to come back into her life. Brigit, at forty, had reached the pinnacle of bloom.

When he received the letter from Maria informing him that his father did not have much time to live, Michele had to return to Sicily.

"You know I love you," he said.

"Not enough to stay," she whispered.

"My family needs me. I'll come back."

She knew he would not; she'd listened to his dreams and knew how much he missed his home and his family.

For Maria, the enormous pressures of dealing with her father's funeral and the realization of the uncertainties the future would bring were brought to a head at the family's crypt. The crypt was ornate, resembling a small villa in a cemetery that looked like a miniature medieval village. The first Parisi buried there was Barone Alfonso Parisi who was given the title from King Frederick, II who succeeded his father, Emperor Henry, VI to the throne of Sicily. Since then the other barones—the Cavours and Contis—built larger and more ornate crypts. The grounds resembled a well-manicured botanical garden where cypresses grew to thirty or forty feet and the trees played music as the wind entered and exited their thick foliage.

It seemed the whole town showed up at the Duomo to show their respect for Barone Salvatore Parisi, one of the favorite sons of Acireale. The Contis made their usual elegant entrance and sat at the right side of the ornate altar, and when Gabriella came in with Donnatella and Orazio, the heir apparent to the barone, they sat on the left side of the altar next to their cousin Riccardo.

Maria wasn't sure if Michele had gotten the letter to come home, but when Michele walked into the Duomo, there was an awkward moment of silence as he slowly walked down the marble path to the altar where his father's body lay. He was greeted by all on both sides of the aisle as Acireale offered its condolences to one of their most benevolent and respected citizens.

And why not? The barone had built a college and a hospital for the people of the town and made the sulfur baths public, but he was endeared mostly for saving the *carusi*, the children of Sicily, from the mines.

After Michele paid his respects to his father at the altar, he turned to the packed church with teary eyes and a hurtful soul. He didn't have to say anything; his sorrow was written in his face.

As he stepped down, the silence was broken as a buzz spread over the church as everyone speculated on which side Michele would choose to sit. His mother, Gabriella, moved to make room for him on the aisle; he stopped for a moment and kissed his mother but walked over to the other side where he was greeted with hugs and kisses from Maria and Don Ciccu.

But the bigger buzz was about Maria and Don Ciccu. It was obvious by their body language that they had become more than just friends. At the crypt Maria had about all she could take. She was about to faint. Don Ciccu, who had been watching her, picked her up. "I'll take you home."

"No. No."

"Where do you want to go?"

'Take me to your apartment." He placed her in the carriage and they rode off to his apartment in the *centro* of Acireale.

He carried Maria out of the carriage and to the front door of his apartment. "You know what people will say if they find out you are here?"

"Do you care?"

"I'm not worried about what people say about me. I worry about what they think of you."

He opened the door and placed her on his couch. "I want you to put me in your bedroom." He hesitated for a moment and then walked to his bedroom and placed Maria in his bed.

He got up to leave. "Don't leave me, please don't leave me. I've never been so afraid in my life. I don't know what's going to happen next, but I do know I want you near me."

"I'm just getting a towel to wipe you down." She didn't realize her clothes were completely soaked. "I think you have a fever."

Maria was diagnosed with walking pneumonia, which eventually would take her life, and for five days he didn't leave her side. He nursed her back to health, and she realized how much she needed him and how much she loved him.

✤ ✤ ✤

CHAPTER 27

A week after Barone Salvatore's funeral, at Maria's request, Michele and Don Ciccu decided to go to the family villa at Corruth for the week and relax at the beach. It had been two years since either of them had stepped foot inside the villa. The barone had closed it up when Florianna died and now it looked gloomy. But Maria was intent on restoring the villa where the family had been happiest.

One night at the beach, Michele and Don Ciccu sat reminiscing. Then they became silent, staring out into the sea at Corruth. At last Don Ciccu turned to a pensive Michele. "I hear she is very beautiful."

"*Bellissimo.*" Michele knew he was talking about Brigit.

Don Ciccu smiled at Michele. He was looking at Etna. "You always had an eye for beauty, but sometimes, like that mountain, beauty can be fatal." Michele and Don Ciccu didn't have to say a word to each other; they always knew what the other was thinking.

Don Ciccu got serious. "Your father loved you very much."

"He looked sad." Michele put his head down.

"He lost his desire to live. He needed you. Michele, you were the only one who got to him, and he made the reforms at the mines because of you. He knew how you felt about it."

Michele looked toward Mount Etna and the tears started to well up in his eyes. "Do you know how many times I've wanted to come back? When I heard that he was reforming the mines and paying to free the *carusi* I wanted to tell him how much I always loved him."

"But you didn't."

"No, I didn't."

"You broke his heart. He loved you so much."

"I know." Michele couldn't hold back the tears. "Why are you doing this to me?"

"Because I loved him too. I had to watch every day that you weren't here; it ate him up. It took a piece of his life away. That's how much he loved you, and I can tell you this because you are my brother." And Don Ciccu took out his golden horn.

Michele reached to his neck and clasped his horn. "You are my brother." With tears streaming down his cheeks, an emotional Michele said, "I love him so much it hurts. Every canvas I paint, he is there. His soul, his spirit consumes everything I do, and our last words were so bitter."

"That's why you ran away and didn't come home to visit? Michele, I told you years ago, this is where you belong, and your family needs you. Your father needed you, and I need you now."

"What has to be done?"

"There are three people that would like nothing better than to destroy us."

"Who are these people?"

"Turiddo, Don Carlo, and the one who holds the strings, Riccardo Conti. Don Carlo and Riccardo were not happy with the reforms. As the largest lease holder, Riccardo's profits were cut in half." Ciccu knew that if Riccardo gained control of the mines the *carusi* would be used as slaves again and hurled back into the caves.

Don Ciccu put his arm around Michele. "It's about time I settle up with Don Carlo." He had murdered his father, used his mother, and sent him to the mines, and had it not been for a large sum of money paid by Barone Salvatore, Don Ciccu knew it was only a matter of time before Don Carlo would have had him killed.

Michele looked at his expression and knew exactly what that meant. Don Ciccu usually didn't say much, but one could read his face when he wanted someone to. "For what he did to my mother," concluded Don Ciccu.

Michele wiped the tears from his eyes and agreed with Ciccu. "Florianna was like my mother too. It's time for me to step up as well."

The next morning after his meeting with Don Ciccu, Michele was at what had been his favorite place growing up: the beach at Corruth. He used to swim to the black lava island about a hundred yards off the beach. It was here that he would listen to his father telling him stories about Ulysses and the Cyclops while watching Mount Etna in the distance, always in the distance. Now Michele lay down on the smooth lava of his childhood and silently talked to his father, now gone.

"I'm sorry if I let you down. I didn't realize how much it meant to you. I never wanted to live your life and I won't. But I will make it up to you. I promise, and if I ever have children, I will always tell them what a wonderful grandfather you would have been."

It was a beautiful morning, and Maria had told Rosa to go to the beach and go for a swim. For a whole week Rosa had worked to get the villa open and ready for them. She was still getting over the vicious beating from the *cornuto*, Turiddo.

She timidly undressed, dived into the sea, and swam to the island rock. Her body glided smoothly through the water. When she reached the island, she boosted herself up, her shapely silhouette sparkling in the rays of sun reflecting from her wet body. She thought she was alone. She sat up on one of the lava rocks.

Michele was mesmerized; at first he thought she was a beautiful mermaid. He said to himself, *I have never seen anything so beautiful. She looks like a Greek goddess. I must know who she is.*

Michele quietly walked to the side of the island where she was resting. He startled her. "Please don't be frightened, my name is Michele."

Obviously embarrassed and self-conscious, Rosa turned her head away from Michele so he couldn't see her face. "I didn't think anyone would be up so early," she timidly whispered.

"Me too. I used to come here every morning. I didn't realize until now how much I missed it."

"I know." She turned and looked at him.

"Do we know each other?" Michele looked at her. He was struggling to remember how he knew her.

"You don't remember?" She almost smiled.

"I feel like a fool. How could I forget a beautiful face like yours?"

Tears welled up in her eyes, and Michele realized something was wrong. "Listen, I'm sorry, can I help you?"

"It's too late for anyone to help."

He noticed the side of her face was bruised and her lip was swollen. Even with that she was still the most beautiful woman he had ever seen. Michele gently touched her swollen cheek.

"You are still beautiful."

"Beautiful enough to be Queen of the Carnival?"

She smiled and gave him a kiss on his lips, and in an instant Rosa jumped into the water and was swimming toward shore. "*Aspetta!* Wait!" Michele yelled out. "When will I see you again?"

She smiled. "Tonight I'll be serving you dinner."

Maria's plan was working. From the day that Michele had crowned Rosa Queen of the Carnival, Santa and Maria knew she had been hit by a lightning bolt. Maria believed that if Michele had not fought with his father and left for Florence and later for Paris, things might have been different.

There were four table settings that night at the Parisis' villa in Corruth. Maria had set the table herself while Rosa prepared the risotto and wild mushrooms. Rosa knew it was Michele's favorite, and only Florianna could make it the way he liked it, but Rosa had Florianna's secrets. Florianna had treated Rosa like her daughter. She had loved the young girl and taught her everything she knew, from picking the wild mushrooms, to opening the sea urchins, to keeping a beautiful *giardini*. Rosa had followed Florianna all day long. They went to the markets in Catania together where certain merchants would sing love songs to Rosa and Florianna, telling them how beautiful they were and how they would love to make love to them.

Back then, the open-door markets were a carnival of activities. The same merchants set up in the same section of the piazza selling anything from fish from the nearby sea to the finest cotton from Egypt and the shiniest silk from China.

"*Che bella donna.* What beautiful women. If you were mine, *Signora*, I would build you a castle in heaven."

"*Femmina mi fa pazzi,* you women drive me crazy. I can't live with you and I can't live without you."

For the most part the merchants were kind and gentle souls, but they loved beautiful women and they loved Florianna and Rosa.

Maria and Rosa had worked for weeks trying to clean out the cobwebs and restore the villa as they remembered it. When Salvatore closed it down two years ago he had left everything the way it was and never went back. A warm feeling emanated from its faded stucco walls and walnut-stained oak floors and natural-beamed vaulted ceiling. The archways opened up onto outdoor patios that brought the outside *giardini* into the room where the family gathered after dinner. In the mornings they were awakened by the fragrance of oranges and lemons, which permeated throughout the villa, and at night they would be put to sleep by the sound of the sea lapping gently against the lava rock.

Michele lit the candelabra on the dining room table. Don Ciccu poured the wine, and in silence they raised their glasses and toasted one another. What a wonderful feeling it was to be back again in the place they all loved and which held fond memories of their youth.

"What are you thinking of?" Maria asked her brother, Michele, while they were eating the risotto and wild mushrooms.

He looked at Rosa and his heart skipped a beat. She was beautiful. "I'm thinking what you all are thinking, about the wonderful times we spent here. About Florianna and our father, Salvatore. Those were special moments that can never be replaced in our hearts. I was so lucky and I never knew it."

"We are still very lucky because we have two people," Maria looked at Rosa and Don Ciccu, "who are our dearest friends, who have become part of our family, who have shared in the good times and cried in the bad times."

Michele spoke softly, "Well, sometimes we don't see the beauty that's right in front of us. We think some far-off intriguing place or some mysterious person has the answers to our lives, when in reality it was here for us all the time."

Maria's eyes were focused on Don Ciccu. When Don Ciccu had heard her say, "I love you," the night when they met with Giuliani and Turiddo challenged him to a fight, his emotions were torn apart. He wanted to hold her in his arms, kiss her, and tell her how much he loved her, and at the same time, he wanted to kill Turiddo for unmercifully beating Rosa.

He never before had been able to love any woman. Maybe the scars from the mines and his hatred for Don Carlo had suppressed all his other emotions. But Maria was different. He had watched Maria grow into a radiant, vibrant, intelligent beauty of nobility. Yet tonight at the dining table she became the simple little peasant girl he had adored.

Michele could not take his eyes off Rosa during the entire meal. He couldn't help but compare her to the only woman he loved, Florianna. They sat there at the table in a trance not knowing that Maria and Don Ciccu had left the table. When they discovered they were sitting alone, they giggled like two school children who just found out what it meant to be in love for the first time.

Later, as they walked through the *giardini*, Michele held Rosa's hand and she placed her head on his shoulder. He sat down in the large armchair and she cuddled up around him. They didn't say a word to one another; they didn't have to. They were sitting in the same chair that Salvatore and Florianna sat in at the end of every night. They watched the stars and Mount Etna erupt, putting on another fantastic show as they fell asleep in each other's arms.

❖ ❖ ❖

CHAPTER 28

D on Carlo had asked for a meeting at his palazzo in Palermo. The aging don had sent out peace offerings to the quarreling aristocratic families in hopes of coming up with a unified protection force to put down the peasant revolt. The Italian army in Sicily was now under the control of Don Carlo.

His plan had been simple. Don Carlo had planted a spy, Turiddo, amongst the bandits. Don Carlo and Turiddo were secretly plotting Giuliani's demise so that Turiddo could take over the peasant army and end the revolt. The carrot put on a string for Turiddo was that part of the Parisi family's estate would be given to him.

"Giuliani is getting soft," said Don Carlo, offering his protection to Turiddo. "Once Giuliani is gone and the peasants are defeated, the Parisi family will fall."

"Get Giuliani to Taormina and we will take over from there." The plot was drawn up and the power-hungry Turiddo had planted the seed. The second part of the plan was to fulfill his vendetta against the Parisi family.

Etna had stopped smoking; that was not a good sign. Everyone held their breaths in anticipation of the explosion.

And now the Parisi family was in serious danger. It was decided that Michele would meet with Don Carlo.

The view from Don Carlo's palazzo was of the magnificent twelfth-century cathedral high up in the hills of Monreale on the outskirts of Palermo. The wonderful russet and brown stone chancel of interlacing arches, gothic rose windows, and Arab windows with pointed arches blended into the beautiful cloister, which some said offered strangely mixed sensations of spiritual meditation. As visitors meandered through the exotic flowers and trees they came to the focal point of the *giardini*, the Arab fountain, and they realized that the history of Sicily was so varied and intriguing it was almost impossible to understand.

Sicily was in turmoil. A Roman senator once said Sicilia would always be in turmoil. "The more things change, the more they stay the same."

"We have come to this point and now we must fortify our position," Don Carlo said to Michele. Don Carlo had aged and had difficulty breathing. He and Michele were sitting on the verandah in Don Carlo's palazzo overlooking the beautiful cathedral in Monreale. "We have a long history, your *famiglia* and I, and now it's *finito*."

Don Carlo was gloating; he knew he had Michele with his back to the wall. Word had come that the bandits had been massacred at Taormina and were no longer a threat. Giuliani jumped off the cliffs to his death rather than be a prisoner to the Italians. "Riccardo Conti and I will control the sulfur mines. If you have any desire to work with us, I could see to it that you will have a position with us."

Michele's mind was racing as he sat there in Don Carlo's palazzo barely listening to him. Michele knew if he didn't accept Don Carlo's proposal he would not walk out of the palazzo alive. That was why Don Carlo needed to be killed.

Michele had insisted that he be the one to meet with Don Carlo. He knew Don Carlo's men would relax if they were meeting with a nobleman, a man of honor. There were also rumors about him being an artist and living in Paris. He wasn't all man, certainly not Sicilian.

"Don Carlo." Michele had a tough time calling him "Don." "How will I know you will honor what you say?"

"Michele, I never had a son, you could be my son. I know you had problems with your father," Don Carlo just kept rattling on. "Let me tell you—I just got word from Taormina. Giuliani and his men are all dead, and I had that traitor Turiddo killed." He paused. "I hate rats, and he was a big one."

When Don Ciccu had made the deal with Giuliani, he had given him most of his men to help him and the peasants. Michele knew now that meant that his family was unprotected, and Don Carlo and Riccardo Conti could do as they pleased. There was no one to stop them now.

The hairs on Michele's skin were standing. There was a pit in his stomach that ached and he started to sweat. He hated everything about this *animale*. It was time to carry out his plan. "Don Carlo, I am honored that you would consider me the son you never had, but you did have a son, Turiddo, and *a marzarto*. You killed him."

Michele looked him straight in his eyes to see his reaction.

"What do you mean?" Don Carlos' cockiness disappeared.

"Your son was the big rat. A *marzarto*. You killed him." Michele got up and took two steps toward Don Carlo as if he was going to embrace him. "And now I'm going to kill you." In that instant he slit Don Carlo's throat and kissed him on his forehead. "That was for Florianna."

Don Carlo's guards were watching from a distance on the rooftop in the next building and thought nothing of the gesture of Michele kissing the don. He walked out, leaving Don Carlo sitting in his chair looking over the cathedral.

Only a few minutes passed before it was realized that Michele had murdered Don Carlo. The guards started shooting, but Michele and Don Ciccu had made their escape.

They were too far away to be caught, but a bullet did manage to enter Don Ciccu's lung. Don Ciccu knew he was dying, but he had to make it back to Acireale. He had to be with Maria.

At Don Ciccu's apartment in the Palazzo Parisi, the candles were lit next to the Madonna and his favorite saint, Saint Francis, his namesake. He lay on his bed prepared to die. "Michele, I just wanted to tell you how much your family has meant to me, but you must be careful. There is still danger here for you and your *famiglia*."

"I understand, but you must rest now and save your energy." From the moment he had brought him to the apartment, Michele had not left Don Ciccu's side.

"Please write this down." Michele took a pen off the armoire. There were pictures of the Parisi family and Michele's paintings around the room, but it was obvious that Maria's picture was the most precious to Don Ciccu. It was placed next to Saint Francis. Michele sat down next to Don Ciccu. They had been through so much together and shared so much history, but the one thing they both had cherished was Florianna. They were bonded by her boundless love for them and they had become more than brothers, they had become best friends.

Don Ciccu placed his hand affectionately on Michele's head. "Are you ready to take my letter?" Michele nodded.

"*Carisimma*, Maria," began the weak Don Ciccu. "I have watched you grow from an innocent child to a beautiful, caring *donna*. You were my first thought in the morning, you were my first smile of my day. I know you didn't love me at first, but I have always loved you. You are the first and last breath that I take, you are my *sciatu mio*."

Don Ciccu stopped talking, closed his eyes, and passed away. He was now at peace and their souls were together again. His beloved Maria had passed away with pneumonia.

Michele lowered his head and whispered to his friend, "I love you, Don Ciccu. *Ti amo, mio caruso.*"

PART III

❖ ❖ ❖

CHAPTER 29

Brooklyn, New York

The wine bin in Santa's cellar was getting cold, and Santa had tasted so much wine that she could not go on telling Michael the story of their family in Sicily.

"But *Nonna*, you have to tell me what happened to all these people." Michael had been intrigued with his grandfather, Michele, and his grandmother, Rosa.

"*Va fan culo*, they are all dead." Michael knew that was the wine talking. "*Ammunini*. Now let's go upstairs before we freeze our asses off down here and the rats eat us up alive." Santa had a strange way of communicating.

That night Michael slept at Santa's apartment on Carroll Street. His father, Giuseppe, slept alone in the apartment on Sackett Street wondering where he went wrong and worrying about his son. They were two blocks away, but they were both dreaming of Sicilia.

Michael tossed and turned. All the characters that Santa had described came walking into his dreams. His grandfather, Michele, and his grandmother, Rosa, had raised his father, Giuseppe. But was Giuseppe Michele's son or was he Riccardo Conti's son? And if he was Conti's son was he entitled to Conti's fortunes? And now Claudia walked in, the mystery lady Claudia Cavour. Did Claudia hold the key? Did she inherit it all?

Michael woke up in a cold sweat. Now he understood why his father had married Anna, his mother. She was Claudia's sister and they looked so much alike. But did Claudia know that Santa was her real mother?

The next day Santa, as was ritual, went down to the cellar to check out the wine barrels. "Come on, *auiti* me."

Michael followed her down to the wine cellar. He figured that maybe she would continue her stories about Sicily. "*Si, Nonna.* What happened to my grandfather and grandmother?" Michael was enthralled with his family's history. It seemed his father, Giuseppe, had been telling the truth, that the family came from nobility. "And why did Giuseppe leave Sicily?"

Michael's mind was full of questions: who had inherited the Contis' and Parisis' fortunes and what happened to Claudia Cavour? And what happened to Santa after Giuliani was killed?

"*Auiti* me." Santa needed help to get up on the stool so she could check the corks on the barrels. The wine was fermenting; Michael could hear it bubbling inside the oak barrels.

"You ask too many questions and my brain needs to rest. Another time I tell you, *ammunini*." She pulled Michael's arm the way she used to, but her strength was gone. Santa was getting frail and was having bouts of Alzheimer's. In the last few years, spinal stenosis had set in, and her chin was almost resting on her chest. She was less than five feet tall now and had lost some of her teeth. Her hair was silver-gray and she tried to keep it in a loose bun, but it would fall apart and she would struggle to fix it, but the arthritis in her fingers did not help.

"Please, *Nonna,* please tell me what happened."

Santa was thinking of him, her one true love, Gaetano Giuliani. How she had become his lover when she was only fourteen years old. In Sicily the peasant girls grow up quickly. And she was thinking of how she was forced to move to Trapani and marry Vito Marsala, a marriage of convenience and a favor returned to Barone Salvatore Parisi for buying the young boy's freedom from the sulfur mines.

Years had gone by since she had to leave Corruth for Trapani. With tears in her eyes Santa remembered consoling Giuliani between her young breasts. He would fall asleep telling her how he was going to get a farm for them to live on where they could raise chickens and plant an orchard of fruit trees.

They would be self-sufficient, make love every night, and have lots of children. That sounded good to Santa.

One morning she had held him tight and pleaded for him not to go. "Please do not go to Taormina. I have a feeling it's a trap. Please don't go."

"I must go, but when I get back I promise we will get that land and get married. I'm making a deal with Don Carlo, and all this fighting will soon come to an end and we will settle down."

He never came back, and Don Carlo had never lived up to his end of the deal. But Santa was having Giuliani's baby.

"*Aspetta*, let me help you with your hair, *Nonna*." They were still down in the wine cellar, and Michael could see that Santa's pain was getting worse. She could barely move her fingers to fix her hair. She had tears in her eyes, but it wasn't from the arthritis, it was from her memories.

Michael knew Santa would not go anywhere without her hair in place even if it meant going from the cellar to her apartment on the third floor. "You never know who you could meet or what could happen." That's why, she insisted, "you must change your underwear every day, because you never know when you could wind up in the hospital. We might be poor, but we are not *caffone*."

"*Nonna,* you have beautiful hair, you are still beautiful." She placed her hands on Michael's face. "*Figlio beddo,* I love you so much." Michael just knelt down and placed his head in his *nonna's* lap and she started to weep.

"I've been through so much I'm tired of living. Everything I loved was taken away from me. You're the only thing I have left, my *sciatu mio.*" And she placed her hand affectionately on Michael's head.

"I love you too, *Nonna,* I love you."

Santa picked up Michael's head and wiped away his tears and looked at him with her faded blue eyes. "As much as I love you, remember this: your father loves you more, and don't ever forget that."

✤ ✤ ✤

CHAPTER 30

That night the starry-eyed Michael dreamed about Sicily again—about the sulfur mines and the *carusi* and about the struggle for control of the mines, and how ironic it was that now there was a struggle for control of the piers. How it echoed the family fight over the mines so many years ago. Maybe the names were different, but the end result was the same. It was all about power. Who wanted it? And how much were they willing to give up for it?

Two blocks away, a sad Giuseppe was wondering how he had lost the only person he had left to love, his son Michael. His mind flashed back to Acireale where it all started and ended.

"I don't want them to control me, and I don't want them to control my son." He remembered his father, Michele, saying those words to his mother, Rosa. "*Forza e un maladia*—the quest for power is a sickness."

Giuseppe lay awake in his green leather chair. The pains in his chest were getting stronger and he found it more difficult to breathe. Giuseppe thought to himself, *before I die I need to settle up. I need to make sure my son gets out of here alive.*

The wars between the five families were still brewing. Carlo Genovese, the nephew of Don Carlo of Palermo, had become the head of the New York families. His extended family included the Gallo, and Gambino families. These families had solidified against the Anastasia family and the Parisi family.

But the thought of scum like Nicky Genovese and his egocentric, sadistic father, Carlo Genovese, not to mention that crazy Joe Gallo with their henchman Ciclopi taking control of the piers and putting the Parisi family out of business, didn't sit too well with many people. This was especially true for Harold Wilson who needed the Parisis and the Anastasias to stay in control for him to maintain power.

Despite the fact that Harold Wilson didn't have too much love for Big Tony or Blackie, it was where his money was, and his money and power needed to be protected. But Harold Wilson realized Big Tony was not capable of bringing the two sides together. He needed someone whom both sides respected, someone who could mediate a peace so that business could resume as usual. Harold Wilson knew he had to get Luigi, Pasquale, and Giuseppe to come together and make peace. After all, it was these three who had brought the Sicilians to power on the New York piers in the first place twenty years ago.

Luigi Genovese, alias Luigi Parisi, was the stimulus to the rise of power and influence of the Genovese family. Luigi was cunning and well liked by the working men, and his reputation as a revolutionist and outlaw in Sicily preceded him. Luigi had very little respect for his mother's brother Carlo Genovese, who had inherited Don Carlo's evilness.

But Luigi's hatred of Big Tony fueled his desire to take control of the piers and bring Big Tony to his knees. But his love and respect for his cousin Giuseppe was greater than his hatred of Giuseppe's half-brother.

Harold Wilson had asked for a meeting with Luigi and made him an offer to take over complete control of the docks. But they would need help.

Luigi did not like Harold Wilson, but he knew Harold was holding the strings. "I will do this because I love Giuseppe and we have a family history that only we two can share and still remember. The workers know this and respect him more than anyone else." Luigi shook hands with Harold. "I don't think you can understand that, can you?" He took Harold by surprise with that question.

"What do you mean?"

"I mean, you were governor, you controlled many businesses, you have money, but the most important thing to you is power. Am I right?"

Harold didn't answer; he didn't have to. Luigi went on, "For Giuseppe it's respect and his son."

The undeclared war had raged for three years in the battlefields, the streets of Brooklyn. But the final straw that brought the feuding sides to the table to talk was the assassination of Albert Anastasia. Albert was the head of the Anastasia crime family, which shared control of the piers with their allies, the Parisi family. Albert Anastasia had been knocked off sitting in a chair getting a haircut and shave at his favorite barbershop in Red Hook.

The press had a field day showing Albert's bloody body hunched over in the barber's chair. The news even made it to Sicily. The politicians and the judges had about enough of these murders and people where getting tired of all the violence. It was bad for business. So the heads of the families in Sicily and the powers that be in the States said that's enough.

Now both sides were ready for a truce, and so was Harold Wilson. They needed a mediator to make the peace, someone who was respected by both sides. Someone who still had the connections in Sicily.

Luigi met with Pasquale, and the two friends worked out the compromise. There was too much bloodshed and neither side was backing down. So Don Pasquale, with Big Tony's permission, sent out a peace offering to the other families. They would meet on Good Friday at the club, and all the players would come and have a sit-down.

There was more security than if President Eisenhower had been at the meeting. Each family sent five bodyguards to keep surveillance. Every roof was manned and every corner for five blocks was patrolled. Nobody trusted anyone else; there was too much bad blood between them.

The snow had turned to slush in the streets, but the black Cadillac limos shone as they lined up along Court Street. The chauffeurs and bodyguards opened doors as the who's who of the Brooklyn underworld made their appearances. They were dressed in three-piece Italian handmade gray or black stripe silk suits, bought from the Jewish men on Baxter Street and made by the Chinese on Canal Street. The black camel hair coats were draped over their shoulders and freshly buffed fedoras were placed meticulously on their heads. Carlo Genovese's chauffeur rolled out a rug over the snow so that Carlo wouldn't dirty the shiny patent leather shoes he was sporting.

As the heads of the families and their *consigliores* entered the club, Don Pasquale greeted each one and assigned him to a seat at the rectangular table. When Luigi walked in, Don Pasquale embraced him. It was more than an embrace of affection; it was an embrace that was rendered to the head of a family. Carlo Genovese was not comfortable watching it.

Luigi had walked in with Paul Castellano. The Castellano family had become one of the five most powerful families in New York after the assassination of Don Luchese. Castellano was different; he was educated, and his sons were lawyers and worked for him in his extensive real estate business in Brooklyn and Manhattan. Castellano was not liked by Carlo Genovese, and Castellano knew he needed someone to keep his business and family protected. John Gotti was his protector.

Carlo Genovese was given the honor of sitting at one end. Next to him sat his *consigliore*, Luigi Genovese, but the other end was left vacant. Even Big Tony was relegated to a side seat.

The aroma of freshly lit Cuban cigars seemed to be winning out over the bay rum cologne. Jimmy Scotto—they called him the undertaker because his father owned Scotto's Casket Company—was wearing a two-carat diamond ring on his pinkie and twisted and turned it so that it would reflect in everyone's eye. Jimmy Scotto was also an underboss for the Gambino family.

Nicky Genovese sat next to his father. He had started to look like his old man more and more, and now he was starting to emulate him. At twenty-two, he had a lot to learn, but the wise guys knew it all. He had the money and now he thought his father was giving the *caffone* the power.

There was an uneasy tension in the makeshift conference room. A long mahogany table had been placed in the middle of the club and the wooden folding chairs had been placed strategically around it as Don Pasquale sat down. The dark-paneled room was filled with smoke, and upright fans ushered the smoke out an open widow. He had organized the families for this meeting as Harold Wilson had instructed him, but he knew he needed help to end the wars and bring peace to the families, not just for Harold Wilson but for the families themselves.

When they all seemed settled and quiet there was a knock on the door. Don Pasquale said, *"Entrare."*

The door opened and a soft voice said humbly, *"Ce' permesso?"* Giuseppe Parisi stood quietly in the doorway waiting for permission to enter. This gentle soul had aged considerably in the past ten years, but he still personified a dignified gentleman of nobility.

They all rose one by one. Luigi was the first one to stand. He walked over to Giuseppe and placed his arm around his cousin, and they kissed. "Take your seat at the head of the table." It was obvious now that Luigi had taken over as head of the Genovese family.

Giuseppe graciously took the seat at the head of the table. There was a moment of silence before he began to speak. He spoke softly and in Sicilian. "It's been a long time since we left our homes in Sicily. Most of us came here with only the shirts on our backs. We didn't speak the language, we didn't understand the customs. We were ridiculed, put in jail, and/or hung for crimes we did not commit. Our businesses and homes were burned down only because we were hard workers and made money and people were jealous. We helped build this country, and they still call our children wops, guineas, dagos. In Sicily, the Italians called us *ignoranti*, burned down our homes, and took away our farms. The Romans two thousand years ago used us as slaves. Some say we are the missing link between the human race and the cavemen."

Giuseppe paused and looked around the table; some were nodding in agreement. But Carlo Genovese and his son Nicky were not.

Giuseppe continued, "I look around this room and see men who have done well financially for their families. I see fancy cars outside; I see fine suits from Italy. I see expensive jewelry. I see men of power. But I do not see men who are respected."

He looked around again and continued, "If we can't respect one another, how do we expect others to respect us? These wars must stop. The shedding of blood in our streets must stop. The killing of our children who are in the middle of this fiasco must end. And we must change our ways so that our children don't glorify the gangsters and Young Turks. Like Mr. Castellano here, his two sons are lawyers; we need to follow his lead.

"Our children should become doctors, lawyers, judges, professors, mayors, senators, maybe one day president, but not Mafia thugs, who one day will be shot down in the street because some wise guy wants more power. I have a son who I have tried to keep away from this world of violence that surrounds us. I have tried. It's been hard, but I want to make sure he gets out of here. I want to make sure he grows up to be a fine young man respected because he is educated; respected because he is *signore,* a gentleman.

I want him to get married and have children, and hopefully those children will be able to be proud to say 'we are Sicilian.'"

Giuseppe stopped again and looked purposely at each and every one of them. "This is all I want. I do not want money. I do not seek power. I want my son to get out of here alive."

All the heads of the families looked at Giuseppe and nodded in agreement.

"Finally we will have peace." Luigi raised his glass of wine, and they saluted Giuseppe. "To the Prince, a salute."

At the end of the meeting the three *paisani*—Luigi, Pasquale, and Giuseppe—came to the center and embraced.

The wars were over for now and peace had come to the city.

CHAPTER 31

Red Hook, Brooklyn

Within minutes of the meeting's end, the news of a settlement between the families spread around Red Hook and Brooklyn like a hot sirocco in Sicily on an August night. The Parisis were to keep control of the piers and, along with the Anastasia family, control of the unions. But they had to share their control with the Genovese and Castellano families.

To the dismay of Carlo Genovese and Nicky, Luigi had become head of the Genovese family and Don Pasquale had become *consigliore* to the Castellano family.

It was reluctantly agreed to have Blackie keep whatever inroads he had made into the drug trade, but he could not expand. The control of the drug and gambling businesses still were in the hands of the Gambino and Genovese families.

At first it seemed a victory for the old-timers, the heads of the families who wanted to return to the good old days before the wars when everyone was making money. Everyone seemed to be pleased with the peace terms, everyone except the young wise guys, Blackie, Nicky Genovese, and Ciclopi, who did not want to wait for their destined thrones. But the last battle of the war still needed to be settled, and that meant more bloodshed.

The settlement came the next day. Ciclopi's body was found in the Gowanus Canal. His heart was hacked out, his *cagliones* stuffed in his mouth, and a U for Ulysses was carved on his back. No one got upset. It was a price to be paid for peace. No one except Nicky Genovese, whose power had just been cut from under his legs. Nicky knew he would be next, and this time his father could not protect him.

Six hours later, the body of Nicky Genovese was found in the canal with a bullet in his head.

The day of the meeting, Michael was still at Santa's apartment. He was having a tough time understanding how his father, this meek, humble man, had the power to bring together some of the most ruthless gangsters in the city. When he heard of the meeting, something inside of Michael wanted to rush to his father's side to tell him he loved him. Michael knew his father would want to hear that more than anything else.

Michael lay awake for most of that night fearing to fall asleep. He was worried about his father. He knew how treacherous and deceitful these people were and was concerned that his father was being set up. He dozed off and dreamed. He was on the piers and Ciclopi was stalking Giuseppe, ridiculing him and calling him "*Vecchio fesso*" and then plunging the hook into Giuseppe's lung. And then Ciclopi had Michael on the ground kicking him unmercifully and laughing like a hyena. Then Michael was in Sicily, and there was Ciclopi by a cemetery and out of a tomb came a little angel. She was so beautiful, pleading with Ciclopi not to kill her.

In the middle of the night Michael got up and walked out of Santa's apartment and over to his apartment on Sackett Street. As he entered he heard the television and could see his father sitting in the green recliner. When he went up to him, he kissed him on the forehead. "I love you, Pappa, I'm sorry."

Giuseppe's head was cold and he was at peace with Claudia's letter in his hand.

The day after Giuseppe passed away, Don Pasquale was sitting very erect in his regular seat at the club, with his back to the wall. He looked at Michael with a strange smile on his face.

"Can I tell you something in confidence?" he whispered to Michael. "Ciclopi and Nicky *sono morti*."

Michael did not show any emotion, "Who killed them?"

No lo so, who knows? Who cares? Giuseppe is dead and we got our revenge. But you and I must talk, sit down and let me tell you a story.

"In Sicily, all your father had to do was go along with Riccardo's plans for him. Riccardo thought Giuseppe was his son and that one day his bloodline would continue thorough him. He could have been set for life, but what a price one has to pay to sell one's soul. To play the puppet while someone holds the strings is not what your father wanted, and he hoped you would understand he did not want that for you either.

"We had a famous puppet show that would come to Acireale during Carnivale. Everyone would come from miles around to be entertained by the master of the puppets, *Signore* Pennisi from Messina. He could control three, four, five puppets at a time, and as kids we would laugh and have a good time. One day your father had tears in his eyes and I asked him what was wrong. He told me, 'That's us. We are the puppets and we are being controlled by the ones who want to keep control of the power.'"

"But too much power can be destructive."

"Etna exploded and unleashed a fury of hot red lava. The earth parted, and the sea became angry with ten- to twenty-foot waves pounding the shoreline and engulfing anything in sight. To some, the end of the world had come. When it was over, the survivors looked for love ones. The lucky ones found them and buried them. That day we didn't have to say anything;

we all understood. The powers that be can make all the plans and try to control, but one day something will come along and wipe it all out. Don't be a puppet was what your father was saying to me."

Don Pasquale continued. "Michael, I am not a smart man. I do not have an education, but I love you as much as your father loved my son, Frankie. And I know one thing for sure—if you stay here you will become one of them, and maybe wind up like Frankie, *morte*. You will just be one of *Signore* Pennisi's puppets unless you cut the strings and leave."

It was a cool April afternoon and the wind was blowing from the northeast, but the sun was shining brightly, and it gave him warmth as he unbuttoned the top of his navy pea coat. The wind played with Michael's charcoal black hair, tossing it from side to side. His cheeks were still red—not from the cool breeze, but from Santa's wine.

Michael had just left Pasquale, and his head was full of questions about his life now that his father was not there. Where would he live? What would he do? How was he going to make it through life with no one there to help him?

He was leaning on the black iron railing staring at the New York skyline on the promenade in Brooklyn Heights waiting for Mary Madison. Since they first met at Lundy's a few months ago, fate seemed to have brought these two special souls together. They had become intoxicated with one another. They would not let a day go by without seeing each other, without hugging,

Two nights before, she had held him tightly, and her kisses were longer and more passionate. "My goodness, Michael, I never thought I could love someone as much as I love you. You are so different than anyone I have met."

"And you—" But Mary Madison wouldn't let Michael finish. "Just hold me like it's our last time together. I just want to be in your arms forever and ever."

Michael looked at his watch; Mary Madison was late for their daily meeting. He had fallen in love. She was so beautiful and different. She came from another world—the world of Donna Reed. She was raised to be a showpiece, a debutante, in Charleston, South Carolina.

Her mother, Elizabeth Wilson, had been a most beautiful debutante in the Hamptons. Raised without a mother since the age of six, Elizabeth's father, Harold Wilson, had given her everything her heart desired—everything except his time and his love, and because of that she was never able to love anyone, including her two husbands until she met him—Giuseppe.

From the moment she laid her eyes on him at Rosario's funeral she knew she had to have him. So Harold conveniently looked the other way and Giuseppe became her lover. But something she and Harold did not bargain for happened. Unlike the rest of her conquests, whom Elizabeth tossed aside once she was tired of them, this time she fell in love. She gave him her '38 Packard, her most prized automobile. She bought him fancy watches and dressed him in the latest styles. Elizabeth and Giuseppe became an item in the Hamptons while her father made detailed plans to take control of everything Luciano left behind. When Luciano was getting too big for his britches Harold called Dewey the New York Attorney General to have Luciano deported.

Mary Madison Brittain never showed up that night. Michael was perplexed. They never missed a day without seeing one another. He wondered what had gone wrong. As he walked along the promenade, a horse and carriage pulled up. The obviously well-to-do gentleman in the carriage asked the driver to stop and open the door. The gentleman pulled out two champagne glasses and gave one to the elegant lady next to him and they toasted to a beautiful moment overlooking the New York skyline.

Who was he kidding? Maybe he just didn't belong; maybe he was just another kid from Red Hook.

❖ ❖ ❖

CHAPTER 32

Mary Madison Brittain was raised a privileged child in Charleston, South Carolina. Her father was Tommy "Bubba" Brittain, a Charleston solicitor. A graduate of The Citadel, he later was elected lieutenant governor of South Carolina. His great-great-granddaddy was James Madison, fourth president of the United States. And Bubba was going to use every bit of his family's influence to become governor. Bubba had it all: his father was a respected Presbyterian minister and his mother was the principal of the finest private academy in the South, the Ashley Academy for young southern white women. But Bubba had one problem: he could spend money faster than a bat out of hell.

Bubba spent money on booze, women, and gambling, and not necessarily in that order. By the time he reached the ripe old age of thirty-five he had gone through his family's money. Bad advice and bad investments left him, as he said, "without a pot to piss in."

But as faith would have it, he was invited to the Wilsons' gala at the one-time President Jackson's palatial mansion in Charleston, which Harold Wilson had purchased. After he stepped down as governor from New York, Harold had sold all his belongings in the Hamptons and settled his family in Charleston.

When he first met Elizabeth he knew why he was invited to the party and also knew what Harold expected of him. They married in Saint Michael's Cathedral where some of the finest southern families were married and buried, including Henry Clay.

Harold Wilson had become the master puppeteer. He had become a modern Riccardo Conti. He would do anything to keep control and to keep his power.

Mary Madison Brittain was a beautiful child, and Bubba became a doting, responsible, loving father. He never became governor, he still drank too much and was a big womanizer, but Mary Madison became the reason he lived and the reason he tolerated the Wilsons.

Bubba made sure that Mary Madison grew up every bit a southern lady and every bit a Charlestonian. He took pride in his southern heritage and looked at the Wilsons as the invading Yankees who came to Charleston with their money and thought they could buy into Charleston society.

According to Bubba he was "southern by the grace of God," and no amount of money could buy this southern heritage. But Harold Wilson didn't look at it the same way. He was living in President Jackson's home and his daughter was married to a descendant of President Madison. They attended the same church as the finest Charlestonian families, a church where Henry Clay was buried.

Tommy "Bubba" Brittain died at the age of forty-seven; his liver just gave up. Mary Madison was just twelve years old and every bit a southern lady. Bubba was a wonderful, charismatic, loving father; he brought joy and laughter to his daughter's world, and when he died, the laughter and joy ended with him.

Elizabeth was despondent and bored with her self-indulgent life; her self-pity became a disease and infected those around her. Harold was always too busy to be concerned about his daughter; after all, she had enough money to make anyone happy, and his granddaughter would have even more.

But fortunately Mary Madison was sent away to boarding school, and since she was still in Charleston at Ashley Academy, her grandmother Mazzella Brittain watched over her and showered her with love and affection to make up for losing Bubba.

One fall, when Mary Madison had just turned seventeen, she came home to find that her grandfather was planning another gala event at the mansion. These events had become the toast of Charleston and every who's who of the city was invited. But this party was different; it was a celebration of womanhood amongst Charleston's finest families. The Forty-fifth Cotillion ball was being held at the Wilsons' mansion, and Mary Madison looked every bit the princess Harold Wilson wanted her to be.

Her escort was Mathew Cooper III, a senior at The Citadel and a direct descendant of Lord Ashley Cooper, the founder of the city of Charleston. It was whispered in inner circles that one day he would be governor of the state of South Carolina. A natural leader at The Citadel, Mathew Cooper III had bigger plans.

It was a ceremony fit for a princess, and Harold basked in the light of his beautiful granddaughter. Her beauty and charming personality was the toast of Charleston. And the next day the *Charleston Gazette* devoted a whole page on the Wilsons and the who's who of Charleston, but one name emerged as the new flower of Charleston; her name was Mary Madison Brittain.

That night she found herself in her mother's bedroom. Elizabeth had gone out partying, and Mary Madison was alone again. It seemed Elizabeth was rarely there for her daughter; ever since Bubba died she was there even less.

A photo album lay open on her bed, and Mary Madison was surprised to see a younger, beautiful Elizabeth looking so happy with her arms around a dark, handsome stranger. They were sitting in an older convertible with New York plates that was parked on a hill overlooking the ocean. She took the photo out and read what her mother had written. "I have never loved and will never love anyone as much as I love you." She could feel the passion in their eyes and saw the red lipstick print her mother left behind, with a tender kiss, on a tear-stained photograph.

Mary Madison had never seen her mother so happy as in that photo, and when she feel asleep, she dreamt of this dark, handsome stranger and her mother and the passion they had obviously shared. When she awoke the next morning the first thing she said to herself was, "I'm going to New York."

✤ ✤ ✤

CHAPTER 33

It was the early 1980's, and Michael was a teacher in New York City and also had a one-man law practice on Staten Island, in the black and Hispanic section of Castleton Ave. Between the two jobs, he barely was able to support his family. They had moved from Brooklyn because Michael wanted to escape his past and hopefully keep his sons away from the stories of Red Hook and the Parisi family. They lived in a modest three-bedroom home on Staten Island where Michael tried to blend in with the rest of the city workers.

But Michael found it hard to blend in and even harder to escape his past. The Parisi family still had some control of the longshoremen, but their influence was fading as new regulations and the use of containers reduced the dependency on longshoremen and with them the power of the Parisi family.

So the younger generation turned to drugs, gambling, and prostitution to make their money. And every once in a while they would make the front page of the *Daily News*. Big Tony's son and Michael's cousin, Blackie, had just been sent up the river for five years for tax evasion. At the time he was living on Todt Hill on Staten Island in a two million-dollar house. Michael had been appointed supervisor of Special Education on Staten Island. That gave him a whopping thousand dollars more a year added to his twenty-five. His cousin Blackie made that in a week in prison.

Sometimes Michael felt he had been in prison living in Red Hook and trying to keep his past and his family name as far as away as possible, but living in New York made that impossible

It was a warm, balmy Monday in June and the beginning of the last week of the school year. Michael was waiting in front of the mental health building at the bus stop. It had become a ritual he looked forward to. The children would be so happy when they got off the yellow school bus to see Michael as he always had a big hug and made them all feel loved.

Sidney was always the first one off the bus. At nineteen he was one of the oldest. He was black, overweight, and had the greatest smile. When Sidney met someone for the first time he always asked for his or her birthday.

"November 30, 1941," Michael answered.

Without thinking, Sidney said, "You were born on a Monday." Michael couldn't believe it. Unfortunately, it was the only thing Sidney could remember. The psychiatrist called it a classic case of idiot's savant.

Dennis Miller would get off the bus holding a stack of five to ten telephone books and God forbid if anyone tried to take one away from him. He would go into a rage. That rage would only stop if he were given a telephone book. The psychiatrist said he was looking up his own telephone number. They nicknamed him ET because he was always trying to call home.

Michael always felt sad at the end of the week. Many of the children would pack their bags anticipating a parent or a family member coming to get them from the state facility of Mount Loretto where they lived, but most of the time no one showed up. Unfortunately, no one wanted these children and now the psychiatrists were telling the staff they could no longer hug the children because the child abuse laws were being enforced. Teachers were being accused of child abuse and no one wanted to lose his or her job, so teachers began to turn their backs. But Michael couldn't turn his back.

"The day I can't hug one of these kids is the last day I'll work here."

Michael looked at his watch. The school bus was late. Through the years as a teacher and supervisor Michael had learned to expect the unexpected. He never knew what to expect from one day to another and this was going to be one of those days.

The bus pulled up at the stop rather abruptly, and out ran Sidney crying hysterically followed by the rest of the Special Education children crying and screaming for Michael to help them. The bus driver and matron got off the bus and refused to get back on unless the foul-mouthed troublemaker in the back of the bus was removed.

Michael was looking at a sixteen-year-old wannabe tough guy. There was a cult thing in certain parts of Brooklyn that young Italians boys mimicked characters in the movie *The Godfather*. Every one of these boys thought he was the don or related to the don. Everyone knew someone, and if you messed with him or her you were messing with the family. When you mentioned the family that meant you were connected, and being connected meant you were in the Mafia.

For the most part, the only thing these kids were connected to was the organ between their legs or their parents' purse strings. These young wannabes chose to be ignorant. They drove around parts of Brooklyn, especially Bensonhurst, in their parents' Cadillac or Mercedes spouting lines from the movie *Grease, The Godfather,* or De Niro in *Taxi.*

"Yo, how you doing?"

"Yo, you talking to me?"

"Yo, wise guy, you know who you're talking to?"

The sixteen-year-old boy in front of Michael in the back of the school bus was the epitome of the wannabe in a black leather jacket, slick black hair, a $200 pair of cowboy boots, and a cigarette hanging off his lip. He had a large golden lion's head diamond ring on his index finger. Three months ago he had been suspended from the regular high school for selling drugs and bringing a gun to school. His suspension was over, but the high school didn't want him, so the system, in its infinite wisdom, placed him in Special Ed with children who were defenseless against such hoods.

Michael looked at him with disgust. He looked like some of the young hoods that he grew up trying to avoid in Red Hook, the ones that hung out with the Gambino and Genovese families.

"The first thing I want you to do is to take that cigarette out of your mouth and get off this bus."

"Who the fuck are you? Do you know who I am?"

Michael was trying to bite his tongue. "I'm saying this again. I want you to take that cigarette out of your mouth and I want you to get off this bus."

"Who the fuck is going to make me, you?"

In a flashback, all Michael could see was Nicky Genovese's face, with a bullet hole in his forehead, and Ciclopi on his knees, begging for forgiveness.

"I am not going to tell you again. If you don't do as I say, I am going to shove that cigarette into your mouth and then I'm going to drag your ass off this bus. Do you understand that?"

"If you lay one fucking hand on me I'll sue you, and besides, my father will come up here and kick your fucking ass."

Michael had had as much as he could take. He slapped the cigarette out of the boy's mouth and proceeded to drag him over every bench seat from the back of the bus to the front. By the time Michael had dragged the young hood out onto the sidewalk the young boy was crying and his leather jacket was ripped apart.

"I'm going to kill you, you motherfucker. When my father comes here tomorrow he'll blow your fucking brains out, you cocksucker."

He kept ranting and raving as Michael instructed the security guard to cuff the youth. Meanwhile the Special Ed children, the bus driver, and the matron were elated that the bad guy lost and the good guys got revenge.

As security was taking the boy away Sidney went up to him and asked him when he was born.

"You fucking retard, get out of my face!" he screamed.

The very next morning a special hearing was quickly assembled by Marvin Cohen, the administrator of the Department of Mental Health of Staten Island. John Lieter had received a telephone call at his home. Evidently the kid's father's attorney, Tony Calvecchio, was also the attorney for mobster John Gotti. The father had called and demanded that the person who had abused his client's son be fired. John Lieter was sure a child abuse allegation would come of it and, even worse, a lawsuit.

John was a conservative Jew from Crown Heights, and the inception of a mental health facility on Staten Island had been his dream. When John's daughter was born autistic, John went on a mission to raise millions of dollars to build a facility to help Special Ed children. John's father was a successful jeweler on

Canal Street until he ran into a streak of bad luck betting on the trotters.

Mr. Lieter's bookmaker worked for the Gambino family, which turned out to be a good thing. The Gambino family needed another way of laundering cash from their illegal business. Buying diamonds on the open market with cash from their prostitution ring worked out well for the Gambino family, but placed a heavy burden on the elder Mr. Lieter. He kept finding himself more in debt to the Gambino family. So one early February morning, he walked into his jewelry shop, put the gun to his head, and pulled the trigger.

When John was getting the bids to begin building the mental health facility on Staten Island, he received a visit from the Gambino family. They wanted John to award the contract to G & G Builders. And even though G & G were the highest bidders for the project, they were given the job. John had to make good for his father's so-called debts.

The principal, Mario Biaggi, was hot-tempered, had been in the system a long time, and knew how to play politics. Mario had managed to work the system well. He was the principal of three different sites on Staten Island, but his biggest prize was the mental health facility. And he wanted it to look good—that's why he had placed Michael in charge.

In private Mario would tell his supervisors, "I don't fucking care what you do, I want complete control of our schools. Do what you have to do to keep order. The last thing we want is a riot like they had in Bedford Stuyvesant." Mario was referring to Jefferson High School, which was looted and set on fire by the students.

Michael looked at Mario and John Lieter sitting across the conference table. "For God's sake, Michael, couldn't you have controlled yourself? He's only a fucking kid." No sooner had Mario finished uttering those words than the secretary opened the door and stuck her head in the conference room and said, "There's an irate man on the phone who wants to talk to the effin' person that beat up his son."

The phone was in the middle of the conference table and Michael went to pick it up. John said, "Don't pick it up; we could be involved in a lawsuit."

Michael picked up the phone and put it on speaker so that everyone could hear the conversation.

"Hello, can I help you?" Michael said.

"Are you the fucking asshole who likes to beat up on kids?"

"What can I do for you?"

"What can you do for me? How about if I come there and kick your ass in for starters?" Michael didn't get a chance as the father became louder and started screaming, "You know who I am?"

Michael said, "No."

"I'm Big Paulie Genovese. I'm from Red Hook. We get guys like you and make them into meatballs, you fucking pussy. When I get through with you, you're gonna wish you never heard of the Genovese family."

"Hey, Paulie, I'm from Red Hook too."

"Yeah, wise guy? Where in Red Hook?"

"Sackett Street."

"You from Sackett Street?"

"Yeah."

"What's your name?"

"Michael Parisi."

"You related to Big Tony?"

Michael took a deep breath. "Yeah, he's my uncle."

There was silence on the other end for a moment as Mario, Marvin, and John just stared at Michael.

Paulie calmed down. "Well, every once in a while he needs a beating."

"Who, my uncle?"

"No, no, my kid. He's got a big mouth. Hey, Michael, were you related to the Prince?"

Michael hesitated for a moment as he got choked up a bit, not expecting this question. "He was my father."

CHAPTER 34

Red Hook, Brooklyn, 1960

It was an unusually warm night in late April, and it seemed all of Red Hook had come to see their prince for the last time. Scotto's funeral parlor was filled with flower arrangements from the Longshoremen Association and from other names Michael had never heard of. It seemed as if there were hundreds of Western Union letters from Sicily expressing their sympathy.

And then there were the flowers from the ex-governor.

When Harold Wilson walked into Scotto's funeral home, Michael couldn't believe his eyes. Seeing Harold and his mother, Anna, together brought back the past. For the first time he realized whose car he had pretended to be asleep in in the back seat when he was six years old. It all made sense now—the limo picking up Michael and Santa in Bergen Beach and Anna living in a swanky apartment in Brooklyn Heights.

Michael looked at Anna. At thirty-nine she was as stunning as ever. She did not look like Michael's mother and she certainly didn't act like it either. Anna had never wanted to be a mother. In Jacksonville when she found out she was pregnant she had tried to abort the child. Had it not been for Neddy and Big Ben, Michael would never have been born. Anna had left Giuseppe heartbroken, knowing the one thing Anna wanted more than anything else was money.

The funeral went on for three days as the mourners poured in. Michael just wondered who these people were and if they really knew his father, but it was out of respect that they came. And because they were Sicilian.

They came from Bensonhurst, Carnarsie, Little Italy, and Hell's Kitchen. They were mostly dock workers and their families, but there were others who knew the family in Sicily and there were some who had just heard the stories and wanted to see the Prince of Sackett Street.

They came because they knew of the benevolent Barone Salvatore Parisi di Floristella, Giuseppe's grandfather. And they knew Michele, his father. And they came because they knew that Gaetano Giuliani, the Robin Hood of Sicily, was there in spirit.

Santa sat next to Michael for most of the time as he stood to greet the mourners. They offered their condolences. "*Mi Dispiace*" or "*Sono molto thristi.*" Some could not say anything but just cried. They all just wanted to pay homage to this humble man.

When Big Tony and Blackie came to offer their respects to Santa, she got up slowly. In a powerful voice for all to hear she went on a rampage as only a hurt peasant woman who has been holding her sorrow in for years can express. *"Disgraziato, figlio di putani, bestia. Male occhi tu e tutti la tua razzi. Hanno marzarto mio Giuliani."* And then she spit in their faces.

Michael tried to calm her down. *"Nonna, basta,* enough!"

Michael continued to plead with her, but to no avail. No one could stop the pain she felt in losing her Giuliani, and she blamed the traitors, Turiddo and his father Don Carlo. And if everyone hadn't known then, they knew now, that Big Tony was Turiddo's son. He had raped Santa's sister, Rosa.

"Che hanno fatto a Giuseppe, questo caffone, un baccala." Then she exploded on how Big Tony had cruelly treated Giuseppe.

"Basta, Santa." Don Pasquale came over to help, but she wouldn't stop.

Big Tony and his son were so humiliated that they had to leave the funeral parlor to the pleasure of many, including Luigi Parisi. But this funeral was also a celebration for Luigi (Parisi) Genovese. As the Genovese and Gambino families were ushered in and out, mixing with the Anastasias and Castellanos from Staten Island, Luigi was anointed as Don Luigi, a head of a family. To the side of the funeral parlor they hugged and kissed, and Luigi became a made man. He would now be the one to control the piers.

When the last of the mourners left, Michael was alone at the coffin when Luigi, Don Pasquale, and the new head of the five families in New York, Paul Castellano, came over. Castellano approached Michael. "We know what you have been through and we want you to know that you are not alone, we are here for you. Whatever you need, you will let us know. Your father wanted you to go to college. The ILA will pay for it for you. We have set up a college fund for you, and when you graduate, if you want, you will have a position with us."

Don Pasquale was the last one left. "Can I tell you something in confidence?" They both smiled, and Don Pasquale put his arms around him. "You must never come back here. Your father was right, if you stay here, you will wind up like my son Frankie."

Don Pasquale had tears in his eyes as he started to walk away. "I don't want to see you anymore. Do you understand that? If you come back, I will have nothing to do with you. *Capice?*"

When everyone left he was alone with his father. He took out Claudia's letter. It had been wrinkled and some of the words he couldn't read because his father's tears had erased some of the ink. He went over to his body and placed the letter in his father's suit jacket and whispered to him, "I love you and I am sorry. Please forgive me."

"The more the world changes, the more it is the same."

❖ ❖ ❖

After the funeral Michael went back to the apartment on Sackett Street. He lay there in his bed completely exhausted and thought long and hard. What was he going to do? What road would he take? If he went to work for the family he would be set for the rest of his life. But how long would the rest of his life be?

And now he heard Don Pasquale telling him that if he stayed, Don Pasquale would have nothing to do with him.

He was exhausted, but he looked through the Western Union wires from Sicily and stopped when he saw her letter. "*Carissimo* Michael, *mi dispiace che e morto il suo padre* Giuseppe. (My dear Michael I am so sorry to hear that your father Giuseppe has died) Unfortunately I am not able to travel, but I want you to know that you are welcome here in Sicily. I would love to have you come and stay with us so you can get to know your Sicilian heritage.

Signed, Claudia Cavour, Piazza Agostino Parisi, 11 Acireale, Sicilia."

In the envelope was a plane ticket to Catania, Sicily.

With the letter still in his hand he was about to fall asleep when he heard a noise—maybe another rat. No, it wasn't a rat, it was Dorothy. The landlady had given her the key to clean up the apartment for Michael.

"Shh, don't say a word. I'm going to make all your pain disappear." Dorothy undressed and slipped under the covers and Michael forgot about everything except her, Mary Madison Brittain. She had never showed up at the funeral.

❖ ❖ ❖

CHAPTER 35

It was the summer of 1960 and it was hot and steamy in Jacksonville, Florida. Michael had left Brooklyn three months after Giuseppe passed away. He had been accepted to the University of Florida and was thinking of becoming a lawyer.

He found out where Big Ben and Neddy lived and showed up on their doorstep in the black section of Amelia Island, north of Jacksonville. Michael realized that if someone had not burned down his parents' gas station he would have been a southerner.

He stepped up to the picket fence and was surprised to see a neat-looking home with a vegetable garden in front. When he was about to knock on the screen door Neddy came to greet him.

"Oh my God, it's Joe's son!" she exclaimed. He was welcomed with open arms and quickly became part of the family

Ben had a little fishing boat. He fished all day, and when the fish weren't biting, he tended to their garden and the chickens. It was a simple way of life and Michael grew to love it.

Santa would have loved it too. Michael called her every week on Sunday and would try to sneak away to visit her during the holidays. She was getting a little senile and started repeating herself. Fortunately for Santa, Anna had left her apartment in Brooklyn Heights and moved in to take care of her mother.

Michael didn't ask any questions and Anna didn't offer any reason why.

Every Sunday, Neddy would make Italian sauce just like Joe and Anna had taught her, with the ground meat and breadcrumbs and fresh Italian parsley she cut from the garden. "Make sure you put in two eggs and mix it up," Anna had taught her. Neddy made the best meatballs in the South. Ben teased her, saying, "She cooks just like an Italian."

Every Sunday they invited their neighbors in for their traditional Italian family dinner. Everyone loved it, and Michael felt at home. Little Joe and Samuel were twins and the same age as Michael. They were both six feet three inches and weighed over two hundred and fifty pounds. They took Michael under their wings.

But things really didn't heat up until that second summer when the Johnson family came by. They brought their niece, Missy, from Charleston. It was obvious that Missy was mulatto, and at eighteen she was the most beautiful thing on Amelia Island.

Michael and Missy quickly became friends one afternoon while they were crabbing on Ben's dock.

"Are you in the Mafia?" she asked.

"Why do you say that?"

"Because some folks say you're Sicilian and all Sicilians are in the Mafia. They also say you're hiding out because you killed someone in New York. Is that true?"

"Well, if I say to you that you're a black person and all black people are just a bunch of lazy bastards, is that true?" he retorted.

"Now looka what we have here. You are a cocky Sicilian, aren't you?" Missy stood up and put both her hands on her hips and fussed at him. "And you better be careful who you calling black because you ain't no white boy."

"Do you like white boys?" The question caught her by surprise. She looked at him with her green eyes like daggers aimed at him.

"Now let me tell you something, Mr. Smarty Pants. I hate white people and I'm beginning to dislike Sicilians."

"Look, I'm sorry. I didn't mean to offend you." Michael could see he had hit a sore spot. "I just don't like it when people think because I'm Sicilian I'm in the Mafia. I guess I hate the Mafia as much as you hate white people."

There was a good reason why Missy hated white people, especially white men. And she told him the story of her mother being raped one night by five drunken members of the Ku Klux Klan in Charleston, South Carolina.

They never finished their stories that afternoon on Big Ben's dock because Neddy called them in for pasta and meatballs. At the end of dinner the Johnsons had to go home. Mr. Johnson had to get up early to tend to his farm and Missy asked to stay and help Neddy clean up. Michael volunteered to walk her home.

There was a beautiful full moon, and they watched their shadows walking closer and closer until they touched. By the time they reached the Johnson cottage, she reached out for his hand and he kissed her on the cheek and she kissed him on his lips and said, "Now I'm looking forward to this summer."

'Me too," he whispered.

That summer was filled with fishing for snappers with bamboo poles at the creek, diving for conch, gigging for flounder, and baiting for shrimp. Missy would make lunch for the two of them and they spent their time on the deserted beach beside the "Colored beach only" sign.

She told him of her family. That they had been taken from noble tribes in Africa, sold into slavery, and brought to the islands and sold again to a wonderful, rich Charleston family. And how her family survived and flourished under the benevolent owners.

And he told her about Santa, Giuliani, Don Ciccu, Florianna, his father, and Claudia, and he read the letter Claudia had sent him when his father had passed away.

She was excited. "I feel that I know these people, and especially Santa. Now let me tell you, she could give us black folks a lesson or two. Nobody is going to get anything over on her."

Michael smiled. He looked at her and couldn't help but compare her to Mary Madison. Missy was different; her skin was as tan as his and she would point that out as the summer went on, how much darker he got.

"Are you sure you don't have any black blood in you?" she teased.

Her eyes were green, she had high, shiny cheekbones, her hair was short and curly, and she was almost as tall as he was. When she came out of the water she looked like one of those exotic models in *Vogue*. Her skin was smooth to his touch, and when they kissed, her lips were soft and wet.

One night Big Ben and Neddy offered to take the entire family out to eat at their cousin Randolph's restaurant called "Fried Fish Only." It was the only thing on the menu and thus it became the name of the restaurant. Cousin Randolph's son, Leroy, worked as a waiter, and he and Michael had become best friends.

When they walked in, Michael smiled and gave Leroy a wink and Leroy winked back. As they settled down around the large table, Leroy came over to the table and pointed to the sign "Blacks only."

Missy quickly responded, "Are you kidding? He ain't leaving."

"Ma'am, it's not him that has to leave, it's you." Everyone started laughing except Missy.

"Now let me tell you something, you little smarty pants." And with a smile on her face she winked at Michael. "Like my Sicilian grandmother Santa says, it takes six people to take a dead person out. Can you imagine what it's going to take to get me out of this restaurant?" And Missy started laughing.

She looked at Michael and winked again. "Santa would be proud. You can't fool me either."

The next summer, Michael started playing baseball in the South Jacksonville league with Samuel and Little Joe. It was an all-black league but they allowed Michael to play because, as the locals said, "He must have some black blood. Look how dark his skin is."

Back in New York Sam Peppe never made it as the starting first baseman for the New York Yankees. He was shot to death, being in the wrong place at the wrong time. Hanging out with the *caffone*.

Michael tried to forget about Brooklyn. He tried to forget about everything. His team was playing the Jacksonville Yankees at home. It was the last game of the summer and this was for the championship of the league.

Michael was at the plate. With two runners on, he hit a shot over the center fielder's head and the ball rolled to the fence. The two runners scored and Michael was waved around third base. The shortstop got the relay throw and threw a perfect strike to the catcher, and as Michael slid in, they collided. The ball trickled out of the catcher's mitt. "Now I'm sure that white boy has some black blood, look how he runs." Little Joe was laughing

Michael was dusting himself off and was being congratulated by his team when Samuel pointed out the white woman behind the fence. "Michael, I believe you have a fan."

"How do you know she's my fan?"

"Because no white woman would ever come and see us black boys play."

He looked up and saw Mary Madison. She was the epitome of a young, beautiful, southern lady on a Sunday afternoon. Michael walked over to her, and with each step he wondered what he would say to her and if he had any more feelings for her. She looked sad.

"This is a long way from Charleston. What are you doing here?"

"This doesn't look like Brooklyn." And she smiled at him.

He was glad to see her, but when he looked in the distance he saw the red Cadillac convertible with a man smoking a pipe waiting patiently.

"How did you know I was here?"

"Some people said there was some white prince playing baseball on a Negro team, and I just had to see that for myself."

"Well, some people don't know what they're talking about. There's no white prince here, just us black folks."

She took a deep breath. "I just want you to know— if you ever need anything, just let me know. I will always be there for you."

"I have everything I need right now." Michael hesitated, looked around at his teammates, who had stop playing and were curiously watching, and at the driver in the red Cadillac. "I waited for you that night."

"I can explain."

"I think almost two years is a little too late for explanations, don't you?"

Mary Madison couldn't talk anymore. As the tears welled up she took out a little package and handed it to Michael. Michael opened the little box. Inside was a golden horn and a note. "Remember the night you thought you lost your horn? I found it; it got caught in my sweater. You will always be my prince and I will always love you. One day you will find those castles in Sicily."

When he looked up she was running to the car.

Mary Madison Brittain had become Mary Madison Cooper of the prominent Charleston family of Lord

Ashley Cooper. Her husband, Mathew Cooper, was running for governor in the fine state of South Carolina.

Mary Madison had never showed up at Michael's father's funeral because Harold Wilson did not want her to. Though Mary Madison finally realized that it was Giuseppe who was the dark, handsome stranger in that photo with her mother, what she still didn't know was that Giuseppe was her father.

Mary Madison had been leaving her grandfather's townhouse in Brooklyn Heights that night to meet Michael. She was in love, and when Harold Wilson found out he went into a rage. But the master puppeteer knew he needed to calm down and think what to do.

As she was leaving, he calmly called Mary Madison into his study. "Mary Madison, please sit down, I need to speak with you." She sat down, checking her watch. She couldn't wait to see Michael.

"We must leave immediately for Charleston. I have our plane tickets and my car is waiting for us." Harold had set the scene and was about to deliver the punch line. "Your life is in danger here. Michael is a marked man and you do not need to be around him.

"What are you talking about? Michael is not in the Mafia." What Mary Madison didn't know was that Harold was about to put a contract out on Michael's life if Mary Madison didn't make the right decision.

"Look," Harold was about to deliver the knock down punch, "your mother is on the line." Elizabeth was on the line as Harold had planned, and when he handed over the phone to Mary Madison, he said, "Giuseppe Parisi is your father."

Mary Madison was speechless as she took the phone from her grandfather and listened to her mother. She heard every other word as her mind went blank. She hung up the phone and said nothing.

"That's why I've been discouraging you to see this Michael. He is your half-brother" If looks could kill, Harold had it. The master puppeteer had regained his control and was happy for now.

CHAPTER 36

Sunday dinner was the same as usual except that the boys were celebrating their win over the Jacksonville Yankees and Michael was the surprise hero.

Missy was sad, for she knew he would be going back to college and she would be going back to Charleston to start nursing school. When the dinner and celebration were over, it was later than usual. They took their time walking back to the Johnson cottage, stopping to kiss.

Missy had seen him talking to the white girl at the ballpark but had never mentioned it to Michael. Now Missy stopped and looked into his eyes. "I just want you to know I never felt about anyone the way I feel about you."

He stopped her and put his fingers on her lips. "I know. I feel the same way." They kissed and each kiss became more passionate.

When they reached the cottage they could not let go of each other. She quietly led him to her bedroom and they made love for the first time. For the next two years they looked forward to spending the summers together.

In September 1964, Missy was killed in a civil rights march in Salem, North Carolina, and her body was brought back to Amelia Island. As Big Ben was leading the small congregation out of the church, the pallbearers stopped in front of Michael and Little Joe motioned for Michael to take his spot.

He looked up with tears welling in his eyes. Choking up, he could barely say, "Thank you."

It was a humbling and eye-opening time in his life. Growing up in Red Hook, he really never felt comfortable being with the young, macho Italians. He avoided them, but he especially avoided his father's family like the plague.

When Giuseppe died, Michael was on his own. But the best decision he made was to listen to his father: "Michael, when I die, I want you to leave here and go to my friend Big Ben in Florida. He will take care of you."

Take care of him was an understatement. They had become the family he didn't have. They were the salt of the earth. They were like Santa.

A year after Missy's death, Michael was in law school in Atlanta when he got the phone call from Anna that Santa was dying. He rushed back to New

York and stood by her side for three days before she passed away. It was at the funeral that he met Linda Favata. Four years earlier, her family had come right off the boat from Bari, Italy, and moved next door to Santa's apartment.

They dated for a month, and Linda's father thought it was time for them to set a date to get married. Michael had decided to enroll in New York University to get his law degree. He was living in Santa's apartment and working as a substitute teacher in Bedford Stuyvesant, Brooklyn.

After a short engagement, Michael and Linda were married. Michael wasn't in love with Linda. Of the two women he did love, one was dead and the other was married to the governor of South Carolina. Linda was comfort; she gave him the stability in life that he needed and that had been missing since Giuseppe passed away. When he finished law school, he opened a small office on Staten Island, in the black and Hispanic section of Castleton. He couldn't afford to stop working as a teacher, because he couldn't support his family on the income from his law practice.

Sixteen years after he married Linda, Michael found himself in a marriage that was falling apart, an educational system that was in turmoil, and a son who wanted to be a wannabe—and an offer he couldn't refuse...

Paul Castellano had become *"Capo di Capo,"* head of the five families, and needed help to operate his business. Paul was going legitimate and wanted to get away from the stereotyped Italians. He was looking to assimilate into the American pie.

The meeting was held at Marco Polo restaurant in Red Hook. Luigi set it up, since Don Pasquale was in a nursing home on Staten Island.

As Michael stopped the car in front of Marco Polo, the young attendant said, "Leave your car here, Mr. Parisi, I will park it for you."

When Michael walked into Marco Polo restaurant he was immediately transformed back to Italy. The walls, made of red brick, are adorned with beautiful hand-painted murals of Venice. The handcrafted arches around the doorways were made from custom hand-painted tiles. Antique chandeliers from the island of Murano hung from the ornate walnut-beamed ceiling. The waiters wore tuxedos and spoke with very heavy Italian accents.

"Signore Parisi, your table is in our private dining room in the back." When Michael stepped into the back dining room he was surprised.

Phil Dressler was there to greet him. *"Ciao, paisano, come stai?"*

"Your Italian is much better, *Paisano."* And they embraced.

"What are you doing here?"

"I didn't leave the neighborhood like some person I know."

"Don Pasquale didn't give me much choice." Michael knew Phil was teasing him. They were still close friends and they shared a past and a secret.

"Okay, okay." Phil was teasing him. "I'm Mr. Castellano's accountant and I'm here to make you an offer you can't refuse." The movie *The Godfather III* had been out awhile and everyone was using its most famous line.

Michael had resigned from the board of education after the incident with the Genovese kid, and devoted all his time to his law practice.

Michael recognized Mr. Castellano immediately since he had been at his father's funeral. And of course his cousin Luigi was there, and they embraced and kissed. A large bodyguard stood by the door, and he acknowledged Michael. He was a massive man with large hands. As he embraced Michael he said in a rough voice, "My name is Paulie Genovese. They call me Paulie G."

Michael looked at him. "So you're the father of—"

He didn't let Michael finish. "Mr. Parisi, I'm so sorry. I apologize again."

"No need, how is he doing?"

Paulie G. lowered his head. "He's in jail."

"I'm sorry."

Phil interrupted, "Come on, let's sit down and eat." There was a feast before them.

Phil Dressler could not marry Sophia Loren, but he did the next best thing: he married Dorothy Tuscano. Dorothy turned out to be the perfect loyal, voluptuous Italian wife for Phil and mother of their four children. After the meeting that day, Michael was asked to be godfather to their fourth child and first daughter, Sophia Dressler.

The day of the christening of little Sophia started out as a joyful occasion. It was early April, and the dandelions were blooming. Phil and Dorothy had selected the cathedral at the Mission of Mount Loretto as the church to baptize baby Sophia. It was where they had sent Dorothy to chill out after Nicky Genovese beat her up and forced her to have an abortion.

"I thank God I didn't have his baby," Dorothy said. And so did Phil and Michael.

Little Sophia was dressed in white like a little bride. Michael was holding her and standing between Dorothy and Phil. As the priest poured the holy water over the infant's head, Phil placed his arm around Michael. "I'm so glad you're back."

When the ceremony was over, they paused for pictures on the front steps of the cathedral. Michael was still holding Sophia, and Dorothy whispered in his ear, "You make a handsome godfather."

Michael smiled as the family members took pictures. "Thank you, and you are a beautiful mother."

"Do you remember our first night together?" Dorothy smiled. "You thought it was a rat creeping around."

"Some rat," Michael smiled.

"Phil told me they arrested Mary Madison's husband, the governor, in South Carolina for dealing drugs."

"I read something about it."

"Phil says Mr. Castellano thinks a lot of you. He's trying to get away from the old wise guy types and businesses. And he thinks you should run for borough president of Staten Island. And who knows? Maybe in four years Senator Marchi will be retiring..."

"I'm not too sure about that. I'm still thinking about it."

"Phil also told me that your marriage is on the rocks."

"Does Phil tell you everything?"

"Almost. There's one thing he hasn't told me." She smiled and toasted his glass.

"What's that?"

"Did you and my husband kill Nicky?"

"If I told you no would you believe me?"

"No."

As Dorothy was about to walk away, she asked one more question. "Did you go to Sicily?"

❧ ❧ ❧

CHAPTER 37

Red Hook, Brooklyn, 1960

The day after his father's funeral, Dorothy was still sleeping in his bed. He left her a note: "I need to find my family in Sicily. I will never forget you." With the plane ticket to Catania in his hand, which Claudia had sent him, he was off to Sicily.

As the plane flew over Reggio Calabria, the pilot announced they were approaching Sicily. Michael looked out the window and before him was the mountain, Etna, puffing rings of white clouds in the distance. It was more stunning than Santa had described. Mount Etna started at the calm blue-green Ionian Sea and slowly made its way up among the green rows of citrus groves and grape vineyards, mixing with fields of orange poppies and intertwining with yellow wildflowers up to the black fields of smoking red-hot lava.

He rented a Vespa, and with Claudia's recent letter in his back pocket, he took off to search for this castle in Sicily.

According to the map there were three routes to take from Catania to Acireale. Michael took the winding scenic road along the coast. He was in awe of the beauty of the island and its contrast to the ugly, dirty streets of Brooklyn.

The oleanders were shooting out their red blooms alongside the hibiscuses, and the scent from the orange and lime groves along the curving road was intoxicating. He was captivated by the majestic mountains to his left and beautiful towns nestling down from them to the sea. It brought a smile to his face as he enjoyed this beautiful adventure.

"Oh my God, I never thought it would be so beautiful."

He stopped three times and asked for directions and each time he was surprised at how good his Italian was. And why not? Between Santa, his father, and Don Pasquale, he had had the best teachers. And with each stop, his heart would pound a little harder as he got closer.

When he turned onto the Piazza Parisi, he saw the castle at the far end. As he drove down the cobbled pavement his heart pounded with every bump in the road.

All he kept saying to himself was, "I don't believe I'm doing this."

It was a magnificent structure built over three hundred years ago. The driveway to the three-story portico was lined with royal palms, a gift from a sultan from the Ottoman Empire. The gardens were well manicured and reminded Michael of a botanical garden in Brooklyn. A massive wall to protect the spectacular opulence of a bygone era enclosed the entire grounds.

He rang the solo bell on the outside wall and could hear it echo into the castle. A soft but affirmative voice answered, "*Che sai?*"

"*Sono* Michele Parisi, I'm looking for my family in Sicily."

"*Aspetti*, wait a minute." The gates opened, and Michael drove his Vespa slowly up the driveway, taking in the ambiance amidst deep breaths.

No sooner had he put the kickstand up than the massive wooden door opened. He was greeted by a kind voice. "*Signore* Parisi, my name is Raiggie." He was from Bombay and was in charge of greeting people, cooking, cleaning, and taking care of Claudia.

"Let me take your bag. You will need to refresh yourself before we have lunch." He spoke British English.

When Michael was refreshed, he walked slowly down a long corridor that joined one massive room to another. The hand-carved wooden doors were at least twelve feet high and there were another ten feet to the arched ceiling. Paintings adorned the dimly lit corridor, and as he looked closely he saw that the artists were Gianni Parisi and Michele Parisi. Many of them were icons depicting scenes of castles and villages along the coast with scenes of peasants working and explosions from the mouth of Etna.

There was a portrait of Maria Parisi on a white Arabian horse in a vineyard in Corruth. And a photo of her and Don Ciccu sitting on a chair—and it went on and on. The history of the Parisi family was being preserved by someone who cherished it.

In the dining room were two massive oil paintings, one of Barone Salvatore Parisi and the other of Gabriella Conti Parisi. And on a mantel below Salvatore's portrait was a photo of Florianna.

When the swinging doors opened, Michael was surprised to see the two people in front of him. The gentleman introduced himself and his wife: "*Sono Orazio Parisi III di Floristella e' questa e mio molglia*, Lina." They were both diminutive in stature, but he spoke in a powerful voice. She was smoking a cigarette and the ashes were about to drop when she walked over to Michael and kissed him.

"You are welcome as our guest," she said in broken English.

They sat down at the carved wooden table to eat; the very same table that the barone and his family sat at years ago. Instead of the beautiful Florianna serving, it was Teresa Zapala, the chubby maid and cook who was missing a few teeth. Michael thought she had the most beautiful voice, and she sang the old Neapolitan songs that he and his father had listened to every night while they played briscola.

Teresa had served the family for many years. She loved her job and she loved doting on Michael. "Michele," she called him in Sicilian, "you are so handsome, *sciatuzzo*. Here, have some more wild mushrooms and risotto. I make it just for you."

She reminded him of Santa, and why not? She was a simple Sicilian peasant.

Michael would soon find out that Orazio II was the oldest son of Barone Salvatore Parisi. Even though Orazio II was the legal heir to the title, it was Michele, his younger brother, whom Salvatore had wanted to be head of the family.

When the dinner was done they retired to the parlor for espresso with anisette and Sicilian pastries served by Raiggie in his butler's attire.

"*Ammunini, facciamo un passagare a giardini.*" Unlike his father Orazio II, this Orazio was more charismatic and loved the Sicilian people, who in turn loved him. Orazio grabbed Michael's arm and ushered him out to the *giardini*. Once he showed him the gardens he said. "now let me show you our town."

Orazio used a cane to walk. He put his arm around Michael's arm not to balance himself but because it was the way Sicilians walked with each other. The men and boys would walk arm and arm together in the piazza, passing women and girls coming the other way. And if there was an exceptional looking *donna*, they paid their compliments.

"*Che bella, signora, che bella donna.*" It was like someone admiring a beautiful work of art. Orazio had an eye for the women. And they loved this adoring man who was so respected in this little town.

"Orazio!" they shouted when they saw him, or just called him "Barone." Not only did the women come over and hug and kiss him, but the men and children did too. He was respected by all, and he glowed with the honor. His small frame became erect with each accolade, and of course a kiss from a *bella donna*.

When they sat down in a café the owner quickly came out. *"Barone, non ho visto in tanto tempo, grazie per venire."* You haven't been here in a long time. Thank you for visiting.

Michael realized that Orazio had difficulties getting around and realized he had made this a special trip for him.

The café owner was curious and asked who this young man with Orazio was. Orazio replied that this was Giuseppe's son and Michele's grandson: *"Questo e* Michele Parisi, *di Stati Uniti. Figlio di* Giuseppe e'*nonno di* Michele."

"Bravo, che bello giovano, me piacere a coniscere—What a handsome young man, it's a pleasure to meet you," he said, kissed Orazio's hand, and proceeded to kiss Michael's hand.

After the gelato, Orazio told Michael, *"Allora ammunini,* okay, let's go."

Orazio was getting bored and needed more action and attention. So up the Via Emmanuel they went. The spectacular *via* was lined with little cafés, boutiques, shoe stores, novelty shops, and plenty of baby stores. And of course *ostarias,* where wines could be tasted before being purchased—or sometimes just tasted.

Michael knew this was where Maria, Rosa, and Santa had shopped as young girls and had fun being admired by the young boys as they strolled the *corso*.

Orazio thought the wines were "too sweet, too bitter, not enough body" and grabbed Michael's arm. "*Ammunini.*" Michael felt like he was shopping with Santa on Union Street.

It was about ten o'clock at night, but the streets were still full of people. At the end of the Corso Umberto they came to the large Piazza Nicolosi surrounded by wagons and carts that functioned as storefronts to sell anything from fresh fruit, to fresh meats, to fish, to household goods. It was ten times bigger than Union Street, but it had the same intensity, and the adventure of finding the best buy became a game. This was where Rosa had been crowned Queen of the Carnival.

Michael stopped at a vendor who was selling watches. "*Quando il prezzo?* How much?"

The vendor responded, "*Centro mille lire.*" Michael instinctively responded that this was too much. "*Troppo sai.*"

"*E quando voglie pagare?*" Michael turned to Orazio and asked him how much should he offer. And the game of bargaining began.

"*Ho fatto bene.*" Orazio complimented his bargaining skills, and Michael silently thanked Santa.

At the Piazza Nicolosi was an entrance to a beautiful park called Parco Vista Bella, and it lived up to its name. The view overlooking the rugged coast lined with villas and vineyards to the majestic town of Taormina was spectacular. In the center of the park was the bust of the three barones: Barone Franco Cavour, Barone Riccardo Conti, and Barone Salvatore Parisi—the heads of the three families of Sicily. And in many ways they resembled the five families in New York. Some were treacherous and would stop at nothing for power.

Orazio's grandfather was Barone Salvatore Parisi. The Parisi family was fortunate that King Ferdinand had bestowed upon them the property called Floristella.

As Orazio stood there admiring the bust of his grandfather, he told Michael the story of how a rare Greek coin was uncovered in an archeology dig between Agrigento and Syracuse. The coin was so rare that no one could place a value on it. So it went up on the auction block. There were three bidders: the international banker J. P. Morgan from the United States, King Emmanuelle from Italy, and Barone Salvatore Parisi.

After three days of bidding there were two left—J. P. Morgan and the barone. The barone won.

When the barone was asked why he wanted the coin he said, "Because it should not leave Sicily." When Salvatore died, the coin was put on special display in Syracuse, where it still makes its home. No one knows for sure how much the barone paid, but it was whispered that he could have bought half of the island of Sicily for what he paid for the coin.

When they asked Morgan to make a comment all he had to say was, "I lost to one crazy Sicilian."

When Orazio finished this tale, Michael detected a tear as he wiped it away. Orazio shouted, *"Ammunini, dommani e un alter giorna."* Tomorrow is another day.

Trying to fall asleep that night, Michael looked around the room and saw his grandfather Michele's paintings and realized he was sleeping in his grandfather's bedroom. Michael thought of his father lying there in the coffin. He remembered the bedtime stories Giuseppe had told him of this noble family in Sicily. At the time, Michael had found the stories difficult to believe, especially because they were living in a cold-water flat in the heart of Red Hook, Brooklyn.

He fell asleep thinking of Dorothy Toscano and how she eased his pain, and when he woke up in the morning, the first thing he thought about was Claudia. Where was Claudia?

❖ ❖ ❖

CHAPTER 38

When Barone Franco Cavour first held the infant Claudia in his arms he couldn't believe how beautiful she was. She instantly won over his heart. "Sometimes things happen for the best."

Franco's wife was Vita Conti, Alfredo Conti's sister. The Cavours had had a string of misfortunes, and with all their wealth and power and influence it made it seem worse, but hopefully now Claudia would change all that.

Franco Cavour was a fancier of wild animals. He had chosen Ragusa to retire to because he had inherited a magnificent estate that at one time belonged to a Roman emperor who had also been a fancier of wild animals.

Once an imposing villa had graced the estate, but Mount Etna had suddenly erupted, burying it along with its inhabitants. It lay buried in lava for hundreds of years until Franco Cavour's father, stirred by his desire to search out the past, began a massive excavation of the area. When Franco took over from his father he concentrated on the restoration of the villa. Drifting from room to room in this rambling villa, he could see life portrayed on the floors in vivid reds, blues, and flesh tones as it had been 1,600 years ago. There were charioteers lashing their teams around Circus Maximus in Rome; men loading elephants, camels, tigers, and rhinos aboard a Roman ship with its rigging portrayed in meticulous detail; a pagan priest in vestments offering human sacrifices to the Goddess Diana; a man leading two hounds around in collars and leashes as he watched beautiful naked women sunning on a beach.

Franco would point out the various expressions of placidity, pain, smugness, and astonishment revealed in these portraits and comment, "The more the world changes, the more it is the same."

He was proud of his estate and of his daughters. Antoinette and Laura were the pride of his life, but his scandalous son Philip had discredited the family. Philip, with his lack of manliness, was not a son Franco could be proud of, so he threw him out of his home, out of Sicily, and out of his inheritance. The one good thing his son gave him was the infant Claudia.

As luck would have it, his two daughters met misfortunes. Antoinette married Riccardo Conti in a prearranged marriage by his father, Alfredo Conti. This marriage was part of his overall plan for more power. The two families would combine their wealth, and their offspring would continue the noble Conti bloodline.

But the best-laid plans don't always go as planned. And so when their first- born was diagnosed as mongoloid and Antoinette could no longer bear children, it struck a major blow to the master plan.

And if that weren't enough, two months later when Laura was riding through the estate in Ragusa, her Arabian stallion bolted and took off, galloping through the woods. Laura frantically tried to restrain the horse, but she was not capable of holding back the mighty beast.

The day of the funeral, *Signore* Cavour took his loaded Lupera down to the stables and blew the head off the stallion.

With the cold fact that the family's bloodline would come to an end it became clear that Claudia must be the one to carry on the Cavour bloodline. And she would become part of the master plan.

Claudia grew up to be a "bijou," a jewel of nobility in Italy. She was educated in the finest schools, where the powerful Medici family once flaunted their wealth, in Florence. The Contis were proud descendants of the Medici bloodline and they now were the ones pulling the strings. Riccardo Conti had become the master puppeteer and he had Claudia on stage.

She was invited to the most prestigious events of the year on the continent. He paraded her around as if she were the most prized filly in an emperor's stable. At the age of seventeen she had her coming out party in Florence, and the opulence rivaled any noble wedding. All of the aristocratic families had come out to meet this newly crowned princess.

"So, Riccardo, what plans do you have for my daughter?" Franco had been blessed the last years with seeing her grow into a *bella donna*. She adored her father and when his wife, Vita, died, Claudia became his sole reason to live. Franco took her all over the continent, and it was only the best for his *bambina*.

"Franco, just watch." As they lined up properly to ask her to dance, Riccardo bent over and whispered into Franco's ear, "This is our stallion, the prince of Savoy, the son of the king of Italy." And what a handsome couple they made as the young prince proudly paraded her around the dance floor. The aristocracy whispered, "What a fine looking couple."

Even the king commented, "Riccardo, you sly little devil, if your intentions are what I think they are, you have done well. She is a thing of beauty."

Riccardo gave his brother-in-law a wink, and Franco's life and dreams for the moment were fulfilled.

But deep down in her heart Claudia knew that one day she would go back to Sicily, the place where she was born. Where life was simple and the people were warm and where she loved to swim. And it was where she first met him.

❖ ❖ ❖

Four years ago, when she was thirteen years old, Claudia first went to Acireale to visit her uncle Riccardo. It was the beginning of the summer, and the nobility were leaving Florence for their holidays in the south. Riccardo had invited his brother-in-law, who was mourning the loss of his wife, to his villa at the beach.

Claudia had been saddened by the loss of her mother. She grew up as an only child, and even though she had every material thing a young lady possibly could have, she was still lonely. In her solitude her heart cried out to someone who could understand; someone who knew her; someone who loved her for being what she wanted to be, not what she was being forced to become.

When she saw the large peasant families gathering for the celebration of the festivals and holidays, she watched the joy they exuded, the love and passion. They basked in the delight of the hot Sicilian afternoons and danced as the summer showers drenched them. They continued dancing and singing until the showers stopped and then they ate and drank and laughed until the children went to sleep. And then they made love.

There was no laughter in the Cavour villa and there was no passion in Florence. But Claudia knew one day she would find it, and the love of her life, in Sicily.

That first morning in Acireale the sea beckoned her to its shore. The fresh sea air was intoxicating. It was magical as it wafted in through the open window. The curtains started dancing like ballerinas and said, "Awake, my princess, and come with me, and you will find your dreams to be."

She loved writing poetry in her little brown notebook: "Walking down the winding steps to the sea, I came upon an old willow tree. I stopped to sit by its side, and felt its wisdom deep inside. He beckoned me to stay a while and told me not to despair, for one day, I will meet him here."

The early morning sun had risen to the center of the sky and it was time to go, but she needed to feel the coolness of the sea and taste the salt for her very first time. There were three little islands made of lava rocks within a good swimmer's reach.

Homer said this was where the Cyclops threw the rocks at Ulysses. She could see the children diving off the cliffs and into the beautiful blues and greens of the Ionian Sea. She looked around and marveled at the simple beauty of this ancient village of whites and pinks. Colorful villas nested down the cliffs, cuddling alongside the silver and green-leaf olive trees that had been there for hundreds of years. The tranquility engulfed her senses, captured her heart, and she knew this was where she wanted to stay.

At first the islands looked closer, but as she swam out a ways and looked back, the beach seemed so far away, but the rocks weren't any closer. She started to panic and cried out for help as she kept swimming toward the rocks. Her arms could not move anymore as she tried to keep her head up and yell once more before she went under for the last time.

She realized that she wasn't in very deep water and if she stood on the tips of her toes, she could jump up and down and breathe. But on her way down her foot got caught between two rocks and she couldn't come back up.

In her last moments before she thought she would die, she had a vision of a woman who was not her mother, holding her and singing in a beautiful voice and crying *"Ti amo, sciatu mio, ti amo."*

Claudia shouted out, "Mamma, Mamma," and drifted off as the salt water entered her young lungs.

She could feel something tugging at her feet and in an instant she was struggling to breathe. She felt an arm around her neck and could hear him saying, *"Respiro,"* begging her to breathe.

When Giuseppe dragged her limp body to the rock, he instantly started breathing into her mouth. He was frantic; it was the first time he had tried to save a drowning person. His father once saved his life and taught him how to give CPR, but when he looked at her face he saw that it was turning purple, and for a moment he thought she was dead. He started to pray. *"Dio mio,* please don't let this girl die, she is too young. Jesus, please?" Now he was breathing his soul into her body, and with every breath he took he pleaded with his maker.

He held her limp body in his arms and looked up and shouted to his God *"Auiti* me, help, please don't let her die, Jesus! If you let her live, I will take care of her forever. Please don't let her die, she is too young." He remembered when he was dying he promised his Lord that he would help save others if he would just give him another chance. And his father had saved him.

"Breathe, breathe," he pleaded.

She started to vomit up the sea and her blue eyes seemed to sparkle and smile at him. "Will you take care of me forever?" she said.

"Grazie, Dio." His prayer was answered, and so was hers as he smiled back.

Four years later, at the beginning of the summer, Europe was ready to explode, and Riccardo was anxious for the fireworks to begin. Italy had signed a pact with Germany and Austria-Hungary, called the Triple Alliance. Now that he controlled the sulfur mines, the Germans were assured of victory and control of the continent. And Riccardo, the master puppeteer, had all the strings in hand—for now.

In Sicily, she awoke in the same room overlooking the sea in Acireale. She had longed to go back, but between her father insisting she finish school in Florence and Uncle Riccardo prancing her around the continent, she had had no time to breathe. But she had plenty of time to think and dream and to write her thoughts down in her little brown book.

Sometimes those dreams were so real she saw herself drowning and someone coming from above to save her and then there was the lady holding her, singing to her. "I will not let you die, I will take care of you forever, you are my *sciatu mio.*" She shouted out, "Mamma!"

But now she was where she belonged. A place where she felt at peace, a place where she wanted to stay forever. The place she met him at the sea—the boy that brought her back to life and had promised "to take care of her forever."

She had anxiously waited for four years for this day to come. As she came upon the old willow tree, she stopped and put her arms around its trunk and secretly wished never to leave.

The summer was just beginning and the staff of the villas above the sea were opening the shutters and sweeping the leaves off the balconies. The gardeners were dusting off the clay pots and replanting the gardenia and hibiscus plants. The purple and red bougainvilleas had draped the villas over the winter, protecting them from winds. The smell from the sweet lemon flowers above permeated the hills and descended down to the sea.

She took a deep breath and whispered, "I am home."

She saw them on the island rocks, the local boys diving off the cliffs and into the sea. Her cousin

Philomena told her he would be there. As she waded into the water she wasn't the skinny little girl anymore, but a beautiful princess who had the passion of a peasant and a heart for one young man.

There was no problem this time reaching the island. As she got up, her long black hair was pulled back, revealing her gorgeous face with deep, dark blue eyes and high cheekbones.

She was the belle of Florence and the twinkle in the prince of Savoy's eye. "*Che bella*," the prince of Savoy said when he paraded her around the dance floor. "Are you spoken for?"

"No, Your Highness."

"Good, then you will be all mine for the rest of the night." And when he passed Riccardo he winked his approval. The marriage arrangements were being made as they continued to dance the night away.

She watched him dive from the cliff above and into the sea, and even from a distance she knew it was him. He was swimming back, and as he was climbing up and out of the water, she knew he was the one. "*Buon giorno.*" She smiled.

"*Conosco*? Do I know you?" He smiled back.

He looked better than she remembered, but more important, he still had those eyes. That was the first thing she saw when he saved her. They were sincere, they were warm and comforting, and she knew he was passionate when she heard him cry out loud for his God, "*Auiti* me," to help him save this girl.

"*Si.*"

"*Ma come?* But how?" he quizzed. She had aroused his curiosity.

"*Non ricordo?* You don't remember?" She teased.

"*Di judo,* no, I swear," but he was enjoying being teased.

She walked closer to him until they were face to face, "*Quada me occhi*—look into my eyes. *Sicuro che non ricordo?* Are you sure you don't remember?"

Now he was beginning to enjoy this mysterious beauty in front of him and the game she was playing.

"*Non ricordo che a ditto a mi?* You don't remember what you said to me?"

"*E che era?*"

"That you will take care of me for the rest of my life." No sooner had she got the words out than she embraced him, kissed him, and immediately dove into the water and started swimming to the beach.

It was like he had been hit by a lightning bolt—he remembered the little girl. He quickly dove into the sea after her, but it took a while for him to catch up. When he did, they stopped swimming and embraced one another, and he kissed her. "I don't even know your name."

"It's Claudia, Claudia Cavour."

"*Mio nomo e*—" He didn't finish before she stopped him.

"I know, it's Giuseppe," she smiled. "I have written it down so many times in my book."

When the second lightning bolt hit, all he could whisper was *"Dio mio"*

❖ ❖ ❖

CHAPTER 39

The next morning Michael could smell the espresso brewing in the kitchen as Lina and Teresa prepared breakfast, Sicilian style, grilling some leftover bread in olive oil with homemade fig and orange preserves. Michael woke up and just followed his nose and ears. Teresa was singing in the kitchen and Lina was grilling the bread while smoking a cigarette, and the ashes were about to drop into the pan.

"*Buon giorno.*" He smiled, feeling better and glad to be away from Brooklyn. His father, Giuseppe, had been dead almost a week, but it seemed so long ago and so far away.

"*Buon giorno,*" they sang in unison. "*Figlio beddo. Settede e mangi?*"

Lina and Teresa sat him down and surrounded him with love, the love he was missing.

The kitchen in the *castello* was bigger than his three-room railroad apartment in Brooklyn. When Michael was finished eating breakfast he found himself walking through the castle, and at every turn he came upon some painting or photo of the family and friends and guests who came to visit.

When Barone Salvatore lived, he entertained the royalty of the continent. They came from Germany and Austria and northern Italy. And once he even entertained Tsar Nicholas and his family from Russia. Back then they had come to Sicily for the weather and because the barone was picking up the tab. The lavish lifestyle they left behind was definitely not an issue once they got to Castello Parisi. Anyone entering the grounds was taken aback by the lush tropical gardens, the paths intertwined around the castle, and the centerpiece—the ornate fountain designed by the famous artist Pelligrino. In the distance were the *pescina,* the pool, and the tennis courts. It was said that the tsar had made a bet that he would beat Salvatore in a chess match.

The tsar was a competent chess player and liked to boast about it. He had recently beaten Chancellor Bismarck in a match that took all day and now he challenged the barone.

"Salvatore, let's see how good you are." Salvatore was up to the challenge and a side bet was made. But to the tsar's dismay he had to pay up, and pay up he did. Two Arabian horses were added to the barone's stables. Anastasia was named after the tsar's daughter and was considered the fastest horse on the continent.

The duke of Winchester had offered to buy the horse a year ago for a small fortune, but the tsar didn't like the British.

Michael looked at the ornately hand-carved chess pieces in the salon. On the marble mantel was another painting of Maria as a beautiful young woman riding a magnificent horse, but this was a different horse from the first painting he saw. The names under the painting identified Maria and her beloved mare Anastasia. Fascinated and enthralled with the history of this family, Michael wanted to know more.

Back in those days, the horse ride to the beach was always a favorite among the ladies. With a snow-covered Mount Etna smoking in the background, the ride through the vineyards and citrus groves down to the beautiful beach was enthralling. "This is the most beautiful place on earth," Martha leaned over and whispered to her husband, Chancellor Bismarck from Germany.

In the spring of 1892, Hugh Lupus Grosvenor, the first duke of Winchester and the richest man in Great Britain, came to visit the barone. He had heard of the barone's political friction with the king of Italy, how he had outbid the banker Morgan and beat the Russian tsar in chess. The duke had heard the barone had some of the finest Arabian horses in the world, and he wanted Anastasia. The duke was passionate about breeding thoroughbreds. For three years in a row his stables had won the Triple Crown in London. He brought his most prized mare, Gideon Hill, to Sicily for a challenge on his two hundred-foot private yacht.

The race would start from the *castello* and go to the sea and back. Maria begged her father to let her ride. They were in the kitchen.

"I can win, you know I can."

"But women don't race, it's not proper."

"Pappa, this is Sicily, not Florence."

"Don Ciccu, what do you think?" Salvatore always turned to Don Ciccu to support him with Maria. She was spreading her wings, and at seventeen she was in full plumage.

"I agree with your father. It's too dangerous."

"You see, Don Ciccu agrees with me."

"You two are becoming more and more alike. I can't stand either one of you. Florianna, what do you think?"

"I think your father and my son think like old Sicilian men. They probably believe women are like eggs, the more you beat them, the better they are."

Salvatore looked at his daughter and smiled, "*Va bene.*"

Don Ciccu was not too pleased that Salvatore had given Maria his permission, but he accepted the family decision. "*Va bene*, if you ride, you must stay behind at first going down to the sea and not make your move coming back until you are a hundred yards from the *castello*. Do you understand?"

"*Si*." She was ecstatic. She kissed her father and said, "*Ti amo*." And then she kissed Don Ciccu and said, "I love you too."

She didn't hear Don Ciccu whisper, "*Ti amo*."

They had two weeks to prepare for the race, and every day she and Don Ciccu would race to the beach and back to the *castello*.

"Remember, just stay close to Gideon Hill all the way, and when you see the gates of the *castello* you make your move. And do not use the whip, she will know. *Capisce*?"

"I understand. Now tell me why do you and my father treat me like a baby? I'm seventeen and have a mind of my own, but you two think I have to be protected all the time. I can think for myself!"

"Listen, Maria, you will always be the baby in your father's eyes."

"But what about you?" She had caught him off guard.

"I don't understand." He was trying to stall, not knowing where she was going. In the past few years he could not think of anyone but her.

"You know, I see you looking at me, and it's not the same look as my father's." She looked into his eyes, searching for the answer that she already knew.

"Maria, I'm like your brother," he retorted.

She stopped him, and with a smile on her face she teased him. "You know it's not the look that my brother Michele gives me."

Don Ciccu was getting uncomfortable. "You know, at this moment, I'm starting to think like a true Sicilian."

"And how is that?"

"A woman is like an egg. The more you beat her, the better she is." A shy smile came across his face.

"So you want to beat me? Let's see who gets back to the *castello* first." And she slapped Anastasia and the horse took off.

She beat him back to the *castello* and was waiting for him. When he got there she wanted to put her arms around Don Ciccu and kiss him, but she didn't. And he just wanted to hold her the way he had when she was an infant.

It was the first time she realized that she loved him. But she didn't tell him—until the day she thought she might lose him when he was about to fight Turiddo.

The day of the big race was an absolutely gorgeous April day. There wasn't a cloud in the sky, and Mount Etna stood majestically in clear view, still with some snow on its peak.

It was as if there was a carnivale in town. It seemed all of Acireale had shown up for this event. They stood three and four deep from the *castello* to the beach. Rosa and Santa were at the finishing line at the *castello*.

The duke was giving his last instructions to his young jockey, and Don Ciccu was trying to settle down a nervous Maria—all the while feeding Anastasia sugar cane. "Remember what I told you, stay back until the end."

As Santa watched Don Ciccu tending to Maria, she saw the same passion in their eyes that she and Giuliani had for each other. Giuliani told Santa that he would be there, and she was searching the crowd when she felt him behind her.

The starter shot the gun in the air and the horses were off. The duke and the barone sat next to each other on the makeshift grandstand. That day the barone and the duke became more than friends when they discovered they both knew the German chancellor's daughter, Heidi, intimately.

They became so engrossed in their conversation, laughing and slapping each other's backs that they almost missed the end of the race. As the horses entered the piazza, Gideon Hill was ahead by two lengths. With a hundred yards to go Maria made her move. She could see Don Ciccu at the finishing line in a bright red shirt waving his arms. She could feel Anastasia responding and moving up head-to-head with Gideon Hill. Then, in the last ten yards, she pulled away, and the crowd went wild. The barone's horse won and Maria was exhausted and thrilled. Anastasia proudly walked over to Don Ciccu for the sugar she knew he had for her.

"So that's how you win over the ladies?" Maria commented.

Don Ciccu smiled and gave Maria a wink. "I've come to realize that you get more results using sugar than the whip on some *donna*."

Maria just acknowledged him with a smile.

Gideon Hill's jockey came over and handed Don Ciccu the reins of his horse. "I believe she is yours."

That night the castle was lit up in all its glory and it seemed everyone with a title in front of his or her name was there, and even the ones without titles were welcomed. It would be the last time the castle hosted such a gala affair.

It was late in the afternoon, and while everyone was taking a nap Michael continued to explore the *castello* and all of its history and past grandeur. He found an iron spiral staircase that led to the roof. The *castello* had four turrets that towered over the town, and Michael stood atop the tallest one. He could see Etna smoking and covered with snow. As he turned and looked toward the sea, he could make out a path that made its way to the sea. It was the path on which Maria rode Anastasia to victory.

Only a few days ago Michael had buried his father. He remembered the stories Giuseppe had told him about his family being nobles and living in castles. Michael had never believed them. He hadn't cried at the funeral, but all of a sudden he realized how much his fathered sacrificed for him and how much he loved him. He went on his knees and started to weep. He tried to stop but couldn't.

✤ ✤ ✤

CHAPTER 40

When Orazio III and Lina got married in 1939 they had to move out of the castle. The war had reached Sicily and the Germans made the *castello* their headquarters in Sicily, and Orazio and Lina were forced to move out. The British bombarded it for months, but the *castello* withstood the onslaught. When the Germans left they raped the *castello*, tore up the gardens, burned down the stables with the horses inside, and took a piece of Sicilian history away never to be seen again.

When they came back after the Germans left, the *castello* was a shadow of the splendor it once was. Orazio held on to Lina and cried *"Desgraziata, animale!"* He fell to his knees and vowed to restore it. But what the Germans started, the communists and the socialists in Italy finished, and an aristocratic way of life was over.

The next morning Orazio shuffled into the kitchen with his cane in hand, Michael had just finished his breakfast. Orazio kissed him and sat down beside him. He seemed taller because Lina had placed five pillows on the seat. As they sat down for dinner the night before, Lina had to put extra pillows on Orazio's chair.

"Orazio is shrinking and one day he will disappear." Lina served him his tea and biscotti while Teresa sang and washed the dishes from last night.

"Allora, questo e' la programma che facciamo oggi, visitiamo con Claudia, che aspetta per noi, ma prima facciamo un gira." They were going to visit Claudia today.

Lina explained to Michael, "Claudia had an apartment on the second floor above the chapel of the *castello*. But now she is at her villa in Corruth and is expecting you to have lunch with her there today." Lina always repeated what Orazio said, trying to improve on her limited knowledge of English.

"Ammunini." He got up and grabbed Michael by his arm and off they went. The Fiat looked like it had seen better days, but it started up. Lina had placed about six pillows on the driver's seat so that Orazio could see above the dashboard, just barely. It was comical as he dashed in and out of traffic, his foot barely reaching the clutch and his arms just long enough to put it in second, beeping his horn to get the pedestrians out of his way and all along complaining that the people today didn't know how to drive.

But everywhere they stopped people embraced him and called him "barone." When they reached the *ostaria*, he instructed Michael, "Go into the trunk and get the empty soda bottles and bring them inside."

The owner quickly stopped what he was doing with another customer and began filling the bottles with the wines from his barrels. No one seemed to mind; in fact they were honored that he came in. They spoke of family members and the weather, and of course they were curious as to who Michael was. "*E famiglia*," he said proudly. Orazio and Lina had never had children, but family was everything to them and Michael was family.

"*Ammunini*." Orazio grabbed Michael and pulled him along, to the butcher and baker, to the fish store, to the *tabaccino*, and they were met with the same responses...

"*E che e questo giovanetto*? Who is this young man?"

"*E famiglia*," and he proudly smiled. Michael smiled, thinking how much this was like going shopping with his grandmother Santa.

When they were at the outskirts of Corruth Michael realized that they were at a special place. Florianna and Salvatore might have called it heaven, but Santa knew it was. The canvases of the artist Gianni Parisi showed an enchanting world in Corruth —the color of the Greek sea, the magma of Mount Etna, the gardens of orange blossoms and jasmine, a vibrant and explosive fantasy where nature in all its richness wrapped itself around this earthly paradise.

Orazio stopped talking and let the beauty speak for itself, and Michael just soaked it in. "Oh my God," he whispered to himself.

The Fiat turned onto a long and narrow driveway and followed the ruts in the dusty dirt road lined with lemon and orange groves. It was a long distance before the villa revealed its hypnotic beauty. When he stepped out of the Fiat, Michael felt he had entered an ancient civilization where the most basic of human instincts was to survive. And it was here that it not only survived, it flourished.

Four thousands years ago, people had left Greece in search of a new home. They had heard the stories of *The Iliad* and *The Odyssey* by Homer and the island of good and plenty, but it flourished beyond their imaginations. And the temples and theaters they built stand today, greater than they left behind, as a tribute to their tenacity.

Raiggie took the food and wine from the car and directed Michael to go to the covered patio as he and Orazio walked into the villa.

"*Aspetta per te.* She is waiting for you."

She was simple but elegant, and he was surprised that she was sitting in a wheelchair. She looked so fragile. She smiled and he felt he had known her all his life. At one time, she had aroused a king and accepted the proposal of a prince, but her heart had belonged to a peasant. When she spoke, it was as if she were angelic; her tones and cadence were that of someone who was not only from nobility, but someone who had suffered and understood the meaning of life.

At one time, when she smiled she had lit up the city of Florence. Now it was this young man before her, this young man whose father lit up her life and answered her prayers.

"*Mi dispiace che e morto tu padre.*"

"*Grazie.*" He went over and kissed her. He suddenly realized why she was in the wheelchair. She had no legs.

Tears welled up in her eyes and as she reached for tissues she touched her brown notebook. "One day I hope you will read this because I see him in you."

❖ ❖ ❖

CHAPTER 41

It was January third, 1986, and Michael had been in a coma for three days in a New York City hospital. The doctors didn't know if or when he would start responding to the medication. He could hear the voices surrounding him and didn't know if they were real or if he was dreaming or if he had died and was waiting for his placement in heaven or hell. Everything was spinning in slow motion in his head. He could hear her southern accent pleading for him to come back.

Three days before, on New Year's Eve, Michael was with Paul Castellano at the swanky uptown Manhattan restaurant, Sparks. He had been invited by Mr. and Mrs. Castellano to their New Year's Eve party. He was sitting at a table with Phil and Dorothy, Senator Marchi and his lovely wife, Matilda, and Don Pasquale.

It had been over twenty years since Michael last saw Don Pasquale at his father's funeral, where Don

Pasquale told him, "Leave New York," and if he came back he would have nothing to do with him.

Don Pasquale was fragile and at times incoherent. "Oh, can I tell you something in confidence?" Michael gave Don Pasquale a big hug. "I missed you, Michele."

Mr. Castellano had arranged for Don Pasquale to get out of the nursing home to be with Michael. The doctors said the cancer was spreading and he didn't have much time.

"I hear you go back to the old country," Don Pasquale said as he held Michael's hand tightly.

"*Si*, I try to go back as much as I can."

"*Bellissimo, ho trovato la famiglia?*"

"*Si, ho trovato la famiglia.*"

"Claudia?"

"*Si, ho trovato* Claudia."

Michael had divorced and, in the past three years, had gone back to Sicily and stayed with Orazio and Lina at the *castello*. He needed "*la famiglia*" and they had welcomed him into theirs.

Claudia never married the prince of Savoy as Riccardo Conti had planned because in the devastating volcanic eruption in 1914 she had been buried alive for three days in a pile of rubble with twenty other people. She had been running through the streets of Acireale looking for Giuseppe because she wanted to tell him that she was not going to marry the prince of Savoy and wanted to run away with him to America.

When she got to the Piazza Nicolosi the red, hot ashes came down like a thunderous rainstorm. Everyone took shelter in *Signore* Nicolosi's café. The café crumbled to the ground with the first shock that destroyed half the town.

Three days later, as they were clearing the debris, the rescuers found three people alive. One of them was a young lady that no one could identify, and her legs had to be amputated.

"Can I tell you something in confidence?" Michael smiled; Don Pasquale leaned over and whispered into Michael's ear, "I missed you very much." Tears started to well as Don Pasquale continued. "When my Frankie was killed I thought I would die. I had nothing to live for, but you came along and you were like my son. Those days we spent at the race track and Lundy's, I never forget, they were special because I had you all to myself."

Don Pasquale paused to wipe his tears, and Michael did the same. "I love you, Michael. I know Mr. Castellano has made you an offer; he's a good man, but remember you will be a puppet."

Don Pasquale paused. "Your father was never a puppet."

"I love you too, Pasquale. I now understand what you and my father warned me about, because now I'm a father and I warn my two sons about the same things. I don't want them to wind up like Frankie."

Michael paused took a deep breath. "And that's why I am not accepting Mr. Castellano's offer."

Don Pasquale got up and bent over to kiss Michael and whispered, "You are my Frankie."

It was only an hour away from midnight and the bandleader announced he had a request from a beautiful lady to play "A Summer's Place" for her prince. Everyone looked around as this beautiful woman walked over to Michael and said, "It's been a long time, my prince. May I have this dance?" Mary Madison looked over at Dorothy and winked "thank you." Dorothy had arranged it all.

Michael got up and she curtsied before him. "I missed you so much."

They were the only two on the dance floor, and everyone sensed this was very special. As the prince and his princess made their way around the floor, they were greeted with applause. It had been over twenty years since they had met in Lundy's.

Dorothy winked and Phil gave the thumbs up. Don Pasquale just looked up to the heavens and said "*Dio mio*" and clapped his hands and threw them a kiss. "*Aguri*."

She held him tightly and whispered in his ear, "This time I am not letting you go." She told him why she never showed up at his father's funeral.

She told him of the lie that her grandfather Harold Wilson had told her over twenty years ago. The lie that Giuseppe was her father and that Michael was her half-brother.

"I'm not going anywhere without you."

"Will you take me to Sicily to search for the castle?"

'I found the castle and a villa, and I think we will be happy there."

"I will be happy anywhere with you."

It was midnight, and the bandleader had counted down to one. "Happy New Year!"

The music played on. They just kept dancing and holding each other, neither one wanting to let go.

In the years that lead up to this long drama, Mary Madison Cooper had become the First Lady of South Carolina when her husband had been elected governor. At the swearing-in ceremony, Harold Wilson sat by his side. Harold was becoming frail, but he still was in control. Like Riccardo Conti, he had manipulated the people around him all his life for one purpose—more power, and with that came more wealth.

From Lucky Luciano, to Albert Anastasia, to Giuseppe Parisi, and now Paul Castellano, it was Harold Wilson who manipulated the strings. Even his daughter and granddaughter were brought into his tangle web of deceit. But it was Giuseppe Parisi who refused to be a puppet and had cut the strings just like

Spartacus who led a rebellion of Sicilian slaves who overthrew their masters. Just like Gaetano Giuliani, who refused to be controlled by the Italians.

But it would be Mary Madison who would get her revenge and end the reign of the puppeteer. She was almost forty and pregnant for the first time. The doctors had warned her she could not have children, but they were wrong. Harold was thrilled, especially when they found out it would be a boy. An heir to his throne.

They had even decided to name the boy Harold Wilson Cooper, and with that Harold had donated fifty million dollars to a search committee for Governor Cooper III's run for president of the United States. Everyone was happy, everyone, that is, except Mary Madison.

In her seventh month Mary Madison hemorrhaged and lost the baby and almost died as well. She needed massive blood transfusions for three days, and after three days she found out that she had been adopted.

Her mother, Elizabeth, could not have children, so she and Bubba secretly adopted a child from an orphanage in North Carolina. They left Charleston for a while and visited friends in New York, and after a year returned with the infant Mary Madison. Only Harold Wilson knew they had adopted the girl.

"So you knew I was adopted." Mary Madison was at the governor's mansion recuperating. The little bassinet was still in her bedroom.

Harold looked at her knowing full well what the next question was going to be. "I did it to protect you." Explaining why he lied to her about Giuseppe being her father and Michael being her half-brother.

"You did it because he wasn't good enough for you. You did it because Michael was Sicilian. You did it because he couldn't be governor or president. You did it because his father had the audacity to challenge the big almighty God, Harold Wilson. You did it because your ego is so big you can't let go."

"Mary Madison, I did it because I love you and did not want you to get hurt."

"You did it because you want to control; that's all it's been with you—money, money, money, and power. I hate you, I hate you for what you did to two young people who were in love and now will never know what could have happened if you hadn't interfered."

"But look at your life: you are married to a man from a wonderful family, you are the first lady, you have it all."

"You just don't understand, do you?" He had a blank look and shrugged his shoulders.

"How many lives have you destroyed? Just start with your daughter. You made her miserable all her life and finally when she found the only person she loved, Michael's father, you tore them apart. You used a young Anna in your deceit, and when you no longer had any use for her you threw her out into the streets."

He was about to say something, but she stopped him. "I have nothing. I don't even have a past now and the only thing I could have had, the only thing I wanted, you took away with one big lie."

She paused for a moment and looked him straight in his eyes. "I hate you. I hate everything about you, your deceit, your money, your life. I do not want to see you again, do you understand?"

He looked at her in astonishment. No one ever talked to him like this. No one would ever dare talk to him like this, and he knew them all. Luciano, Columbo, Gambino, Genovese, Anastasia, Luchese, and Gallo, they were all dead.

She repeated, as calmly as she could but if looks could kill, hers did. "I want you to leave this house. I do not want to see you again, do you understand?"

Harold Wilson lowered his head and turned around and for the first time in his life he was humbled.

CHAPTER 42

It was about one o'clock when the New Year's Eve party began thinning out. The line of limos in front of Sparks restaurant was waiting and the drivers were at attention holding the doors open. Mr. Castellano was just getting in when the shots where heard from a passing car. Mr. Castellano took a bullet to the back of his head and died instantly.

A stray bullet pierced Michael's head and he was taken to a New York City hospital and was operated on. He was in a coma for three days.

The dapper Don John Gotti was now in control of the five families in New York. He was everything that Michael despised. He was Nicky Genovese and Ciclopi rolled into one.

It was the longest three days in her life. Mary Madison sat by his side and refused to leave until he woke up. The nurse came around and gave Mary

Madison the chain and golden horn he always wore. She fastened it around his neck and whispered, "Santa, do your thing and keep the evil spirits away."

She could feel his heart and she knew he wanted to live. She knew he was dreaming and she knew he was sad as she wiped away the tears rolling down his cheeks.

Michael was dreaming. He was by Santa's side before she died and she whispered in his ear, "*Saba che Io e' la mamma?*" Does she know I'm her mother?

He whispered back, "*Si, Nonna, e' anche che Giuliani e il padre,*" and that Giuliani was her father.

"*Allora abbiamo fatto fesso.*" We made fools of them. And fools they were—Riccardo and his father, Alfredo—with all their master plans to keep the bloodline going. They were made fools by a simple peasant woman and her lover, the outlaw Giuliani.

"*Ha fatto bene, figlio,*" Santa whispered.

Michael never told Santa that Claudia had never married, never had children, or that she had lost her legs and lived a lonely life.

"*Un altra cosa...*" One more thing. She was fading fast, but she wanted Michael to answer her last question. "*Venne piu vecinno,*" she bid him to come closer as she did not want anyone to hear. "*Era tu ho marzarto quell animale, che ha marzarto la bicharidda* Dominique?*" Had Michael killed Ciclopi, *quello disgraziato* who raped and killed her daughter, Dominique?

Michael paused and whispered in her ear, "*Si, Nonna, ho marzarto.*" Yes, he had killed him.

"Ha fatto bene, figlio, ha fatto bene, sciatu mio." And with that she took her last breath, knowing she had gotten her revenge on all of them. She died content.

Over a hundred years ago, a cycle of evil had started with the malevolent Alberto Conti and his conniving son Riccardo, who tried to destroy Salvatore Parisi to get control of the sulfur mines. They enlisted the *"disgraziato"* Don Carlo from Palermo who killed Florianna's husband and used her as his *putana*, and spy, while threatening to kill her son Ciccu as insurance for her obedience. But it was Ciccu who killed the "animale" Minicu, Don Carlo's brutal enforcer at the sulfur mines. Years later, the *"disgraziato,"* Don Carlo, was stabbed to death by Michele, but before he died Michele informed him that Don Carlo had murdered his own wicked son Turiddo.

With the death of Minicu's grandson Ciclopi, Michael had ended the cycle of evil that had plagued Santa and the Parisi family for three generations.

His eyes opened and he saw Mary Madison's beautiful face. She was crying but she was happy. "Oh, Michael, it seems we have waited all our lives for this moment."

He just looked at her and smiled. *"Ammunini, e trovare un castello a Sicilia.* Let's go find our castle in Sicily."

Two months later, he was in Sicily at the *castello* recuperating and being doted on by Teresa and Lina. Teresa was singing and Lina was making coffee, the ashes from her cigarette falling in the pot along with the coffee.

Orazio shuffled in with his cane and sat down next to him. *"Senti meglio?* You feel better?"

"Si, si." Michael had recovered well.

Mary Madison walked into the kitchen and they all began talking at the same time. Michael was trying to interpret as best he could and she loved it.

This was where Don Ciccu had held the little infant Maria; this was where Michele told him that he loved him too and Florianna's prayers were answered; This was where Florianna had given Michele and Don Ciccu their golden horns and Ciccu had become part of the family.

Mary Madison sat next to Orazio and he said, *"Tu sai bellissima, se ero giovanno te sposa."*

Michael translated for her: "You're so beautiful if I were younger I would marry you."

"Well, at least somebody wants to marry me," she teasingly looked at Michael.

"Will you?" Michael moved the napkin in front of her and there was the ring. He was on his knees with the ring in his hand and placed it on her finger.

She couldn't stop the tears of joy. "I remember the first day we met. You were on your knees and you called me your princess and I called you my prince."

"I do, and I remember when I was helping you put the skates on I was on my knees again, and I told you they say three times is a charm." Michael kissed her hand.

"Bravo, bravo, bravo!" they all shouted.

The following week they were married in the family's little chapel. Over a hundred relatives wished them well. Orazio was the best man and Lina was the matron of honor. Teresa sang "Ave Maria" and made everybody cry. Orazio and Lina had surprised them both by having Michael's two sons, Joseph and Frankie, flown over for the wedding. Both sons had fallen in love with their Sicilian "*famiglia*" and embraced their newfound heritage.

But the biggest surprise was Anna. After Santa died, Anna was alone. Claudia had found out and insisted she move into her apartment in the *castello*, which she did. The sisters spent a few years together before Claudia died. At first it was hard for them to communicate, but then they didn't even have to talk. They just looked into each other's eyes and knew the sorrows and the loves they once shared. The one love they each had and the one mother that gave them life: Santa.

It was during this time that Anna poured out her heart and soul and told her sister secrets she never dared share with anyone. By now Claudia was bed-ridden as the cancer spread throughout her fragile body. Anna had become her nurse, and for twenty-four hours a day for the last six months, Anna had never left her side.

"I want to thank you for being here for me." Claudia stretched her hand out for her sister. Anna held on to her hand and started to cry.

"Why are you crying?" Claudia put her hand on Anna's head as she wept uncontrollably.

"I don't know where to begin," Anna sobbed.

"Start from the beginning," Claudia said.

Anna was sixteen when she met Harold Wilson. Even at that age she was absolutely stunning. In Red Hook the young men howled and whistled as she walked by and the older men went home and dreamed of her. Wilson was a distinguished-looking man and the former governor of New York. Anna was working as a seamstress on Canal Street in Manhattan. The shop was one of many that Harold owned. When the Jewish manager of the shop pointed her out to him one day, he had to have her and nothing was going to stop him. Harold Wilson always got what he wanted.

It was six o'clock on a day in the middle of summer when the black limo picked her up in front of Santa's apartment on Carroll Street. The only time a limo ever appeared on a block in Red Hook was for a funeral, and this was no funeral. The neighbors' curiosity mounted as the limo pulled up and the chauffeur, dressed in a tuxedo, got out and stood patiently as if he was waiting for someone important. Word spread like wildfire as young and old perched in their tenement windows waiting to see who would enter the limo.

When Anna came out she was dressed like a movie star in a black velvet dress, a gift from Harold Wilson, that accentuated her young, voluptuous body. The driver opened the door for her, but before she got in she looked around and smiled, enjoying every minute of the attention. As the limo drove off, Santa watched from her apartment window.

They drove to Delmonico's in lower Manhattan for dinner where he wined and dined her. And when they had finished they drove back to Brooklyn over the Brooklyn Bridge to an apartment in the Heights.

It was a small studio apartment overlooking the Manhattan skyline. It was extravagantly decorated with the finest furniture from a village boutique— something Anna had only seen in fashion magazines.

"How would you like to live here?" He didn't wait for an answer; he started pouring the champagne and making a toast. "To the beginning of a lovely relationship."

"But Mr. Wilson, I can't afford this." She knew she was way out of her element because this was something girls like her could only dream of.

"I know you can't, but I can."

"But I can't leave my mother. I'm her only source of income. Who will take care of her?"

"I have already made the arrangements for Santa to be taken care of. She will be given some money every month as long as you stay here. I will give you a job in my office in Manhattan and you will be taken care of so long as you remain loyal."

That was the beginning, and for three years Anna was loyal—and then she met Giuseppe and ran off to Florida with him. Harold became enraged when he found out and swore, "I will cut his balls off!"

Nobody, but nobody ever dared cross Harold Wilson. Not even Luciano, but Giuseppe had. And for that Harold put a contract on him. "I want that fucking Guinea dead."

Anna stopped her tale and began crying again. Claudia tried to get up and console her sister, but she was too weak to get out of bed. "Come here, let me put my arms around you."

"Oh, Claudia, I didn't know what I was doing. I was young and he had so much control over me. I thought when we went to Florida we would be free of his control, but I was wrong. He arranged to have our business burned down and he told me that was just a warning. That if I didn't come back he was going to have Giuseppe killed. And I was afraid for Michael too."

"I understand." Claudia held her in her arms. "Don Carlo from Palermo did the same thing to

Florianna. He killed her husband and threatened to kill her son Ciccu." She stopped for a moment, remembering, and then continued. "And Riccardo did the same to us. These despicable men of power think they can control everyone, and when they find someone who will stand up to them, they try to destroy them."

Six months later, Claudia lay on her deathbed. She knew she had only a few moments to live. Anna was by her side holding her hand and wiping her forehead, trying to comfort her. "Tell me, did she ever think of me?" Claudia whispered.

Anna knew she was talking about their mother, Santa. "*Si*, she—" Anna stopped as Claudia interrupted her. "I can't hear you, please come closer." Claudia was fading quickly. Anna put her face next to her sister and said, "I heard her every night call your name in her sleep, Claudia, Claudia, *mia bambina*, my baby."

When Michael walked over to his mother and asked her to dance, the family formed a circle around them—a circle of love, a circle to forgive and forget. Michael wiped away the tears from his mother's eyes, and he said, "I love you, Mom."

"I love you too."

After the ceremony, Mary Madison grabbed his arm and said, "*Ammunini*."

Everyone applauded. Mary Madison fit right in, and they loved her and her southern accent.

"Where are we going?" he asked.

"It's a surprise." She smiled.

"I'm not sure if my heart can take anymore surprises." He was laughing.

"We're going to our villa in Corruth." She was excited.

"Our villa?" He was shocked.

"*Si abbiamo comprato la villa.*" She took out the deed and showed him.

Everyone applauded again. "*Aguri, aguri!*" the well-wishers shouted.

"I didn't know we could afford it." He was bewildered, standing there with his palms up in the air.

"We made her a deal she no refuse," Orazio said in his best English, throwing up his palms in the air.

"And besides we got *il sconto per la famiglia*, the family discount." Mary Madison winked at Orazio. Orazio and Lina embraced them. "*Va va, verdiamo domani.*" They got into Orazio's Fiat and drove off to their villa in Corruth.

Her husband had left her nothing; he was governor of South Carolina and was convicted for being part of a drug cartel from Colombia, South America. All their assets were confiscated by the government.

But her grandfather, Harold Wilson, left her everything.

When Michael and Mary Madison arrived at the villa in Corruth, Raiggie was waiting for them. He had prepared a Sicilian meal at Mary Madison's request. The fresh fish that Raiggie bought that morning in Catania was grilled on the open pit and served on a beautiful hand-painted platter. It was garnished with lemons and limes from their groves and the aroma filled the *giardini*. The warm crusted bread heated from the wood-burning oven was placed in the center of the wooden table, along with a large tray of risotto and wild mushroom soup.

Mount Etna lit up the sky as usual and became their entertainment with its red lava illuminating the sky with the brilliant reds and lavenders that reflected in their eyes. They could feel the wonderful warmth that permeated throughout the villa, warmth that lived on through the wonderful memories of the *famiglia* Parisi and the photos of Maria riding her horse and of Michele on his father's lap and the one of Salvatore holding Florianna's hand.

"Oh, my God, Michael, Salvatore looks so much like you, and look how they are looking at each other, you can tell Salvatore and Florianna were in love." Mary Madison put her arms around Michael, who was sitting in Salvatore's chair, and she sipped from Michael's glass of red wine.

"I just love it here," she sighed.

Years ago, Salvatore sat in this chair there in the *giardini* after a meal like this, thinking to himself, *If I could stop time I would stop it right now.* Seeing his children laughing in front of him and knowing that the woman he loved was by his side, it didn't get better than this.

Salvatore could hear his daughter Maria calling Rosa and Santa, "*Venire a mangare con noi sta sera.*" And they came. For years there was so much joy and happiness in this home.

With the candles lighting up the house and the fire going, they all went to their corner of the villa and giggled and talked of the ones they loved. For Santa there was no one but Giuliani; for Maria, when she finally realized it, it was Don Ciccu, and for Rosa it was always Michele.

One night, when all the children were gone it was just the two of them at the villa, Florianna watched him sitting in his chair—so tranquil sipping a glass of wine waiting for her to come to him so that they could fall asleep in each other's arms while Mount Etna was putting on a show for them. She had been crying knowing she didn't have a long time to live. She walked over to him and sat on his lap and put her head on his shoulder. "*Sciatu mio,* I love you so much you will be the last breath that I take. Thank you for everything." And she fell asleep in his arms and never woke up.

Mary Madison was sitting on Michael's lap in the very same chair. The same chair that Rosa and Michele feel asleep in that first night when they were together with Maria and Don Ciccu.

Mount Etna was putting on a show as Mary Madison clutched Claudia's little brown notebook to her heart. The book was falling apart. Some of the pages were out of place and some were stained and hardly readable. Mary Madison could feel Claudia's presence prompting her to read her secrets, and she started reading.

The book was written in Italian, but in the last year Mary Madison had immersed herself in learning the language and had become quite proficient.

"Oh, Michael, this is so sad." Mary Madison started reading from Claudia's diary. "'Again she came to me in my dreams. I was a baby and she held me in her arms and kissed me and sang me to sleep. I could always feel her close to me. She is so young and sad, but she comforts and protects me and I know she is my mother. One day I will find her.'

"Michael, did she know that Santa was her mother?"

"She knew, but she never met her."

"Oh, listen to this." Mary Madison continued to read. "'I am so happy, tomorrow we go to Sicily. I know I don't belong in Florence, for it is too fancy and too cold for me. I want to be with the peasants. I know that is were I belong. I love Sicily and one day I will live there because I know in my heart that is where I was born.'"

Still in Michael's lap, Mary Madison turned more pages and held her breath. "Oh, Michael, this is when she meets your father." She read on, "'When I first met him I knew he was my *sciatu mio*.'"

FINO

STANDING IN THE BACK, AUTHOR AND HIS WIFE CAROLYN
WITH ORAZIO AND LINA PENNISI.

B orn in 1942 in Red Hook Brooklyn, Frank J. Pennisi is the only child of Sicilian Immigrants. He grew up among the stories of Sicilians and was touched by their plight to overcome the prejudices toward Sicilians in America. He graduated from Long Island University with a B.A. in history in 1964 and started teaching in Bedford Styvesant, Brooklyn. Promoted to dean after his second year, he drove a taxicab to earn money to pay for a master's degree in education. His last year he was coordinator of crisis intervention for Special Ed. on Staten Island. He now lives in Myrtle Beach SC.

Made in the USA
Lexington, KY
30 March 2015